Cut to the Bone

Bone

Roz Watkins

ONE PLACE. MANY STORIES

HQ
An imprint of HarperCollins*Publishers* Ltd
1 London Bridge Street
London SE1 9GF

www.harpercollins.co.uk

HarperCollins*Publishers*
1st Floor, Watermarque Building, Ringsend Road
Dublin 4, Ireland

This edition 2021

1
First published in Great Britain by
HQ, an imprint of HarperCollins*Publishers* Ltd 2020

Copyright © Roz Watkins 2020

Roz Watkins asserts the moral right to be
identified as the author of this work.
A catalogue record for this book is
available from the British Library.

ISBN: 978-0-00-821474-6

MIX
Paper from
responsible sources
FSC™ C007454

This book is produced from independently certified FSC™ paper
to ensure responsible forest management.

For more information visit: www.harpercollins.co.uk/green

This book is set in 11/15.5 pt. Bembo by Type-it AS, Norway

Printed and bound in Great Britain by
CPI Group (UK) Ltd, Croydon, CR0 4YY

For Starsky the dog, whose foul woodland scavenging started all this. And to the animals in intensive farms who don't get that freedom.

1

Meg – Present day
Monday

The road swooped into the valley, its sun-beaten tarmac melting into the hillside. The car smelled of petrol and hot plastic, and the steering wheel stuck to my hands. DS Jai Sanghera was sprawling in the passenger seat beside me, legs thrown apart, head back, and we were embroiled in a pointless argument in which I'd found myself defending his girlfriend for a reason I could no longer remember.

Jai's manspreading was reaching such critical levels it was impeding my access to the gearstick. 'I know you're hot,' I said. 'No need to turn it into performance art.'

Jai dragged himself forward to fiddle with his air vent. 'Let's just agree to disagree, shall we? I think if Suki's serious about me, she should try harder with the kids; you clearly don't. We've got a missing person to focus on.'

'Fine.'

I eased my foot off the brake and let the car accelerate through the treacly air. The wind curled round my damp face, and my shirt flapped against my stomach. I fanned myself, trying to let the tension dissipate.

In the distance I could see the dazzling surface of Ladybower Reservoir. We were heading for a valley to its east that looked like a huge meteorite crater, but had probably been caused by some dramatic event in the last ice age. The hot summer had turned the grass yellow, and the bowl of the valley was surrounded by rocks. They jutted up like teeth, as if we were driving into a gaping mouth. In the centre, where the tonsils would have been, was an ugly industrial building. Gritton Abattoir.

I forced my tone to be friendly. 'What do we know about her?'

Jai took a long breath and when his voice came out, it was normal, not pissed off. 'Eighteen-year-old girl. She was working at the abattoir overnight and when they got in this morning, her car was still there but no sign of her. You know who she is though?'

'No. Who is she?'

'Violet Armstrong.'

I looked at him for a beat longer than the driver should, our disagreement forgotten. '*The* Violet Armstrong?'

'Yep. Bikini-barbecue-babe Violet Armstrong. Poster girl for carnivores everywhere. Missing from an abattoir.'

'Jesus. What was she doing at an abattoir?'

'I think she works there. Bit weird, I know. Especially with someone as controversial as her. It's when "turning up in one piece" is way too literal.'

'Thanks for that, Jai. No doubt there'll be some banal explanation involving a dodgy boyfriend or a runaway pig.'

Jai laughed and I felt the atmosphere loosen. 'Yeah,' he said. 'If I was a pig I'd run away from her and her barbecue tongs.'

On the horizon, tendrils of smoke drifted upwards, reminding me we were near the wildfire. 'This weather's got to break soon,' I said. 'We'll get monsoon rains.'

'Most of which will no doubt end up in my basement.'

I hadn't yet been inside Jai's new house, even though it was round the corner from mine, but he seemed obsessed with his damp basement. Maybe he'd been droning on to Suki about pumps and that was part of her problem.

We followed a narrow lane through gates into a concrete yard. A slab-sided grey building sat in front of us, sanitised and anonymous, giving away nothing about what went on inside.

'Are you going to be okay with this?' Jai said.

My head filled with images from abattoir videos posted by animal rights groups and shared by my friends on Facebook, just to improve my mental well-being and sleeping patterns. I didn't need to see the real thing, especially in my current state of mind. Or hear it. This abattoir did pigs. Pigs squealed.

'I'll be okay,' I said. 'I'm more worried about the missing girl.' But it struck me like an electric shock that I wasn't that worried about the girl – at least not to my usual PhD-level. Was I so worn down from watching Gran die that I'd lost some vital part of myself? It scared the hell out of me. If I didn't care about my job to the point of virtual mania, who even was I?

'You do know she's famous because she barbecues burgers in a bikini?' Jai said. 'A phrase I wouldn't advise saying when drunk.'

'Yeah. She simultaneously dumps on feminism and animal rights in an impressive double whammy.' I could keep the banter going while I had my mini existential crisis, but our camaraderie felt forced. I'd thought I was doing the right thing by being super-nice about his girlfriend, thus removing any question of whether I liked him a little too much for a colleague, but I'd obviously got it all wrong.

We pulled up in the yard and heaved ourselves out of the car. The sun sliced through the hot air, making the car windows so shiny it hurt to look at them. A few uniforms were buzzing around. We had a lot of missing person calls, but this one had triggered a red-button-push.

The door to the abattoir building swung open and a skinny blonde woman came out at a gallop. 'Goodness, it's warm. I hope we're not wasting your time. I'm not wanting to make a fuss, but I thought we should call just in case …'

'Shall we pop inside a minute?' I said. 'I'm Detective Inspector Meg Dalton and this is Detective Sergeant Jai Sanghera. What's your name?'

'Anna Finchley. I own the abattoir.'

I wasn't sure if it was subconscious sexism or ageism, but I was surprised at that revelation. There was a touch of the gangly teenager or new-born foal about her, although she must have been in her thirties. She didn't look like an abattoir-owner.

'Not being melodramatic, but do you think it's the animal rights people?' she said.

'What makes you say that?'

'We've had threats. And someone's smashed the CCTV.' Anna shook her head. 'But surely, they wouldn't … Maybe she went for a walk or …'

I looked at the sun-scorched hills in the distance. A faint smell of smoke hung in the air. It wasn't an ideal spot for a hike.

'How far are we from the reservoir?' Jai said.

The beauty of Ladybower Reservoir seemed to act as a magnet for death. It was well known, to us at least. If some poor soul was planning to slit an artery and bleed to death in north Derbyshire, there was a fair chance Ladybower would be the destination of choice.

Anna said, 'It's just over the hill.'

'Let's take a few details inside,' I said. 'Can we see the smashed CCTV?'

Anna led us through a door into a grey corridor and on into a small room. The building was functional rather than swish, but had been recently renovated. So far, it was mercifully free of butchered animals.

I leaned to peer at the CCTV box, which looked like it had been set about with a baseball bat. I stepped back to let Jai see. 'They've taken the hard drive,' he said.

'Let's get this area sealed off and processed,' I said.

We shuffled out of the room. A man was walking towards us down the corridor. He was lean, toned, and good-looking in a rough, footballer kind of way, and he moved like a man with something to prove.

Anna said, 'What is it, Gary?' I sensed tension between them. A slight narrowing of his eyes; a fractional curling of her upper lip. 'This is my brother,' Anna said. 'He works here too.'

The man held up an expensive-looking, glittery, and clearly now evidentially compromised object. We needed to get the scene under control. 'I found a watch,' he said. 'It—'

'That's Violet's,' Anna said. 'Why on earth would she take off her watch? Where did you find it?'

'If you'd let me finish, I'd tell you. I don't know why she'd have gone there – it wasn't in the area she cleans. It's bloody weird, if you ask me.'

'Just tell us where it was, Gary!'

'It was beside the pig pens.' He shot Anna a look that was almost accusing. 'And there's blood on it.'

2

Anna Finchley led us into an office containing a desk and four chairs. White-painted walls were covered with a surprising collection of abstract art – the kind with blobs of colour that my dad would say a three-year-old could do – and a prominent TV screen. Anna sank down on one of the chairs, crossing her legs and arms as if protecting herself.

'Sit on that side if you want the window-view and the art,' she said. 'I sit here so I can monitor the CCTV. When it's working. And I hate to be negative, but Violet's not careless with her stuff. Why would she have dropped her watch? She shouldn't even have been by the pig pens. And why would it have blood on it?'

Jai and I sat opposite her and didn't answer her questions. She could run the scenarios on her own. I watched her face as she did so. Not giving much away.

'When did you last see Violet?' I asked.

Anna blinked a couple of times and looked to the ceiling. 'The day before yesterday,' she said. 'I stayed late and I saw her at the start of her shift.'

'And how was she?'

7

Anna shook her head and frowned. 'Not that I'd necessarily notice, because I didn't spend long talking to her, but she seemed fine.'

'Could you talk us through this morning? Were you the first to arrive?'

'I got here at about eight. Daniel had come in earlier and fed the pigs. Daniel Twigg. I think he'd messed up the amounts though, because they'd left loads. Maybe it was because he wasn't feeling well – he's gone home ill. I didn't realise anything was wrong at first. Violet's car's parked round the side so I didn't see it.' Anna pushed her hair back behind her ears. 'I got the pigs killed. Then cleaned up their pen. And the lorry arrived to take the Category 2 waste away – that's the animals' innards and other bits we can't use – to be rendered, and when it went round the side, I noticed Violet's car. It's not normally parked that far round, so I hadn't seen it at first. Anyway, I looked for her everywhere I could think, and tried her mobile but there was no answer. I phoned Esther – my partner, who Violet lodges with – and she's not there. I phoned Violet's parents in Sheffield but there was no answer. Then I went to check the CCTV, and when I saw it was smashed, I called you.'

Anna was providing a lot of detail in her descriptions. That could be normal. She might have just been a very helpful person, a kind-of human Lassie dog. Or not. It was too early to tell.

'The Category 2 waste …' I said. 'Would that have included any meat waste from yesterday or last night?' Our assumption was that Violet was alive, but I wanted to know what had happened to those waste products.

'Yes,' Anna said. 'Yes, it would. And from this morning. It's all been taken away. It goes to be rendered.'

'Do you have details of the company that takes it?' I asked.

She froze a moment. 'Why would … Oh, okay.' She reached into a drawer, fished out an invoice and passed it over. If she'd worked out what this could mean, she kept it to herself.

I turned to Jai. 'Do you mind calling them now? And checking on the searches.'

Jai took the paper and left the room.

When I turned back to Anna, her fists were clenched tight in her lap, knuckles shining white.

'Violet was on a night shift?' I said.

Anna nodded rapidly. 'Ten till two thirty. Cleaning. She has a summer job here.'

'Why did she come to work in an abattoir?'

'It's strange, isn't it? When I found out who she was, I was baffled. I did ask her and she was rather vague. I can't say for sure, but I got the impression she wanted to come to Gritton for some other reason, and this job was an excuse.'

'Okay, thank you. And had she worked her shift last night? Could you tell this morning if the cleaning had been done?'

Anna frowned. 'I'm not sure … We have such high standards here, it's not as if she was mopping up blood – it's more of an extra clean. We have what we call a "clean side" and a "dirty side". She was on the clean side – meat only, no live animals – which is why it's so strange that her watch turned up near the pig pen on the dirty side. She's been given specific instructions not to go on the dirty side when she's cleaning.'

'Okay. Could you have another look – the guys will tell you where you can go. See if there's anything to suggest she did or didn't clean up.'

'Yes, of course.'

'Is there any CCTV other than the broken one? Any camera footage that would show if anyone else was here last night.'

She shook her head. 'Sorry, no. Not on site.'

'Where were you last night?'

'At home. But Esther was with me. She doesn't live with me, but she stayed over. She can confirm I was with her.'

'Violet lodges with Esther?'

'Yes. Yes, she does. I helped that girl a lot, even letting her live with my girlfriend.' Was that a hint of bitterness in her tone?

'Did Violet not appreciate that help?' I asked.

'Oh yes, I'm not saying she didn't appreciate it.' A somewhat tight-lipped response.

'Do you get along with Violet?'

Anna swallowed. 'She's all right, I suppose. A good employee generally.'

'Generally but not totally?'

Anna's eyes hardened briefly. A flash of steel. 'Just a turn of phrase. She's fine.'

I paused to write in my notebook. Anna kept her face expressionless. She clearly didn't like Violet. Could be relevant. Could be nothing. I spent half my life wanting to throttle my colleague Craig and I hadn't murdered him yet.

'How long has Violet been working here?' I asked.

'About a month. I can't—' Anna swung her gaze around the room as if Violet might be hiding in a corner. 'Let me ring Esther again. Violet's probably home by now.'

'Okay, you do that,' I said.

Anna fished out her mobile and dialled. The phone must have been picked straight up at the other end. 'Is she back?' Anna's voice was loud and sharp.

I couldn't hear the answer but Anna's face dropped. She spoke into the phone. 'No, nothing.' There was a muffled reply, the words audible though my brain could make no sense of them, and then Anna said, 'Oh, come on, Esther, you don't believe that rubbish—'

Anna frowned at the woman's response and ended the call with a brisk, 'Okay, bye.'

'No sign of her?' I asked.

'No, I'm afraid not.'

'Okay. And what rubbish does Esther not believe?'

Anna shook her head. 'It's nothing. What else do you need to know?'

My brain got there in the end with the words I'd heard. 'Did she say something about a pale child?'

Anna shifted papers around her desk before looking up and staring straight at me. 'Not to cast aspersions on the people in this village, but they don't get out enough. The Pale Child thing is all nonsense.'

'Who is this Pale Child?' I asked.

Anna gave me a strange look. Like somebody remembering a scene from their distant childhood. When she spoke, her voice was cracked, like sun-scorched earth. 'As I said, it's not real. Are we done here? Because I have things I need to be getting on with. It's bad enough you people saying I can't kill animals today, but if I don't make a few phone calls soon, it'll be too late to cancel, and they'll be turning up here. I suspect you don't need a bunch of condemned pigs marauding around the place.' She wasn't in Lassie-dog mode any more.

'You make your phone calls,' I said. 'We'll need to take a formal statement from you later. But first, could you tell me who else could have got into the abattoir last night.'

'My brother, Gary, who you just met, has keys. He's outside looking for Violet. And Daniel Twigg – the one who over-fed the pigs earlier.'

'You said he was unwell, didn't you? What's the matter with him?'

'Said he felt sick.'

'Okay, we'll talk to him. And before we go, even if it is nonsense, what's the story about this Pale Child?'

Anna sighed. 'It's nothing. Just idiot-talk from the people in the village. It's not relevant.'

'Fine. Tell me anyway.'

'People see her in the woods around the village. A girl dressed in white, old-fashioned clothes. Supposedly, if she sees your face, you're going to die.' She lowered her gaze. 'Which is clearly not true.'

'So she's a child who lives in the village?'

'She's not a real child. The whole Pale Child thing is a myth. I don't know why Esther even brought it up.'

'Did Violet see this Pale Child?'

'Of course not. I don't know why you're even asking about this.'

I wrote 'Pale Child' in my notebook and underlined it twice, then looked up and said, 'Okay, tell me about the threats you mentioned earlier.'

Anna's leg jiggled up and down before she stilled it with a hand. 'You obviously know who Violet is. Her videos?'

'I know she's famous for videoing herself cooking meat-based products in a bikini.'

Anna sighed. 'Maybe we used her, you could say.' She fiddled with a loose thread on her vest-top. 'I've been wanting to start a blog for a while, to debate this stuff. Meat, the environment, welfare, etc. Violet helped. She got us attention. I never knew it could be … dangerous.'

'Okay, you'd better tell me from the beginning.'

'It's all so polarised now, like everything. I wanted to have an intelligent discussion. We set the website up – The Great Meat Debate – and put videos and posts on it. Discussions about the ethics of meat, and about how we'd designed the abattoir. Gary does stupid strength challenges with vegans. Lifting vans and ripping up books or whatever. I mean, that wasn't part of the intelligent debate, but people love that kind of thing. As for Violet … well, Violet's just Violet, and she brought us most of our visitors.'

'You've had threats?'

'Yes. I never expected that to happen. It's not like we're doing anything bad, but we attracted a load of attention. You know what it's like – sometimes the more ethical meat producers come in for more vitriol. As if it's almost worse to be nice to the animals before you kill them. People can't seem to handle that. Like that farmer who let kids meet the turkeys at Christmas. It's irrational, but there it is. We get a lot of haters. Especially a group called the Animal Vigilantes. Do you know them?'

I nodded. They'd been on our radar for a while. They wore clothing printed with a design that made it look like their skin had been removed and you could see their insides. They looked like meat. And their violence levels had been escalating.

'Daniel can tell you more,' Anna said. 'He was really worried about it, and he tried to look into the Animal Vigilantes and who was behind them. Maybe he was right to be worried. He said they were getting more aggressive. And he thought they might follow through on their threats.'

'What kind of threats did they make?'

She swallowed. 'They said they were going to slit Violet's throat.'

I left Anna Finchley and made my way through the grey corridor back into the scorching heat outside. This was not our usual kind of missing teenager. For some, going AWOL was practically a weekly occurrence and the police a free taxi service. Violet wasn't one of those. Besides, someone had threatened to slit her throat.

A man was walking down the verge of the lane, heading away from the abattoir. He was bashing at the undergrowth with a long stick, the effort showing in the sweat soaking his shirt under the armpits and down his back. I called to him, and he jumped and spun round. It was Gary. Anna's brother who'd found the watch earlier.

I pointed at his stick. 'You can leave that now. We're doing a search. It's best you don't do it.'

Civilian searches were appalling evidence-manglers. I mentally noted where Gary had been hacking at the undergrowth, just in case he'd been deliberately destroying evidence. He'd already manhandled Violet's watch.

'Whatever,' he said.

'Can I ask where you were last night?'

'In bed at home.'

'Can anyone verify that?'

'My wife can.' Gary smacked his stick against the ground again, contrary to my instructions. His attitude made me suspicious. For people who had never been in trouble, your typical *questioned-by-the-cops* look was a mixture of terror and the eagerness of the schoolkid at the front of the class with their hand up. Gary didn't have that look. This one was hanging around the bike-sheds and claiming the cigarettes belonged to his mate.

I looked at his stick and he let it drop to the ground.

'I don't know why Anna's giving you this *I'm so worried* bullshit,' he said. 'She bloody hates Violet.'

'Anna hates Violet?'

'Yeah. She thinks Violet's a pain in the arse. Always moaning about the way things are done.'

'What kinds of things?'

'Everything. Violet knows best. The way we clean, the way we process the meat, even the way we kill the pigs.'

'Does that cause conflict?'

'You could say. Not my problem though. I'm just the minion, aren't I? Anna's the boss.'

So was that the tension? Gary didn't like his sister being his boss? I had to admit, it was an unusual set-up, practically guaranteed to offend any fragile male egos involved.

'Anna employs you?'

He opened his mouth as if to speak, then shut it again. 'Yes.'

I softened my stance and gave him a conspiratorial smile. 'It's never easy working with family.'

'No. And stuck in this shithole.'

I wanted to know why he would stay at the abattoir, working for his sister, if he hated it so much, but I sensed it wasn't the time to get the truth out of him. Thankfully, when it came to criticising Anna, he was happy to spill all.

'Do you think Anna might harm Violet?' I asked.

Gary laughed. 'God, no. Anna wouldn't have the balls to

do that. She's not what you think, you know. She makes out she's this tough country girl, so at home running the abattoir and hanging out with proper farmers, but you know what she wants? To live in the city, surrounded by poncy art galleries and theatres, where she'd never have to smell pig shit again in her life. But will she admit it? Will she, bollocks! Anyway, that's not your concern. It's the animal rights lunatics who've hurt Violet. I just think Anna should drop the Oscar-winning performance of being all upset about it.'

That was quite a speech to blurt out spontaneously. I didn't comment – it's best to let people carry on when they're mid-rant. But he didn't say any more.

'Tell me about the animal rights lunatics,' I said.

'You know they've threatened to kill Violet?'

'Who threatened to kill her?'

'Idiots online. Posting sicko stuff about her. But they've had a go at all of us. Come to think of it, maybe that's what Anna's upset about.' He let out a sharp laugh. 'She's not worried about Violet – she thinks it's her next.'

'What exactly have these people said?'

'Called us murderers. Said they'd come and slit our throats. Messed-up shit.'

That did sound messed up, even by internet standards. 'Did you take it seriously?'

'It's hard not to, when psychos are threatening to kill you. Daniel's totally freaked out by it, but then he's a right pansy at the best of times. That's probably why he's gone home. When he saw Violet was gone, he must have realised they meant business. You know he's a junkie? Claims it's for his back, but it doesn't do him any favours.'

Gary's phone pinged and he fished it out of his pocket. Pressed a few keys. 'Yeah. Look at this.' He showed me the phone. 'If it's not them, how do they even know to post this?'

I looked at the screen. It was the Great Meat Debate website that Anna had told me about. Gary had scrolled down to the bottom of the comments on the home page. One was posted under the name 'Animal Vigilantes'. It said, *Violet got what she deserved.*

3

'Media are going to go mental for this,' Jai said, as we drove up the lane away from the abattoir. The reservoir sat low in the valley, sparkling turquoise and white in the sunshine, contrasting with the darkly jutting rocks which loomed above us on the gritstone edge.

'I know,' I said. 'The best thing that's happened to the meat industry since the invention of the burger, and she goes missing from an abattoir.'

We were on our way to see Daniel Twigg. To find out what he'd seen that morning and what he knew about the threats from the Animal Vigilantes. To find out why he was so scared.

'Do you think the Animal Vigilantes have done something to her?' Jai said. 'They're quite full-on.'

'It's possible. I've asked the techies to trace who posted the throat-slit comments, and the one that said Violet got what she deserved. Do we know what happened to the waste products from last night?'

'Bit weird, that. The company who'd sent the invoice said their contract was cancelled a few weeks ago. But Anna Finchley claims she didn't know and has no idea who replaced them. She reckons someone must have changed contractors without telling her. She's checking with them urgently.'

'You mean we don't know who took the waste this morning, or where it's gone?'

'Er, no. Not yet. We're on it.'

I didn't want to go there in my mind. For now, the girl was missing, not dead. Missing, not murdered and thrown into a vat with pigs' intestines and snouts and trotters.

There was nothing about Violet on our system. No previous disappearances, no suggestion she'd self-harm, no criminal record, no domestic violence complaints. She was a blank slate. Blank slates were tough. They gave you no clues.

We'd pulled out all the stops to look for her. Her car had been seized and taken off on the back of a truck. We'd arranged dogs and a drone, a unit to her parents' place in Sheffield in case she was holed up there, house-to-house in the village, checks for any cameras, people bagging up all her things from her landlady's house. The local mountain rescue would be brought in if she was missing much longer.

Above us I could see the black speck of the drone hovering like a mutant insect, while in the distance smoke was still rising from the wildfire. Together they induced a sense of end-of-the-world doom. Plagues and fires and all that good stuff. But I was lacking my usual big-case emotions – a mix of excitement and terror akin to what Eddie the Eagle must have felt standing at the top of the ninety-metre ski jump. So far all I felt was the crushing weight of responsibility and a dose of low-level depression.

'Why come to Gritton and work in an abattoir?' I said.

'A beautiful young woman, who must be well-off, yet she's cleaning up pigs' guts in a backwater village.'

'It is weird.'

'Anna Finchley said she thought Violet had come to Gritton for another reason and the job was an excuse. We need to know that reason.'

'Did you talk to the brother?' Jai asked. 'Gary, was it?'

'Yeah. And that's another odd set-up. I got the impression he can't stand this place and he and his sister hate each other. It's all simmering under the surface.'

'It'd be more than simmering if I had to work with my sister.'

'Ha, I'm sure.'

I wished I could have had the chance to simmer about my sister.

'Sorry,' Jai said. 'That was insensitive.'

'It's fine. She died twenty-five years ago. You don't need to be sensitive. In fact, I'd worry about you if you started being sensitive.'

A mile later, we came to a sign: *Welcome to Gritton. Please drive carefully.*

I pulled around a steep bend and looked at the road ahead. A flush of adrenaline hit my stomach and I slammed on the brakes.

'Bloody hell,' Jai said. 'What's that?'

In front of us, the road seemed to have collapsed into a spectacular sinkhole, but as I looked more closely, I could see it was in fact an image painted onto the road. 'Wow,' I said, allowing the car to crawl towards the crater and fighting the urge to shut my eyes as we drove over it. 'That slowed me down.'

'It's good to see that you shut your eyes when things get tricky,' Jai said.

'I just squinted a little! But you wouldn't want to drive here if you had a weak heart. I suppose it must be to slow people down, but it's a bit brutal.'

Once we'd passed the fake sinkhole, the lane rose steeply beside a row of stone houses with freshly painted windows in Farrow & Ball colours. On the other side was a park, tree-fringed and pristine, a children's play area at its centre. Every lawn was immaculately mown and weed-free, every garden fenced with railings, every door beautifully painted. The street lamps were Victorian-style. There weren't even any people, as if they'd lower the tone. The only things that disturbed the look were notices attached to the lamp posts, although even they were tastefully done. *Don't Build on our Burial Grounds! Stop the Development!*

'Is this a real village or a filmset for a period drama?' Jai said.

'It's creepy,' I said. 'And everything's fenced in. Look at the railings by the sides of the road. That would annoy me. You can only cross in designated spots. I'd feel the need to climb over them.'

'That could end in tears,' Jai said.

'I hope you're referring to my dodgy ankle rather than the size of my arse.'

Jai laughed. 'Naturally. But yes, it's almost too perfect.'

'The village or my arse? Because that's far from perfect.' That had popped out before the censorship lobes in my brain had a chance to click in. Trying so hard to get our banter back that I crossed the line into dodgy territory. 'Yes,' I said hurriedly, cringing inside. 'It's quite Stepford. Almost ominous. But there are cameras everywhere. That could help us.'

'There are tunnels in this area,' Jai said, ignoring my babbling. 'I wonder if that's why they have all the fences. Are they scared of kids wandering off and falling into them? I heard they stretch for miles. Old lead mines and stuff. I've seen videos on YouTube. I wondered if you fancied dragging me down there? Maybe at night? In a storm? When they're about to flood?'

I laughed, relieved I'd got away with the inappropriate arse comment. 'Honestly, Jai,' I said. 'One little incident where we nearly die in a flooded cave and you won't stop going on about it.'

We reached the rim of the valley, where the road sloped down again. A sign said, *Thank you for driving carefully through Gritton.* Underneath, in very faint letters as if they had been repeatedly scrubbed clean, were the words, *Village of the Damned.* It was almost reassuring that there were vandalising teenage scrotes in residence amongst all the perfection, but I wondered what the village had done to earn that accolade.

In another half-mile, we drove through red-brick housing which looked more normal and messy, as if people actually lived there, although there were still barriers to the pavements and some of the roads were gated. Ahead was rocky moorland and in front of it a field containing a collection of dubious-looking run-down caravans in various shades of dirt-colour.

'That must be the place,' I said.

I pulled up and climbed from the car, narrowly missing a neatly curled dog turd. The place contrasted so extremely with the main village, it was almost as if it was trying to make a point.

'Nice.' Jai unfolded himself slowly as if he didn't want to get out.

Ten caravans were spread over a field of unkempt grass. No people were in evidence but one or two curtains twitched, and there was the muffled sound of kids screaming and dogs going ballistic inside the caravans.

'The shutters are going down and the hackles are going up,' I said.

'Yeah. The cop-detection radar's good in places like this.'

The largest caravan was aligned in front of the others as if on guard. Its wheels had either disappeared or sunk into the ground, so it looked as if it had sat down. The door squeaked open and a ginger Staffie charged out at us, barking and slavering. Jai and I both took a hasty step back and crashed into one another, demonstrating our smooth professionalism.

A boulder-shaped orange-haired woman emerged from the caravan, lunged forward, and grabbed the dog by the scruff of its neck. It carried on barking but at a more strangled pitch.

The woman gave us the same look I'd given the dog turd. 'What?'

I flashed ID. 'We'd like a word with Daniel Twigg. Which is his caravan?'

'Why are you after him?'

'Which is his caravan please?'

'How do I know you're not those animal activists? They're dangerous, you know.'

I held up my ID again. 'Because we're police. Feel free to call and check.'

'Why aren't you wearing uniforms? You look too scruffy to be police. Well, you do.' She pointed at me. 'He looks okay.'

'Oh, for God's sake,' I said. 'Which is his caravan?'

She frowned at us, causing creases in her face which matched her dog's. After pausing long enough to demonstrate that she was still sceptical about me and was complying out of her good nature and not because she had to, the woman gestured towards a small caravan with trails of green mould drifting down its side. 'He's not well. He's come back from work, so don't go bothering him.'

'Thanks.'

We moved gratefully away from the dog, which was baring its teeth and salivating.

'What on earth …?' On each side of the caravan door was a pile of rocks. But *pile* didn't properly describe it. The rocks were balanced on top of one another in teetering stacks about four feet high, even though the base rocks were smaller than the higher ones.

'Rock-balancing art,' Jai said. 'It's what constitutes a wild time round here. No glue or cement or anything – just gravity and physics.'

'I like them.' I stepped between the rocks, worried about knocking them over.

I tapped on the door. It opened abruptly, causing the entire caravan to wobble and making me fear for the rock art. A man appeared. White-faced, nervous-looking. Mid-thirties. Longish hair. Delicate, unshaven features. Arctic Monkeys T-shirt.

Jai spoke first. 'Are you Daniel Twigg? This is DI Meg Dalton and I'm DS Jai Sanghera. Can we ask you a few questions?'

'You'd better come in.' He stepped back to allow us to climb up.

The inside of the caravan was steaming hot, grubby, and smelled of cooked broccoli. We could only see one side of it, the other being separated off with a partition. Our half had a tiny kitchen area and some benches to sit on, and presumably the other half contained somewhere to sleep and a loo.

We accepted an offer of tea with some reluctance, and Daniel fished cups from the not-very-clean draining board and milk from a mini fridge.

We perched on a cramped bench while Daniel shuffled around

awkwardly in the limited space. He didn't make a drink for himself.

'I've only got oat milk.' Daniel sat opposite and plonked mugs in front of us. He grabbed a lump of what looked like Blu-tack and started fiddling with it. He had a slightly spaced-out look, and I remembered Gary saying he was a junkie, and something about pain in his back. He was moving stiffly.

'Have you hurt your back?' I asked.

He frowned. 'A long time ago. It's okay, but I have to take very strong painkillers. So bear with me. They affect my concentration sometimes.'

'Do you have any idea where Violet is?' I asked.

'No.'

'So talk us through this morning please.'

'I arrived at the abattoir at seven, like I normally do, fed the pigs, then I felt ill. I came home, and I only found out Violet was missing when Anna phoned.'

'Anna thinks you may have over-fed the pigs,' I said. 'Do you think you might have done that?'

Daniel looked up sharply. 'What? No. Of course not. I gave them the right amount for twenty pigs. Why?'

'They'd left their breakfast.'

Daniel's eyes widened. 'I didn't give them too much.'

'Okay, we'll look into that. Have you got details of the new people who are taking the Category 2 waste?'

'What new people?'

'The contractor's been changed. Did you organise that?'

He shook his head. 'No, not me. I don't know anything about that. Maybe try Gary?'

I sat back and let Jai ask questions while I watched. 'When did you last see Violet?' he said.

Daniel was making a miniature version of the balancing rocks – blobs stacked on top of one another. There was a tiny tremor in his hands when he manipulated the Blu-tack. How could he stand the heat in this caravan? 'Friday, at work,' he said.

'How has she been recently?'

'Okay, I think. But I don't know a lot about her.'

'What's Violet like as a person?' Jai settled deeper into his seat and put on his *mates-at-the-pub* voice. 'You know, away from all the internet stuff.'

Daniel swallowed. 'She was all right, I suppose. I didn't give it much thought.' His eyes flitted nervously between Jai and me. *Mates-at-the-pub* wasn't working.

Jai shot me a discreet look. Daniel had used the past tense about Violet.

'Do you know something, Daniel?' I said. 'You seem very upset.'

Daniel shifted back as if I was intimidating him. 'Of course I'm upset. They were threatening her. Really badly. All of us – but Violet got it the worst. It's been horrible. Scary.'

'Tell us about it.'

He looked at his new sculpture – eight or nine Blu-tack blobs balanced on top of one another – and then crushed it with his thumb. 'The website was Anna's idea – I don't know why I got involved. I'm not someone they should be attacking. I *care* about the animals. I suppose I can see why Gary and Kirsty piss people off. And Violet. But not me and Anna.'

'Who's Kirsty?'

'Kirsty Nightingale. She's got a pig farm over the valley.'

'So the people involved in the website are yourself, Violet, Anna and Gary Finchley, and Kirsty Nightingale? Five of you?'

He nodded morosely. 'I wish I'd stayed out of it.'

'What did Gary and Kirsty do that pissed people off?'

Daniel picked up his blob of Blu-tack and rubbed it between his finger and thumb, looking at the Blu-tack rather than at us. 'Gary's just a dick. He was supposed to be doing strength challenges and stuff, but he'd stick in snide comments about vegans and vegetarians, saying they were weak and pasty. And Kirsty deliberately winds people up – it's as if she enjoys it.'

'So you think the Animal Vigilantes are responsible for Violet's disappearance?'

He looked away. A tiny muscle above his eye twitched. Possibly nerves at being interviewed by cops, possibly something else. 'Yes, I do.'

'You believe they would hurt her?'

'To make an example of her, yes. Of us, maybe. She might be just the first.'

'What did you see this morning?'

'What do you mean?'

'Did you know Violet was missing? Did you see something that worried you?'

'No. I didn't realise her car was there.' He looked right at me when he said that, very deliberately. That made me suspicious. Along with mentioning not seeing the car. People rarely mentioned things they hadn't seen.

'Do you know what brought Violet to Gritton in the first place?' I asked. 'It seems a strange choice.'

'I won't argue with that. But no, I don't know.'

I waited a second or two, but he said nothing more. 'Has Violet had any arguments with anyone else that you're aware of? Besides the animal rights people?'

'She was annoyed with Gary.'

'What makes you say that?'

'He comes on to her all the time. He's always been an arsehole.'

Back to present tense. 'In what way?' I asked. In my experience, there were a multitude of ways to be an arsehole.

Daniel shrugged. 'He's an arrogant tosser and a racist. Been like that for years. And he leches after Violet.' A flash of emotion across Daniel's face. Jealousy?

'How does Violet react to that?'

'She didn't dare say anything – he's her boss.'

'But Anna runs the abattoir, not Gary?'

Daniel gave a tiny smile. 'Yes. Their parents left it to Anna. Thought she was more responsible. Even though she doesn't want to be here.'

'Is that a problem for Gary?'

'Yes.'

'Why does he work for his sister if he hates it so much?'

Daniel shrugged. 'Don't ask me how Gary's mind works. But I guess she pays him well and is softer on him than any other employer would be. He's not the most diligent employee.'

'Does Violet have a boyfriend or girlfriend?' I asked.

'I don't think so. If she does, they wouldn't want to see the way Gary fawns over her.' He stood, grabbed our empty cups, pivoted round, and dumped them in the sink. His arm went to his lower back and gave it a quick rub.

'Where were you last night?' I asked.

Daniel ran the tap over the cups, then leaned forward to splash water on his face. 'Here, in bed.'

'Can anyone confirm that?'

'I doubt it. I was on my own. And we don't have twenty CCTV cameras for every caravan here. Not like the main village.'

'Are you from round here?' Jai asked.

Daniel turned to face us, dropping his hands by his sides and leaning against the sink. 'Yes, I grew up in Gritton.'

'Do your parents still live here then?'

'I never knew my dad, and my mum moved away. She won't ever come back.'

'Why not?'

'Can't stand the place.'

Again the strange undercurrents. 'Do you like living in Gritton?' I said.

'You drove through the village?'

I nodded.

Something dark and desperate passed across his face. 'Can you imagine growing up there? Spied on the whole time, fences everywhere so kids can't even leave their gardens, constantly corralled like prize ponies until they go crazy.' That was the most animated he'd been since we'd arrived, his voice quick and forceful.

'Did it drive you crazy?' I said.

'A little. A long time ago.'

The situation with Anna, Daniel and Gary made my detective nose twitch. They all worked at the abattoir and yet none of them wanted to be there. I got the impression they didn't want to be in Gritton at all, and yet they were trapped in this place, bound together somehow.

'Do you know anything about the Pale Child?' I asked.

Daniel gave a small shake of his head.

'If she sees your face, that means you're going to die?' I added.

He clenched his hands together, knuckles tight. 'It's not real. I told you – people here are strange. The old people moved here when their village was drowned under the reservoir in the 1940s. They claim you can still hear the bells of the old church ringing, even though it's underwater and had been knocked down anyway, plus the bells had been taken to Chelmorton and Chaddesden. That's how reliable the locals are. They'll tell you about a vicar who gives a sermon for the dead once a year. The Pale Child thing is just an offshoot from all that. There's nothing in it.'

'What's the story behind it?' I asked.

A muscle twitched under Daniel's eye. 'She's supposed to be a child who died in Victorian times. People see her through the trees. Or her ghost or whatever. If she sees your face, it means you're going to die.'

We were all silent for a moment, then I said, 'Did Violet see the Pale Child?' I recalled that Anna had claimed she didn't.

A flash of fear passed across Daniel's face. Then he gave a quick nod and said, 'Yes. At dusk in the woods on the edge of Gritton. She was sure the Pale Child saw her face.'

4

We pulled up outside the home of Anna's girlfriend, Esther, where Violet rented a room. It was one of a row of stone cottages facing a park. Roses and hollyhocks around the door; full-on chocolate-box front garden. It was in the excessively perfect part of the village, bordering the valley that swooped down to the abattoir, but far enough away that the abattoir didn't make its presence felt.

The bucolic view was ruined by a police van and assorted members of the search team. There was always a conflict in these cases – preservation of life came first, so we had to comb the area with the thoroughness of a Labrador looking for treats. But if this turned out to be a crime scene, we'd have inevitably compromised the evidence. We got out of the car and suited up.

'What was that about a child?' Jai said.

I filled him in on what Anna had told me. 'She was reluctant to talk about it,' I said. 'And she claimed Violet hadn't seen the Pale Child, whereas Daniel just said she had.'

'Hmm. Weird.' Jai struggled with one of his overshoes. 'Daniel likes Violet, doesn't he?'

'Yes. And there was a hint of someone a little less passive under all that hippieness.'

'It's always the quiet ones,' Jai said.

'Except it isn't. It's often the belligerent, aggressive and extremely loud ones. But yes, I wonder what Daniel's like when he's angry. And I think he saw something this morning at the abattoir that he's not telling us about.'

One of the plants in the garden was scenting the air with a sweet and nostalgic fragrance. A memory hit me from childhood. From the time after my sister became ill. Playing in the garden, me wanting Carrie to be her old self and help me make a mud-castle for worms. What a strange child I'd been.

We made our way to Violet's small bedroom. It was simple and serious-looking, not what I'd expected from someone who frequented YouTube in a pink bikini. A bookcase dominated one wall, the bed was covered by a plain white duvet, and a printer sat neatly on a desk in the corner.

I walked over to Violet's bookcase and scanned the titles. A wide range of novels, from detective fiction through to a cluster of magic realism and a whole shelf of orange-spined classics.

'Poncy books,' Jai said. 'Not your *Fifty Shades* type of girl.'

'And look at the non-fiction,' I said. '*Journalism after Fake News, Journalism for the Internet World, The New Feminism, Women and Art.*'

'Feminism?' Jai said. 'She prances around semi-naked on the internet. Does that count as post-feminism?'

I walked over to Violet's desk. There was no sign of a laptop. I leafed through a pile of papers by the printer. Articles from the internet: 'Art and ethics', 'Creepypasta and internet memes', 'When stuff goes mad on the net', 'Why stripping can be a feminist act' and 'Why stripping can never be a feminist act'.

'Looks like there's more to Violet than meets the eye,' I said. 'Nothing about meat though, or the threats from the animal rights people.'

'Hang on,' Jai said, and reached for a paper from the floor. He held it up for me to read: 'When online threats turn to physical violence'.

'Oh,' I said. 'She *was* worried.'

I turned to Violet's bed. The duvet had been dragged across it in a half-hearted effort to make things look neat, but you could still see the indentation in the pillow where her head had been the last time she'd slept there. On the other pillow was a neatly folded cotton nightshirt with a penguin on it.

I stared at the penguin. I could feel the old me starting to come back. Struggling to get to the surface like a drowning swimmer. I wanted this girl to be okay.

Back at the station, I stood in the incident room we'd been allocated, wondering if the temperatures were breaching any health and safety regulations. The place had the ambience of a Turkish sauna. I eyed my team. They were fanning themselves and muttering about the heat, sweating extravagantly.

In front of me, too close, was DS Craig Cooper. Red-faced, puffy, damp. There was a small cut above his right eye. I knew this was a bad thought, but if someone had smacked him, I reckoned he deserved it. Next to Craig – turned slightly away – was DC Fiona Redfern, usually competent almost to the point of being annoying, but currently distracted by a workplace conflict I hadn't got to the bottom of. Then Jai, not looking too bad, but unable to stop moaning about the weather for more than five seconds, partly to wind up Craig, who could never grasp that Jai had been born in England and was not acclimatised to the weather in the Punjab. Then a few more DCs I didn't know well, and then the indexers, including a new civilian investigator called Donna, shipped in and paid a pittance to type stuff into our HOLMES database. She was a retired crime scene officer, so at least she knew the ropes.

I steeled myself to do the briefing. This case had all the makings of being seriously high profile and I knew my boss, DCI Richard Atkins, would be concerned about me. My gran had recently died in circumstances which he knew had pushed all my buttons. But if anything it had left me numb, lacking in emotion, closer to what Richard would find desirable in a detective. Maybe this could be a chance for me to not get too involved. To prove I could follow the rules and do everything by the book. But for now, Richard wasn't around. He was on his way home from sunning himself in a secret location that we were all very intrigued about.

'Okay,' I said. 'Let's get started. Yes, it's a little warm and it would be nice if we had air-con, but we don't, so let's consider all the moaning about that done. We have a high-risk misper, Violet Armstrong, aged eighteen, disappeared from the abattoir at Gritton village yesterday evening. The last person to see her was a neighbour, when Violet went out at around eight.'

All eyes were on the over-sized image of Violet's face – dark eyes bright with expectation, confident straight-toothed smile, peachy skin.

'The *actual* Violet Armstrong?' Craig said. 'Bikini-strutting Violet?'

'Yes,' I said. 'The actual Violet Armstrong.'

'Wow.' Craig licked his lips in an unpleasant manner. 'Her videos are—'

'Yes, thank you, Craig,' I said. 'We're all familiar with her videos.'

Craig smiled. 'Oh, are you? There's a thought.'

'A more pleasant one than picturing you leering over them,' Jai said.

'Enough of the videos,' I snapped. 'She's a high-risk missing person. Treat her like anyone else.'

Fiona gave Craig a look of contempt before turning back to me. 'Why was she at the abattoir at night?'

'Works there. Why she would have chosen to work in an abattoir in an obscure Derbyshire village is one of the things we need to find out. This morning, her car was there, but no sign of her. No note. The CCTV was smashed. And her watch was by one of the pig pens, with the strap broken. There was blood on it, which has gone to be tested.'

'By the pig pens?' Fiona said. 'Was that where she'd been cleaning?'

'No,' I said. 'She shouldn't have been in that area. We don't know why she went there.'

'I don't suppose she was petting the pigs,' Fiona said. 'Given her views.'

'CSI are there,' I said. We were supposed to call them CSI now, just like on the TV show. I felt for the general public when our lot turned up sweating profusely inside their protective gear, instead of a bunch of Hollywood-polished Americans. 'We have her laptop, which was in her locker with her bag and keys. Her purse was there, with her credit cards, and her passport was at home.'

'She didn't leave of her own accord then,' Fiona said.

'There are definitely some worrying signs. Violet had been receiving threats from animal rights activists. Social media comments saying she was asking to have her throat slit, and one this morning from a member of the Animal Vigilantes, suggesting she'd got what she deserved. We don't know how the commenter knew Violet was missing.'

'Shite,' Craig said. 'I always said those animal rights people were nuts. They're the ones that wear those meat suits, aren't they? What do you think, Meg? You hang around with those sorts.'

I sighed. 'Just because I'm vegetarian doesn't make me an animal rights activist, although I wouldn't rule it out for the future.'

'I can't believe you even respond to him,' Fiona said. She'd been short with Craig recently, and she had a point. Ignoring him was usually the soundest strategy, but I had an enduring sense that deep inside (very deep indeed) there was a decent guy trying to get out.

'Anyway,' I said. 'I don't want us to assume Violet's disappearance is anything to do with animal rights. It's much more likely it's a family member or boyfriend.'

'Is she in a relationship?' Fiona said.

'Not that we know of – yet. But that doesn't mean she isn't. Her best friend's coming in.'

'What about family?'

'Her parents are on holiday in New Zealand – of all the inconvenient spots. They're on their way back. No siblings.' I fanned my face and took a swig of water. 'Christ, this weather.'

'Not going to break for a week or more now,' Jai said. 'And the abattoir's not far from the wildfire, so if she has wandered off for any reason, let's hope she hasn't got too close to that. It's not under control yet.'

'It's been a nightmare for the poor firefighters,' Craig said. 'They've been missing their afternoon naps.'

'Well, I'm sure the weather will break soon, and they can get back to posing for calendars and naked kitten-rescuing.' I wiped my forehead. I'd never sweated so much in my life. I was even repulsing myself. 'If it carries on much longer, I might have to dig out my dress.'

Jai fanned himself. 'If it carries on much longer, I might have to dig out mine.'

Craig snorted.

'Why not?' I said. 'It's ludicrous that it's not seen as okay for men to wear dresses. It says all sorts of things about society's attitudes that you really don't want me to go into right now.'

'No, we really don't,' Craig said. 'And we also don't want to see Jai in a dress.'

'Anyway,' I said. 'The people who have easy access to the abattoir are: Anna Finchley, who owns it; Gary Finchley, who's Anna's brother and works there; and Daniel Twigg, who also works there. They all hate each other. Gary said Anna can't stand Violet. He reckons Daniel's a junkie, but he appears to be functioning. I think it's drugs for pain relief – he has a bad back.'

'Gary sounds like a nice chap,' Jai said.

'Yes, God love the bitter ones. Anyway, there's that lot, and others could have got into the abattoir if they were loaned gate-clickers and keys. Or Violet could have let someone in. But if she wasn't due at the abattoir till ten, why did she leave home at eight? It's only a five-minute drive. Did she arrive at the abattoir early, maybe to meet someone? Or did she go somewhere else?'

'Then there's the abattoir waste,' Jai added. 'The Category 2 waste had been taken away before we arrived this morning, and we're having trouble tracking down the company that disposed of it.'

'Make no assumptions,' I said. 'We don't have a body. We're treating this as a high-risk missing person. Okay? We think she was wearing white overalls and DM-type boots. Witnesses say she always wears a brooch on a chain around her neck: a pelican. Never takes it off. There are lead mines in the area – the dogs should find a scent if she's wandered off and fallen into one. There aren't many houses nearby, but in the main Gritton village there's loads of CCTV, so that should help us.'

'Have we got her phone?' Fiona said.

'Unfortunately not.'

'We're on to the service provider to get call records and tower data,' Jai added. 'But if she didn't make any calls, we're screwed. And even if she did, the data doesn't always help – there aren't many towers in that area. But the techies are doing what they can. And before you ask, there was no sat-nav in her car.'

I was conscious of a general shuffling of feet, as if they were keen to dash off. To catch the golden hour.

'Without veering into the realms of the very unlikely, I reckon there are four basic scenarios,' I said. 'One – she's alive and she left the abattoir on her own; two – she's alive and she left the abattoir with someone, possibly against her will; three – she's dead and someone disposed of her body at the abattoir, possibly with the missing waste; four – she's dead and someone took her body away from the abattoir. If she's alive and left with someone, or if she's dead and someone took her away, that would most likely have involved a car. Which somebody may have seen. Do you agree?'

They all nodded earnestly – except Craig, who was looking at me with the expression of a dog eyeing up a lamp post.

'Anything else?' I asked. 'No matter how unlikely.' I tried to soften my tone. I did my best to make the briefings non-scary, so people could talk without fear of having the piss taken, although it could be challenging with Craig and Jai around. I was well aware that if I wasn't careful, I could end up with a queue of introverts at my door straight after the briefing, jostling for space with the folk from intelligence strategy, CSI, forensics, and family and media liaison. That I did not need.

But nobody said anything. They were too far into greyhounds-in-starting-boxes mode.

'Okay,' I said. 'Dismiss nothing at this stage. We'll do a short press briefing later today – get the photos out and an initial appeal. And let's find that abattoir waste before it's turned into puppy food and porky twizzlers.'

5

Violet's friend Izzy sat in one of our nicer interview rooms looking very young and overwhelmed. She had a standard-issue teenage look with long, straightened hair and highly defined eyebrows. I was hoping Jai would turn on his charm and get her talking, because if anyone knew what was going on with Violet, it was likely to be her best friend.

Izzy fiddled with her hair, stroking it like a pet. 'Is Violet okay? She's gone like totally off-grid.'

Jai activated big-brown-eyes mode. 'When did you last hear from her?'

Izzy softened. Brown-eyes mode successfully received. 'Yesterday afternoon. She said she'd come up with more info and she'd be in touch later. But she never called and she hasn't posted anywhere. Something must have happened to her.'

This was kids nowadays. Anyone who was out of the social media loop for more than a few hours was assumed dead or at least in a coma.

'Have you still got the message she sent you?' Jai asked.

Izzy fished out her phone and tapped the screen. 'Here.'

Five p.m. on Sunday: *Think I might be on to something. Let you know later xx.*

'On to something about what?' Jai said.

Izzy sniffed. 'Probably about her real dad.'

'Her real dad?' Jai said.

'Yeah, she was adopted.'

I glanced at Jai. He raised his eyebrows. We hadn't known that. Izzy carried on: 'She doesn't talk about it much. Her real mum's dead, but Violet knew she originally came from Gritton. She doesn't know who her dad was.'

'Is that why she found a job in Gritton? So she could look for her biological father?'

'Yes. But she didn't want anyone to know. With her being … who she is and all that. She was really messed up about it. I told her it might be best to leave it be, but she wouldn't. Do you think she found him and …'

We waited, but she didn't say more. At least that answered the question of why Violet had come to a backwater village in the boonies. 'Did she have any idea who her biological father was?' Jai asked.

'No. She knew her mother's name – Rebecca Smith – but she died when Violet was a baby. So Violet was asking questions in the village, hoping to find out who her dad was. But, like, carefully, not telling anyone why she was asking. I wondered if somebody had told her. And if Violet was going to try and see him. Last night, I mean.'

'If she found her biological father,' I said, 'do you think there's a chance she might stay with him for a while and not tell anyone?'

'She'd contact me. She'd know how worried I'd be. And she'd want to tell me she'd found him.'

41

I was holding on to the possibility that Violet had disappeared voluntarily, even as the likelihood slipped away with each passing minute. 'You know you have to tell us if she's been in touch, Izzy, don't you?' I said. 'Even if she made you promise not to? We're very concerned about her.'

Izzy shook her head, hair flying. 'She hasn't been in touch! I'm not lying. Honestly!'

I should have let smooth-operator Jai carry on asking the questions. I didn't have the knack with this one.

I smiled at her, trying to get her to calm the hell down, and indicated to Jai to carry on. 'How does Violet get on with her parents?' he asked. 'Her adoptive parents, I mean.'

There was a tiny wobble to her chin, but Izzy spoke confidently. 'She's fallen out with them – her dad especially. They never wanted her to go to Gritton. They said it was a horrible place, full of pig farms and abattoirs. That's when Violet started doing the videos. To piss them off. Her mum's vegetarian.'

'She made the videos to annoy her parents?'

'At first, yeah. We were messing around, having a barbecue. Violet had bought steak to irritate her mum, and I videoed her cooking it in a bikini. We uploaded it, for a laugh. And it went crazy. Thousands of views and all these people saying how hot she was. She didn't realise it would get nasty, and part of her liked it. As for pissing her parents off – she hit the jackpot. Plus she's making money now, you know, from adverts. And then some burger company paid her to eat their stuff and put photos on Instagram. But it's not like she was ever a massive meat-eater. So she's being a bit of a hypocrite. Before she was, like, the face of steak, she had a go at some lad at our school about eating factory-farmed meat. Said it was like rape.'

'What did she say exactly?' Jai asked.

'This boy had said the usual thing about bacon, like, *Oh but it tastes so good.* Like the fact he enjoyed eating it meant it was okay, no matter how hideous a life the animal had had. And Violet said, *And that's enough reason? That it tastes good? Would you rape someone, if it felt good to you?* It was harsh, but her reasoning kind of made sense in a Violet sort of way. It got a bit heated.'

That sounded more like the Violet who had the feminist books on her shelves. 'So it's a bit of a turnaround, then, doing what she does with the videos?'

'Yeah, I suppose … But, like I said, she wanted to annoy her parents. She got a kick out of people going on about her and saying she's hot. Violet's … well, she's complicated.' Izzy's face crumpled briefly before she regained control.

'What's it been like for you, Izzy?' I asked. 'With Violet suddenly becoming so well known?'

For a second she looked like she was about to cry. She shoved a strand of hair into her mouth, caught herself, and took it out again. 'It's okay, I suppose.'

It clearly wasn't okay.

'Is Violet in a relationship?' Jai asked.

Izzy's eyes widened. 'No. No, she isn't.'

'Anything casual? Anyone she hooks up with?'

She blinked. 'No. I'm pretty sure there's no one.'

I made a note to follow that up. I didn't trust Izzy's answers. 'Have you visited Violet in Gritton?' I asked.

Izzy reddened. 'Once. We went out for a drink with some people she knew.'

'Oh? Who was there?'

'The people from her work.'

'How did Violet get along with her colleagues?'

Izzy swallowed. 'Same as Violet always does. Being the centre of attention. That guy Daniel was mooning over her.'

That was interesting. Daniel had told us that Gary was the one doing the mooning.

'What did Violet think of Daniel?'

'Not much. I'm not sure she even noticed him. He's like really old.'

'Did Violet talk about anyone else she'd met?' I asked.

Izzy shook her head.

'Did she mention anyone she'd fallen out with?'

Another shake. 'No. But … I think she's in trouble. She's …'

'What, Izzy?'

Izzy swallowed. 'She's my friend, so … I like her despite this, but she does get on the wrong side of people. I mean, she deliberately winds people up, and the threats were getting worse and worse. I think she might have pushed it too far and those awful Animal Vigilantes in the meat suits have hurt her.'

Jai had gone to investigate Violet's parentage while I mulled over progress so far. Violet's parents were still on their way home from the other side of the planet. At least we could rule them out. The obvious candidates for hurting Violet were the Animal Vigilantes, but then again all her colleagues were a bit dodgy, and we'd want to take a close look at the biological father if we could find him. Plus I couldn't let go of my hunch that there was a relationship in the background. Relationships were always interesting, especially ones that people wanted to hide.

I browsed the comments posted on Violet's videos, getting a strong gag-reaction from reading both the enthusiasts ('We want to spit-roast you, Violet') and the haters ('You deserve to spend your life locked up in a cage and then get your throat cut'). I highlighted anything particularly virulent from both sides.

I looked up to see Jai approaching with two cups of coffee. He placed one on my desk. 'We've got her adoption papers. As Izzy said, the mother is Rebecca Smith. No father listed, but we're investigating. You look stressed.'

'Thanks.' I gulped the coffee down. 'Doesn't get any better, does it? I keep hoping one day I'll come in and a rich benefactor will have bought us an espresso machine.'

'Vivid imagination you have.'

'Not as vivid as the people commenting on Violet's videos,' I said. 'Have you *seen* this stuff?'

'I had a quick look. Pretty dispiriting.' Jai perched on my desk and flipped a knee up so his calf was across his thigh.

I recoiled. 'Christ, Jai. Is that some kind of primitive display ritual? Imagine if I did that on your desk.'

'It's a flimsy desk, Meg – British workmanship. I wouldn't risk it.'

I tried not to smile. Clearly Jai and I were getting back on track, but I vowed to avoid mentioning his girlfriend and her conflicted attitude to his children. 'Sit on the bloody chair, with your legs reasonably close together, and shut up.'

Jai hoicked himself off the table and sat unwillingly in my guest chair.

'Right,' I said. 'These comments on Violet's videos – loads have appeared today saying she's been killed, but we're obviously more interested in the ones from before her disappearance was made public. Even the ones who like her turn potentially homicidal if she doesn't respond to their pitiful observations.'

'Yeah, and it's not like they even start subtle. But whether they'd harm her in real life, I don't know.'

'Rejected men do have that tendency, Jai. Although I agree, the online ones usually stay there, where nobody can see how pathetic they are.'

'I'm not sure why the pro-animal ones hate her so much. What has she actually done? She's not drowning puppies.'

'She's making meat look sexy,' I said.

'But it's not enough for someone to harm her, surely?'

'Izzy said she deliberately winds people up, and there are so many people at the moment who are permanently furious, maybe she pushed one of them over the edge and they came to the abattoir to confront her. Anything on the biological father yet?'

'No,' Jai said. 'But we're carrying on with the house-to-house. Hoping someone in the village had told Violet her dad's name. Or maybe we'll find a lead on her laptop. You reckon she might be with him?'

'Maybe,' I said. 'Kids can be remarkably forgiving of some bloke that shot his load two decades ago, as opposed to the poor sods who slaved to bring them up.'

'But why leave the car and go missing in the middle of the night? Why not contact Izzy?'

Fiona poked her head around the door. 'I think we've found out where Violet was between eight and ten last night. Results from the house-to-house. Someone saw a car that matches Violet's.'

'Excellent,' I said. 'Where?'

'Visiting a man called Tony Nightingale. He's the father of Kirsty the pig farmer – you know, the one who's on the Great Meat Debate website with Violet and co. He's a pig farmer as well – with a farm at the edge of Gritton. I've spoken to him and he's confirmed Violet did visit, and apparently she was saying strange things. He's happy for someone to call on him.'

I groaned and looked at my watch. 'Oh God. Why did I arrange for Hannah to come this evening? I'll have to feed her from the freezer.'

'Hannah will be devastated,' Jai said. 'She'll be expecting eight courses of cordon bleu cuisine, based on your past performances.'

'Sod off, Jai. Those chips I got you from George's were a perfectly nice supper. And as I recall, I offered you cereal for pudding.'

'I rest my case.'

'I suppose the lovely Suki whips up fresh and fragrant curries every night?' Damn it, I'd gone there.

Jai looked down. 'She's away at the moment. She'll be glad to miss the kids at least.'

'Right. Okay.' There was a pause while my brain searched for something non-inflammatory to say about Suki and the kids, while contemplating Violet's visit to this pig farmer. 'Listen, Jai … You're only round the corner now. Why don't you come over tonight after we've visited the pig farmer? You could meet Hannah. I can't believe I've never introduced you. You'll like her.' And I'd make sure I didn't mention Jai's girlfriend, and we could go back to being normal with each other again.

'Ah, no, I couldn't crash your party,' he said.

'You may as well. Witness the rare event of me providing food, albeit from the freezer?'

He hesitated, then said, 'Yeah. Okay, I will. Thanks.'

'Good. First, let's see what Violet was doing visiting a pig farmer last night.'

6

Jai and I pulled onto the road out of Buxton. The sun was a vivid orange, and smoke from the wildfire was drifting up from the hills, leaving a hint of bitterness in the air.

'Did you get any more info on him?' Jai asked.

'Tony Nightingale? Pig farmer and all-round country gent, from a long line of similar. Rolling around in cash, by all accounts – and owns a lot of the land around here. Violet turned up at his house around eight, saying she was related to him. Could be a good lead. Maybe it's all a bit Thomas Hardy and he's her biological father?'

We drove through Winnats Pass, a spectacular, steep-sided limestone valley with cliffs on all sides, formed from a long-ago collapsed cave system. It had once been the main route between Sheffield and Manchester, famous for its bad weather and bandits. We went another mile or so in silence, and then ground to a halt in the traffic of Castleton. Tiredness was catching up with me, and I wished again that I hadn't invited Hannah over.

We chugged onwards, leaving Castleton and heading through the Hope Valley and up through Bamford, before reaching the outskirts of Gritton.

A red-brick farmhouse sat by the road, a tree-lined lane curling round behind it. A fence corralled a small garden, and an old path overgrown with weeds led to what looked like the original front door. A sign proclaimed *Mulberry Farm – Rare Breed Pork*. It was a decent-sized house, set apart from the neighbours, but wasn't that grand for a supposed country gent.

I drove round to a yard at the rear, passing a field inhabited by pigs wallowing in mud. I regarded them with envy.

'Nice,' Jai said. 'Shame they're going to end up on someone's breakfast plate.'

'You could always go veggie,' I said, 'if you're feeling bad.'

'But bacon tastes so good …'

I remembered what Violet apparently said. That using the taste of bacon as an excuse for eating it was like saying it was okay to rape someone if you enjoyed it. Definitely an odd thing for our bikini-wearing sausage-sizzler to come out with.

We knocked on a solid, newly-painted door at the back of the house. To the side was a rose garden, overgrown and knotty, with long grasses growing between thorned stems.

The door was opened by a man with the corduroyed, bespectacled look of a university professor. He didn't fit my image of a pig farmer, although I told myself there was no rational reason why a pig farmer should look like a pig. Then I noticed he had a thin covering of light, fair hair, almost like the hair on a pig's back, and I felt strangely reassured.

We showed the man our ID and he nodded calmly, confirmed he was Tony Nightingale, and ushered us inside. The door led into an unmodernised farmhouse kitchen, complete with Aga, non-fitted wooden units, and pungent, aged black Labrador. We sat at a Formica table while Tony Nightingale made tea. The Labrador lay on its side, only raising an eyebrow in greeting.

'Violet Armstrong came here last night?' I said.

'Yes.' Tony placed a teapot, cups, and a milk jug in front of us, and lowered himself into a chair. 'I'm sorry. It's all such a shock. She said some rather strange things.'

'What did she say?' I asked.

Jai fished out a notebook and pen.

'I didn't know who she was. I don't know about blogging and videos or whatever it is she does. But she told me not to tell anyone she'd come because she didn't want any publicity. And then …' He put his cup down with a trembling hand. 'Sorry. She said she was my granddaughter. She said her mother was dead and she wanted to find her relatives. And to find out who her father was.'

'Did you get to the bottom of it?'

He folded his arms. 'She'd been told that her mother was called Rebecca Smith. My daughter is Rebecca and she took my sister's name, Smith, when she went to live with her. But my daughter, Bex, isn't dead.'

'Did your daughter have a baby?'

Tony looked out into the garden. The evening sun was glistening on a climbing rose. A flash of anguish passed across his face. 'If she did, she never told me.'

'How old would Bex have been eighteen years ago?'

'Only sixteen.'

'Was she living with you at that time?'

Tony looked down. 'She lived with her aunt. My sister, Janet.'

'Oh?'

'Yes, I'm afraid so. It was … hard. My other daughter, Kirsty, lived with me.'

'What was the reason for Rebecca – Bex – living with her aunt and not with you?'

Tony jumped up. 'I forgot the biscuits.' He opened a wall-mounted cupboard and fished out a biscuit tin which he placed on the table with a flourish. 'Only Rich Tea, I'm afraid.'

'Thanks.' Jai was straight in there, as was the aged Labrador, who'd done a Lazarus-like manoeuvre and was now sitting staring dolefully at Jai while he rummaged in the tin.

'Ignore him,' Tony said. 'Burglars could maraud through the house unimpeded as far as he's concerned, as long as they didn't open any food containers.'

'Aw,' Jai said. 'He's hard to resist.'

I smiled. He was indeed hard to resist. I blamed those hypnotic eyes. 'So, Bex went to live with your sister?' I said.

'Yes. My wife, Nina, and I split up. Nina was from the Ukraine and she returned there when Bex was only three. I found it difficult to cope with two children.'

'Nina left the children with you?'

He nodded. 'I suppose she thought they'd have a better life here. I was terribly upset with her at the time, but now I think she was suffering from depression. I should have given her more support.'

I spoke gently. 'If Bex didn't live with you, is there a chance she could have had a baby eighteen years ago?'

'She was only sixteen. And Violet was sure her mother was dead. I tried to call Bex, but she hasn't got back to me. Then I phoned Kirsty, to see if she knew anything about it, but she didn't. I can't ask my sister – she died of breast cancer two years ago.'

'I'm sorry about that. We will need to speak to Bex. You say she took your sister's surname when she went to live with her?'

'Yes. Smith. For all intents and purposes, my sister adopted her. It was much easier with schools and things if she took her name.'

'Okay. We'll take her contact details from you.'

'Oh Lord.'

'Before we go, we'd like to clarify – the missing girl, Violet, was born in May 2000. When did you last see your daughter before and after that date?'

A look of shame crossed his face. 'She stayed here for a month the summer before that. I haven't seen her since 1999.'

'Is there a reason you haven't seen her?'

He swallowed. 'She doesn't like coming to Gritton, and it's hard for me to get away, what with the animals.'

'Why doesn't she like coming to Gritton?'

He looked out of the window at the old rose garden. 'I think she just has a very busy life. She's a dog trainer.'

I knew all about fathers who didn't see their daughters, but a 'busy life' didn't explain what was going on here. I was very keen to meet Bex.

'I love my daughter,' Tony said. 'It's just … shocking the way the years slip by.' He pointed to a framed photograph on an old dresser. 'That's her. That's my Bex.'

The photo was small and I had to stand and take a step closer to see it clearly. A slim, dark-haired girl of about sixteen stood next to a huge, spotty pig, smiling with exactly the same radiance as Violet.

'Do you think this Violet might be my granddaughter?' Tony said.

Looking at the photograph, he must have suspected as much. 'We're investigating that possibility.'

Tony nodded slowly. 'Right.'

'What time did Violet leave your house last night?' I asked.

'About nine thirty. She said she had a job at the abattoir. She had white overalls on, so I suppose she planned to go straight there. But she was agitated when she left.'

'Violet didn't react well to your conversation?'

'She was upset. Kept asking me who her father might be. I said I had no idea and she didn't like that at all. I'm afraid she left here in a terrible state.'

7

Bex sat in the back of the taxi twisting her fingers and praying the driver wouldn't start talking again. The closer they got to Gritton, the more her stomach climbed towards her mouth. It took all her energy to clamp her lips shut instead of shouting to the driver, *No! Turn round! Take me back to the station so I can go home!*

The driver lifted his chin. 'Visiting relatives?'

She didn't want to talk. She had no idea what might spew out. His previous comments had required no answer. *Everyone thinks taxi drivers are racist, don't they, love? But I don't mind immigrants. We had a Polish bloke do our bathroom.* She'd been able to sit and smile and nod, while her own private mental battle raged on.

If she tried to speak, would her insides erupt? She risked it. 'I'm visiting my dad.'

'Do you live with your mum then, love?'

'My mum's dead.' The casual lie slipped out. Easier to say than, *My mum left when I was three, and went back to the Ukraine.* Because what kind of mother would do that?

'Oh, darling, I'm sorry. When did she die?'

'Thirteen years ago.' Bex touched the pelican brooch she wore on a chain around her neck. 'It's okay. I live with Aunt Janet in Southampton. She's nice.'

That seemed to satisfy him. He didn't ask the obvious question. *Why don't you live with your dad?* She didn't want to answer that one, even in her own mind. There was only one possible answer: *Because he blames me for what happened.* And she couldn't handle that.

She needed the driver to shut up so she could prepare herself. She knew her dad didn't want her to visit him at all, never mind for a month. Why on earth had she forced herself on him? Her aunt had been against it too – begging Bex not to go to Gritton. But Bex felt a sick desperation to be closer to her dad and Kirsty. A hollowness inside her that she was sure would go away if only she knew them properly. When you've already lost your mum, you need to hang on to the rest of your family. When they'd done *The Importance of Being Earnest* at school, she'd been the only one in her class not to laugh at the joke about losing both parents.

Her dad and Kirsty had visited a few times – she'd last seen them a couple of years ago – but it had always felt unreal, like her dad wasn't really her dad, her sister just a stranger. Surely a month together in Gritton would fix that? So why was the prospect so terrifying?

She'd written instructions to herself in her diary that morning, which now seemed childish and pathetic.

1. *Pretend your dad wanted you to visit.*
2. *Get on well with Dad and Kirsty.*
3. *Make a friend in Gritton.*

She smoothed her dress over her legs. She'd tried to look nice, so they'd be glad to see her. A new yellow coat, a dress instead of jeans, girly shoes. She peered out of the window. It was dark ahead, despite only being early evening.

'Looks like a storm,' the driver said, and the rain came pouring down, pounding the taxi's roof. 'You're unlucky – it's been dry for weeks.'

The taxi splashed through a puddle and the driver turned the wipers up to maximum. Bex saw the sign, *Welcome to Gritton*, but the surroundings were hidden by the sudden downpour. She closed her eyes. She had a picture of Gritton in her mind. The dark woods behind her dad's farm, the rocks standing on the hill like prison guards, the reservoir that drew the light from the sky deep into itself. It must have come from photographs. She couldn't possibly remember it from when she was three, and she hadn't been back since.

The driver interrupted her thoughts. 'You want me to take you right into the village?'

'Yes please.'

'Some people get dropped here.'

'Could you take me to Mulberry Farm please, on the Bamford road?' Why would he not want to take her into the village, when rain was coming out of the sky like bathwater down a plug? When Bex didn't have a raincoat, and had a large case?

The storm had darkened the sky to graphite. A fork of lightning danced over the gritstone edge above the village, and Bex cringed, waiting for the thunderclap. It came a second later, making her jump even though she was expecting it.

The lane that led to her dad's farm had turned to a stream, and the taxi churned up a wave of water on each side as they cruised down. The driver clenched his hands around the steering wheel. 'This village,' he muttered.

Bex told herself it was just the weather. The black skies, pounding rain and cascades of water gushing over the hillside. But she felt it. Something ominous about Gritton.

It would be okay. She pictured herself in her dad's kitchen. He'd be delighted to see her, Kirsty would too. They'd drink mugs of tea and maybe have cake. There would be a reason he'd not wanted her to live at the farm with them. A reason she'd been too young to understand. A reason other than that he blamed her.

The taxi driver finally pulled up at the front of the house, by an old gate overgrown with brambles. He shouted over the noise of the rain against the windscreen. 'Here okay?'

The front door of her dad's house was covered in chipped green paint, edged with moss. The sight of it made Bex want to be sick. The old garden gate was rusting, and the paving slabs were cracked, dandelions thrusting through.

The driver jumped out of the car and darted round to open her door. She sat a moment. 'All right, love?' he said, a hint of nervousness in his voice, maybe wondering if she was going to sit there and refuse to move, rain hammering the roof of the car above her. He moved away, popped the boot open, took out her case and dumped it on the ground.

She dragged herself out and grabbed her case.

'Do you need a hand?' the driver said, already climbing back into the car.

'No.' She shoved a twenty at him. 'Keep the change, and—'

The driver pocketed the cash and accelerated away as if he had wolves at his tail.

Bex took a deep breath, then dragged her suitcase through the rusty gate and up the overgrown path. The rain and wind were so strong it was as if she was at sea, being thrown around by waves. She banged her fist on the door, but it had a dead feel, as if nobody had opened it for years. There was no bell. She kicked the base of the door, feeling her tears hot under the freezing rain. What kind of dad would do this? Not pick her up from the station, not even be at the door to welcome her.

She hauled the suitcase back to the lane and dragged it onto a path that led to the rear of the house. The weight of it felt monstrous and she had a fleeting memory of packing it, folding summer clothes and imagining herself spending mellow, warm days with her family. She swallowed a sob.

She'd expected to see a back door that she could knock on. It hadn't occurred to her that anyone would be outside. But there were people in the back yard, visible through the drenching, buffeting rain. Three of them, encased in huge yellow waterproofs, pulling things around. They were piling up sandbags, trying to stop the torrent of water flowing off the rocks and heading for the house.

One of the people turned towards her. Kirsty, her older sister, her face half-hidden by a huge hood. Bex opened her mouth to shout a greeting, but Kirsty turned away again and carried on shifting sandbags. Had she not seen Bex? She'd stared right at her. Bex felt a flush of humiliation. Had her sister deliberately ignored her?

Bex couldn't make herself call out. Instead she stood in the yard, invisible, rain bouncing off her stupid city coat, her case deposited in the river which gushed towards the house, her shoes engulfed in pig-shitty water, and let the tears flow.

8

Meg – Present day
Monday

I returned from creating a salad – or rather, pouring a bag of salad into a bowl – and found Hannah in my living room watching a cop drama on TV. Hamlet was sprawled over her lap, kneading exuberantly. I handed her a glass of wine and plonked myself on the sofa. My mind kept replaying the conversation with Tony Nightingale, but I tried to put Violet from my thoughts and focus instead on my evening with Hannah.

Hannah shifted Hamlet's paws. 'Good job I'm low on nerve-endings around there, Hamlet. Yay for spina bifida.'

'Oh God, shall I move him?' I could never tell how serious Hannah was being when she said things like that.

'He's fine. But do you need help with the food? Thai green curry. Home-made. I'm impressed.'

'I never said it was made in this home. I got it from the garden centre last week and stuck it in the freezer. I've no time to cook, not with a high-profile missing person case which I can't afford to cock up.'

'Oh wow, you mean that girl? The sexy sausage girl? Are you on that? I'm honoured you're even here.'

Violet's face flashed into my mind. A girl of contradictions. A girl who was starting to wriggle under my skin. 'I nearly cancelled. Whatever you do, don't let me get hammered – I have to be up super-early tomorrow.'

'What's happened to her? Missing from an abattoir? That's seriously disturbing. Is it animal rights people? They hate her guts. I had a look at some of her videos. Strange girl. Why would you do that? I suppose she gets money from adverts.' Hannah was having a conversation all on her own. I wondered if I could avoid answering.

'So, what do you think's happened to her?' Hannah said.

Obviously not. 'No idea, yet.'

'Is it the animal rights people? The ones in the hideous meat suits? I mean, I might have said those little barbecue-dances she does are a hanging offence, but …'

I gave her a stern look.

'Okay, I get the message.' Hannah nodded towards the TV. 'Have you seen this new American one? I couldn't help noticing that the female detective is always beautifully made-up and conducts her investigations in a pencil skirt and high heels.'

'Oh, we all do that,' I said.

Hannah snorted. 'If you wore shoes like those, they'd have had to surgically remove a stiletto from Craig's head by now.'

'We're getting along better these days. I think it's all a cover for deep-seated insecurity.' Although when I pictured Craig with a shoe wedged into his smug, bull-doggy face, the image lingered enticingly.

'Isn't it always?' Hannah said. 'Doesn't make it any easier to deal with.'

On the TV, the detective chased and apprehended a criminal, still in her heels. 'I think they must give her superpowers. Maybe I do need a pair.' I made a Wonder Woman noise. 'Stiletto Woman! She can run really fast without separating her legs at the thigh!'

'How much have you had to drink?' Hannah said. 'I thought you weren't supposed to get hammered.'

'Ah, you know. It doesn't count if you drink it while cooking. Or defrosting.'

'So, been on any hot dates recently?'

'No, Hannah. Seriously. I don't need this in my life. I read this dating blog the other day and you wouldn't believe the stories. You're lucky if the guys you meet have just the one wife and a few of their own teeth.'

'Yeah, I've got to admit, numbers of wives and children does seem subject to rounding errors.'

'The stuff in this blog was mad. Necrophiliacs, people with walls of knives. All that.'

'Sounds like the software engineers at work,' Hannah said. 'Have you noticed if someone fricassees and eats their lover's body parts, the cook is always in IT? And talking of bad dates, one guy greeted me by saying, *You're quite pretty for someone in a wheelchair.*'

'Oh Christ, really?'

'I can't be arsed with trying to meet someone at the moment either. I wonder if looking for men online is more fun than actually meeting them.'

'Much like house-hunting online, as opposed to turning up and seeing the desperation in the eyes of the poor bastards who've spent three hours cleaning away all residue of their sticky children and moulting dogs, and then you realise within two seconds of stepping into the house that it's not for you, but you have to go through the whole sad rigmarole of traipsing round saying, "That's nice," in every room.'

'House-hunting going well then, Meg?'

'I'll get there.' My eyes drifted to the damp corner of my living room. I was fond of my rented place, despite its undoubted problems. It was on a beautiful cobbled street in Belper, and I'd started to see its uneven floors and draughty windows as *features* rather than irritants. It had been good in the hot weather, its perpetual dampness creating a refrigeration effect, although I'd be wandering around in my extra-long scarf tripping over penguins come winter.

'I used to wonder if this cottage was haunted,' Hannah said.

'Whaaat?' She was normally so logical, and yet she thought ghosts might be stalking the property.

'It's cold and there are strange noises. And you always used to look up at the ceilings …' Hannah blushed. 'Sorry. I know why you did that.'

'I think we can lay the blame at the door of the geriatric boiler. You know there's that company called Victorian Plumbing, which I always thought was a weird name. Well, my boiler actually is Victorian plumbing. And as for me looking at the ceilings …'

'I'm sorry. I know.'

'Yes. It's okay. I'm over it. Most of the time I can walk into a room without thinking a family member's going to be hanging from the rafters. It's all good.'

Hannah winced. 'I honestly don't know why I said that.'

'It's fine. And maybe the house is haunted. It's ancient and it has its own microclimate and socks disappear all the time. Maybe there's a poltergeist.'

'Ha. Yeah, why can't poltergeists ever tidy up, if they're in the market for shifting stuff around.' Hannah paused. 'Seriously though, I know you'll battle on and work hard and get far too emotionally involved in your new case, because that's what you're like, but you do need time … you know, to get over your gran.'

'Time to get over being a coward and letting her suffer needlessly, after all she'd been through?'

'It wasn't your fault, Meg. She said she didn't want to go to Dignitas after all.'

'She was just protecting us. And me and Mum knew it. We knew the kindest thing was to take her, but we let her persuade us not to.'

'You'd been through a lot too. And you weren't to know it would drag on so long and so … horribly.'

I felt my eyes mist over with tears. I wanted to tell Hannah how much I appreciated her, how important she was to me, even though I could be prickly. She knew what I was like, knew how I could fall into that pit. I couldn't find the words. 'Hannah, I'm okay. But … thanks for keeping an eye on me.'

She shook her head slightly. 'Someone has to. And how's your mum doing?'

I closed my eyes and pictured Mum rigid with grief and horror at what Gran had gone through. 'She's a lot better at coping than me. Throwing herself at causes like a silver-haired ninja. I'm not sure her reaction's entirely normal.'

'Since when has your mum been normal? For her, heading off to El Salvador on a mercy-mission is quite in character.'

A knock on the door. 'Oh shit, Jai's here.' I blinked and leaped up, negotiating the hallway, which was narrowed by the presence of too many books. The front door had been sticking in the hot weather and I had to give it such a wrench, I stumbled backwards when it finally opened.

Jai looked at me with a slight frown. 'Always so composed and dignified.'

'Yeah, maybe Stiletto Woman isn't my destiny super-hero.' I grabbed the bottle of wine and six-pack of beer he was holding. 'I can barely stay upright in flats.'

'I have no idea what you're talking about.' He caught my eye. 'Are you okay?'

I hurriedly rubbed my face. 'Yes, come in.'

Jai stepped in, surveying the piles of books stacked along the wall. 'Have they been breeding? Asexual reproduction?'

'I had to move them around to do some cleaning. They're reeling from the shock of it, but they'll be fine. Come and meet Hannah.'

I led Jai into the living room and made the introductions.

'I *finally* get to meet him!' Hannah cried, then turned to Jai: 'She's always going on about you.'

'I am not always going on about him, Hannah. Jesus.'

I sat Jai on the chair in the damp corner. Hamlet gave him one of the slow blinks I loved so much, and settled deeper into Hannah's knee, purring furiously. I went to check on the food.

When I returned with drinks, it was obvious they were bonding. Possibly *over-bonding*.

'Does she give you that look too?' Hannah said. 'Like it could freeze boiling oil.'

I put wine glasses on the coffee table. 'I am here, you know.'

'There's the look,' Jai said.

I ignored him. 'I think we'll eat in here. It's too cramped in the kitchen and the garden's complicated.'

'That's fine,' Hannah said. 'Saves me having to move. Are you working on that case too, Jai? The sausage girl?'

'She's a real person,' I said. 'Just because you've seen her eating sausages in a bikini doesn't mean she's pretend.'

'Sorry,' Hannah said. 'You're right. Famous people never seem real.'

I wanted to say, *She's not what you think. She's not just a girl in a bikini. She reads feminist books and appreciates art.* But obviously I couldn't say that.

I nipped out to check on the food and returned with three plates on a tray. I overhead Jai saying, 'Yes, Suki wants kids of her own, but she doesn't like mine very much. It's as if she thinks by accepting mine, she's giving up on having her own. But I don't want more.' How did Hannah get people to do this? I should have had her on the interrogation team.

I handed them plates. 'It's like my silver service days all over again. Guests chatting away to each other; me the irrelevant waitress.'

'Except you haven't chucked boiling-hot soup in my lap,' Hannah said. She was attempting to eat her food without moving Hamlet. There's an unwritten rule in my house about moving cats.

My mobile went. I put my plate down and fished it from my pocket, in case it was work-related. *Dad.* The father I hadn't heard from in months, who hardly ever phoned me and was relatively monosyllabic when I called him. I stared at the screen, frozen. My finger hovered.

'Sorry,' I said. 'It's Dad. I'd better take it. He never calls. Something must be wrong.'

I touched the green button. 'Dad, are you okay?'

His voice came over too loud, as if he was nervous. 'Yes, fine. And you?'

I stood and mouthed, 'Sorry,' to Hannah and Jai. They were already deep in conversation. No doubt Hannah was telling him all my most excruciating stories.

I walked into the hallway. 'What's going on, Dad?'

'Do I need a reason to phone my daughter?'

Irritation fought with that old desire to please him. 'You never normally call.'

He separated his words, as if it was the early days of telephone communication. 'I thought I might visit you.'

I sank onto the hall stairs. 'Visit me? Why?'

'To see you. I know your grandmother died recently. I wanted to make sure you were all right.'

I felt tears welling up. He hadn't visited me for years. 'Have you spoken to Mum?'

'She doesn't like talking to me.'

'But Dad, she tried calling you about Gran and you didn't get back to her.'

'I never got those messages. So is it okay if I visit?'

'Of course it is. My house isn't big though. You know that? Or tidy.'

'I heard. Your mother said you were thinking of buying somewhere.'

'So you did speak to her?'

'Briefly.' No surplus information there. Dad had a tendency to miss out the bits that other people added to conversations without being asked. The bits that kept things flowing and meant you didn't spend the whole time feeling off-kilter. I couldn't remember the last time Mum and Dad had spoken. Dad and

Gran had never liked one another, and he hadn't come to her funeral. I felt out of my depth – the kid who didn't understand her parents' conversations.

'You know what my work's like.' The very thought of managing both Dad and the new case threw me into a panic. 'We're swamped. And I've just taken on a case that could be big. You'll barely see me if you come soon. When were you thinking?'

There was a moment of silence. I'd learned with Dad not to fill these gaps. You got more out of him if you waited.

'I thought maybe tomorrow,' he said. 'It doesn't matter if you're busy, I can amuse myself.'

'Tomorrow? As in the day after today?' I pictured my spare room, the bed piled high with books, the floor covered in old paperwork, the spiders lurking in the corners with long-term tenancy rights.

'Is tomorrow all right with you?'

I couldn't very well say no, but this didn't feel normal. 'It's fine. Just don't expect to see a lot of me. I can't take time off work at such short notice. If you arrive before me, you'll have to let yourself in and make yourself at home. The key's in the key-safe on the left side of the front door, and it's the first four digits of root 3.'

I cursed his unwillingness to tell me what the hell was going on. Because clearly something was. There was no way this was a social call.

9

Meg – Present day
Tuesday

I woke early and flicked on the bedside light, trying to remember how much wine I'd had the night before. At least I was calculating glasses rather than bottles, which was promising. I'd stayed up late talking to Hannah about Gran. Not a sensible move in the circumstances.

Violet was still missing. With each hour, the chances of finding her alive notched down. I crawled out of bed, pulled on my dressing gown, headed downstairs and stuck the kettle on. Hamlet emerged from a cardboard box by the door and stretched a front leg at me. He gave a supportive and rousing commentary while I sorted him out a breakfast of fine fillets of horribly slaughtered animal.

While Hamlet tucked in with enviable guilt-free gusto, I plonked myself down at the table and opened my laptop. Dawn was shining through my grubby kitchen window and suffusing the room with golden pink light, the summer continuing to hold a hot, dry finger up to climate change deniers.

If Violet's birth mother was this woman Bex Smith, who turned out to be alive after all, could Violet be with her? But why not contact her family or friends? It seemed inconceivable that someone so connected wouldn't get in touch with anyone.

I wanted to get a feel for Violet. Who she'd been before she became a case. A few years ago, missing people were like shadows. All the information about them came from others. Hearsay. We didn't see them talking and, unless they wrote diaries, we never heard from them directly. This had all changed. The murdered and the missing were amongst us still, with their blogs and vlogs and social media presence. Violet had taken this to a new level. There was so much online, you could practically resurrect a virtual version of her, like an episode of *Black Mirror*. And since everyone interacted online anyway, it would be almost as if she'd never gone, although she might not be making any new bikini videos.

I went to the Great Meat Debate website and clicked through to one of Violet's YouTube videos. She was cooking chops, wearing the trademark skimpy swimwear and the pelican brooch on a slim silver chain around her neck. Flat stomach, cellulite-free thighs. The evening sunshine cast a rose glow on her lightly tanned skin. I wondered what it would feel like to look like that. She probably took it for granted, like I did my uncanny ability to pass exams. I prayed to the imaginary friend I kept in my head for these purposes – *please let her still be smooth-skinned and beautiful, not seething with maggots in a vat of pig guts.*

Violet flashed a bright smile at the camera and chucked a sausage on the barbecue. She might not be contributing greatly to the sum of human knowledge, but she'd notched up several million views.

I clicked on another video, dated a week later. It was just as well we'd had a good summer – Violet was cooking again, in another bikini. Burgers this time. Music blared in the background and Violet danced along as she tended the barbecue. Halfway through, she reached for a vest-top and slipped it on over her bikini. It was bright pink, with the caption, *This Sexy Bod was Built by Meat*. The comments under the video were mainly enthusiastic, if on the sleazy side. Lower down the thread was the aggression. The assertions that she was a stuck-up bitch. The suggestions that she should try having her throat slit in an abattoir.

Other contributors to the Great Meat Debate website received less attention. Anna had recorded earnest videos about how it wasn't meat as such that was an environmental disaster but the quantities consumed and the way it was currently produced, in low-welfare systems where animals were fed grain instead of grass and straw and other foods which didn't compete with humans. Gary had a few videos in which he showed off his muscles, Daniel explained the design of the abattoir, and Kirsty Nightingale, Tony Nightingale's daughter, talked rather provocatively about the high carbon footprint of free-range farming methods.

I went through everything carefully. Gary did indeed make snide jokes about weedy vegans, and there was a spirited debate in the comments, in which the words *game changers* cropped up with some frequency. Kirsty also came in for plenty of criticism. Anna's videos and posts were thoughtful, scientific and detailed, and nobody commented on them, which pretty much summed up the internet.

Daniel talked about the curved walkways and rubber matting in the abattoir with great passion. Having read the comments – *If anyone ever slits your throat, let's hope they do it on rubber matting* – I understood his nervousness.

I leaned back and closed my eyes. Was this really about meat? Bad stuff was usually more personal, the culprit a family member or boyfriend. Or the person herself. I of all people knew that.

But recently, tempers had been rising. People were angry. About appalling animal welfare in farms and abattoirs. About carpets of pig manure from intensively kept pigs being spread over the countryside (it being particularly tragic when an animal's waste products saw more daylight than it did). About rainforests being incinerated to provide grazing for cattle. People were asking questions. *Why should your desire to eat meat every day jeopardise my child's right to a planet that's not an uninhabitable fireball?* Meat producers had become fair game. Could one of those angry activists have decided to make an example of Violet Armstrong?

I sighed. My money would still be on a boyfriend or family member. I navigated through to Violet's personal website and clicked on a video that looked different from the rest. Violet was fully clothed. She spoke to the camera like a professional. 'In the village of Gritton in the Peak District, there have been strange sightings over the last thirty years. Of a mysterious girl …'

That was weird. I wondered if this was the Pale Child that both Anna and Daniel had been so unwilling to talk about. I took a swig of tea and switched to full screen. Violet carried on speaking: 'The child is thin and light-skinned, and dressed in white, Victorian clothes. Locals call her the Pale Child.' Violet leaned closer to the camera and lowered her voice: 'Stories of strange, silent children are common in urban myths and creepypasta. This one is supposedly the ghost of a murdered child who lived in the beautiful manor house that was drowned under Ladybower Reservoir. People in this village don't like to talk of the child, and are scared of her. The rumour goes that if she sees your face, you'll die.'

How strange. I wrapped my dressing gown tighter around me, even though it wasn't cold.

I moved the cursor to the most recent video, dated three days ago, and clicked to play. Violet looked less composed this time. Strands of dark hair fell over her face and she was wearing no make-up. 'I talked before about the Pale Child,' she said. 'And … well, I think I saw her.'

So it was true: Violet had seen the Pale Child. I crossed my legs and leaned closer to the screen. Violet's voice was quiet, and husky as if she had a cold or had been shouting. 'On the moor in Gritton. A girl, thin and pale with blonde hair, wearing old-fashioned clothes and a creepy Victorian-doll mask. She turned as I was watching and I think she saw my face. By the time I got out my phone to take a photo, she'd gone.'

In the video, Violet reached for a glass of water and took a sip. Her voice was less resolute than her words. She flicked her eyes down as she spoke. 'You're probably wondering if I'm worried now. Worried I'm going to die because of the Pale Child. Well, I'm not. I'm glad I saw the girl. And I'm going to find out who she is. Because I don't believe in ghosts.'

I sat back and studied the last frame of the video: a close-up of Violet's face. I played the video again, pausing it now and then to look closely at her. I stared into her eyes. Behind the professional veneer, she was scared.

I nipped upstairs to shower and dress, then remembered the phone call from Dad. It felt like a drunken dream, but I knew it had been real. He wanted to visit today, of all days. I stuck my head into the spare room. Dad had always been the tidy one – trailing

73

round after me, Mum and Carrie, tutting and putting cereal boxes in cupboards, books on shelves. When Carrie got ill, she'd had a free pass. Cancer trumps having to tidy up. Cancer trumps everything. So his full irritation had been unleashed on me and Mum. The prospect of him staying in this room didn't bear thinking about.

At least I'd changed the sheets, and there was a path to the side of the bed. I frantically piled the books into higher towers, thus freeing more floor space, albeit at the risk of Dad becoming entombed in the night. While I worked, I thought about Violet and the Pale Child. Obviously the child wasn't a ghost, but who was she? Was she the reason for all the fences? The sign about *Village of the Damned*?

The vacuum cleaner enjoyed a largely untroubled life in the corner of the spare room. I plugged it in and shoved it half-heartedly over the areas of carpet not covered by books. It made quite an impact – one advantage of cleaning on an annual basis was that you could see the difference. I reminded myself that I was in my thirties and if I wanted to live in a house with books piled on the floor and cobwebs hanging from the beams, that was my decision. It wasn't that I enjoyed living under layers of dust, surrounded by spiders, but getting the hoover out had never been a priority in my life. Besides, spiders had the right to a peaceful existence.

I folded two towels and placed them on the bed, chucked a hotel shampoo bottle on top, and decided that would do. My eyes were drawn to a pile of framed photographs stacked in the corner. Photographs I'd not felt able to display. I fished one out and wiped the dust from it. Carrie and me on a beach, before she got ill. She was about eleven, squinting into the sun, blonde hair blowing into her eyes. I must have been around seven, although the way I was clutching a red bucket made me look younger. The colours were distorted, as if it was another world where greens were more yellow and reds more purple. I took the photograph and placed it gently on the bedside table. If Dad couldn't cope with it, he could always put it away again.

A noise drifted up the stairs. The cat flap in the kitchen banging open. I left the spare room, resisting the urge to flick my eyes to the ceiling, and headed downstairs. Hamlet came beetling through to the hallway, his little legs a blur. I gave him a cuddle and had a quick look around with the eyes of a parental visitor. Not great.

I picked up a flyer for a pizza place that didn't even deliver to my address, hearing Mum's voice in my head. *You need to stop trying to impress him.* She certainly wasn't trying to impress him with her recent antics. I felt a sharp stab of worry about her. I should visit but had no time. Nothing was more important right now than getting to work and finding Violet. If we didn't find her today, we could virtually rule out finding her alive.

10

Bex – August 1999

Bex cradled a mug of tea. The kitchen was thick with the fug of wet coats and wet hair and wet dog, and she was sitting at a table with Kirsty, her dad, and the boy, plus a black Labrador who her dad had said was called Fenton. She'd tried to help them move the sandbags in the driving rain, and they were treating her as one of the heroic workers, but she knew she hadn't been much use.

Bex had imagined it so many times, being back in Gritton, that it didn't feel real. Kirsty was different to when she'd seen her two years ago – her edges sharper, the addition of something adult to her, a complexity to her reactions. Their dad was older, damper, less vibrant than she remembered.

Bex wanted to be nice, to get along with them, so they'd have no option but to embrace her into their lives. But she also wanted to scream at them, *How could you? How could you send me away and visit me just three times in thirteen years? It wasn't my fault!*

'You chose your moment to arrive in Gritton.' Kirsty gave her what looked like a genuine, open smile. 'An extra pair of hands was good.'

Kirsty was acting as if everything was normal, as if she was oblivious to the chaos of emotions Bex was feeling. But then Bex caught her eye and what she saw in those sharp blue depths made her realise that Kirsty was acutely aware.

Bex shrugged. 'I was rubbish. Wrong clothes – I suppose I'm a townie.' She thought of her lovely yellow coat, now sodden and smeared brown, her pretty shoes, ruined.

Her dad couldn't look her in the eye. 'No, you were fine,' he said.

'The water got into the library.' That was the boy. About eighteen or nineteen, like Kirsty. A dark, gentle-looking sort, except that he was gulping and slurping his tea, and dunking and devouring his biscuits, chewing with his mouth open. He caught Bex's eye, and then quickly looked away.

'It's fine, Daniel.' Kirsty spoke with an edge to her voice that seemed unwarranted, given the innocuous nature of his comment. 'We shifted the books off the lower shelves, so not a problem.'

Daniel looked up from his tea. 'Not a problem? The library's flooded. They're beautiful old books in there. I can't believe they were rescued from the reservoir and then you put them at risk here.'

Kirsty shot him a piercing look. 'The books are okay, Daniel. Why do you get so upset about a few books?'

'But if you'd let me divert the water to the other side of the big field …'

Bex's dad spoke, his voice firm. 'It's fine, Daniel. Let it go.'

Bex flicked her eyes from person to person, feeling for the undercurrents in the conversation. Kirsty saw her and dropped her shoulders and smiled. 'The books were from the manor house,' she said.

'Oh.' Bex knew all about the drowned house. Their ancestral

home, lost under the waters when Ladybower Reservoir was created over fifty years ago.

'Daniel's helping out this summer,' Kirsty added. 'Sometimes he has his own ideas about how Dad should do things. Forgets he's paid to do what Dad wants.'

Daniel looked at Kirsty through narrow eyes, then took a breath and laughed. 'Your dad's put so much effort into making sure the pig barn doesn't flood that the water ends up in the house. I just suggested we divert it.'

'We're not doing that,' said Bex's dad, placing his teacup down in a way that made it clear this was the end of the matter. 'If the house were to flood we can always move upstairs or outside. Pigs don't have those options. They mustn't get flooded.'

Kirsty said, 'It's sweet how much he cares for his pigs.'

Daniel smiled awkwardly at Bex's dad. 'I'm surprised you don't build a robot to move the sandbags automatically when it rains.' He was obviously trying to lighten the mood, but Bex had no idea what he was talking about.

'Dad makes robots,' Kirsty said. 'In fact, normally he gets the robot to make the tea.'

Bex's dad coughed. 'It's a prototype. It takes a little longer than I'd like.'

Kirsty rolled her eyes.

Fenton shoved his nose under Bex's arm, shifting it up so she spilled tea on the table.

'Dear me, Dad,' Kirsty said. 'For a competent animal trainer, you've done a shitty job with that dog.'

'Sorry,' Bex said. 'It was my fault.' She stroked Fenton's sleek head.

'You've just rewarded him for being an arse.' Kirsty's tone was blunt.

Bex felt sick. Had Kirsty become one of those unnerving people who changed from sunny to scary second by second? She pulled her hand back. 'Oh God, sorry.'

Kirsty laughed. 'Relax. It's fine. You weren't to know.'

Their dad grabbed a cloth and mopped up the tea. 'Don't listen to your sister. She's only teasing. She's been so excited about you coming.'

'So excited,' Kirsty echoed. There it was again. Kirsty's voice had two layers, the sarcasm so subtle it was almost not there. Bex could tell that her dad only heard one layer, but Daniel could detect the other one. His eyes flitted nervously between Bex and Kirsty.

Bex had never imagined that Kirsty might not like her, might not want her there.

'You should get your dad to show you how he trains the pigs,' Daniel said. 'He's really into animal training. The pigs are so cool.'

'Wow, yes!' Bex felt a sudden rush of optimism. 'That would be brilliant.'

Her dad smiled. 'Good. We can do that.'

At last, something Bex could do with her dad that would avoid the awkward silences. And training pigs sounded fun.

'Soft in the head, the lot of you,' Kirsty said. But she gave Bex a warm smile, and Bex realised she must have been wrong. Paranoid. She could be like that sometimes. Of course Kirsty was happy she was there. Nobody blamed her. The summer wasn't going to be so bad after all.

11

Meg – Present day
Tuesday

I was at my desk skim-reading the recent statements from the house-to-house. Violet had spoken to so many people in her search for Rebecca Smith, and the residents of Gritton had been so excessively helpful, interested and keen to share their thoughts with our officers, that we were drowning in their contributions. Most of it was tediously irrelevant, the only thing of possible interest being someone's assertion that Kirsty Nightingale – the pig-farming daughter of Tony Nightingale – dealt drugs. Surprising but not obviously helpful.

We'd spoken to Violet's parents when they'd changed planes in Singapore, and they'd had no demands from any menacing folk about Violet, so a kidnap was looking unlikely. The search teams had found nothing, and there had been no sightings from people who weren't attention-seeking and/or deranged, although plenty from those who were. A huge search of the moorland was underway, with help from an over-emotional public determined to get too close to the wildfire. Crime scene officers were at the abattoir, and in Violet's room at the cottage, and the tech team were going through her laptop. There was still no sign of her phone. To use a cliché, she'd disappeared into thin air.

Fiona stuck her head around the door. 'We've got some info from the house-to-house,' she said. 'An insomniac who spends her nights staring out at the lane by her cottage. And her lane's on the main route into the abattoir. She thinks she saw Violet.'

'Sounds helpful.'

'Yeah. She was sure she saw a small, green car drive past in the direction of the abattoir at quarter to ten. And Violet's car's small and green, so that ties in with Tony Nightingale saying she left his farm around nine thirty.'

'Okay, so it looks like he might have been the last person to speak to her.'

'Yes. And this woman – a Mrs Ackroyd – was sure no other cars passed her that night, although there is another way to the abattoir – you just have to go down a really narrow lane.'

Mrs Ackroyd could of course be mistaken, as witnesses frequently were. I'd learned that the more vehement the account and detailed the description, the more likely it was that the large, black man with a beard was in fact a small, white man with a moustache. Still, if Mrs Ackroyd was right, Violet had driven from Tony Nightingale's and gone to work at the abattoir as normal. But then what?

'I've tracked down Tony Nightingale's daughter, Bex,' Fiona said, 'who we thought might be the birth mother. She's a dog trainer who lives just south of Nottingham. She says Violet's not her child and she refuses to go anywhere near Gritton, or to a police station.'

Another one? Hadn't Daniel Twigg said his mum refused to

go to Gritton? What was it about that place? 'Oh great,' I said. 'Do we know why?'

'She won't say, but she was very adamant.'

'And she says Violet's not her child? Did she have a baby at that time?'

'Her answers were evasive.'

'Arrange for us to go to her,' I said. 'This sounds interesting. And let's have a closer look at Tony Nightingale. If Violet is his granddaughter, what are the implications of her turning up out of the blue? Could he have travelled with her to the abattoir? And what about his other daughter, Kirsty? Would it affect her inheritance or anything like that?'

'I'll look into it.' Fiona left in a cloud of competence. Whatever it was that had been distracting her, she'd let it go.

My phone rang. Anna Finchley from the abattoir. 'You'd better come and see this.' Her voice was flat. 'The Animal Vigilantes have put a banner up. Threatening us. It's horrible.'

'We'll be right over.'

I found Jai in our tiny, sticky-surfaced kitchen, making tea. He turned to me, balancing a spent teabag on a fork. 'Never interrupt a man who's mashing.'

'Even for a trip to the abattoir?'

'Crikey, you know how to offer a guy a good time.'

'They've had a visit from the Animal Vigilantes. A threatening banner's appeared overnight.'

'You win.'

'Why are you mashing tea with a fork? Is that where all the forks are going? You're nicking them for tea.'

'No. Today the teaspoons are partying with the forks in the black hole. This is my personal lunch fork.' He dropped it in the

82

sink and followed me out to the car. He'd never see that fork again. He frowned. 'You think the Animal Vigilantes haven't finished yet?'

I pulled out of the car park and took the road towards Gritton. The heatwave showed no sign of abating and the sun battered the dry rocks and scorched grasses of the moors.

'What about that abattoir waste?' I said. 'Please tell me we found it.'

'Um … Not yet I'm afraid. Nobody admits to knowing who took it away,' Jai replied.

'Oh, for God's sake. How can a ton of rotting giblets just disappear?'

'I know, I know. Fiona's on it.'

'This is all highly suspicious. Did you check with the rendering plants?'

'Yes, they all have cameras and an inspection process. They're adamant they'd spot human remains. We alerted the local ones and they've checked cameras for yesterday and there was nothing suspicious, but they'll let us know if any human heads appear.'

'Bloody hell, Jai. All right, I get the message.' I pictured the potential scene at the rendering plant.

'Sorry, I imagine you don't need that this morning.'

'You weren't exactly Mr Sober either. It was only Hannah being sensible. The pair of you got along well.'

'She's great.'

'Possibly a little too well. Did she start telling you about my awful ex, and threatening to locate my fat baby photos?'

'It was most enlightening. You never talk about your ex. Or your fat baby photos for that matter.'

'He was a nightmare. Don't assume arty, creative types can't also be controlling bastards. And my baby photos are fodder for bad dreams. I have horrible taste in men and I was indeed a very fat baby.'

As I'd hoped, an evening of Hannah sharing my darkest secrets had settled my relationship with Jai. We felt more like buddies again, although I'd be steering clear of any conversation about Suki.

We joined the back of a queue of cars behind a car towing a caravan the size of a small planet. 'Tourists,' Jai sighed. 'Why would you want to bring your accommodation with you like a giant snail?'

'Too many terrifying B&B landlady experiences?'

Jai glanced at me. 'I'm not sure I want to know.'

We sat in the queue for another ten minutes, with Jai cursing everyone who had ever visited the Peak District, or even looked at a map and considered it. 'And the bikes are a pain in the arse too,' he said.

'Ah, come on, at least they're doing their bit for the planet.'

'Are they though? Think of the environmental costs of manufacturing all that fluorescent Lycra.'

Gritton came into view, the craggy edge rearing up behind the houses on the hill, the abattoir nestling in the valley, visible through a shimmering heat haze. As we headed down, I could see a shape draped over the concrete of the main abattoir building.

We drove through the gates and pulled up in the car park, outside the taped-off area.

'That's hard to miss,' Jai said.

A huge banner hung from the side of the abattoir. It showed an image of a piglet skewered and being roasted above a fire, a wooden post shoved in its mouth, its dead eyes wide and terrified. Above the image were words in deep red. *Animal Vigilantes!* Underneath the image it said, *Justice for all animals! Who will be next?*

Jai and I climbed out of the car and stared at the banner.

Anna Finchley came rushing across the car park towards us, strands of damp hair stuck to her forehead. 'Who's done this?' She spoke in a staccato rhythm. 'Have they hurt Violet?'

'Have you any idea where this came from?' Jai asked. 'Was anyone here last night?'

'I didn't see anything. Maybe I should have set up a camera, but I thought if anything had happened with Violet, it was already too late. What was the point of a camera now? This is so horrible. Why can't things just go back to normal?'

Another woman popped out of the door of the abattoir and strode across the car park to join us.

'This is Kirsty Nightingale,' Anna said. 'She's involved with our website too.'

So this was Tony Nightingale's daughter. And possibly the local drug dealer, which seemed implausible, but I'd learned that you could never tell. She was also potentially Violet's aunt, and she was aware of that fact, if Tony had phoned her on Sunday night as he'd said. I recognised her from the video I'd watched earlier. She had a grounded look about her – like the junior school teacher who'd know what to do with the kid who'd swallowed a piece of Lego. She waved at the banner. 'Horrible, isn't it?'

I couldn't deny it, but I'd seen similar images cheerily advertising bonfire-night parties or gatherings of boy scouts. Why was this suddenly so horrific? Was it the inference that Violet had been harmed, or just the effect of looking with clear eyes at a young animal being skewered and roasted?

'Apparently there's a bunch of them in the village now,' Kirsty said. 'With placards. Ridiculous people.'

'Kirsty gets loads of abuse,' Anna said. 'They call her a murderer and a rapist.'

'They're disturbed,' Kirsty said.

'Have they been violent towards you?' I asked.

'Yes, they have. Those horrible people wearing the meat suits that make them look like they have no skin. I've had things thrown at me, I've been spat at. I've been worried for my daughter.'

'When did you last see Violet?'

Kirsty wrinkled her nose as if thinking. 'Er … when was it, Anna? We had a meeting about the website. Roughly a fortnight ago.'

'How well do you know her?'

'Not well at all.' Kirsty laughed. 'I'm not sure the glamorous Violet is interested in hanging around with yokel pig farmers.'

'Okay, we'll get someone to take a statement from you. Thank you.' I turned to Anna. 'Have you ever been targeted before? I mean, not just online?'

Anna shook her head. 'Not really. One time a group came here, but they were peaceful. I went and spoke to them. This is a high-welfare abattoir. We've invested huge amounts in making it the best it can be. I mean, you can't make it nice – animals don't want to die. But we don't use carbon dioxide stunning, and we've followed Temple Grandin's principles.'

'Oh? I've heard of her.' I remembered reading about an autistic woman who'd made it her life's work to improve the design of abattoirs. I admired that. Most people just turned away. That must have been what Daniel was talking about in his video with the rubber matting and curved walkways.

'I told the protesters all that,' Anna said. 'And I said we had CCTV that's properly monitored. They didn't exactly agree with me, but they stopped shouting and didn't stay long.'

'Any follow-up? Any contact with any other groups or individuals? Any threats since Violet started working here?'

'Only the ones on the website.'

'Who knew Violet was missing yesterday morning?' I said. 'Someone commenting on behalf of the Animal Vigilantes knew about it almost immediately.'

'Then they must be involved,' Anna said. 'Only Esther, Daniel, Gary and I knew she was missing, and we didn't tell anyone.'

'The Animal Vigilantes are dangerous,' Kirsty said. 'They claim to be anti-cruelty but they see the end as justifying the means. In their minds, if a few of us had to die to save a load of animals, that would be a price worth paying.'

A mobile phone rang, and Anna fished hers from a back pocket and checked the screen. 'Sorry. Better take this.'

I could hear a loud, frantic voice at the other end but couldn't make out words.

'Have you called the police?' Anna said.

More shouting at the other end. Anna let the hand with the phone drop to her side, and turned to us. 'They've come for Gary.'

12

A cloud of dust rose around the car as we accelerated towards Gritton village. The houses ahead clung to the yellow-green hillside, the ridge of rocks standing guard behind an area of moorland speckled with sheep.

The words on the banner kept edging into my mind: *Justice for all animals. Who Will Be Next?* Was Gary next?

Gary lived in Lower Gritton, the brick-terraced area we'd driven through on the way to Daniel's caravan. Washing flapped and scruffy dogs barked in ragged gardens. As we neared the address we'd been given, we turned through open gates into a narrow street. I slammed on the brakes. The car slewed onto the pavement.

Jai grabbed the handle above the car door. 'Glad to see the advanced driving investment paid off.'

'What the hell …'

There was a throng of people in the road, merging into one red mass. Protesters wearing their unsettling meat-design clothing. The Animal Vigilantes. Shouting and waving banners. The mass of meat suits was obscene, and there were flies circling them as if it was real meat. The yelling blended into a wall of noise, but snippets were audible. 'You're evil … Animal abuse … We're not fucking taking it any more!'

I spotted Gary, his back pressed against the door of a red-brick house, shouting back at the protesters. One double-crewed car was parked a few doors down and two uniformed officers were sprinting in Gary's direction.

I turned off the engine and Jai and I jumped out of my car. The noise and the heat and brightness of the sun felt like being smacked on the head.

Protesters surged towards Gary. The meat suits en masse, writhing and pushing together, were truly repulsive. Like the difference between one squirming maggot and a thousand.

The shouting increased in volume and pitch, and someone pushed into me. A flush of adrenaline hit my stomach. If this all kicked off, we'd stand no chance with our Austerity Britain allocation of just two uniforms. These weren't the skinny pacifists we normally found protesting about animal welfare. I sensed genuine menace.

I gestured to Gary to get inside his house, but he stayed put, standing solidly with legs apart, waving his arms and shouting back at the protesters. I pushed into the crowd, keeping my elbows firm, trying to get to Gary, to persuade him to go inside.

The protesters jostled me, forcing me into a man who stood a good foot above me and smelled of sweat and cannabis. He had a tattoo of a rodent on his cheek. A rat? I looked frantically for the uniforms. Others in the crowd must have picked up on the tension and there was an upsurge of noise and movement. A swelling of bodies towards me.

Shouting and shoving. Everyone bigger and taller than me.

Then Jai was beside me. Rat-man pushed him and shouted something I didn't hear. Jai spun round, his face distorted with anger. Everything was happening at super-speed. Someone pushed rat-man aside. Gary. Rat-man spun round to confront him, and Gary lunged forward, fist raised and ready. I couldn't move fast enough to stop him. I waited for Gary's fist to connect with the man's face, for blood to explode from his nose, for the rat to be torn in two. But it didn't happen. Rat-man's body tipped sideways, and he let out a roar. A woman had kicked his feet from under him. He crashed to the ground, his phone smashing on the tarmac. One of the uniforms shot out of the crowd, grabbed him and pulled him up, holding his arms behind him.

And suddenly the mood changed. Placards were lowered, people started drifting away. It felt as if I'd imagined the intensity of the violence, as if the threat had been in my head. But then I saw Jai's face and realised it hadn't. This was real.

Gary shouted at the woman who'd kicked rat-man. 'Mandy, what are you doing? Are you crazy?'

And I realised the woman was wearing a dressing gown. Blue towelling with a tea stain on one arm. She looked confused about why she was out in the road, but she'd saved Gary from getting in deep trouble.

We left the uniforms to deal with rat-man, and said we'd handle Gary. The other protesters dispersed enough that Gary could open his front door safely. My heart was thudding unpleasantly in my chest, as if it hadn't realised things had calmed down and still thought I was about to get my head kicked in.

Jai and I followed Gary and the woman, Mandy presumably, into their house and pushed the door closed behind us. I turned the key to lock it and took a heavy breath. The house felt cool and damp after the hot dustiness outside.

A blur of flailing arms and legs shot down the hall and hurled itself at Gary. 'Daddy!' A small girl leaped into his arms. She must have been about six or seven, with tangled blonde hair. She was wearing pink leggings and a sparkly top.

Mandy said, 'Gary, you're going to get yourself killed!' She had lank brown hair and huge dark eyes, and the kind of thinness that's achieved by drinking and smoking rather than exercise and healthy eating.

Gary spun round to face me. 'Do you see now? They're crazy. They've got Violet and now they're after the rest of us.' He prised the clinging monkey-girl off him and put her down.

The living room was sparsely and shabbily furnished, and smelled like the day after a party – the kind where everyone's smoked and drunk too much and someone's puked in a wastepaper bin. An ancient and wheezy Jack Russell sprawled on the sofa, looking around the room like a feudal lord surveying his property.

The little girl looked up at Jai and me. 'Would you like a cup of tea?' She was so quaintly polite, she seemed out of place in the dingy environment, like if you invited the queen along to your local boozer. I peered through a door to the tiny kitchen. Old plastic milk cartons and unwashed tins cluttered every inch of available work surface, and white dog hairs floated over the vinyl floor. Normally I never turned down a cuppa but …

'I'll make the drinks.' Mandy disappeared into the kitchen.

'I need a beer,' Gary snapped, and followed Mandy, leaving Jai and me with the little girl. She gave us an open smile, unperturbed by her parents having almost ended up smeared on the pavement outside. 'Would you like to watch telly with me?'

'Not today, I'm afraid,' I said. 'We haven't got much time, and we need to talk to your daddy.'

'Nobody ever has time.' Her tone was so tragic I nearly found myself agreeing to watch *Frozen* with her. I sometimes wondered if I was really detective material. 'Mummy's always sad. And Daddy gets angry, and then there's no one to play with me.' I made a mental note of that. *Daddy gets angry.* And he clearly knew how to handle himself.

The kitchen door bashed open and Gary clomped into the living room. I was struck again by the incongruity of him. He was like a Hollywood actor doing his best to disguise his good looks in order to play the role of a scumbag.

Jai stood and held out his hand. 'DS Jai Sanghera.'

Gary reached slowly forward and shook Jai's hand. His face looked like he'd just found a body full of maggots, a look that was regrettably familiar. What was his problem? I remembered Daniel Twigg saying he was racist, and felt anger welling up inside me. Jai had nearly got hurt protecting this ungrateful bastard.

Gary spoke to me, ignoring Jai. 'Are you going to arrest those animal rights maniacs now?'

Jai's expression was unreadable. People still did a version of this to me every now and then. Addressed whatever man was in the room and treated me like a small and rather uninteresting piece of furniture. A dresser or sideboard perhaps. I hadn't seen the racial equivalent done to Jai before, but he'd told me about it. It made me want to put my hands around Gary's fat neck and squeeze until he passed out.

'Let it go, Meg,' Jai said, under his breath.

Gary seemed larger and more belligerent than he had the day before, as if the scuffle outside had released a squirt of testosterone into his bloodstream. It was useful to see – I was getting a much more genuine impression of him than if he'd been stuck in an interview room, minding his P's and Q's, even if we couldn't use it overtly in evidence.

'We have some more questions for you,' I said, rather sharply. 'About Violet. Shall we sit down?'

'Help yourself. I wouldn't get too near Flossy though.'

I walked past the dog, who let out a low growl. I went for a chair near a surprising old-fashioned TV with a wooden surround. The kind of thing you'd pick up on eBay for a quid if you were prepared to drive and fetch it. Gary sat next to Flossy and Jai took the other chair.

'I already told you everything yesterday,' Gary said.

'How well do you know Violet Armstrong?' I asked.

Gary's eyes darted to the kitchen door. 'Not that well. I already told you.'

'What's your relationship like?'

'She's someone I see at work, and we've both done stuff for Anna's stupid website.' He lowered his voice. 'She's a cute girl. I guess she caught my attention.'

So that tied in with Daniel saying he leched after Violet. I felt a flash of sympathy for Mandy. 'Have you any idea where she is?' I said.

'I already told you. No.'

'Did Violet ask you about a Rebecca Smith?'

He looked up calmly, not concerned by this question. 'Yeah, she might have done. Early on. I didn't know what she was on about.'

'Do you know a Rebecca Smith?'

'Nope.'

'What about Bex Smith, or you might have known her as Bex Nightingale?'

The air in the room solidified. This was different. Gary's eyes narrowed. He spoke slowly, with forced casualness. 'I vaguely remember that name. Kirsty's little sister, wasn't she?'

'Have you met her?'

A pause. He was hiding it well, but his breath was coming faster, his chest rising higher. 'I think she hung around a bit one summer when we were teenagers. She didn't live with Kirsty and her dad. I might have met her, I don't really remember.'

I was expecting him to ask if this was about Violet's birth mother. Or at least to ask what it was about. But he didn't, which was interesting.

The kitchen door poked open and Mandy said, 'Who's for tea?'

'Mandy, you should go back to bed,' Gary said.

'I'm fine,' Mandy said. 'Someone needs to look out for you, getting into stupid fights.'

'Well, since you're here,' Gary said. 'Tell them I was with you all Sunday night.'

Mandy spoke with such a lack of conviction I wondered if she actually wanted us to think she was lying for her husband. 'Yes, he was.'

'We'll need you to pop in to the station to make a formal statement,' I said. I suspected she'd talk when she was away from Gary.

'Go back to bed now,' Gary said.

'I'm fine.' Mandy flicked her eyes at Gary. There was a subtext here that was intriguing me.

'We're okay for tea,' I said, 'but sit down a moment.'

Mandy walked across the room and perched on the sofa arm,

giving the dog a wide berth. 'Gary rescued Flossy,' she said. 'She was abused. That's why she's not very friendly.'

Gary looked embarrassed. 'The police don't need to know that,' he said. 'I only did what anyone would have.'

'He loves dogs,' Mandy said.

I hadn't expected that. 'Well, good for you,' I said to Gary.

'Whatever. What else do you need to know?'

'I gathered yesterday that you were concerned about the threatening comments on the Great Meat Debate website?'

'Of course we're concerned.' He put *concerned* in air-quotes. 'You've just seen those nutters. How would you feel if a bunch of eco-terrorist twats were threatening to cut your throat?'

'Do you know anything that specifically links them with Violet's disappearance?'

'Other than saying they're going to kill her and then putting a banner up basically confessing? I told you – they're psychos. There's children starving, and all they're bothered about is a few pigs.'

As if you couldn't care about both children and pigs. Maybe this was to re-establish full macho mode after Mandy's revelation about Flossy.

'I'm worried about Gary,' Mandy said. 'The Pale Child saw his face.'

The Pale Child? I pictured Violet in her video, eyes stretched wide, trying to hide her fear.

Gary spun round to Mandy. 'For God's sake, woman! You need to go back to bed. The detective doesn't want to hear this crap. This is about Violet. And if anyone's going to get me, it's not the bloody Pale Child!'

'What exactly did you see?' I asked Gary, intrigued by his outburst.

'It'll have been some idiot kid running around in the woods,' he said.

'You told me she saw you, Gary.' Mandy's voice was rising. She looked at me imploringly, giving me the impression she wasn't used to being listened to. 'He admitted it last night when he'd had a few drinks. He was in the woods and the Child saw him.'

'The detective doesn't want to hear about this,' Gary snapped.

I noticed the use of the singular *detective*. Did he not even acknowledge Jai's existence?

'Why were you in the woods last night, Gary?' I asked.

'I took a walk with the others involved in Anna's stupid website. To talk about the fact that some maniac has got Violet and that we might be next. And looking at that banner, we were right to think they were coming for us.'

'If the Pale Child sees your face, you die.' Mandy's eyes were wide, her expression vacant.

Gary slapped his hand against the sofa arm. 'Shut up, Mandy!'

Jai spoke to Gary. His voice was icy. 'Perhaps you should give your wife a chance to tell us why she's so worried.'

Gary finally looked at Jai, and then at me. The dog rolled onto her back and Gary stroked her saggy, bald tummy. 'Mandy's not been well,' he said. 'She has mental health problems.'

Mandy whispered, 'We all know how it works – if she sees your face, you die.' She wiped a tear from her cheek. 'She saw Gary and it means he's going to die next.'

13

Jai and I headed out of Gritton and set off for West Bridgford where Bex Smith lived. It was over an hour away but we could talk through the case in the car so it wouldn't be wasted time.

'That was hairy,' I said.

'Yeah. The Animal Vigilantes have definitely upped their game recently.'

We drove in silence for a while, leaving the hills of the Peak District behind and heading towards Nottingham.

'What do you reckon about this Pale Child?' I said.

'Sounds like the over-active imagination of a bunch of villagers who need to get out more.'

I sighed. 'I know. It is strange though: Violet makes a video saying she's seen the child and then promptly disappears. And nobody wants to talk about it.'

We fruitlessly batted ideas around the car as we travelled down the M1 and around Nottingham, before finally arriving at the address we'd been given for Bex. It was a ground-floor flat in an old Victorian house. I pushed a bell, which annoyingly gave no indication of whether or not it had rung, meaning that when a woman pulled the door open, I had my ear pressed against it. She gave me a confused look, while I acted as if this was normal procedure and showed her my ID.

She ushered Jai and me into a gloomy hallway.

I blinked in the dim light, and my eyes came into focus. It was like walking into one of those crazy antique/junk shops where every nanometre of space is crammed with old and bizarre paraphernalia. The walls were lined with gold-framed paintings – portraits, still lives, horses and dogs, landscapes, and even the odd surrealist. Furniture on both sides of the hallway left only a narrow passage for us to walk down, and even that was cluttered with coat and hat stands, magazine racks and an alabaster bust.

Bex was dressed in loose black clothing, and was large, making it even harder for her to navigate her way between all her stuff.

'Sorry,' she said. 'I have a lot of things. Come through to the kitchen if you want. But I can tell you now there's no way that girl's my daughter.'

We stepped carefully along the hallway and into a much lighter room at the back of the house. A dresser was heaving with old plates, jugs and a clutch of strange china dogs playing musical instruments. Kitchen worktops were covered in books, including what looked like art portfolios. Minimalist this was not.

Bex had prepared for our visit: three wooden kitchen chairs were clear, and she gestured towards them. 'Sit down. Sorry it's a mess. I collect odd things without meaning to.'

'I'm the same with books,' I said.

We sat, and Bex took the third chair, blinking as if she'd recently emerged from a dark place, which I supposed she had.

I asked her a couple of questions about the saxophone-playing china dogs, just to settle her down, and then got stuck in. Jai sat with his notebook, exuding calm.

'Did you have a baby in 2000?' I asked.

'Er … yes, but it can't be that girl. She couldn't be more different from me. She's beautiful and confident and slim and … she just can't be mine.'

She said this, and yet I could still see in her a trace of the girl in Tony Nightingale's photograph – beautiful, clear-skinned, wide-eyed. Admittedly the years hadn't been kind. Her skin was rough and her features not clearly defined, almost as if they were out of focus or badly drawn. I said gently, 'Could you confirm your child's date of birth?'

'Nineteenth of May 2000.'

'Violet Armstrong was born on the nineteenth of May 2000 and her mother was Rebecca Smith.'

Bex shook her head and I could hear her breathing coming fast. 'No, she can't be. She's too …'

'Too what?'

And then Bex was sobbing. 'Oh God, oh God, I never really thought … I tried to forget, but I could never stop thinking about her.'

I sat forward and let my breathing come faster to match hers. That way I could slowly bring her down. I usually get a feel pretty quickly whether they're going to bond with me or Jai, and this one was mine. 'It's a very difficult situation,' I said.

Bex let some tension go from her body, and blew her nose loudly on a tissue which looked too pre-loved for comfort. I grabbed a pack from my pocket and pushed them over the cluttered table.

'I'm sorry,' she said. 'I'm disgusting. It's when people are nice

I can't cope. I didn't expect you to be sympathetic. You're the police.'

She must have had pretty low standards of being nice. All I did was shove a few tissues at her. These old-money families tended to run low in the sympathy department. 'We're doing our absolute utmost to find Violet,' I said. 'Most teenagers who go missing do turn up.'

Bex took a tissue and blew her nose again. 'Sorry. How gross. She didn't want to see me. I registered with that thing to get in touch. If you both register, they connect you, but she never did. Sometimes I wondered if she might be dead, but I couldn't let myself think that. It felt like she was alive and dead at the same time, like that physics cat.'

'She'd been told you were dead. But she did want to find her biological family.'

'Oh my God.' She sank lower into her chair.

'It's okay. It's a huge shock for you.'

'I saw on the news that Violet was wearing a brooch when she disappeared – a pelican?'

'Yes. And we've confirmed that she had the brooch when she was a baby. She wears it on a chain around her neck all the time, and her friend told us she has a tiny tattoo of a pelican on her hip.'

Bex softened. 'I left it with her. It's our family crest. Did you know the thing about the mother pelican gouging out its own chest to feed its babies? The pelican image is supposed to represent parental sacrifice, so it's a bit of a joke that it's used for our family.'

Jai and I sat and listened. Most people don't get listened to – not properly. Usually the other person's just waiting for their chance to speak. So, even though we're cops and they know in the rational part of their brain that anything they say could be used against them, the child inside is so grateful to be listened to that it's surprising what people come out with to keep our attention.

'Our family wouldn't win any parenting prizes,' Bex said, 'as you might have worked out. My mother went back to the Ukraine when I was three, and Dad sent me away to live with my aunt in Southampton. I suppose we're a strange lot. Not good with emotions. But Violet's so full of life. It's … it's so awful that she's missing.'

We sat quietly and gave her a moment to contemplate the child she'd never known. 'I've thought about her every day,' she said. 'Wondered if she's okay, what her adoptive family are like, praying she's had a happy childhood – better than what I could have given her. Now I feel like my insides are dropping away. Plummeting down in a lift-shaft. My child. You gave her to me but then took her away.'

'Most missing teenagers turn up,' I said, not believing my own propaganda. This was so far from a typical missing teenager.

'She's the opposite to me,' Bex said. 'I would never have believed she could be mine. Maybe I would have been like that too, if … if my life had been different. I'm glad she has good parents.' It hollowed me out inside, the way this woman felt about herself. The way she'd assumed Violet couldn't be hers because Violet was confident and sparkly and full of life.

'Bex,' I said. 'We need to know who the father of your baby was.'

She wiped her palms on her trousers. Took a few juddery breaths. 'I'm sorry but I don't know.'

My hope of turning up useful information sank a few notches. 'Tell us what you do know,' I said.

She paused. 'It sounds bad …'

'It's fine. Nobody's judging you.' I regretted that as soon as it was out of my mouth. Might as well scream, *We're all judging you*. I settled back in my chair and hoped I hadn't put her off.

'It happened in Gritton.' She leaned back and looked up at the ceiling, searching for the memory. A tiny wince as she found it. 'I'd been to stay for a month with my dad, the first time I'd been back there since he sent me to live with my aunt when I was three. Anyway, it was my last night. I got drunk. Very drunk. I wasn't used to it. And … and stoned. Sorry. The others went off because I thought I saw someone in the trees. And I …' A twinge of embarrassment crossed her face. 'I passed out and when they got back it must have already happened. I'm sorry, but that's all I know.'

I spoke gently: 'You must have been raped, you mean?'

She nodded. 'It's awful, not remembering.'

'Who was there that night?'

'My sister, Kirsty, and her boyfriend, Lucas. My friend Anna and her brother, Gary. And Daniel who was a friend of Gary's.'

Jai tensed beside me. Gary, Anna and Daniel had all been there. I'd known Gary had been shifty at the mention of Bex. Pretending he barely knew her. Could he have raped her? Could he be Violet's father?

'So you were raped by Daniel, Gary or Lucas?' I prompted.

'It wasn't Lucas. He stayed with Kirsty and there's no way … Oh, I don't know, take it from me – no boyfriend of Kirsty's would've dared have anything to do with another girl, let alone … that.'

'Did you go to the police?'

'I tried to, but … I couldn't go through with it.' She looked at us from under a strand of damp fringe. 'The policemen … I heard them laughing and joking about one of their colleagues. The size of her breasts. I couldn't talk to people like that about what had happened to me. I don't suppose they'd get away with it now.'

I felt a moment of shame even though I hadn't been a cop in 1999. That a girl who'd already been so thoroughly kicked by life, who'd been raped by a so-called friend, had encountered the worst kind of macho dickery and hadn't been able to go through with reporting a crime. And unlike Bex, I wouldn't bet against similar happening now. 'Is that why you said yesterday that you wouldn't come to the police station?'

She nodded.

'Did you see any of the boys afterwards?'

'No. I left Gritton and vowed never to go back.'

I pictured her father in his neglected kitchen, with his run-down rose garden outside. 'You haven't been back to Gritton since that night, even to see your family?'

'No. My dad and sister never even knew I had the baby. And imagine coming across one of the boys and not knowing if it was him that did it. Part of me wanted justice, but I couldn't make myself go back there. Something deep inside me was terrified of the place.' She wrapped her arms around her stomach, almost as if protecting a baby in there. 'Please don't ask me to go back to Gritton. I couldn't do it.'

14

I projected an image of the banner onto the white wall of the incident room. The piglet being roasted over the fire, mouth gaping open, terrified eyes. The statement – *Who will be next?* The image was even more grotesque in the confines of the station; the threat even more chilling.

The room filled with shocked muttering, which rose and then died down. A couple of lads at the back laughed at a comment I hadn't heard. I felt a brief spark of annoyance but didn't react. 'This was found draped down the side of the abattoir this morning,' I said. 'In the light of Violet's disappearance, I think we have to take it seriously.'

The muttering died down. The lads shut up.

'Yeah, Violet could just be the first,' Craig said.

'We can't rule that out,' I said. 'There's been a scuffle in the village involving Gary Finchley and the Animal Vigilantes. It's not clear how it would have progressed if cops hadn't shown up.'

'That banner's a clear threat,' Jai said. 'I've spoken to our insomniac, Mrs Ackroyd, and she saw a van drive past her house at three in the morning. It checks out against one seen at Animal Vigilantes protests.'

'Mrs Ackroyd's golden,' I said. 'So we need a serious look at the Animal Vigilantes. They know too much, they've made some very nasty comments online, they put that banner up, and they sent the aggressive mob to Gary's house.'

Jai fanned himself. 'The ringleader of the aggressive mob has a cast-iron alibi for Sunday night. But you've arranged an interview with the leader of the Animal Vigilantes, haven't you?'

I checked my watch. 'Yes. Shortly. There's also been a development on Violet's parentage. We've spoken to Bex Smith, Violet's birth mother. She was raped – she'd passed out and doesn't know who did it. But both Daniel Twigg and Gary Finchley were there at the time. She's sure it was one of them.'

Sharp intakes of breath all round.

'See if they'll submit voluntarily to paternity testing,' I said. 'And there was a third man there – Kirsty's boyfriend. Bex doesn't think it was him, but see if you can track him down just in case. Where are we at with other stuff?'

'We checked Tony Nightingale's alibi,' Jai said. 'A call was made from his landline to Bex Smith's phone at the same time that Violet's car was spotted by Mrs Ackroyd and then confirmed on CCTV. The voicemail confirms it was him. Also, someone watched catch-up TV at his house just after that, and he lives alone, so it's unlikely that he went anywhere with Violet. In terms of the implications of having another relative, his will splits everything fifty-fifty between Bex and Kirsty, so Violet turning up wouldn't make any difference to them.'

'Okay, good. Anything on Violet's laptop?' I turned to Emily, one of our best tech people. When she'd arrived the previous year she'd been so shiny and sparkly I'd practically had to wear sunglasses, but she'd faded. Contact with sex offenders' laptops could do that to a girl.

'We obviously haven't gone through it all yet,' Emily said. 'But she's done lots of research on finding lost parents. Also on whether online comments ever turn to real violence. And on this myth of the Pale Child. We don't have access to all her social media at this stage. We're working through what we have.'

'There's no phone data for her since Sunday afternoon,' Craig said. 'But we've got details of the numbers she called before everything went dead, and there are shedloads of them over the last few weeks, but she made calls in batches. It looks like she might have been trying to speak to everyone who lived in the village in 1999. We're working our way through them.'

'No phone calls after she left Tony Nightingale's house?'

'Not with the phone we know about.'

'Her phoning everyone ties in with what we've found from the house-to-house,' Jai said. 'She's spoken to every bugger in the village, asking about Rebecca Smith. That's why it's taking us so long to get through them.'

'Okay, fair enough,' I said. 'And bank data?'

'She used contactless and phone payments pretty regularly until Saturday. No unusual activity, no withdrawals of large amounts. And then nothing. We'll get alerted if she accesses the account.'

'Right,' I said. 'Anything more on alibis?'

'Mandy maintains that Gary was with her,' Jai said. 'And Anna's girlfriend, Esther, says Anna was with her. But Esther takes sleeping tablets, so there's no way she can vouch for Anna. Kirsty was on a password-protected internet forum, logging in from her home, so hers is reasonably solid. Daniel doesn't have an alibi.'

'What forensics do we have?' I said.

'Nothing of any use so far,' Craig said. 'They all wear overalls – Daniel's are navy blue, because he reckons the animals prefer that, and the rest are white. We found fibres from both blue and white overalls in the pig area and by the smashed CCTV, but that's not exactly surprising. They all work there.'

'Footwear marks?' I said.

'We found marks matching Anna's, Gary's and Daniel's boots in both locations.'

I sighed and turned to Jai. 'What about the abattoir waste? Where the hell is it?'

'Yes, about that.' Jai grimaced. 'Sounds ridiculous, but we still can't locate it. We do know nothing dodgy's turned up at any rendering plants.'

'You haven't been able to find the company that took it away?' I said.

Jai shook his head. 'Not yet. It was clearly an illegal one.'

'Great,' I said. 'I don't like that at all. Keep on it. Someone must know what happened to it. We have to find that waste before it's turned into … whatever it's turned into.'

'Food for our staff canteen.' Jai was alluding to an unfortunate incident involving a man named 'Maggot Pete' who'd sold condemned chicken to the police. It had been a good week for vegetarians when that one came out.

'Evidence of anyone else going to the abattoir on Sunday night?'

'No. Turns out Mrs Ackroyd's the only one in the whole of Gritton who stays up past half nine.'

'Curse these wholesome village folk,' I said. 'But thank goodness for Mrs Ackroyd's crippling insomnia.'

'You're all heart,' Craig said.

The door banged open and Fiona barged in. 'Sorry I'm late. We've had some info from the lab. There were traces of human blood and human hairs in the pig trough at the abattoir, and on Violet's watch.'

Craig let out a low whistling noise.

I felt my insides sink as the hope that Violet was alive settled lower, deeper inside. 'Are you saying the pigs attacked her?'

Fiona said, 'The hair was shaved off, not pulled out.'

'Someone shaved her hair off? Are we sure it's her blood and hair?'

'Should have confirmation soon.'

Jai grimaced. 'The pigs didn't finish their breakfast, did they?'

'We need to know if it's Violet's blood in the trough,' I said. 'Get that sorted urgently, even if someone has to drive down to the fast-track lab in Oxford.'

'No problem,' Fiona said.

Jai was shaking his head and blinking. 'They shaved her hair off,' he said.

'There's another thing,' Fiona said. 'A comment's appeared on the Animal Vigilantes Facebook page. It says, *If you eat pigs, why shouldn't they eat you?*'

15

Bex – August 1999

'You've never seen the drowned village, have you, Bex?' Kirsty's voice sang out and bounced down the rocky hillside towards the reservoir. The sky was a dazzling blue, the air thick and warm in the valley.

'It's normally underwater,' Daniel said. 'It's rare to see any of it.'

Ahead of them were Gary and Anna, whose parents owned the abattoir in Gritton. Bex had been in the village a fortnight and had seen Anna most days. At least she was ticking one thing off her list, because Anna was starting to feel like a friend. It wasn't so easy with her dad or Kirsty. No matter how hard she tried, she couldn't shift the invisible barrier between them. She still felt like an interloper.

They were nearing the path which led onto the flats that were submerged when the reservoir was full. Gary turned and shouted, 'Hurry up!' Bex had to admit he was easy on the eye, but she wasn't sure she'd trust him.

'I've got a blister,' Bex said. 'Stupid sandals. You go on ahead. I'll catch up.'

'I'll walk with you.' Daniel gave a soft smile. 'There's no hurry.'

Kirsty laughed. 'Okay, I'll leave you two to get to know each other better.' And she scampered off down the path ahead of them.

Bex felt awkward suddenly, as if something was going on that she didn't understand. Daniel asked the questions others didn't. He looked at you like he could see through your skin to the bones of you. Bex wasn't used to being looked at like that, and she wasn't sure if she liked it or it scared her.

'Dad didn't want us to come down here,' she said, for want of anything better. 'I don't know why.'

'Does he remember the village being drowned?' Daniel said.

'No, he wasn't even born. But I suppose his parents must have talked about it. About losing their home to the waters. Such a weird thing to happen.'

They were nearing the edge of the reservoir, or at least where the edge usually was. 'Here are the gateposts for the road to nowhere,' Daniel said.

Two stone posts stood in the trees, recalling a time when a grand driveway must have led down into the valley. 'How sad.' Bex walked forward and stood between the gateposts. Closed her eyes.

'Do you remember your mum at all?' Daniel said, reminding her why she found him both exhilarating and scary.

She took a breath, not sure whether she wanted to talk, then decided she did, and shook her head. 'I was only three when she left. Sometimes I think I get a glimmer of a memory, but then it dissolves to nothing.'

'Kirsty said you liked painting and your mum used to do that with you.'

Bex's heart pulsed faster. What else had Kirsty told him? She looked at Daniel but couldn't read anything in his wide, clear eyes. 'I can't remember,' she said.

They took the path through a sprinkling of trees towards the beige expanse ahead. 'Wow, is that it?' Bex said. It looked like buildings that had been bombed. Piles of rubble where walls once were, surprising stone things rising from the mud, layers of silt over old floors.

'Yes. The church spire used to stick up above the water, but they knocked it down.'

'What a shame.'

The destroyed village was laid out in front of them. Bex couldn't imagine what it must have been like to watch the waters rising. Engulfing your home. A buzzard swooped and cried overhead, its voice so plaintive Bex could imagine it singing for everything that had been lost.

'I remember your mum,' Daniel said.

That broke Bex from her imaginings. She turned to look at him. 'What did you say?'

'I was only six, but I remember. I found her exotic. She was called Nina, wasn't she? A foreign name. And I remember a time I went into the shop with Gary to buy sweets. Gary pushed in front of your mum and she smacked him.'

Bex took a step away from Daniel. 'My mum *smacked* Gary?'

'Yes, and shouted at him in Russian or whatever it was she spoke. Gary went nuts. It all kicked off.'

'God.'

'He had it coming, Bex. But the village kind of … turned against her after that.'

What a strange story. 'Why are you telling me this, Daniel?'

He looked straight at her, in that way he had. 'I wouldn't want you to think she left because of you.'

Bex felt a thickening in her lungs, making it hard to breathe. He must know. Her voice felt shaky coming out of her throat. 'Why would I think she left because of me? What has Kirsty told you?'

'Nothing. It's just … that's what kids think, isn't it? If their parents leave. I never even knew my dad, but it didn't stop me blaming myself, thinking he left Mum because she got pregnant. It was stupid.'

'I'm sorry. My mum went back to the Ukraine and left me and Kirsty here, so she can't have cared much about us.'

'I … I'm just saying it can't have been that easy for her. They're quite anti-outsider here at the best of times – and *outsider* includes someone from Derby or Sheffield. I'm not sure they got the idea of someone from the Ukraine, even before the thing with Gary.'

Maybe he didn't know. Either way, it was making her feel worse.

They walked over the silted flats until they reached the remains of what must have been a large house or maybe a terraced row of cottages. Bex climbed onto a stone block and looked around her. As she peered more closely at the remains, she could see it must have been a manor house. Some of the stonework looked precisely hewn. Ornamental. Expensive.

There was a sound behind her, and Bex turned to see Kirsty jump over a channel and step onto an old lintel – the kind of thing that sat above a fireplace. Her clothes looked wrong in the heat. Short black skirt, big boots, and stripy tights. Gary was there too, perched on a pile of bricks.

'This was our ancestral home,' Kirsty said. 'Not much left of it, is there?'

Bex looked at the chunks of stone and brick at her feet. 'It's kind of creepy. Why didn't Dad want us to come here?'

'Maybe he's scared of the dreaded Pale Child.' Gary jumped from a rock and landed in mud, sending splashes out sideways.

'Oh, Gary!' Kirsty brushed herself down. 'Dipshit.'

'This is where the original Pale Child lived,' Gary said. 'She was one of Kirsty and Bex's ancestors. She lived in this big old house.'

'Yes, we know all that,' snapped Kirsty.

But Bex felt a shock go through her. She'd heard rumours about the Pale Child. If she sees your face, you die. But Bex hadn't known she'd lived in their old house. Been a member of her family. She was both fascinated and repelled by the knowledge.

'She comes out in drought years like this one,' Gary said. 'Maybe we'll see her today.'

Gary was talking as if it was a joke, but Bex could sense the unease within the group.

Daniel gave Gary a look that Bex couldn't fathom. 'Why don't you shut up, Gary?' he said.

'Yes, give it a rest, Gary.' Kirsty flashed her blue-eyed gaze at him.

'This is so cool.' Oblivious to the tension, Anna was childishly overawed by the drowned village, and Bex liked her for it. 'The old church is over there. I wish they hadn't blown up the tower.' She ran off over the flats.

Bex wanted to run after Anna, but she couldn't because of her stupid shoes. She'd worn sandals to match her sundress, but all the others had boots on. She stood on one leg to remove a piece of grit from under the ball of her foot.

Suddenly she was shoved from behind. She let out a yell and

slipped from the rock she was on. Crashed onto her hip and then fell onto the rubble, her head snapping back into the mud below.

'Shit, sorry, I lost my balance.' Kirsty reached out to Bex.

Bex grabbed Kirsty's hand and pulled herself out of the mud. Her face was plastered in it.

'Well done, Kirsty,' Gary said.

'Shut up, Gary. It was you that made me lose my balance.'

'It bloody wasn't!' Gary strode over and grabbed hold of both of Bex's hands. He stood in front of her, and looked into her eyes. He had a very intense gaze. 'Are you sure you're okay, Bex?'

Bex wanted to look away, but somehow couldn't.

'Well, anyway,' Kirsty said. 'We need to get Bex cleaned up. She can't walk all the way back like that.' Bex caught her sister's eye. Had Kirsty *pushed* her?

Anna came barrelling over. 'Oh my God! What happened. Get off her, Gary!' She pulled Gary off Bex, and put her arm around her. Bex felt like crying. Thank goodness for Anna. She hadn't really wanted Gary to look at her in that way. She hardly knew him and wasn't sure whether she liked him or not.

'She's not all right,' Kirsty said. 'She's got mud all in her hair and on her face.'

'No, honestly …' Bex said.

'We'll have to nip to Daniel's,' Kirsty said. 'It's the closest house by far.'

Bex looked at Daniel's face. The colour had drained from his cheeks. He said, 'I don't think …'

'It's not necessary,' Bex said. 'I can walk home.'

'No you can't. Look at you.' Kirsty waved an arm as if they weren't all looking at Bex anyway.

'You do look quite bad,' Anna said. 'It would be good if you could get cleaned up. Are you hurt at all?'

Bex shook her head. 'No, no, I'm okay.'

'Dad will know I brought you down here,' Kirsty said. 'And this would just prove he was right to be so over-protective.'

Anna looked at Daniel. 'I suppose your place *is* nearest.'

'If he doesn't want to, then I don't think we should go there,' Gary said, and Daniel flashed him a grateful smile.

'It's not that I don't want to invite you,' Daniel said. 'It's just ... you know.'

Kirsty turned to Bex and stage-whispered, 'It's Daniel's mum. He's embarrassed by her.'

'I'm not,' Daniel said.

'Look, we all know,' Kirsty said. 'It's not like it's a secret. And Bex is one of us now.'

Was Kirsty being nice now because she'd pushed Bex?

'Kirsty's right,' Bex said. 'I can't go home like this.'

Daniel's shoulders dropped. 'Okay. You'd best come to mine.'

As he led them away over the remains of the old house, Bex couldn't help feeling guilty. It was clear Daniel didn't want them at his house.

They trudged out of the reservoir and set off in the direction of Gritton village. Daniel was silent as they walked, and the others picked up on his mood – except Kirsty, who kept up a stream of chatter about having a barbecue in the woods.

Bex was walking slowly because of her blister, and this time Kirsty stayed back with her. Of course she hadn't pushed Bex. It was Bex being paranoid again. She had to give Kirsty a chance and try to talk properly to her, otherwise it would have been pointless coming to Gritton and making herself stay for a month. She wanted a proper sister. One she could confide in. Maybe she needed to talk about more personal things, to try and reduce the distance between them. To start feeling like she belonged in the family.

'Did you know our mum hit Gary?' Bex said. 'Daniel told me.' And she immediately knew it had been the wrong thing to say. This wasn't the way to get close to Kirsty, who was already stiffening, her stride becoming less fluid.

'You shouldn't believe everything Daniel says.' Kirsty's tone was measured.

'I don't,' Bex said, backtracking. 'Does he not tell the truth?' It was easier to talk about Daniel than their mother.

Kirsty sighed. 'It's not that. He's just a bit weird. His mum's an alcoholic. But anyway, this time he was right. Mum did hit Gary, who no doubt deserved it. And now Gary hates all foreigners, which is stupid.'

'Daniel said everyone in the village turned on Mum and virtually drove her out. Is that right? Do you remember?'

'I don't remember much. But I wouldn't be surprised. I don't know why Dad ever thought someone from the Ukraine would fit in here.'

'Sometimes I hate her.' That had just popped out. Bex wasn't sure she even meant it.

Kirsty turned and looked at her. Their eyes met. Such dazzling blue eyes Kirsty had.

'For leaving us?' Kirsty said, and her tone was gentle, reassuring Bex that she was on her side after all.

'Yes. What kind of a woman leaves her own children?' And Bex knew she'd gone too far. Because they both knew why she'd left. Bex was desperate for Kirsty to tell her it hadn't been her fault, that her mum had left for other reasons.

'Dad says she was depressed,' Kirsty said. 'She was thousands of miles from home. People here didn't like her.' Bex felt herself relaxing. But then Kirsty's expression solidified. 'And it was terrible what happened.'

And then Bex wanted to lie down in the dirt and cry, because it was so clear what Kirsty meant. *She blamed you. We all blamed you.* Instinctively she knew it was best not to argue. To accept that blame and see if they'd let her back into their lives anyway. 'Sometimes I feel so worthless,' she said. Even though it hadn't really been her fault. Had it?

Kirsty gave her an appraising look, cocked her head and smiled her sunny smile. 'Well, there are some that would disagree.'

'What do you mean?' Bex was exhausted from trying to fathom the subtext. Was this going to be a nice comment or a dig?

'The boys. I never knew you'd turn out so pretty. Daniel and Gary have both got their eye on you.'

Bex blushed. 'Don't be ridiculous. You're the pretty one. With your lovely blonde hair.' She sensed it was safer to let her older sister keep the upper hand.

They reached the top of the path where it turned into a lane and entered the lower part of Gritton. Kirsty was right that Daniel's place was far closer than their dad's house, which sat high above the valley, looking down on the village as if it was supervising.

They arrived at the end of a row of terraced houses. The others were waiting by a gate which opened into a fenced-off street.

'Why is it gated?' Bex said.

Nobody spoke. They trooped through the gate, and Daniel looked down and fished a key from his pocket.

'It's to stop cars treating it like a rat-run,' Kirsty said. 'And keep the kids safe.'

Daniel was studiously avoiding looking at anyone. He shoved a key into the door of one of the houses, a shabby place with yellowing net curtains in the windows. He kicked an old milk bottle away from the door and pushed it open.

'Come in then.' Daniel led them into a dark hallway, and poked his head quickly into a room on the left. He sounded relieved as he said, 'The living room's there. Go in for a minute. Mum must be out.'

Bex walked into the tiny room. 'I'm a bit dirty ...' she started to say, but tailed off when she saw that ashtrays littered the floor and wine and whisky bottles were piled beside the sofas. A sharp, sweet smell almost made her gag.

'Are you happy now?' Daniel spoke directly to Kirsty.

Kirsty touched Daniel's arm. 'It's not you,' she said. 'We all know you've tried to help her. It's nothing to be ashamed of.' Her words were kind yet hollow. Bex was sure Kirsty had wanted them to come here. To see the house. To make Daniel feel bad. And Bex had gone along with it.

Daniel shook his head and said, 'Wait here.' He left the room and Bex heard him tramping up the stairs and shutting doors.

He was gone for about five minutes. Bex stood in the grim living room, looking at her feet and imagining him frantically cleaning the bathroom. Anna hovered in the centre of the room as if leaving as much space around her as possible, shifting her weight uneasily from one leg to the other. Gary had plonked himself on a green velour sofa and was trying to get the TV to turn on, and Kirsty was prowling around the room inspecting things. A row of unframed photographs were propped on the mantelpiece and she picked one up and examined it. Bex didn't want to be nosy but she could see that all the photos were of a boy of around eight or nine. There were none of Daniel.

The door banged open and Daniel reappeared. 'The bathroom's straight ahead at the top of the stairs. There's a towel in there. I'm sorry it's … probably not what you're used to.'

Bex smiled. 'Honestly, Daniel, it's fine. I'm so grateful. I'll just get this mud out of my hair.'

'Why don't the rest of you sit down?' Daniel said. 'Instead of standing around looking like you're waiting to be executed?'

Bex could hear them shuffling onto sofas as she headed out into the hall. She slipped off her sandals and climbed the steep stairs. The carpet was worn and loose and she trod carefully. The bathroom was straight ahead, and Bex walked in and closed the door behind her. No lock. The lid was down on the loo, but she needed to pee so lifted it and gave the seat a wipe with loo roll. The porcelain was stained brown under the water-line, but she could see Daniel had put some blue stuff in there. The seat wobbled as she sat, and then shifted sideways with a bang. She gripped on to it to keep it in place.

Reluctant to get undressed and venture into the shower with the mouldy curtain, she told herself it was only her face and hair that she needed to worry about. Her dad wouldn't notice mud on her legs and feet. She leaned over the sink, washed her face, and ran water through her hair. There was a bottle of shampoo propped against the hot tap, and she used some of that.

Daniel had left a pale pink towel folded neatly on the side of the bath. She dried her hair and realised that, contrary to Daniel's fears, this experience had made her think more of him rather than less.

She stepped out onto the little square of landing. Voices drifted up from below. The two doors on her right were firmly closed.

She took a tentative step forward. A floorboard creaked and she hesitated. But she needed to see what his room was like. She knew it was silly, but she felt like his room would show her what kind of person he was. Whether his questions earlier had been well-intentioned, or if he'd been trying to needle her.

She wanted to know if his room was neat and organised, a haven against the chaos around him. What books he had, what posters on the wall. Maybe there'd be some drawings he'd done. She could imagine him doing drawings. She hoped there *wouldn't* be that poster of the woman playing tennis with her bottom out.

She carefully twisted the handle and pushed the door open. Poked her head into the room.

It was tidy, the single bed covered in a smooth duvet in a plain black cover, the floor clear, and a few clothes piled neatly on a chair in the corner. And there was a picture on the wall, right by his bed. She took a step closer to it.

She froze.

It was a photograph. A face, zoomed in, blown up large.

Bex shot from the room, pulled the door shut behind her, and ran back into the bathroom, her heart pounding.

The photograph on Daniel's bedroom wall, right by his bed, was of her.

16

Meg – Present day
Tuesday

Leona O'Brien, head of the Animal Vigilantes, sat opposite
Fiona and me in the interview room. She was black, petite, and
well-groomed – not your stereotype of an animal rights activist.
If I hadn't seen videos of her in a meat-pattern boiler suit scaling
the walls of factory farms, I'd never have believed it.

The clue to Leona's beliefs was in her T-shirt, which was pink
with bold white lettering. *If you want to know where you would have
stood on slavery before the Civil War, don't look at where you stand on
slavery today. Look at where you stand on animal rights.*

She had the attitude of someone waiting for a routine dental
appointment. *Been here before, will be here again, it's not pleasant so
let's get it over with, shall we?*

I sorted out the formal stuff for the tape, my mind full of the
recent revelations. Violet's hair and blood in the pig troughs.
Someone had shaved off her hair and then … Was it possible she'd
been fed to pigs? Might the Animal Vigilantes do that? They had
been ramping up their activities recently. And if it wasn't them,

how had they known so quickly that she was missing? And why had they made the comment about eating pigs?

I'd asked Fiona to lead the interview while I watched.

'So, Ms O'Brien …' Fiona began.

Leona interrupted. 'It's "Doctor" actually. You can congratulate me if you like. Finally got my PhD. Analytical thinking in corvids. Very smart are corvids.'

Fiona nodded curtly. Leona was right about corvids. I remembered the video where crows dropped walnuts onto the road for cars to crush, and then used the pedestrian crossing to eat them safely. I had colleagues who couldn't have mastered that.

'I didn't do anything to the girl,' Leona said.

'But you put the banner up?' Fiona said.

Leona leaned back in her chair. 'Did you like it? I thought it was a good effort at short notice. We wondered about using a photoshopped image of a human three-year-old being spit-roasted. They have a similar intelligence and emotional capacity to pigs. But the real image was shocking enough.'

'How did you get into the abattoir?' Fiona asked.

'We popped over the wall.' Leona made a jumping motion with her hand. 'Easy-peasy when you know how. We couldn't have got inside the building. But we didn't need to.'

'The banner suggests that you harmed Violet and intend to harm other people.'

'Oh, I know. Aren't I naughty? I wanted the publicity.'

'So where's Violet?'

'Sorry to disappoint you, but I have no idea.'

'Where were you on Sunday night?'

Leona rolled her eyes skywards. 'Sunday … Sunday … Oh, I think that was a little meet-up with a friend. Yes, that's right.

In Barnsley, of all places.' She gave a beatific smile. 'Yes, I even stopped for petrol on the way up there. I bet you'll find me on the cameras if I check the receipt and give you the name of the place.'

'Yes. Please do that. What time did you stop?'

'About ten?'

'What time were you meeting your friend?'

'About eleven. He's a night-owl.'

'We'll need his details. Where did you meet, and for how long?'

'At his house and I stayed over.' She touched her hair. 'Does that give me an alibi? Phew.'

'Did anyone else see you?'

She tipped her head to the side. 'You think my friend Martin might lie for me? Oh no, Martin's a lovely man. He'd never lie. Super-ethical is Martin. And … you know what …' She leaned forward as if we were conspiring. 'I bet you'll see my van on some CCTV on the way home in the morning too. Wouldn't that be good?'

'What about other members of your group? Where were they on Sunday night?'

'Ah, well, I'm not sure. We're quite an amorphous group. I mean, this isn't my style, but I can't vouch for the others. People are very angry. They're losing patience. Nicey-nicey hasn't worked. The way the meat industry operates is intolerable, both for animals and for the planet. Maybe somebody decided this girl's life was a price worth paying to make it clear they're serious.'

'How did your group know about Violet's disappearance so quickly?'

Leona smiled again. 'I don't know. We're a big group.'

'Someone wrote a comment implying she'd been fed to pigs. Where did that come from?'

'Sorry, I have no idea.'

'What did you mean when you said she got what she deserved?'

'No mystery. We heard she'd gone missing and we speculated. Were we close to the mark? How funny!'

'Are there members of your group who are more inclined to a violent approach?'

'There are indeed. But they know I'm not, so they don't share their plans with me.'

'You know who they are though?'

'Not really. I gather our Lee had a contretemps with Gary Finchley, but I don't think he's the sort to do anything that requires planning.' Lee was rat-man, and I suspected she was right about his planning abilities.

'We'll need a list of group members, please.'

'No problem, but as I say, we're not an official group. And there are more aggressive offshoots. I'll give you a list of people I know.'

'Please do that.'

'I'd be looking at the men she rejected,' Leona said. 'You must have seen the comments on her videos. She wasn't always very polite to the poor boys.' This much was true.

'Anyone in particular?' Fiona said.

'You must know how it works,' Leona said. 'The rejected and humiliated male who turns to violence as a pathetic way to demonstrate his masculinity. Happens all the time in America – look at all those high school shootings. I'd be checking the comments on Violet's website for people like that. The rejected, the entitled, the men who like to control women. So much fury these people have inside them when they don't get what they want.'

'Yes, thank you. We are doing that,' Fiona said.

Fiona wasn't doing anything wrong, but it felt like Leona was running rings around her. And there wasn't much point pushing it until we'd looked at the CCTV and spoken to this Martin bloke.

My eyes were drawn again to the slogan on Leona's T-shirt. I had to admit I found the woman intriguing. It was invigorating to encounter someone with views so different from the norm, and she was clearly bright. I was a sucker for the brainy ones.

'Do you like my T-shirt?' she said. 'I can get you one if you want, although you need to know that some people find it offensive. Obviously they're missing the point, due to their rampant speciesism. It doesn't need to be about slavery. You could think about the rights of women in 1850, or people with mental health problems. Or children forced up chimneys. It's about whether you can stand back from the cultural norms of your society and see that these practices are cruel and wrong. Maybe you can? You're vegetarian, aren't you?'

I didn't respond. How the hell did she know that?

'What about the other people involved in the Great Meat Debate website?' I said. 'What do you think of them?'

'Gary has a nice body for a meat-eater. And Kirsty is quite pretty, in a blonde sort of way.'

'Thanks, Leona,' I said. 'Very helpful. Let us have that information today.'

'You've got to admit,' Leona said, 'if Violet Armstrong was eaten by pigs, you could argue that she got what she deserved.'

'She's a strange one,' Fiona said. 'Did she start the Animal Vigilantes?'

I stepped to the side of the corridor with Fiona. 'I think so, yes. But it's expanded massively in recent years, so I don't suppose she knows everything that's going on.'

'I bet her story about going to Barnsley stacks up,' Fiona said. 'I doubt she's stupid enough to lie about anything so easily verifiable. But she could have arranged for someone else to harm Violet. What have her group done in the past? Anything violent?'

'They did blow up a car once, but nobody was hurt. They've released a lot of animals and got into scuffles, but I don't think they've deliberately harmed anyone. Although she's right about not being able to speak for the rest of the group, and there's definitely a feeling of rising anger in the animal rights world.'

I heard footsteps behind and turned to see Craig striding down the corridor. 'How's it going?' His tone was wrong. Too friendly.

'What's up, Craig?'

'Nothing. I wondered how things were going.'

'Fine, thank you. Are Violet's parents back from their holiday yet?'

'Yes, they're here. Oh, and Jai has something to show you.'

A sick flush of adrenaline. Since the discovery of the blood and hair in the trough, further news was unlikely to be good. 'Has Violet been found?' I said *Violet* but we all knew I meant *body parts*.

'No. But I think you'll find it very … interesting.'

Craig was oozing smugness. Whatever was going on had to be bad, and it involved me, but I didn't want to give him the satisfaction of seeing that I was concerned. 'Okay, thanks for letting me know, Craig. Come on, Fiona.'

'What's he up to, the slimy sod?' Fiona said as I led her down the corridor.

'I dread to think. No doubt we'll find out later. We'd better see the parents. I hope they haven't been anywhere near the internet.'

17

Violet's parents were in one of our more pleasant interview rooms. It smelled of lemon air-freshener, and it even had a window. Violet's father stood stiffly with his chest thrust forward, clearly reluctant to sit on one of our grubby-looking chairs. He wore a suit that seemed to have been bought for a more svelte version of himself, and a polyester shirt that looked desperately wrong for the weather. 'Are you in charge?' he said, making it clear that me being in charge would not be a good thing.

Helen Armstrong, Violet's mother, looked up and snapped, 'Come on, Roy, you're not helping.' She was better dressed than her husband, in linen trousers and a neatly ironed blouse. I'd have bet that she'd been impeccably made-up earlier, but it was falling apart – mascara staining below her eyes and foundation drifting downwards. I realised with a jolt of unease that I was assessing the pair of them for TV-appeal-worthiness.

Fiona was next to me, her young femaleness possibly adding to Roy's feelings that the case was not in safe hands.

Roy threw himself onto the seat next to his wife and sighed loudly. 'Are you doing anything at all to find her?'

I took that as rhetorical. We'd given them huge detail on our efforts. Roy Armstrong would have been well up there with the suspects if he hadn't been so definitively out of the country when his daughter disappeared. Guilt could manifest as belligerence – I knew that for sure.

We'd decided not to share the information about the blood and hair in the pig troughs. No evidence of any other remains had been found, although admittedly the abattoir waste from the morning was still AWOL. My earlier hope that Violet might be alive was seeping away, but I didn't want her parents to realise that yet. 'We need to know everything about Violet,' I said. 'Obviously she has a very public persona, but we need to dig beneath that. The clues will be there. So please tell us anything you can think of.'

Helen dabbed at her eyes. 'She's a lovely girl.'

People who disappeared or died were always lovely. Nobody's parents ever said, *She's a bit of a shit, actually.*

'All this business with barbecuing meat on the internet,' Helen said, 'that's not really Violet. It was just silliness, and then people kept asking her to do more and more. But underneath she's just a normal girl.'

'Was she worried about anything, that you know of?'

'She started getting horrible comments online.'

'We're looking at the people who commented on her videos. Did anyone contact her in person?'

Helen shook her head. 'We haven't seen her since she moved to Gritton. Most people are found, aren't they? Nothing will have happened to her?'

'Most teenagers turn up safe and well.' I tried to give her a reassuring look. 'We understand she was adopted?'

'Did she find her biological family?' Helen's face was tight with anxiety.

Roy lifted his head and spoke, more to his wife than to us: 'I knew it would come and bite us in the arse one day.'

I looked at Helen, sensing we'd get more out of her than her somewhat rabid husband.

'We adopted Violet when she was a baby,' she said. 'It was what they call a closed adoption – no contact between the birth family and Violet. All we were told was that her mother was called Rebecca Smith and she was originally from Gritton.'

'So, Violet went to Gritton to find her biological parents?'

'Yes,' Helen said. 'We told her not to. Begged her, in fact.'

'Perhaps you can help us with one detail we're confused about,' I said. 'Violet was convinced her birth mother was dead, but she's not.'

Helen blushed. Shot a look at Roy, 'We have to tell them, love.'

'We thought it was for the best,' Roy said, his voice stiff. 'We met Rebecca Smith's aunt before we adopted Violet. She told us to keep Violet from having any contact with her natural mother or father, and to keep her away from Gritton.'

'Why would she say that?'

'She wouldn't tell us. She said she couldn't.'

That was strange. A pattern was emerging of people keeping away from Gritton. 'Did Rebecca Smith's aunt know who the father was?' I asked.

'We have no idea,' Roy said. 'Look, nowadays everyone wants to know everything, and there are these shows on the TV with ridiculous sobbing reunions. But it was different even a few years ago. A lot of people thought no contact was best. We told her right from the start she was adopted. But we thought the easiest way to stop her trying to contact her mother was to say she was dead.'

'That seems extreme.'

'If you'd seen the girl's aunt, you'd understand. It was chilling. She said under no circumstances should the baby have contact with her natural parents. Why do you think we were so against her going to Gritton? We were terrified of what she might find.'

18

'This gets stranger by the minute.' I spun my chair round to face Fiona, who was trying to get my sash window to open wider, without much luck. A few flakes of paint fell off, but nothing moved.

'I know.' She gave one last upward shove, and admitted defeat. 'Bloody thing!'

'I've tried, Fiona. It's not moving. Why would Bex's aunt say those things? What was so terrible about Gritton?'

'Do you think it was because she knew Violet's father was a rapist?'

'Possibly,' I said. 'Let's have a recap where we're at generally. Unpleasant as it is, the most likely scenario now is that someone killed Violet at the abattoir after ten on Sunday night, and disposed of her body by feeding it to pigs and/or putting it in the abattoir waste.' I pictured Violet's bedroom. Her pillow with the indent where her head had been. The panda nightshirt. 'Animal rights activists threatened Violet, but the only people with access to the abattoir overnight were Anna and Gary Finchley and Daniel Twigg, none of whom have decent alibis. And it's likely that either Gary or Daniel is her biological father.'

Fiona reluctantly left the window and came over to sit on my much-shunned guest chair. 'Gary Finchley won't consent to a DNA test,' she said.

'Why not?'

'Says he doesn't trust the government not to cock up and accuse him of some random crime, or sell his data to health insurance companies in the future. And since he's not under arrest, why should he give one, and he never slept with Bex, so he's obviously not Violet's father.'

I sighed. 'Fantastic. But Daniel agreed?'

'Yes. That's underway.'

'Good. Okay. I've read so many statements from the good people of Gritton that my eyes are bleeding, but I can't see anything useful. And as for the comments on our missing person Facebook post …'

'I've seen. The psychics are out. She's in an underground place, or she's surrounded by trees, or was it water? She's alive and needs our help, and we can find her if we'd only talk to them.'

'Would that it were so easy. And I see we've got more than the usual complement of victim-blamers. She wore a bikini publicly so she had it coming, whatever *it* might be. Who are these people?'

'I don't know,' Fiona said. 'Although some of them sound like my mum. We're taking those comments down as they appear.'

'Your mum?' I'd never heard Fiona talk about her mum. She'd mentioned a brother who she liked, and her gran, but kept quiet about the rest of her family.

She rolled her eyes. 'Don't ask.'

I decided to take that at face value. 'Okay. So tell me about the possibilities with Violet.'

'Right. Someone could have told her that either Daniel or

Gary was her biological father and possibly even that he raped her mother. That would have been a nasty shock, given that she worked with them. She could have asked whichever it was to meet her at the abattoir. Then confronted him and it got out of hand.'

'Yes,' I said. 'Although she didn't know who her father was when she left Tony Nightingale's farm, assuming he was telling the truth.'

'We don't think she phoned anyone between leaving his farm and getting to the abattoir.'

'No,' I said. 'But we do know there's something odd about her biological family – not just because her father's a rapist but because of what her aunt said. And who told Violet to go to Tony Nightingale's house? Somebody obviously knew who Rebecca Smith was, or at least that Violet was related to Tony Nightingale.'

'We're carrying on with house-to-house on that,' Fiona said. 'And contacting everyone Violet phoned, plus doing media appeals, including social media.'

'Then we've got this strange business of her seeing the Pale Child.'

'Yes. People say the Pale Child appears when the reservoir water level drops so that the remains of the old villages are visible. Like this year.'

'That's creepy. It is amazing what's appeared this year with the drought. I hear mountain rescue have had to hoick an over-enthusiastic explorer out of the mud by the old Derwent village.'

'It's the lowest it's ever been,' Fiona said. 'People are crawling all over it. And have you seen the drone footage of buried gardens and archaeological sites? You can see the outline of a seventeenth-century garden at Chatsworth – all the paths and borders and stuff. And a grid on the grass at Tissington Hall – nobody knows what it originally was.'

'I love Tissington. Remind me when I have a day off to go over there and pretend I'm on a bike ride but actually go to the tea room.' The thought of a cold drink in a tea room was practically making me drool.

'Sounds good,' Fiona said. 'The stuff from Gritton was more mundane, I have to say. Mainly septic tank outflows making the grass greener.' She stood and walked round to my side of the desk. 'Do you want to see?'

'Ooh yes, show me the septic tanks.'

She leaned in and clicked a few keys, bringing up an image of some drone footage. I recognised the abattoir in the centre, and the roads, houses and rocks of Gritton around it. 'No beautiful hidden gardens?' I said.

'Sadly no. But see those darker patches by the rural houses? Apparently, you can assess the health of the septic tanks from the colour and shape of these patterns.' She pointed at a green area fanning out from beside a remote house, contrasting with the scorched yellow grass around it.

'There's a niche skill,' I said.

'You can see where people have converted barns. Look at this one on the Bamford road – there's a septic tank for a big barn, so I guess it's been converted to a house.'

'I might prefer to see the hidden gardens, Fiona.'

The door banged open. Jai was silhouetted in the light shining through from the corridor. 'We've got the background checks,' he said, 'and Daniel Twigg has an interesting past. He's been inside for causing death by dangerous driving and driving under the influence of alcohol and drugs. But it was nearly twenty years ago.'

I pictured Daniel with his rock-balancing art, in his little caravan. 'Okay, let's find out more about that.'

'Will do,' Jai said, in a cautious tone. 'And there's another thing.'

My pulse spiked and I remembered Craig's slimy comments earlier. 'Oh God. What?'

Jai walked over, pulled my guest chair up to my desk, and actually sat on it (at which point I knew things were bad). He shuffled closer. 'Google *Justice for Violet*,' he said.

I typed in the words. Lots of hits. Fiona leaned in so she could see too.

'The Facebook page,' Jai said. 'Go to that.'

I clicked and a page came up. The header was the Animal Vigilantes' poster of the young pig being roasted above the fire, but scrawled over the top in red letters was the phrase, 'Justice for Violet!' Underneath was a photo of five large men wearing black trousers, black T-shirts and, rather ominously, black balaclavas.

I clicked, 'About', and read the description of the page.

> The vegans and activists have shown their true colours. Violet was a symbol for meat-eaters who are fighting back. Red-blooded men everywhere love Violet. We're sick of being made to feel ashamed of what we are. We like meat and we like Violet! Now these maniacs have killed her and fed her to pigs, trying to make some insane point. We won't let them get away with it.

I sighed. 'Uh oh.'

'It gets worse,' Jai said.

I carried on reading. My eyes skimmed over the next few words and I felt a horrible sinking in my stomach at the sight of my name.

> It's clear that Violet has been killed by the Animal Vigilantes, but the police are unwilling to take action! The investigation is being run by DI Meg Dalton, a vegetarian with an agenda! If she won't find Violet's killer, we will! These misguided animal liberation lunatics think they can save animals by killing Violet. They've made it VERY clear they plan to kill more people!! But we're not giving up that easily. Come forward and confess or we're going to start killing animals until you do!

'Wow,' Fiona said.

I slammed my hand on my desk. 'For fuck's sake!'

Jai shifted his chair away from me, as if I might get violent. 'Apparently, if whoever killed Violet hasn't confessed by midnight, they're going to find an animal in a field and kill it on camera.'

My anger was turning cold. 'Who are these people?'

'I suspect they're a bunch of angry blokes who feel they're under attack. These sorts have been after a fight for the last few years. White, heterosexual men who've never read a book in their lives and are proud of it. They eat lots of meat. And they like watching girls prancing around in bikinis cooking it.'

'But we don't even know for sure that Violet's dead, let alone that she was killed by the Animal Vigilantes. And what's me being a sodding vegetarian got to do with it?'

'There's a lot of anger,' Jai said. 'It's been building up for a while. I suppose they see you as aligned with the animal rights people.'

'But that's crazy! I'm not an activist. I've been on the occasional march and I donate to a few animal charities. Why am I even justifying this to you? These people need locking up.'

'They want locking up for the sheer number of exclamation marks in that piece,' Fiona said.

I noticed the time. 'Oh God, we've got the press conference in a minute.'

'Are you going to mention this?'

I shook my head. 'It's only a stupid thing on Facebook. Whose animals are they going to kill? They'll be punishing the very farmers they want to support.'

My stomach twisted at the sight of the long table. Three chairs, three microphones. I shuffled across and sat down. I hadn't had time to prepare properly. I was still reeling from the personal attack on the Facebook page. All I ever did was try to do my job and do it well and yet I always ended up in the firing line. I felt like punching someone.

Violet's parents edged in behind the table, from the other side. Helen was next to me, dabbing her eyes. Roy had been clothed by our adviser in a better shirt, vibrating as if ready to explode.

Flashing lights, sharp suits, phones waving, microphones pointing. A low murmur punctuated by the odd optimistic question directed at Violet's parents. Me hissing, *Don't answer!*

The room was packed. Local reporters brimming with smugness that there was a good story in their area, a bunch from the nationals looking down on the locals, TV reporters with the made-up sheen of the filmable, and a whole load of unidentifiables. I gave them a stare that indicated I was about to speak. The muttering died down.

I filled them in on the timeline and facts, not giving too much away. I repeated what had been released the day before – what clothes Violet had on, that she wore a distinctive pelican brooch on a necklace. I told them the hotline number, and it would indeed be hot with the calls of the attention-seeking crazies, the empty-lifers desperate to be close to the action. And the hotter the victim, the hotter the hotline became.

'Violet was adopted,' I said. 'We believe she may have been in Gritton looking for her biological family. She may have spoken to someone who gave her information. If this was you, please come forward.'

The noise in the room increased, rising upwards and bouncing off the ceiling until it engulfed us. I tried to imagine a bubble of cool, blue calm around me, but it didn't make a lot of difference.

More excited murmuring and shouted questions. 'Has Violet been killed by animal activists?'

The noise that greeted this almost drowned out my response. 'We've no reason to think Violet has been killed. We'll take questions at the end. Now, Violet's mother, Helen Armstrong, would like to say a few words.'

Roy had wanted to speak, but it had been obvious that Helen would be much better. With his entitled voice and ill-concealed fury, Roy would only alienate. The game was all about appearances. If your eyes were too close together, if you looked too upset or not upset enough, if your nose was shiny or your make-up too prominent, the reporters would have you back home burying your daughter under the patio before you could say, *She's a lovely girl and we miss her so much.*

Helen did a good job. Sniffed and wiped her eyes like a pro. Looked straight at the camera. 'Please …' she said. 'If you know anything about where Violet is, call the hotline. We're so worried about her. We know she was on the internet a lot and but she's really just a normal young girl. Please come forward if you know anything at all.'

They were straining to ask questions, a seething mass of them. It felt as if they were advancing on us, as if they might consume us.

Someone shouted, 'Is it true she'd seen the Pale Child?'

A large man in the front row snorted. 'Moronic yokels.'

'If anyone saw anything unusual the night she disappeared, please call our hotline.' I pointed into the crowd. 'Yes?'

'Dick Granger, the *Enquirer*.' I'd come across Dick before. Never one to hold back for reasons of sensitivity, but even he seemed to have a twinge of doubt as he looked at Violet's parents. Then he dived in before he lost his chance. 'There have been suggestions Violet's been killed and fed to pigs. What do the police say about that?'

I felt Helen flinch beside me and cursed myself for not warning them. I should have known a comment like that would shoot through social media like shit off a muck-spreader.

'Violet's been missing less than forty-eight hours,' I said. 'We've no reason to think she's been killed. The vast majority of teenagers are found safe and well.'

Someone shouted, 'But what about the pigs?'

I ignored them, but Roy butted in. 'What's the matter with you people? How do you think we feel, for God's sake?'

Out of the corner of my eye, I saw Helen reach a hand across and lay it on Roy's arm.

Someone shouted, 'What happened to her body?'

'When will you upscale this to a suspected homicide?' Dick shouted.

'We're treating Violet as a high-risk missing person,' I said. 'Huge resources are being put into finding her. There's no question of needing to upscale anything.'

There was so much shouting I couldn't tell who was saying what.

'What about the Animal Vigilantes? Have you arrested anyone? What about Justice for Violet? What if they start killing animals tonight?'

'We won't tolerate abuse of animals,' I said. 'If anybody harms an animal tonight, we will be coming down extremely hard.' I realised that sounded perhaps a little too menacing.

'Are your sympathies with the animal activists, DI Dalton? Are you the right person to find Violet's killers?'

I flicked my eyes to the speaker. A youngish man with prominent glasses and a trendy beard, who looked like he should have known better. I wanted to leap into the crowd and grab him by the throat, and he may have picked up on the vibe because he shuffled back in his seat.

Another shout. I didn't see where it came from. 'Does Meg Dalton have links to animal rights extremists?'

My pulse was racing. This felt out of control.

'Mrs Armstrong! Where do you think Violet is?' The shout came from a local reporter I vaguely knew, an ambitious but decent young woman. I turned to Helen, and she gave a tiny nod and looked out at the crowd.

'I don't know,' she said quietly, tears running down her cheeks. The energy of the room settled, as if the force of her anguish had hammered through the shells of even the most cynical. 'But Violet isn't what you all think. She didn't mean to be the poster girl for the meat industry. She doesn't even eat much meat. It all happened by accident. So if anybody's taken Violet because of that, please let her go.' As she faced the crowd, I caught the edge of a tiny, disgusted look. 'She's also a very beautiful girl. I'm afraid someone has her. Someone has taken her and ...' She broke off and gave a low sob. 'Please give her back. We'd do anything to have her back.'

A couple of hours later, I was sitting at my desk with my head in my hands. I heard a voice. Fiona. 'Are you all right?'

'Strategising,' I said.

She gave me a concerned look. 'Oh. Okay. I took a formal statement from Anna Finchley and she mentioned something weird.'

'You'd better sit down.'

Fiona settled into my guest chair. 'Is that spider plant all right?' She gave it the look a social worker might give a kid they wanted to take into care. 'It looks like it has to walk to get its own water.'

'Thriving. I chuck my tea in it when I've let it go cold or my coffee when it's too disgusting to drink, so it's all good. Anyway, what's weird?'

'It's Kirsty Nightingale. You know, Tony's other daughter who's on the Great Meat Debate website with Anna and Co. She ... she heard about the fed-to-pigs thing.'

'Oh dear.'

'Obviously, if Bex is Violet's mother, then Violet is Kirsty's niece, and she's upset about … it all.'

'Understandably.'

'But then … She told Anna she's doing an experiment. To put her mind at rest that pigs couldn't have eaten … a person.'

'Christ. What's she doing?'

'Anna didn't want to say, but in the end she told me. Kirsty's doing it tonight. Replicating the conditions in the abattoir and feeding the pigs …'

'What the hell is she feeing the pigs?'

'A whole sheep. Fifty kilos.'

I was struggling to get my head around this. She was feeding a Violet-sized sheep to pigs. 'Get in touch with Kirsty Nightingale and tell her we'd like to be there,' I said. 'We'll come to her farm.'

19

The moon glistened on the rocks of Winnats Pass as Fiona and I drove through. It was nearly midnight, but so bright it might as well have been daytime. I felt a twinge of guilt that I hadn't yet been home to see Dad, but he'd understand. The key was in the safe so he could get in. And Hamlet would hopefully rouse himself from a postprandial sleep on my neighbour's knee, welcome Dad, and show him around the kitchen, or at least to the cat food cupboard.

An owl – pale and solid, lit by the moon – glided in front of the car and then swooped through a gap between the silver rocks.

'I asked my granny if she knew the story behind the Pale Child,' Fiona said.

'Oh yes?'

'It originated from a murder in the 1870s. But the weird thing is that it involved this well-off family who lived in a big house in Derwent village, and they were called Nightingale. Tony must be descended from them.'

'Now that is weird. So how does the story go?'

'The people in this house had a daughter.'

'Oh God, the girl's wearing a red T-shirt, isn't she?'

'What?' Fiona said.

'Oh, you know … *Star Trek*. Never mind.'

'Right. Anyway, the woman – the mother of the girl – was apparently involved in the first wave of feminism. The early suffragists. Gran was obviously impressed, even though she claims not to be a feminist.'

'I don't see how anyone can not be a feminist.'

'She is quite old, I suppose. Thought you had to burn your bra.'

'That mass bra-burning didn't even happen. Great way to trivialise an important issue though. But anyway …'

'Anyway, a lot of people didn't like this woman because her views were pretty radical at the time. They claimed she neglected her child, even though it was normal for children in rich families to be brought up by a nanny. And they said she was unwomanly and against God and so on. Of course there was no concept of the father neglecting the child.'

'Lord, no. It was probably *against nature* for him to look after them. Separate spheres. There was an article in the *Lancet* around that time saying that if you educated women, their ovaries shrivelled up and they grew beards.' If Jai had been around I'd have felt compelled to make a crack about the women who studied science at Cambridge. I was relieved he wasn't.

'Really?' Fiona said, because she wasn't a wisecracking idiot. 'Well, this poor woman had taken the girl out to get some air in the countryside and she got mobbed by a bunch of anti-suffragists. She argued with them, and took her attention off her girl, who was with a nanny anyway. And the nanny was knocked unconscious and the girl strangled. Nobody saw anything, and the woman got the blame.'

'Bloody hell. A child was murdered in broad daylight and nobody saw anything? And they blamed the woman?'

'You have to wonder, don't you? It did happen though. I checked the archives.'

The reservoir slid into view on our left. Black as ink, sucked into the base of the valley by the drought. The drowned villages weren't visible, but I pictured them. The houses swallowed by the waters. Including the house where this poor murdered child and her mother had lived.

'Is the Pale Child supposed to be the ghost of this dead girl?' I asked.

'Yes. After she died, the story goes that she haunted the big old house. But she was benign. She just wandered around asking for someone to look after her or be her friend.'

'So what changed?'

'It was after the reservoir was built. The house that the child haunted was flooded along with the rest of the village, so she lost her home and got more desperate for friends and for someone to look after her. That's why, if she sees your face, she claims you. But you have to go and be with her on *the other side*.'

'Blimey. Is this from your granny?'

'Yes. I had tea with her earlier. She says the Pale Child appears in times of drought, like this year, where the water goes low and reveals the old house where she lived.'

'Your gran's like a one-woman historical society, isn't she? We should get her to start a museum. With a tea room.'

'She can't remember where she left her glasses or whether she fed the cat, but she remembers all this stuff.'

'So the Pale Child was a Nightingale?' I said. 'That would mean she really is related to Violet.'

'I suppose so, yes.'

'How strange.'

'I hear Mandy Finchley's panicking,' Fiona said, 'because Gary saw her too.'

'Yes. If anything happens to him …'

'Then we freak the hell out.'

I laughed and looked at Fiona. An image flitted into my mind. She and Craig at the briefing. The way they looked at each other. 'Fiona, are you and Craig getting along okay? I mean, I know with Craig it's never easy.'

Fiona hesitated and then spoke quickly. 'We're fine. Same as usual.'

'Has anything happened?'

'No, nothing. Honestly. I stand up to him more these days and he doesn't like it. I had to toughen up when I was in charge of the tea-fund.'

'Ah yes. The assertiveness boot camp that is the tea-fund.'

I wondered whether to persist. Things clearly weren't fine. But if she refused to talk, there wasn't much I could do.

'We're nearly there.' Fiona pointed out a collection of buildings on our left. 'I can't quite believe what we're here to see. I guess she's hoping to show it's not possible.'

'Yes. And I suppose it helps us too. I mean, we all know there have been cases, but for the pigs to leave so little in the trough …' I had to admit I was intrigued. I wanted to see what would be left of fifty kilos of meat fed to twenty moderately hungry pigs.

20

We pulled up in front of a modern brick farmhouse. An outside light cast a dull glow onto a lawn, which was fenced off from a concrete yard. To our right was a vast barn, and beyond that another one. Behind them were the woods, separated from the barns by an area of scorched grassland.

We left the car and walked up to the house. Moths buzzed around the light, and the smell of manure hung in the still air.

Kirsty pulled open the door. 'Come out to the barn,' she said. 'It's all ready.' She reached behind her and lifted a plastic bag full of something solid and lumpy. She shoved it at me. 'Give us a hand with this.'

I took the bag, shocked at its weight and the feel of it. It was room-temperature, possibly warmer, and part of me resisted – told me it should be chilled. Kirsty passed me another one, and then gave Fiona a couple of bags.

'I'm sorry,' I said. 'This must be hard for you.'

Kirsty gave a low laugh. 'Yes, nicely done in the press conference. Not the best way to get the heads-up that one of your relatives might have been eaten by pigs. I shudder to think how her adopted parents felt.'

'It was unfortunate.'

'But for me, I never knew I had a niece so I haven't exactly lost anything.'

'That's admirably logical,' I said. *And weird,* I thought.

Kirsty added, 'It's very upsetting, obviously.'

'This is the sheep?' I said.

Kirsty pulled the door closed behind us with a sharp click. 'Fifty kilo roughly butchered, with all the bones and skin, but no wool. Very fresh. It's not been refrigerated.' I could imagine her accidentally lopping off a little finger or popping out a baby or two while making the kids' suppers.

We followed Kirsty across the yard to one of the barns. A gentle breeze drifted over the grassy area between the barn and the woods. We waited while she removed a combination lock and pushed the door open. 'This is intensive pig farming. Some people don't like it, but there's a demand for cheap pork.'

We walked into the barn, and through an area stacked high with straw. As my eyes acclimatised, I saw that the rest of the barn was full of metal cages. Each housed about twenty young pigs, crammed in together, lying on slatted floors. They were slumped in piles, grunting softly.

'They don't have a lot of room,' Fiona said.

'It's all perfectly standard,' Kirsty said. 'Red Tractor approved.'

I'd seen enough videos on YouTube not to be surprised. But what hit me was the smell. Ammonia that tore at the back of my throat, despite the overhead fans that shifted the thick air around the barn.

'Don't they get any bedding?' Fiona said.

'If the slurry system doesn't allow for bedding, we don't have to provide it,' Kirsty said. 'Slatted floors let the waste drop through. But that lot at the end get straw. They're on a new system I'm trying, thanks to pressure from welfare people.'

Kirsty led us to the far side of the barn, to a pen that was bedded down with straw. 'I've set it up exactly the same as at the abattoir. The same size, with straw, and with twenty six-month-old pigs.'

As we approached, the pigs roused themselves, grunting and pushing to the front of the enclosure. They had much more room than the others, presumably to replicate conditions in the abattoir.

'They look hungry,' Fiona said.

Kirsty nodded. 'Pigs are always hungry. But these had a smaller supper than usual. I gave them the same as Anna said the pigs had on Sunday evening.'

'Okay,' I said. 'It won't hurt them, will it? Eating so much raw meat?'

'No,' Kirsty said. 'They have stomachs of iron.'

'Okay. You're being admirably scientific about this.'

She hesitated then nodded. 'I suppose it's my way of coping with the situation.'

Kirsty opened up one of her bags and dumped the contents into a trough in front of the pigs. I winced. A sheep's head, its wool removed. And some large chunks of leg. 'I got the feet taken off,' she said. 'But left the head.'

I opened my bags and dumped the gruesome contents into the pigs' trough. Mine contained a stomach and glistening intestines, which slid into the trough with a slap. Fiona winced and did the same with hers. The smell brought bile to my throat.

The pigs let out delighted grunts and shoved their snouts into the meat. They ripped into it, jostling against each other, pushing and shoving in their enthusiasm.

'Shall we have a cup of tea and we can come back and check later?' Kirsty said.

I looked at the pigs tucking in. They were approaching the problem with an extremely positive attitude, but it would surely take them a while to get through the bones, assuming they managed that, and I needed to get away from the smell. I nodded.

Kirsty took us back to the house and led us inside to a large kitchen. It was scruffy and homely and smelled of fresh bread, a relief after all the meat. A chunky pine table filled the centre of the room. Sheets of drawing paper were spread over it, along with some pencils and a box of charcoal.

I checked my watch: 1.03 a.m.

Kirsty made tea, pushed the charcoal, pencils, and paper into a pile in the centre of the table, put the mugs down, and sat opposite us. She exuded an easy charm and I relaxed into my chair. I pictured the pigs in their brutally small cages and wondered how she could do that for a living. As if reading my mind, she said, 'Everyone has this idea of happy pigs rolling around in the mud – which is fine if you're a hobby farmer and you already have money, like my dad. But to make a living, you have to do it commercially, I'm afraid. And pigs don't think like us. They'll often choose to go back into small crates rather than be in a larger area.'

I didn't want to get into a debate with her, given that her experiment was helping us. She'd convinced herself that what she did was okay, and the way she kept the pigs was entirely legal.

We chatted casually for another half hour, and then Kirsty stood. 'Stay here if you like. I'll nip over and see how much they've eaten.' She headed for the door, leaving us in the kitchen.

'This is the weirdest night,' Fiona said. 'I keep seeing Violet's face in my mind. How could someone do this to her?'

A noise from inside the house. I turned my head. 'What was that?'

The kitchen door pushed open and a girl walked in. About eleven or twelve years old and wearing pyjamas. Sleepy-eyed with messed-up blonde hair. She jumped back when she saw us. 'Where's Mum? I heard a noise.'

'It's okay,' I said. 'Your mum's outside.'

'Why are you in the kitchen?' She was holding what looked like a sketchbook in her hand. It dangled towards the floor.

'Your mum's just … checking on a pig. She'll be back in a minute.'

'Okay.' Once she'd got over her initial shock, the girl seemed quite unfazed by two strange women in the kitchen. She came and sat at the table with us. Reached and took a pencil and opened her sketchbook, her hair falling forward over her face.

I looked at Fiona, and she shrugged.

'Would you like a drink of anything?' I said to the girl.

She pushed her hair off her face. 'Some milk?'

I jumped up, grabbed a glass from a shelf, and took milk from the fridge, only briefly running a scenario in my head in which the girl was allergic to milk and went into anaphylactic shock in the kitchen.

I put the glass in front of the girl, and looked at the drawing she was working on. A spike of coldness shot through me. It was a drawing of a pig in a tiny individual cage. Lying on her side, her piglets next to her, but separated from her by a barrier.

'Is that one of your mum's pigs?' I said.

The girl nodded. 'When they have their babies.' She flipped

to the page before. 'And then the babies get bigger.' The drawing looked like the set-up we'd seen – groups of pigs housed together in larger cages.

The girl reached and took her milk. Glugged it all down. She flicked back through more pages of her book, talking almost as if to herself. 'We have lots of pigs here. Mummy pigs, baby pigs.' She flicked the pages fast, and the drawings all looked similar. I wondered what her teachers must think if she drew like this at school. The drawings were creepy when all seen together. No houses, no birds, no dogs or cats or images of her family. Just pigs – lots of pigs.

And then a different drawing. Trees, shaded charcoal–dark, and amidst them, facing away from the viewer, a person. A girl drawn with white chalk, wearing a pale, old-fashioned dress, shining with a luminous brightness out of the page.

'What's that one?' I pointed to the picture.

The girl looked up from the page. 'The Pale Child,' she said.

I sensed the hairs on the back of my neck standing up.

The girl flicked through a few more pages of pigs, and then paused at a strange image, almost reminiscent of Escher. There was what looked like a lake, but in the water was a circular hole, bounded by a concrete wall so water couldn't get into it. The internal surface of the hole was convex and lined with steps, leading down, as if you could climb into it.

'It's an edge you can't see over,' the girl said.

I looked again at the drawing. The hole sucked in your gaze, so you imagined walking down into it, except the steps got narrower as they went into the hole. If you walked down them, you'd soon be in trouble. You'd want to turn around and shuffle down backwards, but as the steps got narrower it would be impossible to go further without falling. The girl was right. You'd never be able to see into the hole.

'That's a brilliant drawing,' I said.

'It's in the reservoir where the boy fell,' the girl said. 'Years ago.'

The front door pushed open and Kirsty appeared. 'Frankie! What are you doing?'

The girl shut her sketchbook. 'I heard a noise. I found these people in the kitchen. They gave me milk.'

'Okay. Well, go back to bed now.' Robust parenting.

The girl got up and trailed out of the kitchen, taking her sketchbook with her.

'Sorry,' Kirsty said. 'Frankie's not very mature for her age. She's thirteen, but sometimes she acts like a little kid.'

'She showed us her drawings,' I said. 'They're very good.'

'Yes. All the damn pigs,' Kirsty said. 'The poor girl gets grief about what I do – you know, keeping the pigs in cages. From other kids at the school, I mean. It's sad. She's so desperate to be popular but she has to learn to stand up for herself.'

'Her drawings are great. The one of that hole in the water …'

Kirsty looked up sharply. 'Did she talk to you about that one?'

'She mentioned a boy. What was that about?'

'Oh, nothing. She talks nonsense. It's the bell-mouth spillway in the reservoir. The overflow. It's spectacular in full flow. But yes, Frankie is good. I keep trying to get her to enter an art competition. She's lost her confidence though. It's terrible what happens to girls at that age. She used to be so exuberant. Didn't care what anyone thought. Now it's all about being thin and pretty and getting likes on bloody social media.'

'It's awful for teenagers,' Fiona said. 'My younger brother's the same. I know people think it's not as bad for boys, but he's obsessed with videoing himself doing stupid things to get attention.'

Kirsty shook her head. 'Anyway, it horrifies me to say it, but those pigs are doing a spectacular job on the lamb. Do you want to see?'

We stood and followed her from the kitchen, out of the house and across the yard into the pig barn.

All was much quieter now, with some of the pigs lying down and others licking at the trough.

I'd been sure they'd leave fragments. That the pigs at the abattoir couldn't have eaten a person, because more would have been left. That they wouldn't have chomped their way through the hips, the femurs, the backbone, the skull.

'Wow,' Fiona said.

I fished out my camera and took photographs of the trough, the straw, the pigs. The trough was smeared with blood, like the one at the abattoir had been, but there was no bone in it.

Nothing was left of the person-sized sheep.

21

Bex held the plastic toy cone near the pig's face. The pig reached forward and touched it with her nose. Bex made a clicking noise, gave the pig a pellet of food, and held the cone target out again.

'Perfect,' her dad said. 'You're a natural.' He was sitting at the picnic table that overlooked the pig field. It was another warm, shimmery day, the air touched with the smell of a rose that drifted across from the garden. They'd been her mum's roses. They were neglected now, unpruned and straggly, grass and bindweed growing through their thorny stems. Bex wondered how her mother could have left her beloved roses. But that was a ridiculous thought, given that she'd left her children.

Bex threw a few pellets down for the pig and stood. Maybe she was a natural. There wasn't much she was good at. It gave her a warm feeling inside to think she might be a natural pig trainer. And that her dad might be proud of her.

'We can get her doing fetch next,' he said. 'It takes a bit of work to build up to that, but she's well capable of it.'

Bex left the pen and sat opposite her dad, squinting into the sun. The thought of a pig playing fetch was funny, but she wasn't sure why. She knew they were clever. And they recognised her too. She was already growing attached to them.

Bex adjusted the parasol to stop the light dazzling her. Her dad had rigged up an electric motor, so it could take itself up and down. She wondered if he'd have been happier as an engineer. He made his bizarre household robots, and he'd taught himself plumbing and electrics and woodwork. But she supposed he'd never questioned that he'd take over the family farm.

'Why do you train them?' Bex asked.

'It's fun and it makes them easier to handle. It's less stressful for all concerned.'

'Are they as clever as dogs?'

'They're certainly very trainable. I'm not sure comparing intelligence between different species is helpful.'

'Why not?' She didn't want the conversation to end. He felt like a proper dad when they were training the pigs together, and discussing it afterwards. At other times they couldn't talk. There were silences you could drive a tractor through.

Her dad looked at her and spoke as if he cared what she thought. 'Take the "mirror test" that humans are so fond of. An animal passes the test if it recognises itself in a mirror. Do you think that makes an animal intelligent?'

Bex thought about it. 'I guess so ...'

'But is it not biased towards visual animals? Imagine if there was such a thing as a "smell mirror" that reflected back your own unique aroma. Do you think you'd recognise your smell reflection?'

Bex laughed. 'I kind of hope not.'

'So does that make you stupid?'

She was desperate for him not to think she was stupid. To take her seriously like he did Kirsty. 'I get your point. We look at it from our perspective all the time, not giving animals much credit for stuff they do better than us.'

The pig she'd been training had finished the pellets and collapsed into a muddy puddle, settling down as if she was on a spa day, readying herself for a massage.

'We mustn't anthropomorphise them either,' her dad said. 'They're different from us and they want different things.'

Bex nodded and picked at a knot in the wood of the bench. There was so much she wanted to ask him. About her past, her mum, the family. But she didn't want to ruin the mood. She wanted to grab the good time with her dad, and Anna was due any minute. Bex had asked her over, partly because she wanted to find out more about Daniel. She couldn't ask directly, but she wanted to know about that photograph of her.

Her dad stood. 'Anna's here. I'll leave you to it.' He flicked a glance at the pigs, and headed back towards the house.

And there Anna was. Early, which was typical of her. She flung herself onto the bench opposite Bex. 'Hiya. You been training them?'

Bex smiled. She liked Anna. She wasn't very cool, but neither was Bex. It was good to spend time with someone who didn't care what she looked like, and didn't go all pathetic around boys. Bex's friends at school went all ditzy any time a decent-looking boy approached them. It was too boring.

'Yeah,' Bex said. 'Dad's been showing me. He gets them to follow targets to move them around. Reckons they're super-quick to train and it's a better way to do it. Doesn't scare them, and it's safer for him too.' It felt good to be the expert, even just between her and Anna.

'That's good,' Anna said. 'I see them at the abattoir sometimes and it's awful … They're terrified.'

'What's it like having your parents run an abattoir?' Bex looked at Anna to see if she'd got too personal. They'd only known each other a few weeks, even though they'd hung around together most days.

Anna said, 'I think they might want me to take it over when they retire.'

'Not Gary?'

'They think I'm sensible and responsible.'

'You are. Is Gary not?' Bex pictured Gary walking over the stones of the drowned village and felt a tingle in her stomach. But she wouldn't be going all stupid about him, she knew that for sure.

'He's not great with money,' Anna said. 'I guess he'll grow up.'

Bex wasn't sure what to say. Was it good that Anna would take over the abattoir? Or bad that she'd have to kill animals for a living, and that Gary was no good with money.

'There's not much to do for entertainment in Gritton,' Anna said. 'Gary and Kirsty placed a few bets for fun, but I think Gary's still doing it. You have to watch out for Kirsty. Did you realise she deals?'

Bex felt a stab of confusion. 'Deals?'

'I know she's your sister, but you may as well know: she makes a bit of money dealing drugs.'

Bex blinked into the sun. 'No! Not Kirsty! Dad would kill her.'

'She's not scared of your dad. She's a risk-taker and she enjoys the thrill of it. But anyway, Gary gets led astray, and my parents don't think it bodes well. They trust me more than him.'

Bex felt the need to defend her sister, even though Kirsty never defended her. 'Maybe he leads Kirsty astray.'

Anna laughed. 'I don't think anyone leads Kirsty anywhere.' There was a hint of admiration in Anna's voice.

Bex wanted to change the subject. She was sure Anna must be wrong about Kirsty. 'Do you want to take over the abattoir?' she said.

Anna sighed. 'It's a good business, I suppose …'

'You shouldn't feel you have to run it if you don't want to.'

They were getting further from Bex being able to ask about Daniel. It would sound odd if she just shoved it into the conversation now. If she asked whether she should be worried about him.

But then Anna changed the subject: 'Are you getting on all right with your dad?' she asked. 'It must be strange. When did you last see him before this summer?'

Bex felt a stab of embarrassment. 'A couple of years ago. He comes to visit me at my aunt's. Not that often – but it's not because he doesn't want to see me. It's just … he can't leave the animals, and my aunt doesn't like coming to Gritton. So it's hard. But we get on fine.'

'It's not awkward then?'

Bex hesitated. Pictured her dad showing her how to hold the cone out for the pig, when to click, how to offer the food away from her body so the pig wouldn't mug her. He wasn't a great talker but she was sure he cared about her. It had been worth coming to visit. 'It's been all right actually,' she said.

'Why won't your aunt come to Gritton?'

'I don't know. She and my dad fell out years ago. She doesn't like to talk about it and nor does he.'

Bex looked up to see Kirsty walking across the field from the house, hand in hand with a boy. It was Lucas, Gary's friend. The nice-boy sidekick to bad-boy Gary. Any of the girls who didn't fancy Gary had Lucas to gush over. Daniel walked next to them, slightly apart.

Bex noticed a rabbit hopping across the field. It moved in a weird way.

'I think Lucas might be too wimpy for Kirsty,' Anna whispered. 'She'll eat him alive. Gary likes you, by the way.'

A flush of adrenaline in Bex's stomach. 'He does not.'

'Yep. He does. Do you like him?'

Bex wasn't sure of the answer to that. But before she'd had a chance to reply, Kirsty skipped up to their bench and stood in front of them in the sunlight, her golden hair back-lit so it looked like she had a halo. 'We're going to have a barbecue,' she said. 'In the woods over there, on Bex's last night in Gritton.'

Anna smiled up at Kirsty. 'Brilliant!'

Lucas put his arm around Kirsty and pulled her to him. 'Isn't she fab?'

Anna nodded. Bex wasn't sure organising a barbecue warranted this level of adoration but she was happy that everyone was getting along.

'I can sort out the booze,' Lucas said. 'Kirsty can sort the—'

Kirsty shot him daggers and then pointedly looked at Bex. 'What?' Bex said.

'Nothing,' Lucas said. 'Who's being invited?'

'Just our gang,' Kirsty said. 'Me, Lucas, Daniel, Gary, and these two babies here.'

'Hey,' Anna said. 'We're not babies.'

Now Bex had no chance of asking Anna if Daniel was a weirdo. He was standing right in front of them smiling at her. She gave him an uncertain smile back, thinking about the photograph on his wall.

It felt humid and thundery as if it was about to rain.

'Definitely not babies,' Lucas said, and winked at Bex.

Kirsty untangled herself from Lucas's arm and gave him an icy look.

'It's good that Dad's being okay with you, after what happened,' Kirsty said to Bex.

Bex felt like she'd been hit. Where had that come from? She felt hot and cold and sick all at once. Every time she thought Kirsty was being nice, she'd come out with some awful comment and ruin it. Was it because Lucas had flirted with Bex? That hadn't been her fault. And had he even been flirting? Something brushed against her foot. She looked down and jumped. It was the rabbit. 'Oh my God! What's up with it?' she said.

'Oh no, it's got mixi,' Anna said. 'Poor thing. You can see from its eyes.'

Kirsty took a step away, but then moved back and leaned in close. 'Ugh. Look at that.' Her voice had taken on an odd tone. Almost as if she was enjoying the drama.

'We've got to kill it,' Anna wailed. 'It's awful. It'll be in horrible pain. Poor thing.'

Bex had never seen a rabbit with myxomatosis before. Its eyes were swollen and covered in growths, and it was clearly blind. Looking at it made her want to cry. 'Won't it recover?' she asked.

'Not when it's got to that stage.' Lucas had moved away, un-volunteering from the role of executioner.

Anna's voice was shaky. Panicky. 'We've got to kill it. It's in agony. How can we kill it?'

'Bex, run and get a shovel off Dad,' Kirsty said.

Daniel stepped forward. 'The quicker the better with these.' And he lifted his booted foot and smashed it down on the creature's head.

22

Meg – Present day
Wednesday

I flipped my eyes open, heart pounding, breath coming in sharp bursts. I'd been dreaming I was trapped in a cage. It was so small I could barely move, like the pigs in Frankie's first drawing. I'd been thrashing around, begging to be let out. Then the dream had morphed into me being bricked into a hole in a wall, unable to sit up or lie straight, like a display I'd seen at the London Dungeon as a child and never been able to forget. All I could hear were the screams of another prisoner.

I lay and let the relief wash over me. It was morning. None of it was real.

There was another sound. Also terrifying. Hamlet vomiting on my bedroom floor.

'Oh God!' I jumped up. 'Come on, Hamlet. Downstairs.'

It was too late.

Hamlet sat washing his face and looking proud of himself, while I used toilet paper and an old sponge to tackle the furball on the wooden floor, and to stop the more liquid part of the contents of Hamlet's stomach going down between the cracks. I hoped this wasn't foreshadowing the day to come.

I checked my phone, and there were no significant developments. I had a feeling that Violet was alive somewhere and in need of our help, despite us finding her blood in the pig troughs and now confirming that the pigs could theoretically have eaten her. I felt I should be racing somewhere to save her, but I didn't know where. The evidence pointed to her being dead, which put me in a similar category to the psychics. But I was relieved I cared. Talking to Hannah about Gran had clearly helped. I was moving back towards my reassuringly normal level of neurotic workaholism.

Noises were coming from the kitchen. Dad. Why was I so damn nervous about meeting my own father? My pukey cat and I walked downstairs and into the kitchen. Dad was sitting at the table with a newspaper laid out in front of him. He looked up and smiled. 'Meg.' He seemed older than I remembered, the creases deep on his forehead. And his eyes were open too wide, as if he'd recently had a shock and hadn't yet changed his face back to normal.

'Dad.' I reached forward and gave him a hug. He smelled of clothes that hadn't dried properly. 'Sorry again I was so late. High-risk missing person.'

He stood up. 'Don't be silly. Hamlet welcomed me and I was fine. She even sat on my knee. I gave her some chicken.'

All cats were female in Dad's world, even when they shared a name with a tragic Danish prince. I didn't bother to correct him. Hamlet didn't care, especially if chicken was involved.

'I'm proud of you working so hard,' Dad said.

I couldn't help smiling. He was proud of me. I was so pathetic.

'Go on. Sit down,' he said. 'Let me make you tea.'

I flopped onto one of the chairs while he pottered around. I'd been influenced by Mum's negative thinking. He wasn't that bad any more. He'd softened.

I moved the paper aside. He'd always been an aggressive paper-reader when I was young – laying it out flat and taking up the whole table or holding it up to his face while Mum tried to talk to him. I'd never have dared shift the thing in those days.

He put down a mug of tea and sat opposite me.

'Was the spare bed okay?' I said. 'Sorry about the book sculptures.'

'It was fine. I'm fine. It's a nice house.'

'Did you sleep all right?' I wanted to ask why he was suddenly visiting now. I'd barely heard from him in fifteen years, never met his girlfriend, Pauline. I knew nothing about his life. He didn't look quite right. I wanted to know if he was unwell, or if anything was wrong. But I couldn't make myself be that direct. 'How are things with you?' I said instead.

'Good, good.'

That wasn't giving much away.

'Is Pauline okay?'

Pauline had been *She-who-must-not-be-spoken-of* for so long in Mum's house that I could barely get her name past my lips. It felt like Hamlet coughing up the furball.

'Oh. Yes, I think so.'

What the hell did that mean? He was still with her but didn't know if she was okay, or he'd split up with her and didn't even know what country she was in? Had she dumped him for a younger man, as predicted by Mum when they'd first got together? And why was I fine interviewing people who stuck screwdrivers in each other's throats but couldn't get out of my dad whether he was still with his girlfriend?

'She didn't mind you coming down here on your own?' Why was I incapable of just coming out with it?

'No. Yes. As a matter of fact, we separated.'

There it was. 'Oh no! I'm so sorry, Dad. When?' That would be why he looked anxious and ill.

'A few weeks ago. It's all fine though. How are things with you?'

'Why did you split?'

'Oh. Ah. You know. Grew apart.' He shook his head rapidly. 'Nothing in particular. Nothing you could put your finger on.'

I frowned. 'You can talk to me about it, you know.'

'No, no, it's all fine. Tell me about yourself.'

'If you're sure, Dad. I can see it's not been easy for you. Are you okay? You look a bit under the weather.'

'No, no, it's fine. It had been coming a while. What's new with you?'

It was such a novelty to have him ask me questions that I couldn't help but go with it. And at least he wouldn't grill me about whether I'd found a man to have kids with. I had friends who couldn't set foot in their parents' houses without having to provide a dissertation (with references) justifying their failure to reproduce. Mum had given up on me and Dad had never been bothered.

'I'm half looking to buy a house,' I said. 'I've got enough for a deposit with my savings and the money from Gran.'

'How exciting.' He didn't look very excited. 'Have you found anything?'

'There are a few I want to look at. I've got no time or ability for DIY, so I should get a newer one, but they're so bland and soul-less, and half of them are built on actual swamps.'

'I'm surprised you want to tie yourself down. You know what you're like.'

I looked up. What a strange thing to say. 'I like it here. And it's near to Mum.'

'I suppose it is. If she stays here and doesn't do anything ridiculous.'

'Besides, I like my job.' Craig's bulbous face slid into my mind. 'Mainly, anyway.'

How much did he even know about my job? He'd never taken much interest. I'd hoped he'd be proud when I became a DI but there'd been no evidence of it. And then there was the shameful matter of having time off with stress when I was still in Manchester. Not the kind of thing a member of the Dalton family should indulge in.

'What have you got planned today?' I asked.

He examined his fingers. 'Do you think your mother would see me? I'm worried about her.'

'Oh, Dad, I don't know. She was pretty upset that you didn't call back when Gran was dying.'

He didn't bother to repeat that he hadn't got the messages.

'Shall we talk about it later?' I said.

'But we can't let her do this crazy trip.'

'I think she has to do what she wants. It's nothing to do with us any more.'

'Come on, Meg. She's in her late sixties. It's ridiculous.'

I didn't want to admit I'd had similar thoughts. My friends were worrying about their parents not getting out enough, and mine was planning a trip to El Salvador. But Dad had no right to intervene.

'It's dangerous, you know.' Dad shook his head. 'She never used to be like this.'

'She was too busy looking after us, wasn't she, Dad? We should let her live her own life now. Do things she cares about.'

He sighed and looked strangely forlorn. 'I'm worried she's going to get into trouble. But okay, I won't contact her. I could do a spot of gardening for you?'

I looked out of the window. The unkillable shrubs that I'd planted the previous year were thriving, but the rest of the place was more wildlife safe-zone than garden. I shrugged. 'All right. If you fancy it. There are tools in the shed.'

'I worry about your mother,' he said again, prompting me to wonder if he still loved her, deep down. 'What if she never comes back?'

My phone buzzed. I fished it out. A message from Jai: *Have you seen Justice for Violet FB page?*

23

I left Dad moping at the kitchen table and walked out of the house into another day that belonged on a Greek island, with me in a tummy-control swimsuit by the pool, sipping a mojito. My Wi-Fi had been playing up and I'd not been able to see Facebook via the terrible Belper mobile phone signal, so I was keen to get into work and see what Jai had meant about the Justice for Violet page.

I clicked open the car and shoved my bag in. A noise behind me. I looked round. Was it Hamlet? It sounded like a baby crying. I pushed the car door shut and stood very still. Definitely a baby, not Hamlet, and it sounded as if it was coming from the patch of scrubland by the railway.

I locked the car and walked towards the noise. A baby crying from within a house was common enough, but I didn't expect one to be bawling from the direction of the railway, especially this early. I followed a route which was clearly popular with incontinent dogs. The crying was getting louder.

And then I saw it. My breathing quickened. A Moses basket.

I ran towards it.

Someone grabbed me. I spun round. A man had hold of my wrist. A man in a black balaclava.

'Get the fuck off me!' I shouted.

Another man grabbed my other wrist. I kicked at his knees, but he didn't let go.

There were four of them in total. All in black, and wearing balaclavas and leather gloves. One of them had a knife. 'Don't scream,' he said. 'If you keep quiet, we won't hurt you.'

What an idiot I was. Falling for the crying baby. Not exactly original. The crying had stopped.

They had both my hands and now there was a knife near to my face. The light caught it and I saw it was smeared with blood. I tried to calm my breathing. I couldn't reach my phone or radio. Should I scream? They were nervous, jittery, probably not used to doing this kind of thing. The sort that might panic and actually stab me. I couldn't risk screaming.

A pulse throbbed in my ear. 'What do you want?' I tried to keep my voice steady.

The one with the knife shifted round so he could see my face. I couldn't see his, because of the balaclava. He was the most confident, the most intimidating. 'We want to show you we're serious,' he said. 'So you know what'll happen if you let the Animal Vigilantes get away with what they did.'

I wrenched my hand, trying to scratch the gorilla that had hold of it so we'd have DNA, but he gripped tighter and the only bits I could reach were covered in leather gloves. The ringleader shifted the knife nearer to my neck.

'This isn't helping us find Violet,' I said. 'She may be alive and now we're wasting resources on people like you.' I wanted to say more, and with more colour, but the knife was too close. Whose blood was on it?

The fourth man walked over to the Moses basket and fished something out of it. A phone. He tapped the screen. Twisted it so I could see.

A video was playing.

I could hear the men breathing. A car door slammed in the distance. I wondered again if I should scream. But I daren't take the risk of panicking them when I had a bloodstained knife hovering around my jugular.

The mobile phone was close to my face. I watched the video.

It showed a field at night, lit brightly by the moon. A pig – one of those short, fat ones whose bellies drag on the ground – was dozing outside in the warm night. A man was sneaking up behind it. The pig had heard him – I could see from the twitch of its ear – but it was trusting, and it didn't move. The man lunged forward and grabbed it by a hind leg. It kicked out but he held fast. He was in the same black clothing and balaclava as these people. There was flash of metal from his knife – long and sharp, glinting in the pale light. I felt sick.

A squeal.

I couldn't watch. It was the trust the pig had displayed that really did for me.

The blood on the knife at my throat made sense.

My breath came faster. 'Did you do that?'

'Yeah. And we'll do more.'

I wished so hard for a super-power. If I could spontaneously combust them, or send an electric current through my fingertips, or squirt acid from my eyeballs, how wonderful that would be.

Instead I tried to keep my fury hidden and said, 'All you're doing is taking resources away from finding Violet. Is that what you want? There'll be more than pig's blood on your hands if we don't find her.'

'Finding Violet, finding Violet, why do you keep saying that? You know she's dead. They killed her and fed her to pigs.' I wondered if knife-man was on drugs. His energy felt unstable. Unpredictable.

'If she is dead,' I said, as calmly as I could, 'this will divert resources from finding her killer.'

He pushed the knife closer. It touched the skin of my neck. 'No,' he said. 'It'll punish those fucking Animal Vigilantes. Because everyone knows it was them that killed Violet.'

I shrank away from him but my hands were held firm by his two cronies. I could see his eyes through the holes in the balaclava. Grey and bloodshot. 'It won't bother the Animal Vigilantes,' I said. 'They know what you're doing is irrelevant. They already spend their lives thinking about the millions of pigs who get their throats slit every single day. What you're doing is punishing ordinary people who don't think like that. And the owner of that poor pig.'

A noise in the distance. I flicked my eyes towards it. A woman had appeared at the end of the path which led from my road. She froze for a second, then started running towards us. 'What are you doing?' she shouted. 'Let her go!'

Knife-man looked at me and then at the woman, who was getting closer, undeterred by the balaclavas and the knife.

I realised she was familiar. I'd only seen photographs, but this looked very much like Jai's girlfriend, Suki.

Knife-man spoke. 'Let this bitch go.'

They dropped my hands and shot off down the railway track.

'Suki?' I said weakly.

She ran the last few steps and grasped my arm, supporting me as my knees weakened. 'DI Dalton? Are you okay? Oh my goodness, what were they doing?'

My heart rate slowed. 'Don't worry, I'm fine. Thank you for intervening. That was very brave.'

'How could I not? What awful men. Are you hurt? Shall I take you somewhere?'

'No, thank you, I should get to work.' I gently removed my arm and took a step in the direction of my house. She came with me.

My mind was swirling with images of balaclavas and knives, but through some bizarre quirk in my personality I was almost more stressed about what Suki was up to. She didn't have a dog. Why would she be walking near my house?

'Lucky I was here,' she said.

'Yes, thank goodness. Thank you so much.' I almost didn't want to ask why she'd been around. I had a horrible feeling it had been to see me and have an awkward Jai-related conversation. 'I should get going. We'll need a statement from you, but we can deal with that later.'

We reached my road and I eyed my car. While I was very grateful to Suki, I wanted to be in it and on my way to work.

'Oh no,' she said. 'You must be in shock. You should have a drink and a sit-down before you drive. Or I could drive you to the station. It's no bother.'

'No. Honestly. I'm fine.' I leaned against the hot metal of my car.

'Actually, I did want a quick word,' Suki said.

'It's not the best—'

'I know how close you are to Jai.'

'We're not especially close. We just work together.' I absolutely did not need this.

'He thinks I don't like his kids.'

A sinking in my gut. 'Listen, Suki, I know nothing about kids. I mean, Jai's kids probably are pretty annoying. I don't blame you if you don't like them that much.'

'Would you tell him? Tell him he's got it wrong? I do like them.'

I wanted to be alone. In my car. Driving to the station. 'Okay,' I said. 'I will. I'll tell him you like his kids.'

I'd been through multiple layers of bureaucracy in relation to my incident with Justice for Violet, repeating my story so many times it now felt bigger in my mind, more important, more scary than it had at the time. I tried to tell myself it wasn't a huge deal. That they'd never meant to hurt me. But the emotional part of my brain – the ancient lizard part – wasn't convinced. And now to top it all, DCI Richard Atkins wanted to see me.

I found him at his desk, looking like he'd dressed in clothes fished out of his suitcase. 'Sorry,' he said. 'Not feeling my best. Couldn't sleep on the plane. Bloke on my left snored like a buffalo. You can sit—' He waved towards his guest chair. 'Oh.'

Someone had put a sign on it. *Condemned.*

'What on earth's going on?' Richard said. 'What's wrong with the chair?'

Did he really not know? The chair was notorious. Only the youngest and fittest in the force could get out of it unaided.

'It's like a chair version of Charybdis,' I said. 'Sucking the unwary to their deaths. I'm fine standing anyway.'

'Are you all right?' he said.

'I'm fine. Absolutely fine. They didn't hurt me. It was all very silly. Unfortunately I didn't see any faces, but we might have got a hit on CCTV, you never know.'

Richard sighed. 'It's to do with the missing person case, is it? I hear she's an "internet sensation". Not that I'd ever heard of the girl.' Richard was like one of those famously out-of-date High Court judges who used to ask who the Beatles were or if 'Gazza' was an opera.

'It's certainly high profile,' I said.

'Right. Well, from what I've heard, it sounds as though you have it under control.'

I wasn't about to argue, but that was hardly an optimum summary of the situation.

Richard rearranged the pencils on his desk into the shape of an 'H'. Was he sending subconscious messages? Was it a cry for help?

'How was your holiday?' I asked.

It was a mystery who he'd gone with, and one that Jai was determined to get to the bottom of. Richard had been so cagey that we suspected romance was in the air. 'It was good,' he said.

'Where was it you went again?'

He took one of the tiny cactus plants which adorned his desk and examined it. 'South Africa.'

'Wow. Amazing. On a safari?'

'That's right.'

'Did you go alone?'

He popped the cactus down and looked straight at me. 'Nope.'

'Anyone we know?' I was pushing my luck, baiting Richard because it took my mind off that video. Stopped me thinking about the gentle manner of the pig before it died, and the silver knife at my throat, still wet with the pig's blood.

'Hasn't anyone watered these while I've been away?' Richard said.

'Er ... Aren't they supposed to live in the desert?'

'Meg ...'

'Yes?' He made me nervous when he adopted that tone. 'Craig's wife's been in touch with some concerns.'

My insides sank. Not more from the WAGs. 'What did she say?'

'She was worried he'd been attacked. Did you notice the injury?'

'I did notice he had a small cut above his eye. I don't know where he got it from.'

'She's under the impression he'd sustained the injury at work.'

I frowned. 'I'm almost certain he didn't.'

'Maybe you could have a word with him?'

'I'm not sure that's the best idea.' Richard clearly didn't know Craig very well if he thought I could go all pastoral on him. The last thing I needed was a pissed-off Craig on the rampage.

I stood in front of the team, still struggling to get the image of that knife out of my mind. Violet's sparkly smile beamed down at us. The air in the room felt too heavy, as if it had been replaced by an alternative atmosphere from a planet not quite right for human habitation. And someone had forgotten to wash. This was not the week to experiment with *eco* deodorant and cycling to work, or with one of our new special-issue 'wicking technology' tops.

'There's no sign of Violet Armstrong,' I said. 'We're now extremely concerned about her.'

'But are *you* okay?' Jai said.

I gave him a robust smile. 'I'm fine. I've passed on as much info as I could about the men. But they were all in balaclavas and were wearing leather gloves.' How calm and tough I must have sounded. How unaffected by it all. But inside I was shaking. Nothing felt solid. If someone touched me lightly, I'd fall down. To admit this, to walk away from the briefing and let someone else take over for a few moments, seemed impossible to me.

'Well, if you're sure you're all right,' Jai said. 'It sounded nasty.'

The feeling subsided. I was okay. 'Honestly, I'm fine.'

Jai shrugged. I wondered if he could see through the shell to shaky-me. 'Okay,' he said. 'It's not looking so great for Violet. We've had confirmation it was her blood and hair in the pigs' trough.'

'Oh no,' I said. 'Last night Fiona and I saw what twenty young pigs can do to a fifty-kilo sheep, so they could have, in theory, eaten a girl's body.'

Shocked murmuring went round the room in a wave and drowned out me saying, 'I said "in theory"! But, okay, we're now looking at the serious possibility that Violet was killed that night at the abattoir, and her body was fed to the pigs and/or put in with the missing abattoir waste.'

Craig expanded his cheeks and then let the air out with a puff. 'Wow.'

Sick soul that I am, the talk of death was making me feel better. 'We're obviously looking for her blood on the abattoir equipment and in other areas,' I said. 'For the pigs to leave so little mess, whoever did it would have had to … chop her up.'

'Ouch,' Jai said. Helpfully.

'We've got back the paternity results for Daniel Twigg,' Fiona said. 'He's not Violet's father.'

I felt a small jolt of relief. I wasn't sure why, given that we wanted to know who Violet's father was.

'Since Gary Finchley refused to take the test,' Fiona said, 'I think our working assumption should be that it's him.'

'Interesting,' Jai said. 'I wonder if he knows. Maybe not – otherwise he wouldn't have made it so obvious that he fancied her.'

'We are talking about the wilds of Derbyshire here,' I said. 'But I'm inclined to agree. Let's have another good look at Gary. I don't believe his alibi.'

'The Animal Vigilantes are the no-brainer suspects,' Craig said. 'We need to push them harder. What about that Leona woman?'

'She has a strong alibi,' I said. 'She was spotted on CCTV and her friend confirms she was with him. It's not watertight, but it's solid and we've got nothing to suggest she was at the abattoir.'

'The Justice for Violet people are going ballistic that we've not arrested anyone from the Animal Vigilantes,' Jai said. 'And Frazzles the pig definitely had her throat cut last night, live on camera, and it's all over social media.'

The irony wasn't lost on me. As I'd pointed out to my balaclava-wearing assailants, millions of pigs had their throats cut every single day, and most people didn't give it a moment's thought. But the nation was up in arms about Frazzles. Frazzles was kept as a pet by a family who owned a bit of land. Frazzles was a friend, not a meal.

'Her owners named her after a bacon-based snack product?' Richard said.

'Yes,' Jai said. 'But apparently they loved her very much. She had a huge personality and was great with kids. It looks like there'll be others tonight. We've got enraged Violet supporters saying they'll keep attacking random animals until whoever killed Violet confesses.'

'But we don't even know for sure she's dead,' I said weakly.

'The animal people are furious about Frazzles,' Jai said, 'and talking about revenge. They've been smashing the windows of butchers' shops.'

Craig snorted. 'They're more concerned about bloody Frazzles than they are about Violet being killed and fed to pigs.'

'We don't know that's what happened,' Fiona said.

Craig rolled his eyes. 'Oh come on.'

'It's not the only scenario,' I said. 'We haven't found Violet's clothes. The pigs wouldn't have eaten overalls and Doc Martens boots.'

Jai coughed and fiddled with the collar of his shirt. 'We're still having trouble finding the company that took the abattoir waste away that morning.'

'Seriously? How hard can it be?' Richard used the phrase I always found myself using about DIY projects. The ultimate answer was generally, *Extremely Bloody Hard*. Nobody responded.

'Okay,' I said. 'I was thinking about Violet's movements before she disappeared. That's not the only route from Tony Nightingale's to the abattoir, is it? Past Mrs Ackroyd's, I mean?'

Jai gave a side-to-side non-committal head wobble. 'No, but it avoids a narrow lane that's a bugger to drive down.'

'What about forensics in Violet's car?'

'There are fibres in the car from clothes that have been matched to Violet's, and from the type of overalls she wears at the abattoir. Nothing that points to another person.'

'So the driver's seat was at its furthest forward setting and the passenger's at its furthest back – is that right?'

Jai nodded.

'Violet was five foot six. Why would she put her seat at the furthest forward? I'm shorter than that and I don't do that.'

'Maybe she liked to sit far forward,' Jai said. 'Some people do.'

'Can you check with Izzy? And see if she knows what Violet's feelings were about driving narrow country lanes. And see if anyone at the abattoir knows which way she normally drove to work.'

A uniform popped his head around the door. 'A weird call came in,' he said. 'An old guy said he thought he saw someone dumping something in the woods in Gritton. He said the bloke looked suspicious.'

My stomach dropped. 'What kind of something was he dumping?'

'It sounded like a bin liner full of stuff, dumped out of a small lorry. We've tracked it down and the company's owned by a bloke called Mick Tyler. A bit of a scrote, by all accounts.'

'Why do we think it's relevant?'

'The same lorry's been seen coming and going from the abattoir.'

24

Bex – August 1999

Bex leaned against the wooden fence, watching the pregnant sows snuffling around in the dust. Kirsty stood beside her, scraping her boot against the sandy ground and giving off bored vibes.

'Where's the pig with the spots on her face?' Bex asked. 'I've been teaching her to fetch.'

Kirsty looked up. The sun was behind her, leaving her face in shadow. 'Gone to farrow.'

'Why doesn't she farrow here?'

'She has to go to the maternity barn. Do you want to see?' The shift in Kirsty's tone of voice roused a small worm that squirmed in Bex's stomach. It was Kirsty's sing-song voice. The one Bex had realised she used when she tried to make a mean comment sound like a compliment.

'I suppose so,' Bex said.

'She'll have had her piglets. It'll be cute. Dad normally keeps it locked but I saw he forgot just now.'

'Why does he keep it locked?'

'To keep the pigs safe.'

'We should tell him he forgot then.'

'We will, once you've had a look.'

'Oh, okay,' Bex said. She'd been paranoid about Kirsty's sing-song voice. Kirsty was just letting Bex see her favourite pig.

Bex followed Kirsty along a track which led away from the farmhouse. The day was warm and humid and the air smelled faintly of pig manure. 'Is this the barn Dad was worried about flooding the day I arrived?' she asked.

'Yeah. It would be awful for the pigs if water got in. They wouldn't be able to get away.'

After a few minutes they arrived at the barn – a huge, old-fashioned one – and Kirsty slid the door open carefully.

Inside it was dark, and the air which drifted out felt cool, although it smelled of ammonia. Noisy fans whirred up above.

'We'd better not go in,' Kirsty said. 'But you can look.'

Bex peered into the gloom. As her eyes adjusted, she could see a row of metal cages. The pig with the spotty face was in one. Bex breathed in sharply. This wasn't what she'd imagined. The cage was so small, it was as if it had been built around the pig. She couldn't even lie comfortably, let alone turn around. The bars were digging into the flesh on her back.

'But it's …' Bex couldn't speak. More detail came into view. The floor of the pig's cage was made of slats. There was no bedding. She knew mother pigs made nests for their babies, but this pig couldn't make a nest. She was on her side and her piglets were next to her, under a heat lamp, separated from her by bars. There were about ten – so tiny they must have only been a day or two old. Some were suckling on the sow, but she couldn't reach to sniff them or lick them. Her face was pressed against the bars. Bex watched, feeling her breathing quickening. How could it be designed like that?

A shout from behind them. 'Kirsty! Bex! What are you doing?'

Kirsty hurriedly slid the barn door shut and turned to their father. 'Just checking,' she said. 'I thought you'd forgotten to lock up – and you had.'

Their dad was gasping for breath and he sounded furious. 'Kirsty, you know … You shouldn't have opened the door.' He took a key from his pocket and locked the barn door.

'Why do you keep them like that?' Bex said. 'She can't even turn around or touch her babies.' It came out before she had time to think. To wonder if this was the best time to ask, when he was clearly angry.

Her dad grabbed her arm and pulled her away. 'Come on. Come away.'

They walked back to the house in silence. Their dad dragged them into the kitchen and shut the door behind them. 'Sit down,' he said. 'Both of you sit down.' Bex had never seen him like this, at least as far as she could remember. There was a coldness to his anger that was scarier than if he'd been shouting and slamming doors.

They sat in silence while he made tea, in a pot, and placed cups and a milk jug on the table. Finally he sat opposite them and looked at them for much longer than felt comfortable. Bex poured tea for herself and Kirsty, her hand shaking.

Eventually her dad spoke. 'I'm going to tell you about an incident that happened when I was a child.' His voice had softened. Some of the anger had drained away. 'I was only ten. I wasn't supposed to go in the farrowing barn, just like you're not. My father had told me. But I wouldn't listen.'

Bex lifted her tea and took a sip. Kirsty sat looking sheepish.

'I went into the barn,' her dad said. 'And I saw what you've just seen. And I didn't like it. I was a very silly little boy and I thought I knew best.' He sighed and shifted on his chair. 'I reached into the farrowing crate of my favourite sow, and I pulled out the barrier that separated her from her piglets.'

Bex felt a glimmer of respect for the ten-year-old that her dad had been. She'd wanted to do the same.

'I pulled out the barrier,' he said. 'It was heavy for a child, but I did it. And I watched while the sow nuzzled her piglets. It was a lovely moment.'

Bex had a solid feeling in her stomach, as if her insides had turned to stone. The story wasn't going to end well.

'My father appeared. It frightened the pig. She heaved herself to her feet and spun round. But she fell.'

'What happened?' Bex whispered.

'Her legs went from under her. She fell and crushed five piglets to death.'

The kitchen was too quiet.

There was a bump from behind and Bex jumped as if she'd hit an electric fence, but it was only Fenton bashing his way into the kitchen. He must have picked up on the atmosphere – he wandered nervously from Kirsty to Bex to her dad. Snuffling against their legs, trying to mediate.

Bex's dad ignored Fenton and carried on. 'And then I understood that sometimes you have to do things that might appear bad to those who don't understand. To keep the piglets safe.'

'He's right,' Kirsty said. 'Sometimes you have to be cruel to be kind.'

25

Meg – Present day
Wednesday

'Doesn't Bex's rape story strike you as odd?' Fiona stood and leaned against my guest chair. 'She gets raped, but instead of finding out who did it and bringing him to justice, she just goes back to her aunt's and forgets about it.'

'You can sit down, Fiona.' I sat back and crossed my legs. A cup of tea would have been nice, but the man who'd dumped the bag in the woods had been brought in and I wanted to interview him. 'You're displaying an enviable faith in the criminal justice system,' I said. 'This was 1999. She'd passed out wearing a short skirt. You think the rapist would have been *brought to justice*? Have you seen some of the comments about Violet? There are people out there who think filming yourself in a bikini constitutes offering yourself up to be chopped into pieces and fed to pigs. Besides, Bex didn't say she forgot about it. She tried to report it to the police but a bunch of dick cops rattled her and she couldn't go through with it. So she did the most sensible thing: moved on. But then she realised she was pregnant, poor cow.'

Fiona sat down tentatively, also crossing her legs, and it occurred to me how compact she was compared to Craig or Jai, with their sprawling limbs. We should occupy more space, me and Fiona. 'I think there's more to it,' she said. 'Bex's aunt says all that weird stuff to Violet's adoptive parents and then Bex doesn't see her dad and her sister for eighteen years.'

'I'm not saying you're wrong. I just don't think it's surprising she didn't report the rape. You're young. You don't remember what the courts were like twenty years ago. She'd have been ripped apart.'

The door pushed open. Craig. 'Mick Tyler's here.'

'Thanks, Craig,' I said.

'I'll get on.' Fiona practically leaped out of her chair and whipped out of the door.

'Apparently it's all kicking off in Gritton,' Craig said. 'A bunch of balaclava-clad Justice for Violet psychos are kicking the shit out a bunch of meat-suit-clad Animal Vigilante psychos. Or it might be the other way around. Uniform are there trying to get it under control.'

'Wonderful.'

'And the great British public are helping search for Violet, but some of the searchers got too close to the wildfire and had to be rescued, and another one got heatstroke and needed the air ambulance.'

'That sounds like a huge help. Bravo British public.'

Craig shrugged. 'And us cops get accused of being thick.'

I swallowed. Contemplating the idiocy of the general public had obviously put Craig in an amiable mood. I seized my chance. 'Look, before we go in, I just wanted to have a word.'

Craig took a step towards me. 'What?'

'That cut above your eye. Tamsyn's been in touch …'

Craig stiffened, and anger flashed across his face. 'For fuck's sake.'

'She thought you got the injury at work.'

Craig muttered, 'The stupid cow.'

'Craig! Don't speak about her like that. She's worried.'

'You don't know what you're talking about.'

'I know you're sounding like a disrespectful—' I stopped myself.

'You don't know anything about my situation,' Craig said. 'Let it go.'

I forced myself to speak calmly. 'But did you get the injury at work?'

'No.' Craig's lips were tight. 'Can we drop it? I'm fine.'

'I can't ignore this, if it happened at work.'

'It's fine. I'll square it with Tamsyn. Leave it be.' He suddenly looked almost childlike. 'Please?'

Mick Tyler was in our interview room, sprawling in his chair, hefty thighs apart, the absolute opposite of Fiona earlier. He couldn't have given off a less respectful vibe if he'd stuck his boots on the table. A tattoo of barbed wire ringed his neck, and when he blinked you could see that he'd had his eyelids tattooed to look like eyes. He'd stare sightlessly at you even when he was asleep. So, all in all, I wasn't getting the best vibe off him, but he represented a chance to finally establish what had happened to Violet, and for that I was desperately grateful.

I'd checked Mick's records and he'd been done for petty theft and minor acts of violence, mainly towards his supposed friends, and had been in prison a few times for short spells. He'd brought a lawyer in, who was only slightly less thick-necked and dodgy-looking than he was.

'What's this about?' the lawyer said, after we'd taken them through the formalities.

Craig spoke at Mick rather than the lawyer. 'We'd like to know where you were on Sunday night.'

A spasm of relief flashed across Mick's face. He sat up straighter and corralled the thighs somewhat. 'With my girl. She can tell you that.'

'Your girlfriend or your daughter?' Craig said.

Possibly both, I thought, rather uncharitably.

'Girlfriend. I was with her all night.'

Lucky woman, being stared at all night by the bloke's eyelids.

Craig checked the interview plan and then gave Mick an appraising look. 'And what about Monday? Can you tell us where you were?'

'Working. What's this about?'

'Did you go near Gritton Abattoir?'

'I do some work for them. I might've done.'

'You've been linked with an extremely serious offence.'

Mick's breathing was coming faster. 'What offence?'

Craig worked the pause, looking at Mick like a lion about to take down a gazelle. A very ugly gazelle. 'Somebody saw you in the woods,' he said. 'Dumping a bag.'

Mick closed his eyes briefly, showing us his second set of eyes in full creepy technicolour. 'Bloody hell,' he spat.

'What was in the bag?'

Mick shook his head. 'I didn't do anything wrong. It wasn't me that did it.'

We all stiffened.

The lawyer said, 'I'd like a word with—'

'It's all right.' Mick turned to him. 'I know I was bloody stupid. I panicked. Wasn't thinking straight. I didn't have anything to do with killing her.'

The lawyer moved his arm towards Mick as if to advise caution. The air in the room felt thick.

'You'd better explain,' Craig said.

'I take the Cat 2 waste away, don't I? From the abattoir. I found a bin liner in with the waste. With hair and stuff. Gross. A load of long, dark hair and clothes and boots, and that weird necklace with the bird on it. And a smashed-up phone. I realised it must be off that girl. The girl that does those videos.'

So that was it. She really was dead. Craig slammed his hand on the table. 'You didn't think to call the police at that point? Given that you knew a teenage girl was missing?'

I shot Craig a look that said, *Keep your shit in order*. No emotions required on our side of the interview room. But inwardly I was furious. So much time had been wasted. So many hours gone.

'Where does the waste go?' Craig asked.

Mick hesitated. 'Pet food and that.'

I felt a mixture of revulsion and anger. Violet's hair had been dumped with the abattoir waste, with the snouts and trotters and stomach contents, the diseased animals and scrapings off the abattoir floor. And her necklace was there too, in case we were in any doubt whose hair it was.

'Are you licensed to dispose of abattoir waste?' Craig said.

Mick sniffed. 'The permit's not come through yet.'

'That's why you didn't report this. You're not licensed.'

Mick said nothing.

'Isn't Cat 2 waste supposed to be rendered?' Craig said. 'It's not for pet food.'

'Er …' Mick hardened his expression. 'Maybe it was Cat 3 actually.'

We all knew more than we'd ever wanted to about the correct process for disposing of meat by-products, following the Maggot Pete case.

'We can find out easily enough,' Craig said.

'It's a bloody shame,' Mick said. 'Why not use it for dog food or whatever? Some of it's perfectly fine. You don't expect to find a dead girl's hair. Gave me the shock of me bloody life.'

Craig gave Mick a look of disgust.

'I wasn't selling on stuff that was really bad. Not stuff with maggots in and that.'

'What happened to the rest of the waste?'

'It's gone to my mate's company. It'll be dog food by now.'

'We'll need details of your "mate",' Craig said.

There went any chance of us analysing the pigs' stomach contents. They'd be inside someone's spaniel.

'It's a very serious offence taking animal by-products and putting them back into the food chain,' Craig said. 'But murder is an even more serious offence.'

'I didn't kill her! I just found that bin liner in the lorry after I took the waste. Which is weird because you can't put plastic in if it goes to be rendered. It's dangerous. Toxic fumes. So I had a quick look inside and it was … that girl's stuff.'

'When did you pick up this waste?'

'Monday morning.'

'And where did you take it?'

'I took all the waste back to the depot at first. Then when I saw that bin liner and looked in it, I freaked about what was in there. So I took the bin liner to the woods. I didn't do anything to her.'

'Who did you deal with at the abattoir? Who arranged for you to pick up the Category 2 waste?'

Mick rubbed his nose.

'This is extremely serious,' Craig said.

'Some bloke arranged it over the phone a couple of weeks ago. The one who's in charge of the abattoir.'

'He must have given you a name.'

Mick sniffed. 'Gary Finchley.'

Jai marched into my room, in full-on mission mode. 'The tech people have found evidence that Gary Finchley was at the abattoir on Sunday night. We confronted his wife with it and she started crying and admitted he went out.'

'He was at the abattoir the night Violet disappeared?'

'Yes. He logged on to the computer. We think Gary was Violet's biological father, don't we? So she might have talked to him about the rape.'

I nodded. 'And they could have got into an argument. Bring him in. Have we found the bin liner? The one that Mick dumped? That should give us the forensic evidence we need, and then if it's him, we'll have the bugger.'

Jai shook his head. 'Not yet. But we've only just started looking. Do you know how big those woods are?'

'But he told us where he dumped it!'

'It's been moved. Or he got it wrong. Or he lied.' Jai walked over, perched on my windowsill, and jiggled his knee up and down.

'Sit still, Jai,' I said. 'I can't handle your jittering today.'

'Sorry. Are you okay? It sounded horrible this morning.'

'I am. Did Suki tell you she was there? She pretty much rescued me. She's brave.'

'What the hell …?'

'She appeared when they had a knife at my throat.'

'What? Why?'

'She wanted to talk to me. She wants me to tell you she does like your kids.'

'Oh, for God's sake. You're going to be even more on her side now, aren't you?'

I clenched my fists, feeling my fingernails press into my palms. Maybe if I stopped being so damn reasonable and turned into one of those cliched, psycho-bitch, ice-queen bosses then this would stop happening to me. 'I'm on nobody's side, Jai. I just want everyone to be happy. Suki's nice. She's very brave. And she says she likes your kids. End of.'

'Okay,' Jai said. 'I'm sorry she's been hassling you.'

'She didn't so much hassle me as rescue me, Jai.'

He smiled. 'Fair enough. I'll give her that. She has guts.'

'She does indeed. Anyway, we need to find this bag. We don't know if this Mick bloke's telling the truth. What his agenda might be. He's not been Mr Honesty and Integrity so far.' I grabbed a hole-punch that was sitting on my desk and punched a few random holes in a sheet of paper.

'Now who's being annoying?' Jai said.

I punched a few more holes, then shoved the hole-punch away. 'It's bad enough that she's most likely dead, but if Gary Finchley fed her to pigs and chucked her hair in with the toxic waste … It's awful. And imagine if he did that knowing she was his daughter.'

'Horrific. Although if he'd been relying on TV tropes for pig-info, he'd have pulled her teeth out as well as shaving off her hair, so it could be worse.'

'Bloody hell, Jai, all right.'

'Sorry, sorry. It's my way of dealing with it. Won't this window go any wider?' Jai stopped jiggling his knee and started fiddling with the window instead.

'No. It's buggered. Just leave it. So, if Gary Finchley killed her and put her hair and clothes in with the waste, are we saying he thought nobody would look at it? Or he had a deal with Mick to dispose of it and Mick botched it?'

'Maybe the deal was to dispose of it,' Jai said, 'but when Mick looked inside, he freaked out. Maybe he hadn't realised what he was getting into.'

My phone buzzed. A message from Hannah: *I've got something to show you. Will you be in Gritton later? x.*

What was she up to? But I was planning to go up to Gritton and could afford a half hour coffee. I texted back. *OK. 6pm in Gritton tea room? x*

A smiley emoji pinged back.

My internal phone rang. I snatched it up. 'Yes?'

'They've found a body.'

26

The trees were dark around the clearing, the evening humid, preparing for another storm. The fire blazed yellow and orange in the centre of their circle, making the air electric and dangerous. It was Bex's last night in Gritton.

The boys were there, doing boy things. Drinking beer, talking without saying anything, playing with the fire, eyeing up the girls. Gary's hair was golden in the firelight, his eyes bright, his jeans singed where he'd let ash fall on them. He poked a stick into the fire and the flames shot towards his face. He didn't move away.

Bex took a swig of beer and allowed herself to admit it. There was something about Gary. Lucas was all square-jawed magazine looks, and Daniel was good-looking too, with his chiselled androgynous face, but she was weirded out by him after seeing the photo of herself in his room. No, it was Gary she was drawn to.

It somehow felt like Bex had been in Gritton forever but also as if she'd only just arrived. She'd done okay bonding with her dad, especially when they were training the pigs, and she'd tried hard with Kirsty, but there was still a distance there. It was like

Kirsty was a foreigner, an alien even. She wondered if it was because their mother had been foreign, but that made no sense because she was Bex's mother too.

Smoke drifted up from the fire. Anna was beside Bex. The boys were opposite and Kirsty slightly apart from everyone. They weighed each other up over the shifting flames.

Bex had drunk too much. She was new to drink but she sure as hell liked it. Drink toned down her anxieties, made her feel detached from them. So what if she was all messed up inside? Maybe everyone was messed up and it wasn't just her. Why did she worry so much about everything? Why did she feel guilty about things that had happened when she was only three? What did it matter if Daniel had been taking photos of her? She should be flattered.

It was late. The empty bottles were piling up by the fire. The stories were getting more raucous. Bex was laughing too loudly at the boys' jokes. She rarely felt attractive, but that night, all three men were looking at her as if she was a magnet that was drawing them in. She sensed Anna could see it too, but Bex couldn't work out Anna's reaction. Was she jealous or was it something else?

Daniel shouted over the blaze of the fire. 'Get us another beer would you, Anna?'

Anna stood and walked to the pile of beers under the trees. She should have told him to get his own beer. Even Bex had realised you didn't make them like you by being nice to them.

Daniel put a hand on the ground and pushed himself up, skirted around the fire, and plonked himself next to Bex, where Anna had been. She saw Gary mouth, 'Wanker,' to Daniel through the smoke before turning to whisper to Lucas.

Bex knew Daniel shouldn't have stolen Anna's place, but she

was too drunk to care. 'Come sit here, Anna.' She patted the ground on the other side of her. Anna folded down and chucked the beer at Daniel, narrowly missing his head. His shoulder jerked back when he caught it.

Bex took a sip of beer. She had to stare into the fire to stop it spinning away from her. Daniel was too close, letting his leg fall against hers.

She could feel his arm creeping round the back of her, trying to draw her in, and suddenly it struck her as funny. 'No, Daniel,' she said, and pushed his arm away. 'Why would I want to do that?' She laughed in a stupid, hysterical way, knowing it was the drink making her like this but unable to stop.

Daniel wrenched himself away from her and stood. 'You're a stuck-up little cow!'

'No, Daniel, I didn't mean ...' She reached towards him but she was still convulsed with laughter. Daniel turned his back and marched off towards the woods.

Gary leaped up and took Daniel's place. 'Try this.' He waved his hand in Bex's direction.

She reached for the firefly spark of orange light.

She'd only smoked a couple of times. She'd hated the taste of it in her throat. But she took the joint, tried to hold it in a cool way, stuck it between her lips and sucked in. Didn't cough. Felt the spinny unworldliness overcome her.

Bex passed it on to Anna. A fizzy feeling rose up inside her and she didn't care any more that she'd upset Daniel. She laughed at the craziness of everything and nothing. She rocked back onto the mossy ground and giggled like a five-year-old.

'I like her when she's stoned.' Gary was speaking from miles away. She could feel his gaze. On her body, not her face. Her dress had ridden up her thighs. That was funny too. She laughed some more.

'Yeah,' Lucas lowered his voice but she could still hear him at the edges of her consciousness. 'Wouldn't kick her out of bed.'

Bex knew that should bother her, but she couldn't find it in herself to care.

She let her head drop sideways, and caught sight of a figure in the dark woods. A girl. Pale, thin, wild-haired, dressed in white. Fear surged through her. The Pale Child. And she was looking right back at her.

Bex scrambled into a sitting position. The world spun and she clutched the ground with curled fingers and tight toes, as if she might fall off. She pointed and said, 'It's the Pale Child.' But when she looked again, the girl was gone.

She collapsed back onto the soft earth.

27

Meg – Present day
Wednesday

'It's quickest to go into the valley,' I said. 'Past the abattoir.'

Fiona accelerated down the hill. The air was dense with the heat, shimmering over the rocky moors around Gritton, and smoke from the wildfire sat low above the trees. It was the kind of weather that could turn a body into a seething, seeping mass of maggots and flies within days.

'What do they know?' Fiona asked.

'No detail,' I said. 'Just that they found a body in the woods and we should get there.'

Fiona studied me from the corner of her eye. 'Are you okay?'

'I suppose I'd been hoping she was still alive, despite everything. While we didn't have a body …'

'I know. It's awful. Poor girl.'

I pictured Violet's adoptive parents, who'd been warned all those years ago. Who knew Violet shouldn't have come to Gritton but couldn't stop her. And Bex, who also knew to keep away from Gritton, weeping silently for her lost daughter. 'At least if we find her body, we should get some evidence. Everything points to Gary, and we're bringing him in, but we've got nothing concrete on him yet. It's all circumstantial.'

'But if Violet's his daughter …'

'I know.'

'How horrible.' Fiona did a rapid shake of her head. 'Oh, and I see they're laying into us on Facebook again.'

I gave a bitter laugh. 'Laying into me, you mean.'

'Mainly, to be fair. They're going nuts that we haven't arrested anyone from the Animal Vigilantes.'

'For Christ's sake.' I knew I shouldn't care what these people thought but it made me feel wretched. 'It's wonderful to get an ongoing critique of the investigation from a bunch of gammons who know nothing about police work and wouldn't recognise the CPS if it smacked them in the face.'

The woods were behind Kirsty Nightingale's pig farm in the valley. We drove past a huge barn behind a high fence topped with barbed wire. 'It looks like a concentration camp from outside,' Fiona said.

'Having seen the cages she keeps them in, I reckon it feels like one from the inside too.' I wasn't in the mood to invent a bright side. 'But then I would say that, because I sympathise with animal rights extremists.'

The road bent away from the farm and passed into trees. Fiona slowed. 'Round here somewhere?'

A glimpse of white in the distance. We pulled closer. Police vehicles on a verge. Fiona slotted our car in behind them. 'Am I blocking the road?' she said anxiously.

'No.' I didn't even look.

An approach path had been marked out, and we followed

it deep into the woods. It had been hacked between brambles and nettles. The foliage above us was so thick it absorbed all the brightness from the sky. Some woods were beautiful – dappled light on swaying branches, easy wide paths through bluebells. This wasn't one of them. It was a tangle of ugly plants that either stung or spiked you.

I tried to focus on the path ahead and not think about Violet. Her smooth skin in the light of a summer evening, her earnest face reporting that she'd seen the Pale Child. What would she look like now, after two days in this heat? I didn't want to see.

We reached a small clearing, and the blue tape of the cordon came into view. Just outside it, was Mary, the pathologist, talking to a uniformed cop. She looked up and saw us. 'It's quite interesting actually,' she said.

My heart always sank when Mary said a case was interesting. I looked beyond the tape into a clearing.

I blinked a couple of times, not sure if I was seeing correctly.

'Oh my God,' Fiona whispered.

A body was propped against a tree, slumped sideways. Where there should have been a face, instead there was a pig's head.

28

Bex – August 1999

Bex opened her eyes. It was morning and she was in her room at her dad's house. The world spun catastrophically. She clamped her eyes shut again, but that was worse. She opened them and stared at the antique dressing table by the window. *Don't be sick, don't be sick.* Her breathing was fast. She swallowed. *Oh God.*

She leaped out of bed and raced for the bathroom. Threw herself at the toilet and retched and retched until her stomach was bruised and her throat raw. *Oh God.* She collapsed onto the cool floor tiles.

The sickness again. She clawed her way up and bashed her head into the porcelain of the toilet bowl. How could there still be stuff to throw up?

She dragged herself to her feet and rinsed her mouth again and again. Raised her head and looked at herself in the mirror. *Oh God.*

She stumbled over and locked the bathroom door. Sat on the side of the bath with her head between her knees. This was not good. Maybe if she brushed her teeth?

The side of the bath was hard.

And she was sore.

He heart beat faster. What had happened the night before?

She stood and walked to the toilet. Sat and reached her fingers tentatively to touch herself. She gulped back a sob. She was sore. Very sore.

What the *fuck* had happened the night before? She couldn't remember.

She collapsed onto the floor again. Something had happened and she didn't remember. *Fuck, fuck, fuck.*

She stood, but the room started spinning. She sank onto the toilet. Dropped her head forward and let herself cry.

She spoke to herself. *Okay, okay, so this has happened. Don't panic.* Her breath was coming in short bursts. *Don't panic.*

She didn't want to use the word, even to herself. *Raped?* That was the sort of thing that happened to other people. How could it have happened to her? She was a virgin. She'd *been* a virgin. She wanted to scream. If she hadn't felt so sick, she'd have been screaming. How the *fuck* could this have happened?

She stood again. Leaned against the wall. The last thing she remembered. The flash of fear. Seeing the girl. The Pale Child. That was it.

Then what? Did she pass out?

It must have been one of the boys. *Oh my God*, one of her *friends*. A jolt of memory. The way Gary looked at her with narrowed eyes. Daniel calling her a stuck-up cow. Lucas winking and saying, *I wouldn't kick her out of bed.*

But what about Kirsty and Anna? Why hadn't they protected her?

It must be a dream. She kept saying it to herself. *This hasn't happened.*

But she wasn't waking up. She was still there, in the bathroom, wanting to puke, wanting to scream, wanting to die.

Fuck, fuck fuck. She clutched her head and rocked to and fro.

How was she supposed to deal with this? She wanted Aunt Janet. She wanted her mum. She didn't remember her mum, but she wanted her anyway.

She had to speak to Kirsty. She mustn't have a bath or a shower. She looked at her fingernails. Maybe she'd scratched him. Evidence. She couldn't let him get away with it. He wouldn't get away with it.

How could she not know who it was?

She'd talk first to Kirsty. Kirsty always knew what to do.

Bex pulled open the bathroom door and walked onto the landing. She looked out of the window at the yard below. A police car. Her pulse spiked. Did they know? Had Kirsty reported it already? Were they coming to talk to her?

And then she heard Kirsty's scream.

29

Meg – Present day
Wednesday

I stood at the front of the incident room trying to look composed. I was talking to the team, but half my mind was elsewhere, spinning fast and out of control. Images flooded my brain. That hideous pig mask, the body slumped sideways against a tree. A little girl asking us if we wanted tea, her voice polite and clear and unexpected. A feeling of utter dejection came over me. Why hadn't I watched *Frozen* with her? Why couldn't I have let humanity and kindness beat efficiency and professionalism?

They were staring at me. I needed to speak, rather than stand at the front of the room sweating and looking distressed. 'Gary Finchley was found dead in the woods at Gritton,' I said. 'We haven't confirmed the cause of death, but it appears to be blunt trauma to the head. He had … a pig's head mask on.'

'Bloody hell,' Jai said. 'Wait for the hysterical hordes to get hold of this one.'

'They already have,' Craig said. 'It's on social media about the pig's head. Someone got a photo before we secured it.'

'Oh Jesus,' I said. 'So we've got that to contend with as well.'

'Two in one week,' Jai muttered. 'Did some bastard say it was *quiet*?'

I smiled grimly. There was a veto against using the word 'quiet', its mere utterance being guaranteed to plunge the station into an explosion of activity, albeit generally affrays in Chesterfield and sheep on Snake Pass rather than serial murders.

'Focus on your police work,' I said. 'We don't know for sure that this is part of an ongoing pattern. Don't assume it's about the abattoir, or meat, or even that it's connected to Violet. Cover all bases. At least we have a body. Forensics. Some chance in hell of finding who did this. We even have his phone, although it's locked and we're not in it yet.'

'But it is starting to look more like somebody making … a point,' Fiona said. 'A body eaten by pigs, a body with a pig's head mask on.'

'And both people who supported the meat industry,' Jai said.

'Yes,' I admitted. 'The way they've been killed, if indeed Violet is dead, does seem to make a point.'

'It is about meat, surely?' Fiona said. 'The Animal Vigilantes are protesting outside another abattoir today. Loads of them. All wearing meat suits and carrying placards with pigs' heads on them.'

'Oh God,' I muttered.

Craig said, 'Are you happy it's not Gary now?'

'This isn't about point-scoring, Craig. It's about finding whoever did this.'

'Do you think they're picking off people from that Great Meat Debate website?' Fiona said. 'Could Anna and Kirsty be in danger? And Daniel?'

'Talk to them about protection,' I said. 'And we carry on investigating. We don't assume Violet's dead, although it's probable. We don't assume that Gary Finchley's death is connected to Violet's disappearance, although we accept it's likely. Okay? And let's crack on, because if someone is making a point, I doubt they're finished.'

Gary Finchley's wife, Mandy, was staying with a friend while her house was being taken apart. An elderly woman pulled open the door of the terraced cottage. 'You'd better come in.' She was wearing two pink cardigans despite the heat.

Walking into the cottage was like entering a fridge, and I heard Jai sigh with relief as we made our way into a dark hallway. Cardigan-woman's attire started to make more sense. She ushered us into a tiny living room and disappeared.

Mandy was slumped on a worn green sofa in her dressing gown, so drained of life it looked like she might disappear. The child, Kelly, lay with her head on Mandy's knee, face turned away from us, sobbing quietly. The dog was leaning into her, its upper lip curling whenever Jai or I made any movement.

We sat on a matching sofa opposite them. It was so small that Jai and I were squished together, thighs forced awkwardly close.

'Is someone killing people involved with that website?' Mandy whispered. 'First Violet, now Gary. Animal rights people. And oh my God ...' She wrapped her arms around Kelly's ears as if shielding her. 'A pig's head!'

'I'm sorry you saw that,' I said. 'I'd advise you to stay off social media and please don't discuss this with anyone. It could jeopardise the investigation.' I wished we could shut down the whole of the internet, so people could tell us what the hell they actually knew, rather than parroting some crap they read on Facebook.

'But why?' Mandy said. 'Why would they do that to Gary? He's not a bad person.'

'Do you know anything else that makes you think this is aimed at people on the Great Meat Debate website, other than what you've seen on social media?' I asked.

'I don't know. I don't know anything. Gary saw the Pale Child too. I told you. He saw her on Monday night in the woods.'

I remembered Fiona's comment. *If anything happens to Gary, we freak the hell out.* Should we be freaking the hell out? We hadn't looked into the Pale Child myth in any detail. It had seemed like nonsense. Just an unhappy coincidence that Violet had seen her and then gone missing. Now I wasn't so sure.

'What do you know about the Pale Child, Mandy? Who is she?'

'I don't know!' Mandy cried. 'I don't know who she is!'

'Okay. This must be very difficult for you.'

I let her cry for a moment, and indicated to Jai that he should carry on. He kept his voice soft. 'Why did Gary go to the abattoir on Sunday night?'

'He said he was doing extra work.'

Jai frowned, but in a friendly way. 'In the middle of the night?'

'Yeah.' She looked down at Kelly.

'You need to tell us, Mandy. Don't worry if you're not sure if it's relevant.'

Mandy fiddled with a strand of Kelly's hair. 'I suppose you may as well know. What does it matter now? I think Gary had taken some money from the abattoir business.' She looked up, and shifted herself upright. 'We should have been entitled to it anyway. Why should Anna have been left everything instead of Gary? And Tony Nightingale — Kirsty's dad — gives money to the abattoir as well, but even then Anna can't make it profitable. She's not capable of running it. She spent all that money doing the place up, just for some pigs that were going to die anyway. Gary was sure he could have done a better job.'

I exchanged a look with Jai. 'Did Gary take the money for anything specific?' Jai said.

Mandy sighed. 'Gary wanted to buy Anna out. It should always have been his anyway. Most parents leave a business to the older sibling, or the boy. It was never fair.'

'Gary was stealing money from the abattoir, because he wanted to buy the abattoir?'

'Yes. That's why it wasn't really stealing. He took some money and then invested it to get more. And he changed the people who took the waste away to one who did it for free, and kept the money. Why pay someone when another company will do it for free?' So that made sense of Maggot Mick. Mandy was watching us, silently acknowledging that she knew exactly why you might pay a reputable company to take away your diseased and discarded animal matter. 'He did sometimes lose a bit on the horses. You must have noticed all our decent stuff's gone.'

And there was your clue as to why the business might have been left to Anna.

'Why does Tony Nightingale give money to the abattoir?' I asked.

'I'm not sure. He wants everything in the village to be nice, I suppose. Like those Victorians used to with their villages. His family's been in charge here for a long time.' I pictured Tony

Nightingale in his old-fashioned kitchen, the dog's laser-like focus on the biscuit tin, the roses going wild outside.

'And did Gary see Violet at the abattoir on Sunday?' Jai asked.

'He didn't tell me. But he was in a funny mood yesterday.'

As we waited for Mandy to elaborate, Kelly sat up and nestled herself into her mum's side, back still to us, drawing Flossy to her. I thought of the bright kid asking us to watch TV with her, and my heart broke a little. Even if Gary had been a dodgy bugger, he'd loved his daughter.

'On Monday night, he went out and met Anna, Kirsty and Daniel in the woods. That was when he saw the Pale Child. I knew ...' Mandy wiped away a tear. 'I knew something awful was going to happen. The Pale Child is back because of the drought. The old village has come to the surface again.'

The drowned village. The Pale Child. I shook my head. How could it possibly be relevant?

'And they met in the woods to discuss Violet?' I said.

Mandy hit us with her hollow-eyed look. 'Yes. They thought the animal rights people had hurt Violet and they would be next. But then yesterday evening, Gary told me all our troubles were over.'

'All your troubles were over? Did he tell you what he meant by that?'

She shook her head and looked down again. 'I thought he must've come on some cash.'

'How?'

'I don't know.'

'You didn't ask him?'

She sighed. 'I assumed it was a win, so he wouldn't have told me – he'd sworn he wouldn't gamble any more. Besides, I didn't expect to see much of it.'

How depressing. I could imagine why Mandy might not feel like getting dressed most days. But had it been a win, or something else?

'Did Gary meet anyone else yesterday?' I asked.

'He went to work. Apart from that, I don't know.'

'Last night, what time was it when he went out?'

'About midnight. He never said where he was going.'

'Do you know what prompted him to go?'

Mandy reached an arm around the child and pulled her closer. 'No. He went off without telling me. I had a bad feeling but I didn't stop him. I should've stopped him. But Gary never seemed that scared. Not like he thought he was going to be killed.'

'Why would Gary not have been scared?' I said. 'If he thought the Animal Vigilantes were after him?'

'I'm not sure.'

I had a theory. What if Gary knew who'd killed Violet and it wasn't the Animal Vigilantes? He could have seen someone at the abattoir on Sunday night and been planning to blackmail them. But who had he seen?

'What the actual fuck is going on?' Hannah was sitting at a cramped table in Gritton's only tea room, looking extremely hot. The place was packed full of people who I suspected were not there for the catering. Outside were more people, milling about and rubbernecking their way around a shocked Gritton, mobile phones held aloft.

'Hi, Hannah, good to see you too,' I said. Jai had grabbed a lift back with one of the cops who'd been doing the interminable house-to-house enquiries, leaving me free to meet Hannah.

She grabbed my arm, pulled me close and whispered. 'Is it true? Violet's been fed to pigs. That other bloke had a pig's head mask on. Have the Animal Vigilantes gone completely mental?'

'Let me get you a drink.'

'Thanks, yes. It's not the most disability-friendly spot. And it's hotter than the actual bowels of hell.'

I couldn't argue with her assessment. The place didn't appear to have been modernised in about thirty years and was cluttered, doily infested and chintzy, festooned with notices telling you not to do things. *No Muddy Boots PLEASE! Dogs NOT Allowed. Please keep your children under CONTROL!!*

'Makes you want to turn up with six large dogs and a feral pack of children in muddy boots,' I said.

Hannah shifted on her wooden chair. 'It doesn't even have a proper coffee machine. And that woman over there gave me the evils when I managed to lever myself out of my wheelchair to shift onto a chair. She thinks I'm faking to get a good table.'

'Oh dear. Bad choice of eatery.'

'Don't worry, I'm used to it. Get us another crappy coffee and a gallon of water will you?'

I battled my way to the counter and bought a tea for me, a coffee for Hannah, and a couple of cakes covered in butter-icing that looked like it could cause death on contact.

I squeezed myself in opposite Hannah. 'Anyway, good to see you. What did you want to show me?'

'Is it true though?' Hannah said. 'I can't believe what I'm reading.'

I sighed. 'Don't believe everything you hear, but … there have been some worrying developments which I can't discuss—'

'You sound like a politician, but I'll take that as a yes. My God.'

'It's quite challenging. I can't be long.'

'I know, I know, but I do need you to tell me how it's going with your dad and the rare parental visitation.'

'I'll give you a full run-down, Hannah, but not right now. It's going okay though.'

'Did you find out why he's suddenly visited you, after all these years of total silence?'

'He wants to see me.'

Hannah raised her eyebrows.

'And he's split up with Pauline.'

'And I bet you've totally forgiven him for being such a shit dad for so long, haven't you?'

I felt a spark of irritation that she'd speak about him like this. I was allowed to slag him off, but she wasn't. It was in the official friend rules. 'He's being lovely. Making me food, buying nice gin and wine, asking me about stuff.'

'Well, be careful. I know what you're like.'

'Christ, you're as bad as my mum. Now what did you want to show me?'

She fished her phone out of her pocket, tapped the screen, and passed it to me. 'I know I could have emailed you this, but I wanted a look around the village and I thought you'd be coming up here. See this video I found. I've been researching Violet and I saw her video about having seen that Pale Child. I thought it was a bit creepy, so I had a look for more Pale Child stuff and found this. I don't know how relevant it is, but it's called "Pale Child Sighting".'

I shielded the screen so nobody else could see it. A video played. A rocky moor at dusk, the camera sitting low and at a slight angle as if it was resting on a makeshift tripod. A glimpse of white in the distance. A girl, clambering away over the rocks. She stopped. Turned to face the camera. I felt a jolt of unease. She was wearing an old-fashioned white dress and a doll's face mask, just like Violet had reported in her video. The girl turned and ran away through the heather.

'I think it was filmed above the reservoir,' Hannah said. 'Near Gritton, below the gritstone edge. I had a drive around to look, and I'm pretty sure I'm right.'

'When was it posted?'

'Last week. Which is interesting, isn't it? It was before Violet went missing. I'm sure the thousands of views are more recent, but someone was posting videos about the Pale Child before Violet put it in the public eye.'

'Okay. We'll get our tech people to have a look at it. Trace who posted it. Because that's no ghost, so who the hell is it?'

My phone buzzed in my pocket. I grabbed it and answered.

'It's Daniel. Daniel Twigg.' He sounded as if he'd been running. 'They're coming for me next.'

30

I dropped my death-by-cake and pressed the phone to my ear. Hannah looked at me wide-eyed.

'They've … it's horrible …' Daniel's voice was shaking. 'They've put … stuff on my caravan. My friend's called the police and they're on the way, but I thought … after what they did to Gary …'

'I'll come to you. I'm in Gritton. Get yourself somewhere safe with other people.'

I phoned to check that uniforms were on their way, gulped down a glass of water, grabbed my stuff, and said a hurried goodbye to Hannah.

I pushed through the tea room door, and my phone rang again. Jai. I answered while running to my car.

'I just finished talking to Violet's friend, Izzy,' Jai said. 'Remember we both had a feeling she wasn't telling us the whole story? Well, we were right. There was a secret relationship. Violet made Izzy promise on her mother's life not to tell anyone, but eventually my charm was too much for her.'

'All right, Jai,' I gasped. 'We all know about your charm. Who the hell was it?'

'To be honest, I'm not sure if it was my charm or the fact she's totally bloody terrified because he's now dead with a pig's head mask on him.'

'Gary? But we think he's Violet's father! She was having an affair with him?' I tried to imagine Violet's feelings if she'd discovered that the man she'd been having a relationship with was not only her father but had raped her mother. And what about Gary? How must he have felt if he found out the girl he was sleeping with was his daughter?

'Not sure you'd call it an affair,' Jai said, 'but she hooked up with him, according to Izzy.'

'God.'

'There's more. Gary told Violet a secret. He made her swear never to tell anyone.'

I arrived at the car and clicked it unlocked. 'A secret? Do we know any more than that?'

'Violet told Izzy it was a secret about the Pale Child.'

I hopped into my car, opened all the windows and drove rather too fast up the main road through the village. A secret about the Pale Child. Everything kept coming back to the Pale Child. But it made no sense. Who was the girl in Hannah's video? Wasn't the Pale Child supposed to be a ghost?

I drove down a side road. A sign for a school hung from a red-brick building, and a couple of children stood on the grass outside. They were oddly still. I looked again. Not children. Bollards in the shape of children, positioned firmly in the uncanny valley. Like the sinkhole in the road into the village, they were presumably intended to slow drivers down and prevent accidents, but I nearly crashed into a railing, freaking out at how sinister they were.

I called Jai back, and talked over his attempt at a greeting. 'What the hell is it with this village? All the railings and gates and ways to make you slow down. We've been sidetracked by the whole meat thing and the Animal Vigilantes. I think this is about something else completely. It's about this weird village and the bloody Pale Child.'

'All right. I'm getting the message. I'll find out what I can about the Pale Child.'

I thanked Jai for putting up with me, ended the call, and drove through Lower Gritton, before pulling into the campsite and parking by the sat-down caravan. I shouldn't have been going alone but this was me, and anyway uniform had been called. I got out of the car and headed for Daniel's caravan. The rock-balancing art had been kicked over, the stones lying forlornly on the dry grass. On the side of the caravan, daubed in red paint, were the words PIG TORTURER. YOU'RE NEXT.

The door of the sat-down caravan crashed open and Daniel jumped out. 'Look what they did! They're coming for me!'

'Did you see them?'

'No. Dotty saw. She's called the normal police, but I thought you should see. She said they were dressed in those horrible meat suits. Went right up and did it. She set the dog on them and they ran off.'

'Did they get inside your caravan?' The edge of the door was dented as if someone had tried to lever it open.

He shook his head. 'No. No they didn't.'

I looked more closely. 'It does look like someone's broken in, Daniel.'

'No. It was already like that. But someone's going to come and kill me in the night. They fed Violet to the pigs. They put a pig's head on Gary's corpse. What are they going to do to me? This is so wrong. I do my best for the animals. Why are they targeting me? I love animals!'

I was sure his door had been messed with, and it hadn't been like that the other day. Why would he lie to me?

'I try to make things better,' Daniel said. 'Why can't they see that?'

I gave him an encouraging nod and made it clear I was listening. His anxiety was making him eager to confide, and that was rarely a bad thing in my game.

'Nobody gets why I would work in an abattoir,' he said. 'But I help animals when they really, really need it. Surely the best thing you can do is to give them a bit of kindness before they die? To make sure they're led gently to their end, not pushed or prodded, shouted at or threatened.' He looked me right in the eye. 'Who does more good for animals – someone who has nothing to do with farming or the meat industry at all, or someone like me who's actually *there*? Who makes sure the animals are treated with respect? Those people who go undercover and expose the horrors in normal abattoirs, they despise me, they're even threatening to kill me, but I do good.'

'I understand,' I said. And I did. I couldn't do it myself, but if what he said was true, I respected him for it. I wondered what had happened to him to make him like this. So determined to do the right thing even though it put him in an unbearable situation, having to watch the animals he cared for being killed every day.

Beyond Daniel, in the far distance on the moor behind the caravan site, a flash of white caught my eye. 'Hold on,' I said, 'that looked like the Pale Child. Over there on the face of the rock. Can you get onto the moor from here?'

'You can, but—'

'Show me!' Two people had known a secret about the Pale Child and now they were both gone. There was no way I was letting this pass. I grabbed Daniel's arm and pulled him in the direction of the distant white figure.

It was so far away it was hard to see, but it looked like someone scrambling up the side of one of the gritstone edges. The place rock climbers went, but it didn't look like a rock climber. Rock climbers didn't wear white dresses.

We took a path onto the moor, me stumbling along on my dodgy ankle, desperate to find out who this person was, and Daniel following reluctantly.

The path took us towards the higher ground. Ahead were looming cliffs, and stones in bizarre piles as if arranged by an immense rock-balancing artist. Bracken and heather and tussocks of grass made it hard going, and the ground was pitted with rabbit and badger holes. A sheep bleated in the distance. I was panting with the effort of running up the hill.

As we got closer, I could see it was definitely a child in a white dress. She was hanging down over the cliff, but while we watched, she hauled herself up and shot out of view.

'We need to get to the top of that edge,' I said. 'Do you know the way?'

'That path.' Daniel gestured to our right. 'But you'll never catch her now.'

I was determined to try. My breath rasped in my throat as

I followed the path towards the higher ground, Daniel behind me.

'I have a bad ankle,' I said. 'I know your back's not good but feel free to go past if you can.'

Daniel overtook and ran ahead, eventually reaching the edge where the girl had been. He scanned the landscape, and shouted, 'No sign of her.'

I caught up, and he was right. She was gone.

The lone sheep was bleating louder. The sweep of Ladybower Reservoir was far below us now. In the distance jutted the peak of Mam Tor. I felt a stab of fear when I realised how close we were to the place where the ground dropped away into a cliff. I'd tried to work on my fear of heights but it hadn't gone completely.

'We've totally lost her,' Daniel said.

'Who was it? And what's up with that sheep?'

'Must have got separated from its lamb,' Daniel said. 'They're buggers for getting themselves in trouble.'

I caught a glimpse of movement ahead. 'That's not her again, is it?'

Daniel looked where I pointed and we both ran a few steps before seeing it was the sheep.

'She looks really upset,' I said. 'She's too close to the cliff. What on earth's she doing?'

The sheep was on a higher part of the rocky edge, bleating hysterically and shifting to and fro, approaching the edge and then backing away. Daniel scrambled up to get closer to her.

'Oh God,' he said. 'It's her lamb.'

I inched closer to Daniel. 'What's the matter with it?'

'It's fallen over, but it's on a ledge. Quite a long way down, so it can't get back up. And it's quiet. It shouldn't be quiet. I think

218

it's been there a while. It looks like a runt. It can't be less than two months old at this time of year, but it's small.'

'Oh no,' I said. 'It's not dead, is it?'

A faint bleat came from below.

'Good,' Daniel said. 'It's roused itself. Hang on, I'll move away. I'm freaking it out.'

The mother sheep joined in the bleating, seeming half scared of us, half outraged that we hadn't yet done anything constructive. Daniel and I moved away from the edge to perch on a flat rock and the sheep quietened. The village of Gritton was far below us, its areas of woodland like green velvet in contrast to the dry yellow grassland. It looked idyllic from above, the clashing protesters, hordes of journalists, and grieving families a world away.

'I'll call someone,' I said. 'I don't have time to faff around trying to save a lamb.'

'It's very weak,' Daniel said. 'I'm going to climb down and get it. If we wait for help to arrive, it'll die.'

I wanted to scream at the ridiculousness of this. The Pale Child was getting away, I had one missing presumed dead and one definitely dead, the Animal Vigilantes and Justice for Violet were marauding below us. Was I really going to waste valuable time and terrify myself senseless helping Daniel rescue a runt lamb?

31

'How far down was the lamb?' I said.

'I think I can get to it,' Daniel said. 'If you stay at the top, I can pass it to you.' There was none of the spaced-out quality about him now. And all concern for his own welfare seemed to have dropped away at the sight of a lamb in danger.

I pictured the headline. *Animal Activist Detective Bounces on Head and Dies Trying to Rescue Lamb.* 'Okay,' I said.

'It'll be fine. We'll keep everything really quiet. Keep the mother relaxed.' Daniel smiled and I couldn't help smiling back, despite my panic about being near to the edge.

'I'm not too good with heights,' I said. 'But I'll be okay.'

The lamb let out a weak, heart-rending cry.

We shifted towards the edge, keeping low. The sheep stayed calm and even began to approach us. 'These moorland sheep get fed in the winter,' Daniel said. 'So they're not terrified of people.'

My heard thudded. We were near to the edge.

I shifted onto my stomach and peered over. The lamb was about six feet below us, on a narrow ledge. Below, the cliff fell steeply down to rocks underneath. If the lamb slipped off, it would be a goner. The same applied to us, of course.

'Are you sure you want to do this?' I said. 'That ledge is so narrow and it looks crumbly.'

Daniel laughed. 'I'd rather be taken out by a lamb than by the Animal Vigilantes.' He turned round and shuffled backwards. 'I just hope it doesn't suicide off the edge when it sees me coming.'

The sheep let out a throaty bleat, but the lamb had calmed down. It eyed Daniel sceptically as he inched his way slowly towards it. Finally his feet touched the ledge. The lamb stood frozen. The ledge was so narrow, I couldn't see how Daniel was going to reach down without risking falling. I could grab one of his hands, but he'd need both to pick up the lamb.

'Hang on, I'm coming forward.' Heart pounding, I shuffled right to the edge, stretched out, and grabbed his collar. 'Right. I've got you.'

Daniel squatted slowly, talking softly to the lamb. I allowed myself to go a little lower, so I could keep hold of him. He reached around the lamb, lifted it smoothly into his arms, and then stood tall again. It struggled briefly and then gave up. 'Got it. You can let go of me and move back a bit, then take the lamb from me.'

I let go of his collar, shifted back and stabilised myself, reached and took the warm, squirming thing from Daniel's outstretched arms. It was surprisingly heavy, and softer than I'd expected. As I took it, I caught sight of a white object snagged on a root that protruded from the cliff below the ledge Daniel was on. I twisted around to let the lamb go, and looked back down. 'What's that, Daniel?'

The sheep let out a bellow. The lamb's four legs straightened and it stood blinking and looking baffled. Finally it let out a bleat and charged to its mother without so much as a thank you.

Daniel reached below him, towards the thing I'd seen. 'I can't get it,' he said.

I shuffled nearer to the edge and peered down. It was a doll's face mask. 'It's what the girl was wearing,' I said. 'The Pale Child.'

'Just a kid's toy,' Daniel said. 'Could be anyone's.'

'Can you reach it? It might be important.'

'Er … not without risking falling off the cliff.'

'Don't do that.'

He sighed and moved into a squatting position and then onto his stomach on the ledge.

'No, it's okay … Daniel, don't kill yourself.'

He reached down and managed to grab the mask. Then stood and passed it to me, before scrambling up from the ledge and brushing himself down.

'Thanks,' I said. 'I didn't mean you to put yourself in danger.'

The mask was thin plastic with a stretchy cord to go round the back of the head, like the one the girl in Hannah's video had been wearing. Presumably the girl we'd followed up here had been wearing it. Was she the Pale Child that Violet and Gary had seen?

The lamb was suckling from its poor mother in a way which looked borderline abusive. They were closer to the cliff edge than I'd have liked. 'It had better not go over again,' I said. 'Or it's staying there.'

Daniel laughed.

'Is that the first time you've dragged a lamb off a cliff edge?' I asked. 'You seemed quite the expert.'

'I must be a natural. Perhaps I've finally found my vocation. How about you?'

'Part of a normal day in Peak District policing.'

We headed back across the moor. A surprising wave of well-being washed over me. It had been good to forget about everything for a few minutes and focus on saving the lamb. And I realised with a jolt of discomfort that I'd enjoyed spending time with Daniel. I remembered the research that showed you were more likely to be attracted to someone if you met them on a high bridge. Your brain mistook adrenaline from fear for adrenaline from attraction. It was probably just that.

I forced my mind to clunk back into standard operating mode.

'Daniel,' I said. 'You need to tell me what you know about the Pale Child. What's going on? You saw her in the woods on Monday night, didn't you? When you met Gary, Anna and Kirsty?' I held the mask up. 'Was she wearing this?'

Daniel sighed. 'Welcome back, Detective.'

'I have to do my job.'

'Well, I didn't see her, I'm afraid.'

'But you saw the girl on the cliff just now. And this mask is real. You grew up in this village. What's it all about?'

Daniel strode faster, kicking his way through a clump of bracken. He didn't answer my question.

I hurried to keep pace. 'What is it?' I touched his arm. 'What do you know about the Pale Child?' I thought of the secret that Gary had supposedly told Violet. Did Daniel know what that was?

His shoulders dropped and he slowed and turned towards me. 'We saw her in the woods the night of my car accident all those years ago. But it wasn't the Pale Child who was responsible. It wasn't the Pale Child who got in a car when drunk and ended up killing someone. It was me.'

I didn't say anything, but slowed my pace, hoping he'd slow with me and continue talking.

'I live with a lot of guilt,' he said. 'I try to do *good* things. Try to put things right.'

I couldn't argue with that. He'd risked his life to save a lamb. 'I can see that. Guilt from your accident, you mean?'

He nodded miserably. 'I was nineteen. I'm a different person now.' He snatched at a clump of tall grass as we walked past. 'I couldn't feel worse about that night. Someone died because of my stupidity. I've spent the rest of my life regretting that, but there's nothing I can do to change it.' He rubbed his lower back. 'And every time this twinges, I remember.'

Instinctively, my gaze dropped to my ankle. And as always, I remembered. The day I was partly responsible for my sister's death was the day I broke my ankle. So I understood exactly what Daniel meant.

'You saw the Pale Child?' I said. 'The night of your accident?'

'Yes. But I don't know who she is. Er … I need to tell you something. I should have done it on Monday, but I hadn't realised it was important. Should I come into the police station tomorrow?'

That was a definite and clearly deliberate change of subject away from the Pale Child, but I wanted to hear what he had to say. And I certainly wasn't going to wait until tomorrow. I felt like saying, *Are you mad? Have you never watched* Midsomer Murders*? If you tell me you have important information and don't spit it out THIS MINUTE, you're a dead man!*

'Give me the gist of it now,' I said. 'And we'll take a full statement tomorrow.'

A gust of wind tickled the bracken, and brought a waft of

224

smoke with it. The fire blazed on the distant moor. It was creeping closer to Gritton.

'I was the one who told the Animal Vigilantes that Violet was missing,' Daniel said. 'On Monday morning. I'm sorry. I was worried about Violet and I panicked and contacted Leona in case they'd taken her.'

'You realised she was missing first thing?' I'd had a feeling he was lying about that.

'I saw Violet's car. And she wasn't there, but I saw her watch. I'm sorry. I rushed home and contacted Leona. I thought they'd done something to her. Leona wouldn't tell me whether they had or not. But she said I mustn't let you know I'd been in touch with her or you'd think I was in league with the Animal Vigilantes and that I'd hurt Violet. I didn't think it was a big deal. Anna had raised the alarm by then anyway, and I knew you'd find the watch. But now I can see Leona wanted you to think it was them. To think that it must have been them because they knew about it so early. She wanted the publicity. But they only knew about it because I told them, not because they did it.'

I sighed. 'Yes, that was quite unhelpful, Daniel.'

'I'm sorry.'

'How did you have Leona's contact details?'

'I'd been in touch with her before. When we were getting threats. I wanted to tell her that we weren't the bad guys. That the Animal Vigilantes shouldn't be targeting us.'

'Right. We will need a statement from you, but thanks for telling me.'

This was useful. It reinforced my view that the Animal Vigilantes hadn't hurt Violet or Gary. Whatever was going on

225

had nothing to do with meat. It was connected to some secret about the Pale Child.

'I realised I should tell you,' Daniel said. 'You're a good person and you're on the side of the animals. You won't immediately suspect me just because I was talking to the Animal Vigilantes. I told you because I know I can trust you.'

We arrived back at Daniel's caravan, and the orange-haired woman strode into view. Dotty, I assumed. She gave me a suspicious look. 'Police have been and gone. No effort spared. Oh wait, I meant no effort expended.'

'Good. Okay,' Daniel said, not picking up on the dig about my esteemed colleagues.

'We're getting you protection,' I said. 'In the meantime, don't be alone, okay?'

'He's staying with me,' Dotty said. 'So do I get a cuppa or what?'

Daniel looked at his caravan. 'Well, I suppose …'

'Come on, Dan, don't be tight.' Dotty waved her arm at the caravan. 'Invite us in.'

'No, I … Sit out here. There are deckchairs.'

'Hoity-toity, doesn't want us inside.' Dotty settled herself on a deckchair that looked to be nearing the end of its natural life.

Daniel sighed and looked at me. 'Would you like a drink?'

Daniel's desperation for us not to go inside his caravan had made me equally determined to see inside. I remembered that he hadn't wanted me to investigate earlier, when I'd noticed the damaged door. 'Yes please,' I said.

Daniel slid inside, and I sat on a second moribund deckchair next to Dotty, the plastic mask on my knee. Dotty tutted at the red paint on the caravan. 'Fuckers.'

I nodded.

'There's no way our Daniel's a bad person,' she said. 'Heart of gold, he has. He tries to do his best for the animals. If any of those bastards come back, I'm letting my other dog out, that'll sort them out. He's a pit bull.' She broke off and looked at me. 'Not a real pit bull – he just looks like one.'

The door of the caravan popped open and Daniel appeared with two mugs of tea.

'Grand.' Dotty reached to take one. 'It's not that weird milk, is it? What were you doing haring off over the hills anyway?'

'It's oat milk, Dotty. Remember? You liked that.' Daniel perched on a rock from one of his ruined art installations.

'Don't you drink milk?' I said.

'No, I don't have meat or dairy.'

He was *vegan*. Seriously? A vegan whose job was slaughtering pigs in an abattoir? He was one of the most baffling people I'd ever met. I suspected his behaviour was driven by an even more toxic and powerful dose of guilt than the one I lived with. And I didn't want to admit it, even to myself, but I liked him.

I took a sip of my tea. 'I thought I saw the Pale Child,' I said, wondering what Dotty's reaction would be.

'Ooh, you don't want to let that Pale Child see your face,' Dotty said.

I looked at her. 'You believe that?'

'Yes, I do.'

I took a swig of tea and looked back at Dotty. 'Who do you think the Pale Child is, then?'

'I don't know, but I know she'll not be seeing my face.'

'She was a Nightingale, wasn't she?'

'That family have never been quite right,' Dotty said. 'Too much in-breeding.'

'What's not right about them?'

'Ah, it's probably just the way the rich classes are. I wouldn't get on the wrong side of that girl Kirsty, but Tony's decent enough. His mother took all that compensation from when the manor was drowned and put it towards the village instead of spending it on another fancypants house, and he's carried on the same way.' Dotty stood and handed her mug to Daniel. 'Thank you for that. Things to do.'

Dotty headed off over the rough grass to her guard-caravan, and I got to my feet. 'Any chance I could use your loo, Daniel?'

His face went white. 'Oh. No, it's not … It's not very good. Chemical loos aren't good in this weather.'

I smiled. 'Honestly, I backpacked round India. I'm not fussy.' I took a step towards the caravan, taking the plastic mask with me.

Daniel put his arm against the door. 'I'd rather … Maybe you could use Dotty's?'

'I think I'll use yours, please.'

His whole body sagged, and he let me pull the door open. I stepped into the half of the caravan I'd been in with Jai. The divider between the two halves had been smashed.

'Look, I need to tell you something,' Daniel said. 'About the Pale Child. My little brother, Charlie—'

A noise outside. A shout and the sound of running footsteps. Daniel spun round and yelled, 'No!'

Two men in gruesome meat suits, carrying something. They

228

flung it at me. I shut my eyes and put my hand up to protect my face. Tripped on a board on the caravan floor and crashed to the ground.

Daniel screamed, 'Fuck off and leave me alone!'

I took my hand away from my face and saw that it was covered in dark, thick liquid. Sticky and red. Metallic.

Blood.

32

After Kirsty screamed, Bex had hidden in her room, listening to the low murmurs from below, too scared to go downstairs and discover what was happening. But now the police had gone and she knew she had to face her family.

She crept downstairs and pushed open the living room door. Kirsty was on the sofa, their dad next to her, ashen-faced.

Bex's eyes flicked around. Everything was wrong. A vase left smashed on the floor, Kirsty's expression solid like concrete, their dad's brow pulled down towards his eyes. Whatever had gone on here, it wasn't about what had happened to Bex. Her stomach felt cold.

'Come and sit down,' her dad said. 'Sit down, Bex.'

'Just tell me what happened,' she whispered.

Her dad started to speak but his voice didn't come out. All she could hear was the ticking of the grandfather clock, too loud and intrusive. Her dad coughed and tried again. 'Daniel's car was found on the edge of the woods. It had gone into a tree. The two of them weren't wearing seat belts.'

'Lucas is dead,' Kirsty said. 'Lucas was killed.'

Bex staggered back as if she'd been hit.

'Daniel is in hospital,' her dad said. 'He's broken his back.'

'Oh my God.' Bex walked over and sank into the uncomfortable old armchair opposite her dad and Kirsty.

'They found a lot of alcohol in Daniel's bloodstream. We don't know why he was driving.' Her dad's voice was controlled. She couldn't work out his feelings. Lucas was dead. Was that Daniel's fault? Daniel was in hospital. A broken back. Did that mean he'd be *paralysed*?

Her dad stood, hauling himself from the sofa like a much older man. 'I'll make us some tea.'

Bex looked at Kirsty's bleached face. 'I'm so sorry,' she said.

'I can't believe it's happened,' Kirsty said. 'It feels like a bad dream.'

Bex shifted on her chair, her physical discomfort seeming like nothing now, compared to her sister's pain. 'Why would Daniel drive?' she said.

Kirsty looked up and her face hardened. 'It was because of you. You'd passed out. It started throwing it down. You were cold and we needed to get you inside quickly. You know how he feels about you, so don't pretend otherwise. He drove us home and then took Lucas.'

Bex felt the breath leaving her body. It was as if the air had left the room too, as if there was no longer any oxygen. 'I didn't know it was raining,' she said, a stupid, irrelevant space-filling comment.

'What is this? *Four Weddings and a* fucking *Funeral*? It was raining. You'd passed out.'

'Did we see … the Pale Child?' Another stupid comment. But wasn't the Pale Child always there when bad things happened?

'You thought you saw it. Sent us all off on a stupid wild goose chase. We split up to look for it, and Lucas thought he saw it too, but there was nothing there.'

They split up. They left Bex and split up. Any of them could have raped her.

'When we came back it had started raining. You were passed out. You looked terrible. We had to get you home. Daniel decided to drive us home, and Lucas said he'd come too. To help with you.' The last sentence stabbed into Bex.

The door pushed open and their dad walked in with a tray. He placed it carefully on a low table, poured with a shaking hand, and passed cups to Bex and Kirsty, before sinking down onto the sofa next to Kirsty. Nobody said anything.

Bex sipped her tea. Her lips wouldn't work properly and she spilled it down her front. Opposite her, Kirsty took one sip of tea and then slammed the cup down on the table, splashing tea all over it. 'I don't want fucking tea.' She jumped up and stormed out of the room.

Bex sat with her dad, desperately aware now that they were strangers. The silence between them was too solid to break. Bex looked at the tea on the antique table and wondered if she should mop it up. What a stupid thought, with everything else that was going on.

'I'm so sorry, Dad,' she eventually said.

'It's not your fault.'

But it was her fault. Kirsty clearly blamed her. She'd seen the Pale Child, sent them running off. She'd passed out, got too cold and wet, made Daniel drive despite him being drunk and stoned. It was her fault. And what about the rest? Was that her fault too? Was it her fault that she'd been raped? She couldn't tell her dad about that.

'Why don't you go and check on your sister?' her dad said.

Bex stood. She was no comfort to him, that was clear. She left the room and climbed the stairs. Knocked gently on Kirsty's door and pushed it open. Kirsty was on her bed. She looked up. 'Oh. Hello.'

'Can I come in?' Bex said.

Kirsty waved towards a chair beside an old dressing table. 'Sit down.' She looked a little better.

'Are you okay?' Bex said.

Kirsty nodded. 'I'll cope.'

'I'm sorry.'

Kirsty sighed. 'I know. It's not really your fault. We shouldn't have let you get so drunk.'

They sat in silence. Bex couldn't think what to say. She hoped being there might help Kirsty but there was no indication that it did.

Eventually Kirsty said, 'Seriously, Bex, don't look so tragic. I shouldn't have said it was your fault. You didn't force Daniel to drive. And they could have dropped us and then left the car here.'

Bex looked up and caught her sister's eye. 'I suppose so. Thank you.'

'Life is random and shit,' Kirsty said. 'Get used to it.'

'Kirsty, I …' She looked at her sister's porcelain face.

'What?'

'There's another thing. I know it's nothing compared to losing Lucas …' Was that true? It felt like the right thing to say, when Kirsty was suffering so much, collapsed on her bed like she'd been shot. Bex hated to make it worse but she had to do it. Because she couldn't let him get away with it. 'Kirsty, I wish I didn't have to tell you this now, but I …'

Kirsty looked blankly at her. 'What?'

'I was raped. Last night I was raped.'

Kirsty frowned and shook her head. 'No you weren't. You can't have been.'

'But I was.'

'Jesus, Bex, I can't cope with this now! What is it with your attention-seeking behaviour all the fucking time? I've just lost Lucas. Can't you give me that?'

Bex felt the tears slipping down her cheeks. 'I'm not attention-seeking.' She stood slowly, and stumbled towards the doorway, but her dad had appeared in it. 'Are you girls okay?' he said.

Kirsty's voice was loud. 'She says she's been raped, Dad. It's not true.'

Her dad looked so out of his depth, she almost felt sorry for him. He touched her on the arm. 'What, Bex? What happened?'

'She's making it up,' Kirsty said. 'She can't stand that the attention's not on her for once.'

Bex tried to push past her dad, but he grabbed her arm. 'What happened, Bex?'

'It doesn't matter.' She snatched her arm away and ran along the landing to her room, the gossamer-thin family connections she'd made tearing apart as she slammed the door behind her.

She threw herself onto the bed and sobbed, listening to the soft voices of her dad and Kirsty drifting through the wall. She couldn't hear what they were saying.

The door opened, then closed gently. The bed shifted with someone's weight. 'Please, Bex, tell me what happened.'

She gulped and twisted round to look at her dad. He handed her a tissue and she dragged it across her face. 'It doesn't matter.'

'It does. Who raped you, Bex? Tell me. Kirsty's just terribly upset about Lucas. Forgive her. She doesn't mean what she's saying.'

If he'd been her real dad, a proper dad, he'd have hugged her and she'd have sobbed into his shoulder. But he sat awkwardly as if desperate to get this over with, like the stranger that he was.

'I don't know who it was,' she said, as clearly as she could. 'I passed out. I had too much to drink. I know that's bad.'

'Oh heavens. Yes, that is bad. That's very bad.'

'We need to go to the police. They'll take DNA. They can test the boys and find out who it was.'

'But, Bex …' Her dad laid his hand gently on her arm. 'You were wearing an awfully flimsy dress. You had so much to drink that you passed out.'

Bex's eyes crept up to his face, searching out the shape of the betrayal. 'What are you saying?'

'We can't go to the police with this, Bex. Nobody will have any sympathy for you. You drank yourself unconscious. You don't remember. The best thing is we all pretend this sorry incident never happened.'

33

Meg – Present day
Wednesday

I pulled up on the cobbles outside my house and scrambled from the car. All I could think of was getting properly clean. I'd washed the worst of the blood off in a communal shower block and bundled my clothes and the doll's face mask into evidence bags, and Daniel had lent me clean jogging bottoms and a T-shirt, but I could still smell the metallic tang. So much blood. Every time I shut my eyes, I saw it flying at me in a pungent wave of red.

I pushed open my front door, feeling that old twinge of anxiety. I hadn't quite recovered from having dead-sister dolls shoved through it earlier in the year, and now I was being attacked all over again. Attacked by Justice for Violet for being a vegetarian and now attacked by the Animal Vigilantes because I'd happened to be with Daniel. I was in danger of giving in to self-pity.

My spirits lifted when I smelled cooking. The post had been piled neatly on the bookcase and it even looked like the floor had been vacuumed.

I shouted to Dad, 'Hello! I'm just having a wash,' and legged it upstairs and into the shower before he could see the state of me. I turned my face into the warm water and replayed what had happened. I hadn't seen the faces of the people who'd thrown the blood at us. I remembered Daniel had started saying something which had felt important. About his little brother.

I felt a whole lot better when I'd cleaned myself up. I headed for the kitchen. 'Wow, Dad, are you making food?'

'Yes. Sit down, let me pour you a gin and tonic to start and then you can have a glass of wine with the meal. I got us some nice local gin and a bottle of Chablis.'

I certainly needed alcohol. 'Blimey, you can stay more often.'

I folded myself onto one of my kitchen chairs, still orange pine despite my best intentions, and let him pour me a large gin. When I closed my eyes, I saw blood flying at me, and then the pig's head on Gary's shoulders. My mind was full of the case but I felt the need to pretend to Dad that I was a normal human who could forget about work for a while. 'How was your day?' I asked.

'I tidied up the garden and did a bit of cleaning.'

'That's very good of you.'

'It's fine. You work hard. I'll leave that to simmer.' He sat opposite and raised his glass. 'Cheers.'

'Cheers.' I tried not to feel suspicious. This was almost too much. But it made a nice change to eat a meal with actual vegetables instead of my normal fare of cereal or beans on toast, with a bit of cheese if I was working at peak domestic goddess.

'How are you getting on at work?' Dad asked.

I sighed. 'Okay. Slow progress.' I should have been able to

share with him how hard this case was, how horrible it was being criticised online, to have a knife at my throat, to see a pet pig being killed because people didn't think I was doing my job, to be doused in blood. But he'd been out of my life for so long, he was a stranger. I couldn't confide in him.

'Oh dear. I hope there won't be more animals killed tonight.'

I gulped a large amount of gin. 'Me too, Dad. Me too.'

Dad swallowed loudly. 'I wanted to talk to you, Meg.'

'That sounds ominous.'

'No … It's not. I've been thinking a lot about … when your sister died.'

That old image flashed into my mind. Carrie the day I found her. Feet dangling where feet should never be, sending an immediate stab of horror into my brain. Her neck bent, her head dropped forward, the rope taut above her. I blinked and pushed the image away. I'd been doing so well. Not checking the ceilings. Not having flashbacks.

Dad never talked about Carrie. That had been one of the problems between him and Mum. Not many marriages survive the death of a child.

'It's a long time ago now,' he said, 'But I still think about her.'

'Of course. So do I.'

He seemed so far out of his comfort zone he was in *Here-Be-Dragons* land. He coughed. 'I thought I might try to help people who've been affected by teenage suicide. It's such a hard thing to deal with.'

'Okay …'

'I know our situation wasn't typical. Poor Carrie was dying anyway, but we all still felt …'

'Guilty?'

'Yes. We all felt terribly guilty.'

Oh, yes, I'd felt guilty. I tested myself. Searching for that familiar heaviness in my gut. It was much better now. But it had taken over twenty years.

Dad stroked the side of his glass. 'I hadn't realised how badly it affected you, Meg. I didn't realise you felt responsible. I'm sorry. It was never your fault.'

I sighed. Maybe he would have realised if he hadn't absented himself so thoroughly from my life. 'I know it wasn't my fault,' I said. 'But I was horrible to her the day she did it.'

An odd look flitted across Dad's face and he moved his mouth as if he was going to speak, and then didn't.

'What is it?' I said. 'What else happened that day?'

He paused, then said, 'Nothing. You were ten. It wasn't your responsibility. But we know first-hand the effect it has on families. I want to help other people.'

I remembered all the times Mum had tried to talk to him about Carrie, before he left. All the slammed doors and seething silences. Maybe Pauline had been good for him. He seemed to have genuinely softened over the years. 'What do you want to do?' I said.

'There's a group with an office near where I live. They man phone lines, but they keep having to move premises so they're trying to buy somewhere. They need to raise quite a bit of money. I was going to donate to them.'

'That's good of you.' I wondered if he'd had a win on the poker. After he retired, he'd taught himself memory techniques and with his mathsy brain and knowledge of probability, he'd turned into a bit of a card-shark.

'Your mother said she might donate some of your gran's money too,' he said.

I was relieved that Dad was finally talking about what had happened, that he was doing good, that he was in touch with Mum and she approved. Maybe our family wasn't beyond salvation.

34

Meg – Present day
Thursday

It was early morning and the station felt empty and echoey and smelled of disinfectant. I was torturing myself looking at the Justice for Violet page, which Facebook in their wisdom had still not taken down. We hadn't caught the balaclava-men yet.

I scrolled through the newsfeed. Lots of incoherence, and a video which involved a pet goat. I couldn't watch it. I clicked on a different video. A thick-necked man wearing a black T-shirt and a balaclava. His face was covered but anyone who knew him would surely recognise his voice. He spoke to the camera and I realised it was the same man who'd held a knife to my throat.

'I can't be responsible for what our followers are doing, but I blame the police. Why haven't they made an arrest? Two people have been killed in the most horrible of ways, and no doubt more to come. We wouldn't stoop so low as to threaten people, but until the murderer comes forward, animals are going to keep dying.'

I made the mistake of reading some of the comments. *The*

detective in charge is Meg Dalton. That useless cow's a vegetarian, promoted too fast because she's a woman. Remove Meg Dalton from the case! Put someone competent in charge!

I pictured them sitting at their keyboards, spouting their venom, not caring about the effect it might have, not even thinking of me as a real person. There were no consequences for them. They didn't have to look me in the eye and justify their behaviour. One thing I vowed – there would be consequences for anyone who killed an animal.

I tried to do a spot of therapy on myself. These arseholes couldn't hurt me unless I allowed them too. Why should I care what they said about me? I was always so quick to jump to feeling guilty, taking responsibility, but it wasn't my fault they were killing animals. My mind flipped to Daniel, who also lived with guilt. He was so far from the kind of person anyone would expect me to be interested in. He lived in a grotty caravan, he worked in an abattoir, he appeared to be dependent on opiate painkillers. He'd been done for causing death by dangerous driving, for God's sake. He was not what one would call a *good catch*. And yet on some level far deeper than any of that, he was like me. We were the same.

I closed my eyes and saw blood. Remembered that Daniel had started to tell me about his younger brother. I tried phoning him but there was no answer.

Jai wandered into my room, stuffing a pasty into his face. 'Hey, are you okay?'

'Yeah, you know. Just an average week. A knife to my throat, a gallon of pig's blood on my head ...'

'It sounded horrific.'

'I'm fine, honestly, Jai.'

'You'll have seen the online brigade have worked themselves up into a frothing frenzy,' he said. 'We've got a confirmed serial killer, apparently. An enraged vegan activist picking off meat-industry workers.'

'God, do you feel nostalgic for the good old days when we could get on with our jobs without all this crap?'

Jai shoved in another mouthful of lard. 'Sorry. Didn't get breakfast. But yeah, bring back the days when Enraged of Eldercliffe had to get off his arse, buy stamps, and write to the bloody paper to express his bigoted and unfounded feelings.'

I sighed. 'Exactly. But could you make sure we've got protection in place for Daniel, Anna and Kirsty. I'm sure the Animal Vigilantes aren't the killers, but they're pretty unpleasant. And we should look again at Mandy. Maybe she found out about Gary's relationship with Violet. Maybe she's not what she appears. Also, I saw the Pale Child. A girl in a white dress with a doll's face mask on. I got her mask. It's gone to forensics.'

'She's a real person?'

'She was real yesterday, and Hannah found a video of her from before Violet went missing, so it's not just some kid cashing in on the whole thing.'

'How odd. I thought she was supposed to be a ghost.'

'I know. We need to find out who that girl is. Also, before I got doused in blood, Daniel was telling me about his younger brother. I can't get hold of him, but can we check it out?'

'I'll look into it,' Jai said, and headed off.

Seconds later, the door bashed open again and Fiona hot-footed it in.

'Christ, it's like Piccadilly Circus this morning,' I said. 'How am I to have my nap?'

243

'Ha, ha, morning,' Fiona said. She leaned closer and lowered her voice. 'You know that cut above Craig's eye?'

'Yes. He won't say how he got it.'

'I heard a rumour that Jai hit him.'

'Jai?' I'd never seen so much as a twitch from Jai in the time I'd known him, although when I arrived, I'd been told he had very occasional violent outbursts that everyone seemed to know about but nobody had witnessed.

'Yes,' Fiona said. 'Jai.'

'But that's ridiculous. How are we supposed to run a murder investigation when they behave like primary school children? I'm already being mobbed by their wives and girlfriends as if I'm some kind of marriage guidance counsellor.'

Fiona opened her mouth as if to speak, then hesitated.

'What is it. Fiona?'

'Just tell me if this is none of my business. But … you do know Jai doesn't want you to stick up for his girlfriend?'

'Sorry?' I said.

'I think he wants you to agree that she's being unreasonable.'

'But I'm not sure she is.'

'I don't think that's the point,' Fiona said. 'But it doesn't matter. Forget I said anything.'

I closed my eyes for a moment. I was too tired to manage the investigation, let alone deal with the labyrinthine goings-on of the team social dynamics. I could hardly tell Fiona that I worried I'd got too close to Jai. That by defending his girlfriend I was making it very clear that I was happy he'd found someone. That I wasn't at all interested in him.

The door pushed open and Craig poked his head round it. Fiona gave him the look Hamlet gives next-door's cat when it approaches his cat flap, but Craig wandered in, oblivious. I really was flavour of the morning.

Craig took a breath, about to speak, and I wondered if he was going to get some mileage out of the blood-dousing incident. I could do without any *Carrie* jokes, especially with that having been my sister's name.

But it wasn't that. He said, 'They've found something in the woods.'

I froze. 'What kind of something?'

'Bits of that poor girl, by the sound of it.'

35

Bex – October 1999

The River Itchen was dark grey, far below her, reflecting the rain-filled sky. Cranes and industrial buildings sprawled over the flat areas to the side of the river, and a dirty brown boat chugged through the murky water, looking impossibly tiny.

Bex took her backpack from her shoulder and removed the Sainsbury's bag, dumping the backpack on the ground beside her. A gust of wind grabbed her hair and whipped it around her face.

She hadn't been able to look at the plastic strips in the toilet in the cafe. But she'd done four tests, and shoved them straight into the Sainsbury's bag without looking. It was gross if she thought about it, but she was way past caring about a bit of pee.

She looked at the bag. It was wrong that this mundane object should contain such life-changing information. Potentially life-ending information. Because she couldn't have the baby of a rapist. And she couldn't face having an abortion either. So that was that. She was worth nothing anyway. Her mother had left her and her dad and sister didn't want her. It made sense that someone should value her so little that he'd destroy her life for a few minutes of … what? Pleasure? Gratification? A few trivial minutes for him, that he'd probably forgotten about months ago. She hoped it had been Lucas, because he'd died. But deep down she knew it wasn't him. The world didn't work like that. People never got what they deserved.

She would have coped with the rape, she thought, if only her family had supported her. Helped her find out who did it, made him pay. But no, her family blamed her. Because wasn't she always to blame?

So she'd find out now. In this place. And she'd deal with it.

The water was laid out far below her and nobody was around. Not in this freezing weather.

A flash of fear. But she could do it. She was strong.

Her heart was thudding in her chest, her breath coming fast. A gust of wind pulled at the plastic bag as she opened it and fished out the first test.

She snatched a breath of cold air.

There were two lines visible on the test.

She blinked and reached into the bag for the second test. That had two lines.

The third test. Two lines.

And the fourth. Two lines.

So this was it. She was pregnant. She dropped the bag and the wind grabbed it and carried it away over the side of the bridge. It hovered in the air high above the river for too long, before swirling its way down to the water.

Her hand relaxed and she dropped the last test onto the cold concrete. A seagull cried overhead, sounding too much like a baby.

She leaned over the barrier, her stomach pressing against

it. Was this thing really inside her stomach? How could it be? Growing inside her. Part of her and not part of her. Part of *him*.

Bex felt her knees go soft and she collapsed onto the concrete. She realised she was sobbing.

It was growing inside her.

She was one of two again.

If she jumped into that steely water below, it wouldn't only be her she killed. It would be this thing too. And she realised she couldn't do it. Not again.

36

Meg – Present day
Thursday

Jai and I were in the car, heading for the woods. I couldn't remember another summer where the hot weather had stretched on like this. Where I'd gone weeks without even throwing a cardigan in the car in case of a Peak District reversal where sun turned to fog and rain in an eye-blink. There'd been nothing quite like it since 1976, according to those who remembered, and no doubt it was lovely if you didn't spend your days tackling wildfires or searching for decomposing bodies.

'Are you okay?' Jai said.

I pictured Violet's face, the energy of her, young and strong, filled with so much life it seemed to burst out of her. 'It's good, I suppose. We need forensic evidence. But I'm not sure I'm ready to have it confirmed that she's dead.'

'I think we all know she's dead,' Jai said.

'I'd hoped I was getting better at being detached, but I'm not.'

Jai sighed. 'You don't want to be detached. You're a better cop when you're riddled with stress and anxiety.'

'Oh, cheers.'

Jai paused and then said, 'They're so far off the mark about you.'

'I know. But even though they're dicks, it hurts.'

We drove in silence for a while. My mind drifted back to the Justice for Violet group. The dead animals and the comments about me and my competence, or rather lack of competence.

'I don't think you have any idea,' I said. 'Not you personally. I don't think anyone has any idea what it's like to be publicly castigated until it happens.'

'I suppose not,' Jai said, happy in his status as un-publicly castigated.

'I think of all the times I've read about politicians and celebrities, people coming off Twitter because they can't stomach reading about themselves any longer, and I didn't have a clue until it started happening to me last year.'

'Any dickhead with a computer can have a voice now,' Jai said. 'That's the problem. I don't suppose they have the first idea what it's like to be on the receiving end, having never done anything in their sad lives that puts their heads above the parapet. To have a go at you – someone who works so tirelessly to do the right thing.'

'Wow, save that phrase for my eulogy. But thanks.'

We took the road up past the reservoir. The low water levels gave the impression that the huge spillways had grown, as if they'd sprouted up in the hot weather.

'Jai,' I said. 'I heard a rumour ...'

'Oh God, is this about Craig?'

'Yes.'

'Okay, yes, we had a minor scuffle, but he already had a cut above his eye. I didn't do that.'

'You had a *scuffle*? What is this – infant school? Did you hit him?'

'He hit me first. And he was deliberately goading me. I think he wanted me to hit him.'

'God, Jai. You can't go around hitting people. What were you arguing about?'

'I can't say. I had a theory but he denied it.'

'So you hit each other. And it appears you hit him harder than he hit you.'

'He hasn't complained about it. He already had that cut.'

'So where did the cut come from?'

'I don't know, Meg. He won't say.'

'No, but his bloody wife's been asking about it, and I get the job of talking to him.'

'Okay, okay. It was pretty bad what I accused him of, but he denied it. Can we leave it for now?'

I was somewhat intrigued but didn't have the energy to pursue it. 'Okay,' I said. 'Just try to behave like adults, can you? Adults who don't hit each other. Maybe adult women – they rarely hit each other even when things get really bad. Try to behave like an adult woman.'

Jai turned to me and frowned. 'Fine, Meg. I'll do that. Just for you.'

'Right. Good. That's settled. Where are we going?'

'Back towards the village,' Jai said. 'There's a road runs along by the reservoir and then down into the woods.'

We drove towards Gritton, the windows of its houses shining like glitter on the hillside, the swarms of reporters and rub-berneckers looking like ants on spilled honey. I'd been told that Violet's poor parents were down there, doing their own relentless and desperate house-to-house enquiries.

I diverted towards the reservoir. The abattoir formed a strange focal point for this area, always visible, sitting glumly at the base of the valley.

There was just one CSI van and a marked car, but they'd drawn attention. People were hovering around the perimeter, raising their phones to get surreptitious shots.

I parked badly by the side of the road. Even though I was desperate for evidence, part of me didn't want to know what they'd found. I pictured Helen Armstrong and hoped I wouldn't be the one to tell her.

A steep common approach path had been marked with crime scene tape. Jai and I walked down, me shuffling sideways because of the slope and my ankle, and were met at the bottom by a uniformed officer.

'We found a black bin liner, consistent with being dumped from up there.' He waved towards the road, which was on a bank above us.

My stomach was churning. 'What was in it?'

'There's a lot of hair,' he said. 'Long dark hair. And clothes, including underwear. And that pelican brooch is in there, on a chain.'

'Shaved hair?' I said.

'Yes, shaved. And a razor, which I suppose was used to shave it. I'm afraid the stuff is absolutely covered in blood.'

Richard was no better than Craig in hot weather – his flesh seemed to sink downwards, as if you might turn round one day and find him pooled on the floor, still shouting orders up at you. He was sitting heavily on a chair at the front of the incident room.

Fiona was pacing, with arms crossed and a vexed expression.

The pictures of Gary in the pig's head mask stared at us, *Lord of the Flies* style. And the photograph of Violet's face taunted us, her radiance dulling everything else. The team sat in stunned silence. Even Craig sat quietly waiting for instructions.

I could feel the droplets gathering on my upper lip. I wiped them off surreptitiously, and stood at the front of the room with Violet's face behind me.

'A bag has been found in the woods, in the general area where we found Gary's body, but nearer to the road. It contains clothes and boots that have been confirmed as Violet's. And it contains her hair and a brooch which we've confirmed was hers. Also a razor, which we assume was used to shave her.'

'Christ,' Craig said. 'That's it then. She really was fed to pigs.'

'There's a lot of blood on the clothes and hair and on the bag,' I said, 'although we think some of it's animal blood. The lab have agreed to fast-track it. But it's nearly the weekend.'

'God forbid that the outsourced lab workers should do anything on a bloody weekend,' Craig said. 'Never mind the poor girl's parents are in hell.'

'We've spoken to her parents and to Bex Smith. Explained that we haven't found a body. But obviously everyone's talking about the pigs.'

'How horrendous,' Fiona said. 'Her parents must be in bits. And Bex.'

That had been an unfortunate turn of phrase, but nobody commented on it. Bex had been calling, desperate for news. But she wouldn't go to Gritton.

'Eighteen,' Craig muttered. 'A kid. What's the matter with people?'

'I'm hopeful we'll find prints or DNA on the bag or the boots or necklace,' I said.

'It's unbelievable,' Craig muttered. 'I still can't believe someone would feed an eighteen-year-old girl to pigs. That's seriously fucked up.' I'd never seen Craig like this before, but he did have kids of his own and Violet was barely more than a child, bikini-prancing notwithstanding. She'd got to him.

'Come on, Craig.' Richard hauled himself out of his chair and stood radiating heat. 'We treat this like any other case.'

'Looking at the slightly less photogenic Gary for a minute,' Jai said, 'we've confirmed he was killed by blunt force trauma to the head. He was struck with a rock from behind and then hit several more times. He was propped against the tree post-mortem, and someone put a mask on his head. A mask made from real pigskin. The good news is we found fibres on him, and a hair that wasn't his. And we've got his phone, so I'm confident we'll have more leads to follow up soon.'

'That's great,' I said. 'And I want us to have a good look at Mandy. She had a motive to kill both Violet and Gary if she found out about the affair. Also Anna and Daniel. And Kirsty. There's this secret to do with the Pale Child. And I suspect they're involved. What else do we have?'

'I found out what Daniel must have been about to say about his brother,' Fiona said. 'Charlie Twigg died back in 1995 after saying he'd seen the Pale Child. He was only eight, and for some reason he wandered off to the reservoir. He managed to climb up to the rim of the spillway. Fell down it and died.'

'Oh God, that's awful,' I said. 'That must be what Kirsty's kid, Frankie, referred to. She mentioned a boy and that hole at the reservoir.' Poor Daniel. I'd been trying not to think about him but he'd kept creeping into my mind. Flashes of him saving the lamb. Confident and compassionate. 'Is that the reason for all the fences?' I said.

'Yes. And then in 1999, Daniel's friend Lucas died after the barbecue where Bex was raped. The car accident that Daniel went to prison for. Lucas also claimed he'd seen the Pale Child in the woods that night.'

'So people have actually seen the Pale Child and then died,' I said. 'It's not all made up. Why didn't we check this before?'

'Because it's totally bloody irrelevant?' Craig said. 'Coincidences happen. Or people make stuff up after the event. *Oh yeah, he definitely said he saw the Pale Child.* People love that shit.'

'There was also a three-year-old kid who died back in the Eighties after seeing the Pale Child,' Fiona said, 'but I don't have full details yet.'

'It's bizarre,' I said. 'Three people have died in the past after seeing the Pale Child – Lucas, Daniel's younger brother, and this toddler. We know there's a secret about the Pale Child that Gary told Violet, and now they're both gone too. The Pale Child isn't completely made up – we have the mask I found on the moor and the video, but that clearly can't be the same person who was seen in the Eighties or Nineties, unless she's no longer a child. So what the hell is going on? What's the secret? And is someone so determined to keep it that they're prepared to commit murder?'

I always made a point of chatting to the indexers. They sat at the end of the incident room typing everything into the HOLMES database. Statements, exhibits lists, forensic reports, etc. A good indexer knew a lot about the case. They knew the exact words witnesses had used, they listened to the briefings, they made connections. But historically they'd been ignored, so they didn't always come forward. Some of the old-school detectives even used to send 'the girls' out of the room for the briefings. Very unwise.

I wandered over and perched against one of their desks. 'Noticed anything?' I asked. 'Particularly about a secret in the village, or anything to do with the Pale Child?'

Donna looked up. The new indexer. Ex crime scene officer. 'There was a reference to it,' she said. 'Might not be relevant, but ...'

'Doesn't matter. What is it?'

'I was typing a statement in the other day,' she said. 'From one of the house-to-houses. The woman was a talker. You know the sort.'

'I do indeed.'

'She was going on about her friend who used to live in the village but left years ago. Saying her friend had a son who went off the rails and there was a secret involving the son. That her friend had left the village because of it. The friend's name was Gwen. And I saw a reference somewhere else to Daniel Twigg's mum being called Gwen. I think it might be the same woman.'

My heart pumped a little faster. A secret. Possibly involving Daniel. 'Okay. Potentially interesting. I've tried to read everything but don't remember making that connection.'

'It all sounded a bit mad and irrelevant, but if the son was Daniel Twigg, then I just thought ... You never know.'

'Daniel said his mother won't come to Gritton,' I said. 'And we know he had problems – he's been done for death by dangerous driving. And we now know his younger brother died after apparently seeing the Pale Child. Then there's this supposed secret that Gary told Violet. So, yes, I'm definitely interested.'

Donna blushed. 'I thought you might be.'

'Thank you, Donna. Can you print a copy of the statement out for me?'

Donna pressed a few buttons and a printer started whirring. She passed me the statement. 'There you go.'

I took the papers. 'Thanks, Donna. Well spotted.' But all I could think was, *Please don't let the secret be something bad about Daniel.*

37

It was a bright, cool day, and the light coming through the leaded windows of Bex's aunt's living room felt harsh. Bex's dad and Kirsty had come all the way to Southampton to persuade her to do what they wanted.

Her dad sat on the large sofa, Kirsty beside him. Aunt Janet was next to Bex, but it wasn't clear if this meant anything in terms of allegiances.

A pot of tea was on the low wooden table between them, and Bex realised she'd lined up the milk and sugar in front of her like a defence.

Her dad coughed. 'You can't have the baby, Bex.'

Bex touched her stomach. Did her dad not care that she felt destroyed? That him sending her away aged three had started the process, the rape had carried it on – demonstrating in the most compelling manner how worthless she was – and his lack of support afterwards had finished it. She was literally nothing. There was no reason to live now other than the baby.

'So that's agreed then,' her dad said.

258

'I don't think anything's agreed, Tony.' Aunt Janet folded her arms and shifted in her seat as if squaring up. She was on home ground, surrounded by her chunky wooden furniture, her acres of dusty books, the wall-hangings she'd brought back from her travels around the world. She wasn't about to be bullied by her older brother.

Bex's dad hurled her an irritated look. 'I don't want the girl to ruin her life.'

Janet said, 'Nobody wants that. But you haven't been a parent to her since she was three years old. You can't just storm in here and demand she does as you say.'

Silence around the table. A collective breath-holding. Bex felt as if she might float up and out through the window, away from it all. None of them would understand. But she couldn't kill it. She needed to be one of two again.

'I might want to keep the baby,' she said.

Kirsty breathed out abruptly as if she'd been hit in the stomach. 'You can't have the baby of a rapist, Bex.'

The air settled down over them, still and heavy.

Bex felt a spark of anger, and the part of her that was drifting above looking down was glad that she still had it in her. 'So he's a rapist now, is he? I thought it was all my fault.'

'I was upset about Lucas.'

Bex took the sugar bowl, grabbed a teaspoon and started making patterns in the white granules. Nobody spoke.

Finally Bex looked up at Kirsty. 'I won't tell the child about the rape, so that doesn't matter.'

'You wouldn't be able to keep a secret like that,' Kirsty said.

'Or we could find out who it was,' Bex said. 'And ... do something.'

'You can't use your baby as evidence in a rape case,' Aunt Janet said. 'It's not fair.' And that at least was true.

And anyway, Bex had tried to go to the police and she'd failed at the first hurdle. When she'd heard the cops joking about how shaggable some young woman was, she'd freaked and bottled it and gone home. She wasn't going through that again.

'You'd passed out,' Kirsty said. 'How could we *do something*? Can you imagine what the police would say? We didn't report it at the time, it's your word against his, and you don't even remember what happened. It wouldn't even count as rape.'

Bex looked again at Kirsty and felt that familiar shift inside her. Kirsty's expression was wrong. 'Do you *know*, Kirsty? Do you know who it was? Who raped me? You need to tell me.'

Kirsty looked straight at her and her expression changed to concerned, as abruptly as a TV channel-change. 'Of course not, Bex. I told you. You said you'd seen the Pale Child, we all went off looking for her, and then we came back and found you. I know it wasn't Lucas. He was with me the whole time. I don't know about the other two.'

'But you said my dress was rucked up. Did you know what had happened? Did you see who it was?'

Bex had been over it in her head so many times. She'd humiliated Daniel, laughed at him. He'd been furious with her. They said rape was more about power than sex. And Gary – he was used to getting what he wanted, and she'd sensed a darkness in him.

'No!' Kirsty said. 'We'd all split up, apart from me and Lucas. We came back when it started lashing it down, and you'd passed out. You were cold and we had to get you home.' She spat the final words. 'You know the rest.'

Bex flicked her eyes between her dad and Kirsty. Had they

exchanged glances? What did they know? Why would her dad and Kirsty protect the boy? It hit her that growing up with Aunt Janet had been a blessing, not a curse. Escaping Gritton and her family. Why had she resented her dad for sending her away? She should have thanked him.

'Quite honestly, Bex, I don't know why you allowed yourself to get so drunk,' her dad said.

'Oh? Was I *asking for it*?'

'Well, yes, you were to an extent.'

'Oh for God's sake, Tony!' Janet's voice was low and scarily angry. 'What century are you living in?'

Bex felt a thickness in her throat. She hated the stress, the arguments. 'I could have the baby adopted,' she said. 'The child wouldn't need to know who its father was.'

Her dad thumped his cup down on the table and stood, his bulk filling the small room. 'We have to get back for the animals. But Bex, you are not having this baby.'

'Okay,' Bex sobbed. 'Okay, I won't have it!'

Kirsty was staring at her black boots and saying nothing. Finally she stood too, and cast a sideways look at Bex. 'It's the right decision, Bex. You're doing the right thing.'

38

Meg – Present day
Thursday

The evening sun was burning through my office window and hitting me directly in the face, but I didn't have the energy to move. There was so much that was unspoken in Gritton. It felt like we were skimming the surface while huge currents whooshed beneath, affecting everyone's lives but never mentioned. I felt it in my bones that they were relevant to Violet's disappearance. And was there really a secret from years ago involving Daniel? Fiona was tracking down Gwen Twigg so we could try to get to the bottom of it. Was it the same secret Gary had supposedly told Violet? The one about the Pale Child?

The door of my room banged open and Jai scooted in and skidded to a stop in front of my desk. I felt a jolt in my stomach. He clearly had news, and I was like a mouse in some hideous experiment, trained to expect an electric shock every time a light flashed. Jai appearing with news hadn't been good for as long as I could remember. 'Christ, Jai,' I said. 'You're making me nervous.'

'We've got some results back from the lab. You know that razor?'

'The one in the bin liner?'

'Yes. There were skin cells on it. And we got a match.'

'Okay, go on then, spit it out.'

'I don't think you're going to like it.'

'What do you mean? I just want to solve the case.' But tendrils of fear were forming in my stomach. *No. Not him.*

'It's Daniel Twigg's.'

It felt both shocking and inevitable at the same time. I wanted to sob with frustration at my own stupidity. Because Jai was right. I didn't like it. 'You'd better sit down,' I said.

Jai shifted towards my desk.

'On the chair,' I said.

'Okay, okay.' Jai sat on my guest chair, uncharacteristically still. 'There's more. Violet's clothes were in the bin liner, but there was also a set of overalls with Violet's blood on them. Dark blue overalls. The only one who wore dark blue overalls was Daniel.'

I remembered holding Daniel's collar while he reached down to rescue the lamb. The infusion of well-being I'd felt afterwards. The pleasure I'd taken in his company, even if I didn't want to admit it to myself. 'It's so out of character,' I said.

'We don't know his character.'

But I'd thought I did know his character. I'd watched him risk his life for a lamb. He worked in an abattoir to help the animals even though he hated it. 'Have we brought him in?' I asked.

'We've tried, but we can't find him. He's disappeared. His van's gone, there's no sign of him at the caravan park, and he's not answering his phone.'

'You think he killed her?'

'The evidence certainly suggests that. We know he liked Violet and she wasn't interested. What if he found out she was sleeping with Gary? He was upset the morning after she disappeared, plus he referred to her in the past tense.'

I sighed. And his mum was keeping secrets for him. Possibly. I told Jai about my conversation with Donna.

'He's definitely dodgy,' Jai said.

'Okay. Pull out all the stops to find and arrest him. We'll release a statement. Maybe the Justice for Violet crazies can spend the night hunting for Daniel Twigg instead of committing atrocities.'

I'd decided to visit Mum on the way home. I wasn't going to achieve anything staying longer at work, and the revelations about Daniel, on top of all the online criticism I'd received, had left me feeling like I'd been kicked in the head. I needed a few hours away from the case.

I pulled up in Mum's driveway and hauled myself out of the car. Mum's lawn was tinged yellow from the hot weather but the damn thing hadn't stopped growing. It was ironic that, back when she'd been rushed off her feet tending to Gran, Mum had never let the garden go, but now triffid-like things were appearing in the herbaceous borders.

I let myself in and nearly fell over a parcel in the hallway. 'Mum,' I shouted.

I found her at the kitchen table, reading glasses on, scrutinising paperwork and drinking tea.

'Have you been buying more stuff from eBay?' I said.

'Just a lamp.'

'You have to stop, Mum, there's no room.'

'I have stopped now I've decided what I'm doing with your gran's money.'

'Okay …'

'But why did she do that, Meg? She had that money and she never told us.'

I filled the kettle and sat down opposite her. 'I don't know, Mum. It makes no sense to me either. Maybe she wanted to leave it to us rather than have us spend it on her. That would be like Gran.'

'All that time we were fretting about paying for care for her, or the cost of taking her to Dignitas, and she had thousands squirrelled away. She can't have spent any money. Ever. In her entire life.'

'We should have taken her,' I said. 'We knew it was best for her. I'm sure she only said she'd changed her mind to save us the grief of taking her and getting into trouble.'

'You're right. I hate myself for putting her through it.'

'Me too.' If there was guilt to be shared out, I was having my bit.

Mum sighed. 'At least you have some money towards a deposit on a house.'

'I'll have to put a plaque up outside, or a memorial bench.'

The kettle pinged so I made myself tea, grabbed a pack of biscuits, and sat back down. Mum might be letting her garden go, but if the biscuit cupboard was ever empty then I'd know she was in real trouble.

Normally she'd be grilling me by now. Asking about work. 'I'm on that case,' I said. 'You know, at the abattoir in Gritton.'

What a fine conversation-starter. Straight out of the book, *How to Deal with a Grieving Parent*. Serial killer on the loose, feeding victims to pigs. Although I had read that the emphasis on positive thinking was making us more depressed.

'Oh, how awful,' Mum said. 'It was on the news. Aren't they killing animals every night until you solve it? Terrible business.'

She obviously hadn't seen my performance at the press conference. Part of me felt petulant about this. Wanted to say, *I was on TV, Mum. Aren't you impressed?* But another part was relieved she hadn't seen. I didn't want sympathy about the veggie-detective accusations, speculation on what a pack of hungry pigs could do.

'And how's Jai? Still with that girl?'

'He is, although he does spend every day moaning about their incompatibility. She doesn't like his kids but she wants him to have more with her.'

'Oh heavens. Poor Jai.'

'I know. I shouldn't laugh.'

'Some people just like being unhappy,' Mum said.

'You have to wonder. Given that his previous wife was a social-climbing monster. He must surely have seen through her before they stuck rings on each other.'

'He was probably pressurised into getting married by his family.'

'Better to marry a total cow than just to live with her? Though from what he's told me, they're desperate for him to marry a nice Sikh girl. Aren't families a delight?'

'Not sure how to take that, Meg. Has Hannah found someone for you yet?'

'No, despite her best efforts to hook me up with the deranged of Derbyshire.'

'I'm sure she just wants you to be happy.'

'I am happy. Why would I need a man to be happy?'

Mum opened her mouth to answer.

'That was rhetorical,' I said, and I wished I could talk to her about Daniel, but of course that wasn't possible.

'I suppose you are a bit of a workaholic. Not everyone would put up with that.'

'Oh for God's sake, Mum. Nobody ever commented on Dad being at work all the time. And male cops are positively applauded for working so hard their kids are people they meet occasionally on holiday. Anyway, I'm not a workaholic – I'm just conscientious and prefer to catch murderers rather than leaving them free to rampage around the countryside slaughtering people.'

'That's what workaholics always say. But you still deserve someone nice. You don't have to compromise.'

Not sure exactly what that meant, I decided to change the subject. 'Um … did Dad mention he'd come to visit?'

Her head shot up. 'To visit you? Now?'

I nodded. 'He's staying for a couple of days.'

'Well, well, that is very suspicious.'

'Why can nobody accept that he wants to see me? It's so unfair on him.'

'You need to keep an eye on him, Meg. You really do. Why's he suddenly visiting now? I don't want to be hurtful but he's taken zero interest in your life, and we have no idea what he's been up to in Scotland. Anything could be going on in his life.'

'He's split up with Pauline,' I said.

Mum pursed her lips. 'I knew that would end in tears.'

I didn't mention the fact that Dad had been with Pauline for over fifteen years and that Mum had been predicting the demise of the relationship for all of them.

'He's split with his girlfriend,' I said, 'and maybe he actually wants to see me.'

'There'll be more to it, you mark my words. He's barely acknowledged your existence for the last fifteen years.'

'I suppose so. But I think he's genuinely worried about you. About your … trip.'

'I doubt that. What did he say?'

'He's worried about your safety. Are you definitely going?'

'I am, love, yes.'

'To the murder capital of the world?'

'If it was a civilised country with decent laws, there'd be no need for us now, would there? But I'm sure it's not as bad as you say. I checked the foreign office website and it's okay.'

'Seriously?'

'It's mainly gang-related crime, and I won't be getting involved with that now, will I?'

'Nothing would surprise me.'

'You do know in El Salvador a teenage girl was sentenced to thirty years in prison after she had a stillborn baby?'

'I've read about a few cases.'

'She was still at school. She'd been raped. Hadn't realised she was pregnant and gave birth in a toilet. The baby died and the court ruled that failing to seek ante-natal care amounted to murder. Thirty years in prison.'

I put my mug down with a thud. 'I looked into it. It makes me want to rip people's throats out.'

'She's not the only one. Another woman was given a thirty-year sentence after she had a late miscarriage, because they claimed she'd induced it. Honestly, Meg, the poor woman wanted that baby. All her relatives testified that she was devastated to lose it. How do they think you induce a miscarriage anyway? If only it were that easy. Now she's locked up for the rest of her life. You can't even have an abortion if you're raped, or if your life's at risk or if the baby's going to die anyway. Even if a *child* is raped. Can you imagine? A right-wing Catholic group are trying to take the sentences up to fifty years.'

'I suppose when you only rape choir boys you don't have to worry about pregnancy.'

Mum shook her head and tutted, but she couldn't argue with the sentiment.

'I get it, Mum,' I said. 'I understand you wanting to help.'

'It will be only this once on the actual abortion ship. We're getting set up with drones that can deliver pills. It'll be easier for the women. I want to do it, Meg. It's got to be better than just getting furious and feeling helpless, surely?'

'I wish I could go with you.'

'You do good things here.'

'Not everyone thinks so at the moment, but yes. I'm proud of you, Mum. As far as I'm concerned, you should go for it.'

'Thank you. I have the time now. And I'm good at dealing with bureaucracy and legal matters.'

'And if all else fails, you know how to kill people.'

'Not funny, Meg. What I was going to say was that, thanks to your gran, I have a bit of money.'

I smiled. 'Gran would be proud of you too. I know she would.'

I had to support her. How could I not? But all the same I was worried about her going to El Salvador. I'd already lost Gran. I wasn't sure I'd cope if anything happened to Mum.

'I'll be careful,' she said. 'The teams of women know what they're doing out there. But what's the point of life if you can't do what you believe in?'

39

Dad had made supper and was in a perky mood when I got home, bouncing around the kitchen muttering about salad dressing. I collapsed onto a chair and he poured me wine, while Hamlet stalked over the countertop throwing me an occasional *I-know-you're-too-knackered-to-get-me-off-here* look.

'Dad, I'm sorry we haven't had more chance to chat,' I said. 'This case—'

'Are you making progress?' He sat at the kitchen table and looked at me, waiting for my answer. He'd never asked me questions after Carrie got ill. He'd told me his views, expressed opinions on my life choices, explained why string theory was all wrong, but he'd never sat down, looked at me, asked me questions, and listened properly to the answers. Him doing it now felt like he'd grabbed my inner seven-year-old by the arm and dragged her back to that bright, shiny time before everything went to crap. The time when he'd say, *How far away do you think the sun is, Meg? What happens if you go into a black hole?* And when he'd wait for the answers with a proud smile twitching the edges of his mouth.

'It looks like my instincts might have been wrong,' I said, expecting his eyes to wander, the food to need checking.

Instead he carried on looking intently at me, a neat furrow between his brows. 'Why so?'

Hamlet gave Dad's vegetarian chilli a final contemptuous sneer before hurling himself off the counter and landing with a solid thud. I stood and found him a tin of cat food priced as if it included gold flakes and caviar, spooned some out, and sat back down at the table. Dad was still looking at me, waiting for an answer. He hadn't seized the opportunity to start telling me stuff.

I took a breath. 'The evidence leads to someone, but he's disappeared. So now there's a man-hunt going on. And ...' I couldn't bring myself to admit I'd liked Daniel. 'Oh, never mind, I got it all wrong, and it's stressful. Let's change the subject. I'm sorry I've not been around. I haven't asked you anything about your life. How are things in the world of theoretical physics?' Or rather, *Let's get back to our familiar pattern*.

'Mad as ever,' Dad said. 'It's hard to keep abreast once you're retired, but it looks like time doesn't go forward after all – everything sort of co-exists, so the future can influence the past.'

I took a swig of wine. 'Right. That could come in handy.'

'It's unlikely to affect your day-to-day life.'

'Shame. And how's the poker going these days?'

He shifted on his chair. I caught a fleeting expression on his face that sent a shiver down my spine. 'Not too bad. Yes, fun. How about you though? You say it's stressful. Do you want to tell me about it?'

I hesitated. This was so unlike Dad I was almost joining the *What does he want?* camp. And should I ask more about the poker? His response had definitely been a bit odd. But he seemed genuinely interested in what I had to say. 'You know that joke about the engineer, the physicist and the mathematician who see a black sheep in Scotland?' Even though Dad was giving every impression of wanting to listen, I couldn't stop myself introducing the problem in *Dad-terms*. Giving him the opportunity to be just a bit clever, right from the start.

'Yes. The engineer says, *Oh, the sheep in Scotland are black*; the physicist says, *No, some of the sheep in Scotland are black*; and the mathematician rolls his eyes and says, *No, in Scotland, there is at least one sheep, at least one side of which appears to be black when viewed from here, at least some of the time.*'

'That's the one. Well, I feel like the mathematician.'

'How so?'

'There's an explanation that fits the facts. And everyone's assuming it's true. Assuming the sheep is black. But what if it's just one side of the sheep? Or only when viewed from this angle?'

Because if the sheep wasn't black, we could be assuming Violet was dead when in fact she was alive and desperate for our help.

'Do you want to talk about it? I'm the soul of discretion. I don't talk to other humans, and I find quantum physics more comprehensible than social media, so I think you're safe.'

'I can't, Dad, but I do appreciate you being willing to listen. Really I do.'

'Okay, maybe you can't tell me about it,' Dad said. 'But you've got a good brain. If it's telling you to dig deeper, there'll be a valid reason why.'

40

Meg – Present day
Friday

My eyes popped open. I was tangled in the covers, sweating with the humidity of the night. The rain still hadn't come.

A noise had woken me. I looked at the clock: 3.14 a.m.

I pushed the covers aside and climbed out of bed. Walked over to the window and peered out. The night was a deep black, the moon hidden behind clouds. But I sensed movement in the garden below.

I pulled on knickers and jeans under my nightshirt and crept down to the kitchen. The light was on. My pulse quickened. I was sure it hadn't been on when I'd looked out of the bedroom window, or I'd have been able to see more of the garden.

There was no sign of Hamlet, which sent a thrumming unease into my veins. I checked the cardboard box which was his current preferred sleeping place, vastly favoured over his expensive bed, but there was no sign of him.

The back door was slightly open – not ajar, but not completely closed. I thought I heard voices coming from the garden.

I grabbed my friction lock baton from my harness, crept to the far side of the kitchen, and peered out of the window.

Someone was standing in the garden, the light from the kitchen highlighting their edges.

Dad?

What was he doing? I was about to push open the door and go to him, but I stopped. His body was rigid and stone-still. And someone else was there.

Dad's voice was audible through the slightly open door, sounding husky and anxious. 'Put him down now.'

I looked to the far end of the garden, where the light from the kitchen barely reached.

A man. Standing in the shadows. Wearing a black balaclava. Holding something.

A flash of white from the thing he was holding. I gasped.

Hamlet. He was holding Hamlet.

I twitched with the urge to run into the garden, but stopped myself. These people had knives and had killed pets. It would only take a second for the bastard to slit Hamlet's throat right in front of us and escape into the shadows. At the moment he was hesitating.

Clutching the baton, I ran into the hallway, unlocked the front door, and dashed out. There was a path which went around the side of the house, and brought you into the garden from the rear. If I could get down there, I'd be behind the man.

I gasped. I'd trodden on a stone. Luckily the path down the side of the house was paved. I slowed as I got nearer to the gate into the garden.

I could hear low voices. Dad and the man talking.

'Get me a hundred quid and maybe I won't kill the stupid cat.'

Then Dad's voice. 'Come on, you know you won't get away with this.' Why wasn't he just getting some money?

'I mean it,' the man said. 'I know it's the detective's cat. The one that's protecting Violet's murderer.'

'Hold on,' Dad said. 'She's not protecting anyone. You've got it wrong.'

My grip tightened on the baton. I crept forward. The wooden gate was open. The man had his back to me.

Dad looked in my direction. His eyes widened and his mouth opened a fraction. I frowned at him and put my finger to my lips. He looked away, back to Hamlet, who was struggling in the man's arms.

I raised the baton, stepped forward and brought it smashing down on the man's head.

He screamed, dropped Hamlet, and flung an arm at my face. I ducked and grabbed at him, managing to get his hand. I could feel a bit of skin, and I scratched my fingers on it as hard as I could as he slithered from my grasp. He spun round and ran across the garden before barging through the hedge and disappearing.

Hamlet crashed through his flap into the kitchen. My breathing was coming fast, my heart pounding. Dad was standing in his dressing gown, looking at me in stunned silence. I walked across the lawn to him. 'Let's get inside.'

I followed Dad into the kitchen, closed the door firmly behind us, and swivelled Hamlet's flap to 'closed'.

Dad lowered himself onto one of the chairs. 'I heard a noise,' he said. 'In the garden.'

I picked up the kettle and took it to the sink, hands shaking. The tap was too tight. I couldn't work it with one hand. I put the kettle in the sink and realised I was crying. I turned to Dad.

'Oh my God, they had Hamlet. Why didn't I keep him in? I'm so stupid.'

I put the kettle down, and swooped over and grabbed Hamlet, holding him tight. For once, he tolerated it, although he wasn't purring. I buried my head in his fluffy fur and tried not to sob.

Hamlet finally decided enough was enough and grappled his way out of my grasp, landing with a thud on the floor.

'Careful now,' Dad said. 'You wouldn't want him injuring himself.'

I laughed. 'Oh God. No, he's not the most graceful.'

I turned back to the kettle and managed to fill it and stick it on its base. The image flashed into my mind. The man holding Hamlet. Hamlet who was so innocent and trusting. Who'd most likely gone up to the guy for a stroke. My voice was cold. 'I'd fucking kill him,' I said. 'Seriously. I would not rest until he was dead.'

'Sit down a minute,' Dad said. 'Hamlet's fine.'

'What if they're killing other people's cats?'

'They won't do that. It would alienate too many people. Sit down. There's nothing you can do now. Have a cup of tea.'

I found my case, dug out an evidence bag and carefully scraped under my fingernails.

'Do you think you got his DNA?' Dad asked.

I nodded. 'Just hope he's on the database.'

I made us each a tea, dished out some food for Hamlet who I figured deserved it even though he was getting fat, and plonked myself down at the table. 'You're right,' I said. 'There's nothing I can do now, but I will get that bastard. Thank God you heard him and Hamlet's okay.'

'I haven't been sleeping well since I split from Pauline. Silver linings.' He looked into his tea. 'Meg, I know I haven't been the best father to you. After Carrie died, it was … difficult with your mother. I know I'm not very good at talking about things.'

'It's okay.' I swallowed. 'I didn't talk about things either. I should have told you and Mum what I said to Carrie that morning, instead of carrying it around inside me for twenty-five years.' I remembered an exercise a therapist had made me do, where I'd imagined going back in time and telling my younger self that it wasn't her fault. That Carrie had decided to kill herself, that she was actually saving herself from a huge amount of pain and anguish. That nothing a ten-year-old had said would have made any difference. It had helped, but not enough. 'I guess I'll always feel guilty,' I said. 'But it's manageable these days.'

Dad cleared his throat. 'It wasn't your fault she killed herself. You do know that, don't you?'

The shift in his tone triggered alarm bells. I knew there was more to this. 'Did something else happen that day that I don't know about?' I said. 'You need to tell me.'

Dad's eyes widened and he shook his head rapidly. 'No, of course not. But it was our fault so much more than yours. She told us she wanted to die and we didn't listen. We were selfish. We didn't want to lose a single day with her. We're the ones who should feel guilty for making her go through that.' He touched his eye. 'For making her do it all on her own.'

He'd finally said that to me. After all these years. 'We should help that charity,' I said. 'I can give you some of Gran's money. Why do I need to own a house anyway?'

41

Meg – Present day
Friday

I was pursuing Hamlet through a busy city centre, people jostling and pushing me, Hamlet getting further and further away, me shouting in desperation.

I snapped my eyes open and waited for my breathing to slow, my heart to stop jumping in my chest.

It was still early but I got straight out of bed, slipped on my dressing gown, and padded downstairs to reassure myself that Hamlet was okay.

Dad was already in the kitchen, doing the crossword in a three-day-old copy of *The Times*. I smiled at him. 'Where's Hammy?'

'Oh, I let him out. He was bashing his head against his flap. I thought he needed a pee.'

'You let him out? Bloody hell, Dad, people are trying to kill him! He's got a litter tray.'

'They won't try anything in the daytime, Meg.'

A spark of anger. 'Why didn't you just give that bloke a hundred quid anyway, Dad?'

'What?'

'Yes, I heard.' I grabbed a box of dry food – stuff Hamlet loved but didn't often get because of his kidneys and the size of his belly. I opened the door and shook it.

I pictured the cheque I'd written the night before. Made out to my dad, because he needed to confirm the exact details. The cheque I'd written after our heart-to-heart about Carrie, when I was flushed with thinking he was a good person after all. A creeping sense of unease was rising inside me.

'You can't give in to people like that,' Dad said. 'If I'd agreed a hundred, he'd have asked for two hundred.'

I shook the box more frantically.

A little black-and-white face popped out of a shrub at the bottom of the garden. I released my breath. 'Oh, he's here.'

Hamlet trotted over, undercarriage swaying, and shot into the kitchen.

I poured him some of his crack-cocaine-based snacks, shut the cat flap and shoved a chair against it. 'He's going to Hannah's. He knows he can't go out when he's there. And I'm off to work. I'll see you later.'

Hamlet was in his basket on the passenger seat next to me, face pressed up against the grille of his cat carrier, clawing plaintively at it, wailing like he was being tortured. I had to stop at the lights on the A6 and a concerned passer-by peered into the car, obviously thinking I was molesting a small child. I smiled nervously at her and pulled away. I was heading for Hannah's, having exchanged a few texts and confirmed she could have him.

The phone rang. Mum. I pressed to accept. 'Meg, love, you haven't given your father any money, have you?'

I blinked a couple of times. 'Hi, Mum, nice to hear from you.' I slowed the car, a sense of foreboding gnawing at my stomach.

'Are you paying attention?' Mum spoke rapidly. 'I've had Pauline on the phone.'

'Pauline whose name must never be spoken?'

'As it turns out, I think she's a decent woman. It's not her fault about your father. I should never have blamed her.'

'You know they've split up now. Whatever she's said to you – it might not be true.'

'He's broke, Meg. He lost all his money gambling.'

Everything went white and silent, except for a roaring in my ears. Mum must have still been talking but I couldn't hear her. I pulled into a side road and slammed the car to a stop.

My brain was splintering into fragments, but my hearing had come back.

'Stupid man,' Mum was saying. 'He always thought he was so damn clever. Thought he could beat the odds. Well, it turned out he couldn't. Pauline's been supporting him for years, while he kept promising to give it up. She finally decided she'd had enough. So he's come to try and scrounge off us. Your gran's money.'

I swallowed a gob of phlegm that was forcing its way up my throat. How pathetic I was. How gullible, how desperate to believe he cared about me, that he was proud of me. The bright flash of insight about myself was making me physically ill.

'The charity …' I croaked.

'All made up. It was for him. Has he given you a load of rubbish about that, Meg? Please don't tell me you gave him money. Not your gran's money.'

'No, Mum, I won't give him anything. Look, I have to go – I'm taking Hamlet to Hannah's.'

I indicated and pulled out in front of an Audi which was clearly speeding because it hadn't been there a second ago. The driver's face shone red in my mirror, inflamed with rage. He beeped his horn and swore. I gave him the finger, past caring if I was the star of his latest dash-cam video, and headed for home.

I juddered the car to a halt on the cobbles outside my house. Dad's old VW had gone. I should have known he was skint from the geriatric nature of his car. He'd always liked his cars.

It was too hot to leave Hamlet, so I grabbed his carrier and headed into the house at a swift, furious lollop. I plonked him in the hallway, and he gave me an outraged look.

The house was silent, a slight smell of toast and a few crumbs on the table the only evidence Dad had ever been there. His bag and wallet were gone. The cheque I'd given him last night, that he'd shoved under a mug on the windowsill, was gone. He must have been halfway to the bank by now.

I charged up to the spare room. Dad's suitcase was on the floor, no doubt with all his stuff neatly packed so he could leave as soon as my cheque cleared. I grabbed it and hurled it at the wall. 'You fucking bastard!' A tower of books came crashing down. I kicked the suitcase.

I opened the window. It was only a small, leaded one and Dad's suitcase wouldn't fit through it. I ripped the case open, grabbed his clothes and hurled them out. They fell like dead things onto the tiny garden area outside the front of the house. I went into the bathroom, grabbed his toothbrush, and chucked that out of the window too.

I crashed down the stairs and sat on one of the kitchen chairs, panting. I flipped open my laptop, logged into my bank account and cancelled the cheque. Then deadlocked the front door and put the chain on, and let myself and Hamlet out of the back. Dad wouldn't be coming into my house ever again.

Mum's car was parked in the wide road outside Hannah's.

I grabbed Hamlet's carrier, which felt heavier each time I picked it up, and staggered up the ramp to Hannah's front door. It was flung open as I arrived. Mum.

'Oh, love,' she said.

I put Hamlet's case down and she folded me into a hug. I stood for a moment in her arms, then pulled away, shut the door, and released Hamlet from his carrier.

'Come to the kitchen,' Mum said.

A mug of tea was already on the table for me. Hannah sat by the window. I went over and gave her a rough hug, then sat at the table with Mum.

Hamlet came trundling through and jumped onto Hannah's knee. 'Aw, he's such a sweetie,' she said, as he disgorged hair onto her black trousers. She looked up at me. 'Are you okay? Your mum told me about your dad. She wanted to see you.'

I wiped my eyes, determined not to be upset any more. He wasn't worth it. 'Yes, he got me,' I said. 'How can he be such a fucker?'

'Did he ask you for money?' Mum said gently.

I nodded. 'For his made-up charity. Last night when I was vulnerable. Someone tried to hurt Hamlet.'

Hannah leaned forward and rubbed under Hamlet's chin. 'Who would hurt little Hammy?'

'Well, I must admit I was tempted on the way over. He's practically shattered my eardrums. But anyway, no, it's those deranged Justice for Violet bastards. They loathe me. It's such a mess. And I need to get to work.'

'You can take time for a cup of tea,' Mum said. 'You've had a lot to cope with.'

'I think it's upset me more than I realised,' I said. 'They've been posting all this stuff about me. Saying I was promoted too fast because I'm a woman. Saying I'm incompetent and corrupt and don't want to catch Violet's killer because I'm a vegetarian.'

'What a load of nonsense!' Mum snapped.

'I know it's nonsense,' I said. 'But it's … horrible. It feels like a bunch of strangers have walked up to me on the street and kicked me in the face. I try not to take any notice, but … And now this with Dad. Maybe I was blind to him because I had so much else going on, and I so wanted him to be a good person.'

'Yes, he caught you when you were vulnerable because of all this Violet stuff,' Hannah said. 'You needed to believe that he really cared about you.'

'What kind of a person does that to his own daughter?' I said.

Mum reached forward and put her hand over mine. 'I know you like to think the best of him, but your memories aren't right, Meg. He was always manipulative and controlling. We would have split up sooner if Carrie hadn't fallen ill.'

'What?' I said. 'I thought it was Carrie's illness that split you up.'

Mum shook her head sadly. 'No, if anything it kept us together.'

I took my hand away, not sure what to make of that. Had I been fooling myself all these years about what Dad was really like? Wrongly excusing his behaviour because of Carrie's illness?

'I can't believe he used Carrie to try and get money from me,' I said. 'Talking about how guilty we felt and how we should try to help others who felt the same way.'

'That is seriously shitty,' Hannah said.

I gulped the last of my tea. 'I have to go. This murder … I'm already on a knife-edge. I'm not letting him screw up my career too.'

42

I scanned the incident room. Everyone looked shattered. Hair was unwashed, clothes unironed, eyes bloodshot. My team were starting to resemble me. The desperation for a positive development was sucking the life from us. I realised I'd brought a mug of tea in with me and it still had an economy teabag and a spoon in it. I gave it a squish to try and extract some small amount of tea-taste.

'Are you all right?' Jai said. 'You look terrible.'

'Thank you, Jai. Very motivational.' I fished out the teabag and threw it at the bin. The fact that it went in felt like my biggest achievement for quite some time. 'Justice for Violet tried to get Hamlet last night.' I didn't mention that I'd also had to chuck my dad out of my house. I'd tell Jai and Fiona later when an entire murder investigation team wasn't looking at me. I felt a stab of guilt and pity for my dad, before reminding myself what Mum had said. I put my mug down and picked at a broken nail on my thumb, almost relishing the fact that it was going to *really hurt* any minute.

'Oh no!' Fiona said. 'Is Hamlet okay?'

'He's fine.' I was aware of a buzz of interest from the room.

'And is the perp still alive or have you captured, tortured and killed him?' Jai said.

'Believe me, if I'd caught the bastard, he'd have wished he was dead. I smacked him and he ran away. I got some of his skin under my nails. It's with the lab. But anyway, we need to talk about the case. Where are we at?'

'We've not managed to locate Daniel Twigg,' Jai said. 'On the plus side, Justice for Violet took a night off from killing animals to stampede around the countryside hunting Daniel.'

My judgement was so far off I was like an inverse lie-detector. I'd trusted Dad, and I'd thought Daniel was a good person. How pathetically wrong could one woman be? 'I shudder to think what they'll do if they find him,' I said.

'It's a bit alarming,' Jai said. 'With the weather and the rival gangs in balaclavas and meat suits, it all feels quite post-apocalyptic.'

I knew what Jai meant. Everything was getting out of hand. Civilisation felt more precarious than it ever had in my lifetime. As if it could suddenly fall apart and we'd be killing the aristocracy, looting, plundering, and eating rats.

'For God's sake,' Craig said. 'Are we going to discuss the case?'

'Sorry, Craig,' Jai said. 'I used a grown-up word.'

'Some of us have been doing our job,' Craig said. 'I've found out Gary had a lot of enemies. Owed a lot of people money. Pissed a lot of people off. We're going through it all. But if Daniel killed Violet, he's the obvious suspect.'

'It could be a copy-cat killing,' Fiona said. 'They put the pig's head on to make it look like it was connected to Violet.'

'We're waiting on analysis of the fibres and the hair we found on him,' Craig said.

'And in relation to Violet,' Jai said. 'We know Daniel's razor was in the bin liner with Violet's clothes, Violet's blood was on Daniel's overalls, he has keys to the abattoir, and he had no alibi.'

'Yes, Jai, but do we have any actual *evidence*?' I said.

Jai shot me a look.

'I know, I know, I'm kidding. The evidence currently leads to Daniel having killed Violet.' I hoped they'd put the tremor in my voice down to lack of sleep, and not shame at what a fool I'd been.

Jai fiddled with his tablet. 'It also turns out that Donna was right. Gwen Twigg is Daniel's mother. She moved away from Gritton but told a friend she knew a secret about Daniel. We don't know if it's the same secret that Gary told Violet shortly before they were both killed – the secret about the Pale Child. Anyway, we're bringing her in. But look what we found inside Daniel's caravan.' Onto a screen behind us came photographs of what had been discovered in the secret half of the caravan. The half Daniel hadn't wanted me to look at, just before I got doused in blood. The internal walls were plastered with pictures and newspaper articles.

About the Pale Child.

The headlines jumped out at me. *Pale Child claims another victim. Pale Child returns to village. Just a toddler when the Pale Child came for him.* The images were artists' representations. Girls in white dresses running away through the trees, or over the rocks. Except one, which looked like a Victorian photograph. I peered more closely at it. A girl of about seven, leaning back on a chair, her eyes closed.

'Is that the original girl who died?' I asked.

'We think so,' Fiona said.

'She doesn't look very lively.'

'I think it's a post-mortem photograph,' Fiona said. 'Taken after she was strangled.'

'Jesus Christ.' I stepped back from the photograph. I'd heard about the Victorians doing this, but it was unsettling to see the real girl. The original Pale Child. Dead. And to think that Daniel had chosen to put her on his wall, in the area where he slept.

'There's another weird thing,' Fiona said. 'We found DNA on that doll's face mask you rescued from the cliff, and there's a familial relationship with Violet.'

'What? The girl I saw dressed as the Pale Child is related to Violet? How closely?'

'Not as close as a sibling or parent. But almost certainly a relation.'

'As was the original Pale Child,' I said.

I had a flash of memory. Blood flying at me. The words Daniel had spoken about his younger brother.

'Maybe that's why he started telling me about his brother falling down the spillway,' I said. 'Because I insisted on going into his caravan, and he realised I was going to see this. Maybe he was trying to explain.'

'Daniel was obsessed with the Pale Child because of his brother?' Jai said.

Craig cleared his throat. 'He could have killed his brother as well. That could be the secret. Why Gwen Twigg never comes to Gritton and never sees her only son. She can't stand to see him because he killed his little brother.'

The energy in the room rose. The team thought we had our man.

'He may use the Pale Child as an excuse,' Jai said. 'A way to feel that the killing isn't his fault. *The Pale Child saw them and then they died*. A way for him to reconcile his image of himself with being a killer.'

This was running away from me. 'I don't see his personality like that,' I said. I'd been wrong, but surely not that wrong? They were making him sound like a serial killer.

Craig let out a soft snort. 'Your poncy psychology degree letting you down this time?'

I pictured myself picking up my laptop and smashing it on his head. I settled for saying, 'If you can't contribute positively, please keep your mouth shut.'

Fiona said, 'All this doesn't make him the killer. He might just feel guilty about his brother's death and about Lucas, the boy who died in the car crash, and has become obsessed with the Pale Child because they both supposedly saw her before they died.'

Craig sighed. 'No, the pictures of the Pale Child don't prove Daniel Twigg's the killer. But luckily, we have a shitload of forensic evidence that does, plus the fact that he's buggered off. It couldn't be much clearer. And more than likely he killed Gary too. So now we need to find the bastard before anyone else dies.'

'It does fit the facts,' Jai said. 'Are we warning the public?'

'We are indeed,' I said. 'We have a huge operation looking for him and a press release going out shortly.'

I took another look at the photographs of the caravan's interior. 'What's that one?' It looked like a map. Gritton woods? A spot was marked with an 'x' and there was a tiny image of a gravestone. On it were the words, '1999 RIP'.

'Another murder?' Jai said. 'That's clearly a grave.'

'Bex was raped in 1999,' I said. 'And Lucas died in a car crash that same night. Maybe it's about him.'

'But why show a gravestone in the woods?' Fiona said. 'Lucas wouldn't have been buried in the woods.'

'We'll investigate,' I said. 'But the map's pretty imprecise. We can't justify the resources to dig up the whole of the woods.'

I didn't want to be hunting Daniel. To be talking about whether he'd killed his own brother as well as Violet, and Gary, and possibly even someone buried in the woods as well. He was the first person I'd felt anything for in years, if I discounted my completely inappropriate and thoroughly suppressed feelings for Jai. Everyone sometimes got people wrong. We could all be misled. In fact it always made me laugh watching the TV shows with the 'genius' detectives who could supposedly spot a killer at ten paces. *You gave me a funny look or blinked in a weird way, so you're clearly a murdering psychopath who slaughtered your entire family, including the dog.* Nobody could reliably identify a killer, and we had to follow the evidence. But that didn't stop me feeling utterly dejected about my appalling judgement.

Daniel's mother, Gwen, sat very still while Fiona sorted out the tape and took her through the formalities. She had a thick sweep of long grey hair and eyes that had the same faraway look as her son's.

'He didn't do those things, you know.' She spoke slowly as if checking each word as it came out. 'I'm sure all mothers say the same, but he isn't a killer. He just gets a bit … over-focused.'

'Do you have any idea where he might be, Gwen?' I asked.

She shook her head.

'Any special place he might go? Any idea at all, no matter how unlikely.'

'I'm sorry. I haven't seen him for so long.'

'What happens when he gets over-focused?' Fiona asked.

Gwen looked down. 'Nothing bad happens. Nothing bad happens when Daniel gets over-focused.' Her voice had an almost hypnotic tone, as if she was repeating a mantra. It made me nervous.

'Any places he used to go as a child?' I said.

'No. I don't know. I just keep praying I didn't put that Violet girl in harm's way.'

Fiona said, 'How would you have done that?'

'She called me. The girl Violet. She found out that I lived in the village in 1999. She asked me if I knew who Rebecca Smith was. I told her that would be Tony Nightingale's daughter.'

So that solved one mystery. Gwen had put Violet on to Tony Nightingale.

'The poor girl,' Gwen said. 'I pray for her every day.'

'When did you last see Daniel?' Fiona asked.

Gwen blinked a couple of times. 'Many years ago. I can't visit Gritton.'

'Why not?'

'Terrible things happen in Gritton. My little boy. Nothing was ever the same after my little boy ... After Charlie died.'

Fiona waited a moment and said, 'Charlie fell down the spillway in the reservoir?'

Gwen was quiet and I didn't think she was going to answer. Then she spat the words out, fast and shocking compared to her previous calmness. 'She killed him!'

'Who killed him?' I asked. Fiona and I sat very still, all our attention on Gwen.

'The Pale Child.'

Fiona shot me a look. I felt my spirits sinking with the realisation that Gwen wasn't quite all there. Maybe it was the years of alcohol abuse, but her relationship with reality seemed non-exclusive.

'Who is the Pale Child?' I asked.

'Nobody knows who she is, but she was there that other terrible night too. When Lucas died. I told Daniel not to associate with those Nightingales. I didn't want him to get fixated. I know what he can be like. Those girls were so pretty. Violet's the same.'

'Was he fixated on someone that summer?' I asked.

'Bex, of course. It was all about Bex. And then Daniel hurt his back and went to hospital, it was such a terrible night. His clothes all covered in mud. I don't know what went on that night but it was an awful thing, and he would never tell me.'

I felt the strange lightness that I sometimes get in my head when we're near to a breakthrough. 'His clothes were covered in mud?' I pictured the map. The little gravestone. What had happened that night? Was this the secret in the village? The reason that Daniel, Anna, Gary and Kirsty were forever bound together, stuck in Gritton.

'Yes, covered in mud. And Daniel would never say why. He wasn't the same after. I know I drank too much in those days, after Charlie. Before I found a better way. But I remember how he changed.'

'You said you didn't want Daniel to associate with the Nightingales. Why was that?'

'Those girls had the devil in them, especially the older one. The way they got the boys doing their bidding. I don't know what happened that night, but it would have been down to them.'

'Have you any idea what happened? Why Daniel's clothes were so dirty?'

293

'I knew it was bad. So bad I had to leave the village and never come back. So bad I had to stop having contact with Daniel because what if I found out? I didn't want to tell on my poor boy. They'd find a way to blame him, just like he's being blamed for Violet. So I didn't say anything. But now he's missing and I'm telling you. So you can work out the truth and use it to find my boy.'

Jai chucked the remains of his tea into my spider plant in an over-flamboyant manner, and leaned against my windowsill. 'We know Daniel has these fixations. He was fixated on Bex. Maybe he was fixated on Violet in the same way.'

'He obviously didn't kill Bex,' I said. 'And according to the DNA evidence, he wasn't her rapist.'

'But something happened that night. Involving Daniel. I spoke to Bex again. She's adamant she doesn't remember anything else, and I believe her.'

The door opened and Craig stuck his head in. 'We've got it. The evidence that Daniel Twigg killed Gary Finchley. We found Daniel's phone. He sent a text to Gary asking him to meet in the woods the night Gary was killed, and fibres from his overalls were found on Gary's clothes. And one of his hairs.'

'What time was the text sent?' I said.

'Two p.m. Gary texted back to ask why Daniel Twigg wanted to meet, but there was no reply. And we found Daniel's overalls – the ones that had left fibres on Finchley – in a bin not far from Daniel Twigg's caravan. His boots were in his van, and they had blood on them, which we've analysed and found to be Violet Armstrong's.'

'Right.' I wanted them both to go. I wanted to crawl under the table and cry for the person I'd thought Daniel was. That person hadn't been real. He'd been entirely my creation. 'Thanks, Craig,' I said, and he headed off.

'That's it then,' Jai said. 'We just need to find Daniel Twigg.'

'We still don't know for sure that Violet's dead,' I said. I'd lost Daniel and my father. I had to hang on to the possibility that Violet might, just might, be alive. 'What if Daniel became obsessed with her, and he's kidnapped her and is keeping her somewhere? He could be with her now.'

Jai raised an eyebrow.

'There are a few things that bother me about Violet's drive to the abattoir,' I said. 'Is there a chance someone else drove that car? Mrs Ackroyd didn't see the driver and there's nothing on CCTV to identify who was behind the wheel.'

'It's not impossible,' Jai said. 'I managed to speak to Izzy. She didn't know how far forward Violet has her seat, but she was sure Violet didn't mind driving down narrow lanes. Nobody knows what route she normally took.'

'Right. So why did Violet go that particular way to the abattoir? Maybe she didn't. Maybe someone else drove that way precisely *because* there's a camera. Because they wanted us to think Violet went to the abattoir. They might have known about insomniac Mrs Ackroyd – in a village that size, it's possible. Also, Anna said Violet's car was parked slightly further round than normal. Maybe it wasn't her who parked it.'

'But if she's still alive, what's with all the blood in the pig trough?'

'Let's say Daniel took blood from Violet, and shaved her hair, and then put the blood and hair in the trough to make us think she'd been killed and fed to pigs?'

'Wouldn't the blood clot?'

'Not if he added anticoagulant. I'm going to see if it's possible to test for that.' I sighed. This sounded nuts even to me and I had a high bar. Was I just grasping at straws trying to keep Violet alive?

'But why would he do that?' Jai said.

'So he could keep her?'

'Christ. We need to find Daniel.'

'He's already being hunted by half the Derbyshire police force, Justice for Violet, assorted do-gooders, and the usual nutcases. So how about we do what his mother suggested, and talk to the people who were there that night in 1999. I don't know how, but this somehow relates to that night. Let's talk to Anna and Kirsty.'

43

Anna lived in a Victorian terrace in a small row of similar houses set strangely on their own, on the road between Gritton village and the abattoir. I pulled up outside and Jai and I walked up a flagged pathway. Anna opened the front door and stared at us for a moment as if she had no idea who we were, but then gestured us in.

'We're very sorry for your loss,' I said.

'Is that the standard-issue wording?' she said. 'Or does it depend how close the relative is? Are brothers different from husbands or partners?'

I didn't reply, but followed her down a wood-panelled hallway to a room at the back of the house. It overlooked a hedged garden, the lawn scorched to yellow, and the room was bathed in sunlight. Two of the walls were lined with books, and the third featured abstract pictures similar to the ones we'd seen at the abattoir.

'Sorry,' Anna said. 'I'm not meaning to be difficult. I'm just upset. Sit down, I'll get tea.'

I wanted to grab Anna and shake her until she told us what she knew, what happened that night in 1999. But that wasn't the way with people like Anna. You had to play the long game or you got nowhere. A few extra minutes at this stage could save hours. I took a deep breath and told myself to chill the hell out.

It helped that the room had a calm feel, making it seem implausible that there had been so much death in the village. White walls, an oak-planked floor, minimal furniture, and plenty of books. The kind of room that my mirror-me would have – the me who existed in a parallel world in my head and who lived in a serene, organised, cobweb-free house, ate vegetables, and read great works of literature instead of slumping in a near-coma with a glass of wine in front of *Bake Off*.

Jai and I sat on a beige sofa by the window. I eyed the books. You could learn a lot from people's books – it would be such a shame if it all went to e-books. It was an eclectic mix – psychology, art, classic literature, but mainly utilitarian philosophy and books on food and the meat industry. This wasn't someone who'd gone lightly into running an abattoir.

Anna returned, put mugs of tea on a wooden coffee table, and perched on a chair opposite us. She'd brought cupcakes and flapjacks with the drinks. I marvelled at the kind of person who could produce cupcakes after her brother had been murdered, or even have cupcakes in the house and not devour them all in one frenzied sitting. 'I've been baking,' she said. 'To take my mind off things. The kitchen's piled high with food I can't touch. Please eat some of it.'

I took a piece of flapjack. How could I not? 'Thank you.'

'Is it true Daniel's missing?' Anna picked icing off a cake and dropped it onto her plate.

'Yes,' I said. 'Do you have any idea where he could have gone?'

'No. Did he kill Violet and Gary?'

'We're looking into various possibilities,' I said, and she caught my eye and nodded slightly, as if to say, *Thanks – very helpful.*

'There's a small chance Violet may still be alive,' I said. 'And that Daniel may have taken her. So if you have any idea where he might be ...'

'Good heavens.' She shook her head. 'But I haven't any idea, no. He rarely even leaves the village.'

'Where does Daniel like to go within the village then? Any special places?'

'Oh ... I don't want to be unhelpful, but I don't know him that well.' A sense of information left out.

'Any special places?' I said again.

'Well ...' She sighed. 'Maybe the woods.'

'Where you had the barbecue in 1999? The night Lucas was killed?'

She nodded slowly.

We'd already looked for Daniel in those woods, and found no trace of him. But what happened that night? What was the secret? I felt sure it would help us find Daniel and possibly even Violet. I took out a copy of the map we'd found in Daniel's caravan and showed it to her.

Anna went very still and clutched the arm of her chair.

'Does that mean anything to you?' I asked, pointing to the image of the gravestone with the words *1999 RIP*. 'What does that refer to?'

'I've never seen it before.'

'But you know what it means, don't you?'

I could feel the tension coming from her. I'd met her a few times now and knew she wasn't one of life's over-reactors. This was big.

'You need to tell us, Anna,' I said. 'This is really important. It might help us find Violet alive.'

Anna looked down at her hand, which was still clutching the chair arm, knuckles white as bone.

'We know Gary told Violet a secret about the Pale Child. We will find out what it is. We're asking Kirsty as well.'

Anna snorted. 'Good luck with that. Getting the truth out of Kirsty.'

'You buried someone in the woods,' I said.

This was a guess. I was expecting a shocked denial. But instead Anna sighed, leaned back and closed her eyes.

Jai and I sat in silence, waiting.

Anna popped her eyes open.

Jai and I were both still, breathing quietly. It was like approaching a wild animal. One false move, startle the creature, and it would bolt, leaving you with nothing.

'You think Violet could be alive?' Anna said. 'You think this might help find her?'

I nodded.

'Yes, we do,' Jai said.

Anna's whole body sank in the chair, as if she was letting go of the tension she'd been holding for years, decades even. Then she gave a sharp humourless laugh. 'Gary told Violet,' she said. 'What an idiot. A besotted, pathetic idiot. After all these years.'

'What did he tell her, Anna?'

'Oh fuck it. I'm so fucking sick of this secret. And of Gritton. Of not letting the others out of my sight. Of everything. Now Gary's dead anyway, so what's the point? And Daniel's gone insane. As for Kirsty … I'm not protecting her. It's all going to come out anyway when they dig up the woods for that crappy new development.'

I remembered the signs in the village. *Don't Build on Our Burial Grounds! Stop the Development!* I nodded, encouraging her to continue.

Anna closed her eyes and slowly opened them again. 'It happened the night Lucas died.'

I held my breath.

Jai spoke gently. 'Go on.'

'It was Bex's last night before she went home. She'd been here a month, with her dad and Kirsty. I'd become friends with her. We had … quite a good time, but … anyway, we had this barbecue in the woods.'

'"We" being you, Bex, Kirsty, Daniel, Gary and Lucas?'

Anna nodded. 'Kirsty was in charge, as usual, the boys doing what she told them. I knew Gary fancied Bex, and Daniel was besotted with her. Bex was being irritating, flirting with them. She got way too drunk, and stoned as well. She wasn't used to any of that.'

I nodded. This was in line with what we knew.

Anna sighed. 'Have you been told about that night?'

I put my mug down on the table and sat back. 'Tell us in your own words.' I was always annoyed by the TV detectives who put words into people's mouths. You don't do that. You wait for them to tell you in their own way. People let things slip out when they choose their own words.

'Bex was practically passed out, and then she sat up and pointed into the woods and said, "It's the Pale Child." We'd all been brought up to be scared of the Pale Child. *Don't go into the woods or onto the moor or down to the reservoir. The Pale Child might see your face and then you'll die.* Daniel's brother, Charlie, had died after seeing her. So although we didn't believe in ghosts, we were pretty wary of her. But that night we were too drunk and stoned to be scared. I caught a glimpse of someone in white, and we all ran off, not noticing that Bex wasn't following us. We scampered around the woods looking for this person in white, and Lucas was sure he actually saw her. We ran for ages, you know the way sometimes when you're drunk, you get a burst of speed?'

I nodded, although that didn't happen to me. Bursts of speed weren't my thing.

'It sounds terrible now, but it turned into a kind of game. We were dashing around in the woods trying to find this thing, but of course we didn't find her.'

I was leaning closer to Anna, willing her to tell us what she knew. The Pale Child had been in my mind for so much of the last few days, hovering at the edge of my consciousness, taunting me with questions about her identity, what she wanted. I was sure she was at the heart of this. She could lead us to Violet.

'It started to rain,' Anna said. 'And we realised Bex wasn't with us. So we walked back to the bonfire. And …' She took a deep breath. 'I didn't believe my eyes at first. Thought I was hallucinating even though I'd hardly smoked. It made no sense … Sorry. I need another drink. Wait a minute.'

Our intense focus had been too much. I cursed myself for not keeping it in check. Anna jumped up and left Jai and me sitting in her bright living room, minds full of the Pale Child.

44

Bex – October 1999

Her dad and Kirsty were gone. Bex was still on the sofa, tears streaming down her face. She couldn't make herself move, as if leaving the scene of the conversation would mean she'd accepted the conclusion.

'So the rapist gets away with it, my baby gets killed, and my life gets ruined,' she said.

Aunt Janet reached a hand over and placed it on Bex's arm. 'Now, come on, Bex – your life won't be ruined.'

'I think Dad and Kirsty know who did it. Why would they let him get away with it?'

'Oh, Bex, they don't know anything. They don't want him to get away with it any more than you do, but sometimes it's best to let things go. Do you have any idea which of the boys it was?'

Bex pictured the three of them, faces uplit by the orange flames of the fire. Sinister now in her memory. 'No. I mean ... I believe Kirsty when she says it wasn't Lucas. And I can't imagine Daniel ... I suppose Gary is the most likely, but that's not fair. Daniel was angry with me because I'd laughed at him. The truth is I don't know.'

'Look, Bex, if you knew for sure …' Janet hardened her face. 'Even if you knew for sure, I still wouldn't encourage you to go to the police. But I'd help you.'

'Help me do what?'

'Hunt him down and kill him.'

Bex looked up. Caught her aunt's eye. Laughed nervously.

Janet said, 'I'm only half joking. You know the conviction rates?'

'I should have reported it at the time,' Bex said. 'While there was still evidence.'

Janet poured more tea for them both. 'Don't let your life be ruined by this. How you react to it is in your own hands.'

'But it's not fair. He's the one who caused all this, and he gets away with it.'

'Life's not fair. You may as well get used to it. But he won't be a happy person, whoever raped you. That's not the action of someone who's okay. Console yourself with that.'

'I still don't want to kill my baby.'

'Bex,' her aunt snapped. 'Stop it! It's not a baby. It's smaller than a blueberry. They miscarry all the time at this stage. If human life's so bloody precious, nobody told nature.'

Catching the expression on her aunt's face, Bex asked 'Aunt Janet, did you …'

'I didn't have a miscarriage, I had an abortion. And it did *not* ruin my life. Okay?'

Bex swallowed. She'd been so wrapped up in herself. 'I'm sorry.'

'It was years ago, Bex. It's fine. It was a contraceptive failure and neither of us wanted a baby. It wasn't the easiest decision, but once it was made, it really wasn't that huge a deal. That's what I'm saying. It absolutely won't ruin your life. Don't give that amount of power to the rapist.'

'You didn't want kids and then you ended up lumbered with me anyway,' Bex said.

Her aunt sighed. 'I always thought I could be happy with kids or happy without kids. I've loved having you, but I didn't want to bring one into the world, okay?'

Bex smiled. 'I'm like a rescue dog then. Adopt don't shop.'

'I suppose if you choose to see it like that, yes.'

Aunt Janet was so sure of her opinions. Bex knew she could never be that strong. 'Okay,' she said. 'I know what you say makes sense.' She couldn't explain. Nobody would understand how good it felt not to be alone. 'It's not just me. And …' She wiped a tear away. 'Sorry, it's silly.'

'Oh love.' Janet shook her head slowly. 'You feel like it's two of you again?'

Bex nodded, trying not to sob with the relief that her aunt was beginning to understand. 'It never ever felt right,' she said. 'It being just me.'

'Bex, I should have made this clear from the start. An abortion is absolutely not going to ruin your life, but I'm not going to make you have one if you don't want one.'

Bex looked up, eyes blurry. 'What then? I told Dad and Kirsty …'

'It's your decision. If you keep the baby, I suspect it will cause irreconcilable problems with your dad and your sister, but it's up to you. Or I can help you get it adopted.'

'Yes, I want to have it adopted.'

'Okay, you can do that.'

'And I'll never tell Dad and Kirsty that I had the baby.'

Aunt Janet gave Bex a faint, reassuring smile. 'I think that's for the best.'

45

Meg – Present day
Friday

Anna came back and put more mugs of tea on the table. 'Sorry, you probably don't want tea. Displacement activity.'

I picked up a mug and took a sip.

'We thought the Pale Child was a girl,' Anna said. 'People always spoke of a girl. And … also we thought it was a younger child …' She shook her head rapidly. 'But it wasn't a girl, despite the long hair and the dress. It was a boy, and when we came back to the bonfire, Bex was passed out and this … thing was on top of her. Raping her.'

'Oh my God,' Jai said.

'Lucas ran forward. I was just staring. I couldn't believe what was happening. I was frozen. But Lucas ran forward and … I think Kirsty told him to. It was always Kirsty in control. He ran forward and grabbed a rock from beside the campfire and he … he smashed it on the boy's head. Hard.'

Anna paused and the room felt very quiet. I could hear Jai breathing beside me, and a pulse thudding in my ear.

Anna took a breath. 'Right. Yes, he smashed the rock on the boy's head, and then the rest of us sort of came alive and we all ran up to him and … the boy was lying there on his back now, and we could see his face, and he was only about thirteen or fourteen and he was wearing a dress and he was deathly pale and … Seriously, it was like a dream. We were all drunk and a bit stoned and it was all so … unreal. He wasn't breathing, and Kirsty tried mouth-to-mouth and pushing on his chest, and I was crying and Lucas had collapsed on the floor and was saying, *fuck, fuck, fuck*, over and over, and Gary was standing staring, and … Well, the boy or whatever he was – he was dead. He was dead and there was nothing we could do to bring him back.' Anna wiped a tear roughly from her cheek and carried on. 'Like I said, it felt unreal. How could the Pale Child be a boy? How could he be dead? Kirsty said, "We can't tell anyone about this." Lucas was no use, he kept rocking backwards and forwards saying, *fuck*, and Daniel was no better, and Gary was looking to Kirsty for what to do, and Bex hadn't even woken up, and it was raining harder by then, coming down in huge blobs, and cold too, I just … I just kept thinking I was going to wake up. That was why Daniel ended up driving the car – to get Bex home because she was freezing and soaking … and drunk-driving seemed trivial compared to what we'd done. Only it turned out it wasn't. Because Lucas died that night too. Lucas killed the Pale Child and later Lucas died.'

Was this real? Anna had seemed so helpful and reliable before, so solid in her views. Now she was unravelling before our eyes. I didn't know whether to believe this story or put it down to the stress of Anna's last few days. Surely she and her friends couldn't have seen the Pale Child, and *killed* the Pale Child. But it tied in with the terrible secret, the little grave on the map. And with the four of them bound together, doomed to remain in Gritton, watching each other, too scared to leave in case one of the others told.

Jai was holding his mug tightly. 'What did you do next?'

'Kirsty said we should bury him. She said nobody need ever know. Who would miss him? I mean, nobody acknowledged his existence. We were the sons and daughters of farmers and abattoir owners. We could do this. The ground in the woods was wet with all the rain. Kirsty went back to her dad's house and got forks and shovels and we carried him between us into a dark bit of the wood that nobody ever goes in – the old burial grounds … and we dug a hole and put him in it.'

'This was you, Kirsty, Daniel, Gary, and Lucas?'

She nodded. 'Bex was still passed out.'

We were all silent. In my mind's eye I could see the teenagers carrying this dead boy through the rain. The boy who looked like a girl. And burying him deep in the woods.

'That's partly why we're campaigning against the new development,' Anna said. 'None of us want that area of the woods dug up. He's been there for the last nineteen years, and everything was fine until this summer when the reservoir dried up and the old village reappeared and the Pale Child came back, and everything started going wrong.'

'Did you have any idea who he was?'

Anna shook her head. 'No. I still don't.'

So this was the secret. The reason Daniel's clothes had been covered in mud. The secret that Gary had told Violet. Was Violet missing because she knew this secret? Was Gary dead because he told her?

'Gary told Violet this secret and now they're both gone,'

I said. 'And Daniel's missing. You have to tell us if you've got any idea where he is, or what's going on.'

She took a long, slow breath. 'Look, not wanting to speak out of turn, but Daniel is a bit unstable. I know he takes drugs for his pain, because Kirsty supplies him. Maybe they affected him. If he found out Gary told Violet, maybe he felt doubly betrayed – he liked Violet and I know he would have hated the idea of her being close to Gary. But Kirsty's always been in charge. If anyone knows what's going on and where Daniel is, it will be Kirsty.'

We climbed into the car and set off in the direction of Kirsty's farm, Jai driving, Formula One style.

'Christ,' I said.

'Indeed. So Violet could be the daughter of that boy. But who the hell was he?'

I called Fiona. 'Any sign of Daniel?'

'No,' she said. 'But ANPR picked up his van, heading out of Gritton to the north. We're on it.'

'Okay. Anna Finchley thinks Kirsty might know more about where he is, so we're going there. But in the meantime, could you follow up another lead for me? Anna claims there are human remains in the woods. In the old burial ground, where it was marked on that map. The map's not super-precise, so could you liaise with her to find the right spot and get it checked out?'

There was a moment's silence and I wondered if we'd lost the signal. Then Fiona spoke. 'Violet's remains?'

'No, no, sorry. Not Violet. Historic.'

'Whose then?'

'We're not sure yet.'

309

I thanked Fiona and ended the call.

'Let's think about this,' I said. 'If Anna's right, then the Pale Child that they saw in 1999 was real. A real boy. And now the Pale Child is back, and it's another real child, related to Violet.'

'Someone must know who these children are,' Jai said. 'Anna reckoned the boy who raped Bex was thirteen or fourteen. If that same boy was the "Pale Child" Charlie Twigg saw before his death in 1995, he'd only have been nine or ten back then. He must have lived locally, maybe in the village itself.'

'If so, how come nobody knew who he was? A boy running round in a dress – there'd have been talk about it. And why did nobody report him missing after his death?'

'Maybe his existence was a secret,' Jai said. 'A secret child. I know … it makes no sense.'

'I think Kirsty Nightingale might know who he was,' I said. 'Based on Anna's description of the way she reacted to his death.'

We took the road that went past the reservoir, heading for Kirsty's farm.

'God, this heat!' Jai said. 'It's like the weather's been taken over by a madman. What happened to nice, normal summer days?'

'Maybe God's pissed off with recent events in politics. It'll be water turning to blood and plagues of frogs next.'

'I think I've already got that going on in my basement.'

'I need to see this basement. Though I expect it'll be a big disappointment.'

'I'm getting a sump pump. You'll have to see it soon if you want to witness the full spectacle.'

'Ooh, a sump pump! How would Suki feel about me delving around in your basement?'

I looked up and the bell-mouth spillway at the edge of

Ladybower Reservoir caught my eye. It dragged my attention against my will, as if pulling me towards it. I caught sight of a flicker of white.

'Yeah … About Suki … Hang on, what was that?' Jai slowed the car.

'I only saw a glimpse. What did you see?'

'It looked like a girl. Dressed in white. Blonde hair. Running over the dam.'

'Like the Pale Child, you mean?'

46

Jai pulled over to the side of the road, flicking on the hazard lights. I could see her now. In a long white dress. She was holding it up as she sprinted along the path at the southern edge of Ladybower Reservoir.

The girl ran across the dam and through a metal gate at the end. She turned sharp right and started heading up the far side of the reservoir.

'Uh oh,' Jai said. 'What's she doing?'

I squinted into the distance. Trees rose up behind the water, darkening the area I was trying to see. The girl was climbing down a stone slope that led to the reservoir base. 'Oh, for God's sake,' I said.

The girl reached the bottom of the slope and was now on the stone area that surrounded the spillway. This area would normally be covered by water, but the drought had left it dry.

'That's the same thing Charlie Twigg did,' Jai said. 'Daniel's brother. He managed to climb up somehow.'

'We'd better go after her,' I said.

I jumped out of the car, and Jai did the same.

'Go, Jai,' I said. 'You're faster than me.'

Jai sprinted ahead and I ran across the dam, as fast as I could with my old ankle injury. To my left, the scorched grass sloped steeply down to the river far below. Even with the levels so low, the weight of water behind the dam seemed monstrous.

Panting and cursing my ankle, I arrived at the gate, pushed through it and turned right. Jai was shimmying awkwardly down the slope to get to the dry concrete area around the spillway.

Up close, the spillway was vast. About eighty feet across and twenty feet high. Designed to be hard to climb into when water levels were low. I could see the internal steps leading down to the immense hole within.

As I ran towards where Jai had gone down, I realised the girl was on the rim of the spillway. She must have climbed the pile of stones that was propped against the vertical wall. I stopped and watched her. She seemed familiar.

She took a step towards the gaping hole and turned, about to start climbing backwards into it. She was wearing a doll's face mask, just like the one I'd found on the gritstone edge, but even so I was convinced I knew her.

My phone rang. Unknown number. I hesitated. She was poised on the rim of the spillway. I answered. A male voice. Panicky. 'Meg Dalton?'

My breathing quickened. 'Daniel? Daniel, is that you?'

'It doesn't matter about me any more, but you need to talk to Kirsty.'

'Where are you, Daniel?'

'I'm sorry …' The signal was bad. I couldn't make out his words.

'Have you got Violet?' I shouted. 'Where is she?'

I lost the signal. 'Fuck.' I dialled the number he'd phoned on but there was no answer.

I looked back at the girl on the spillway. With a jolt I realised it was Frankie, Kirsty's daughter, producer of impressive drawings, including of this place. She started shifting downwards, into the spillway.

'Frankie!' I shouted. 'No!'

She was holding her phone in front of her, presumably videoing what she was doing. The steps were mossy. Slippery. And they got narrower as they descended. One hand was on the phone. If she slipped, she'd fall into the hole, just like Daniel Twigg's little brother had.

Jai appeared at the base of the pile of stones. He looked up at me.

'Go up,' I shouted, while trying to call Daniel again. 'But carefully.'

Jai scrambled up the stones and stood with his hands reaching up to the edge of the spillway. He twisted his head towards me and yelled, 'The rim's curved. I'm trying, but I can't get any purchase.'

'I think she knocked the top stone off the pile,' I shouted.

I looked again at Frankie. She'd shifted lower in the spillway, still videoing. 'Frankie, come on out!' I shouted. 'You've got your video.'

Jai was scrabbling with a stone, heaving it to the top of the pile, climbing again. He bounced up onto one leg and dragged himself onto the spillway rim. He said something to Frankie, but his words were carried away by the wind..

I stood frozen. What if she slipped now? Would it be our fault for going after her?

Frankie dropped her arm and looked at Jai. He shifted closer.

314

She hesitated and then shifted one foot upwards. A scraping on stone and she fell back a step. I felt a spike of adrenaline.

She righted herself and crawled up out of the hole. Jai took Frankie's hand and led her away.

We walked back across the dam towards the car, Frankie beside us. She'd taken the mask off.

'I need to phone the station,' I said. 'Daniel called me.'

Jai's head whipped round. 'Daniel? What did he say?'

'He said we should talk to Kirsty and that he was sorry, but then he got cut off. I've got the number he called on. Go on ahead.'

I tried Daniel again. No answer. I called Fiona and gave her the number he'd called from, then ended the call and ran as fast as I could to catch up with Jai and Frankie.

Frankie was talking. I slowed and slipped in beside Jai.

'I know what you're thinking.' Frankie projected her voice away from us, in the direction of the water.

Jai's voice was soft. 'What's that?'

'Why am I dressed like this?'

'You can dress however you want,' Jai said. 'But I suppose we are wondering if people might mistake you for the Pale Child.'

She stopped and turned to face us. 'I liked the dress when I found it in Grandpa's attic, and he said I could have it and I thought I could pretend to be the Pale Child, so I went and videoed myself. But I didn't mean for that girl to die. Or that man.'

I tried to speak casually. 'What do you mean, Frankie?'

'I went on the moor in this dress, to video myself. Just messing around, but I got a load of likes when I posted it.'

I wondered if that was what Violet had seen, and the video Hannah had found, from before Violet went missing. Frankie pretending to be the Pale Child. 'Okay,' I said. 'It's okay, Frankie. You're not in trouble.'

'But I saw that girl. Violet. I know I scared her. And then I went in the woods and I saw the man who died with the pig on his head. I'm the Pale Child now. But I didn't mean for him to die.'

'Was your mum okay about you going into the woods at night?'

'Yes.'

'We're going to see your mum now,' I said. 'Shall we give you a lift back?'

'I don't know whether I should go with strangers.'

'We met though, didn't we, in your kitchen? So we're not strangers.'

I took her hand to cross the road, and unlocked the car. She lifted her skirts and shuffled into the back. Her white dress was stained at the front where she'd leaned on it as she shuffled into the hole. She could so easily have caught a foot in its folds and fallen.

Jai and I got into the car, and I pulled out and accelerated away from the reservoir towards Kirsty's farm. Frankie sat quietly.

My phone rang. Fiona. 'Meg!' She sounded in a panic. 'The wildfire has spread to Gritton!'

'Oh no. Whereabouts?'

'In the woods. It's so dry at the moment ... I've alerted everyone, but I thought I should let you know.'

'Thanks, Fiona.'

I looked at the rocks beyond Gritton. Smoke was rising through the air, veiling them. The fire looked close.

'Do your parents know where you are?' Jai asked Frankie.

'Mum doesn't care.' Frankie didn't sound petulant – she just stated it as fact. 'She doesn't get bothered like other people's mums do.'

'What about your dad?'

'I never had a dad.'

Frankie lifted an arm and pointed at the horizon. 'Look at the smoke.'

It was now billowing above the trees in the base of the valley.

Frankie's voice was calm. 'It's coming from our farm.'

47

The car skidded to a halt and Jai and I jumped out. The fire had spread from the woods across the scorched grasses to Kirsty's barn. The one we'd been in a few nights previously, watching pigs devour flesh. It looked like some straw had been dumped outside the barn, which must have helped the fire spread.

A vast, searing heat came from the barn. And a sickening squealing.

Kirsty was standing staring at it.

Jai took Frankie's hand and led her away from the barn towards the house. Tears were streaming down her face.

'What's happening?' I shouted at Kirsty.

'The fire brigade are on their way,' Kirsty said. 'It's because of the straw. I shouldn't have listened to those silly animal people. There's nothing we can do. I have a pond they can take water from. We can't do anything until they get here.'

'But the pigs …' I pictured them all in their cramped cages. Screaming in pain. Burning.

'The advice is not to try and get them out,' Kirsty said.

I moved towards the barn, but Kirsty reached out and grabbed my arm. Her tight fingers pressed into my muscle. 'We can't open that door,' she said. 'The fire's in the straw at the end of the barn by the door. If we open the door, it will give it oxygen and make it far worse. You need to stay away!'

I turned and caught her eye. She looked as confused by my reaction as I was by hers. She pushed her phone at me. A screen showed a page from a website – The National Animal Disease Information Service. I scanned the words. Kirsty was right. The advice was to leave the pigs to burn. *The fire brigade's primary responsibilities in dealing with a fire are the preservation of human life and protection of property by limiting spread of the fire. Animals are not a priority in such situations.*

'Well, that's pretty chilling,' I said.

'The fire brigade are on their way,' Kirsty said. 'You want to endanger their lives trying to save pigs which are only going to be slaughtered for food anyway?'

'But they're suffering,' I said.

A look of concern formed on her face, almost as if she'd willed it there. 'They'll pass out because of the smoke,' she said. 'They won't be in pain.'

I wanted to say, *They're screaming.* But she had a point. Why save them? It would only prolong their miserable lives and do nothing about the inevitability of their deaths.

'Honestly,' Kirsty said. 'If we could get them out, I would. But it will make it much worse if we open the barn doors. I'm not letting you do that.'

We stood staring at each other for a moment and I realised I wasn't going to win this one. 'Kirsty, do you know where Daniel is?' I said.

'No.'

'What about Violet?'

'Violet? She's dead.'

Out of the corner of my eye, I saw someone running towards the barn. I spun round to look. Frankie, with Jai running after her.

'No, Frankie!' Kirsty was shouting but she didn't sound panicked. She jogged towards the barn, but Jai was already there, stopping a sobbing Frankie from touching the hot doors.

Kirsty grabbed Frankie's hand and dragged her towards the house. 'I'm calling the fire brigade again. And getting Frankie inside.' As she ran away, she shouted over her shoulder, 'I'm not risking my property and firefighters' lives having you open that door! Stay away!'

The pigs were squealing in the barn, a terrible noise that broke my heart in two. It was almost human.

Or *was* that human? I ran closer to the barn, moving to the end furthest away from the door, and the piles of straw and the worst of the fire. 'Hello!' I bashed on the barn wall with my palm. Listened for a moment.

'Jai, I thought I heard a scream. A human scream.' The words spilled out in a panic.

'What the fuck—' Jai said.

'Hello!' I shouted. 'Is someone in there?'

The pigs squealed louder. 'Is anyone in there?' I shouted again.

The barn wall was slatted, with tiny air gaps between wooden boards. I thought I saw movement on the other side. A person?

The noise of the pigs died down and I heard it. A human scream.

I could see fingers now, between the slats, desperately tugging at them.

I put my face close to the barn wall. 'Who is it? Who's in there?'

'It's Bex! Help me!'

Bex? Was I imagining things? It couldn't be Bex. She refused to come anywhere near Gritton. I put my head to the barn wall, trying to hear over the crackle and roar of the fire. 'Is that you, Bex?' I yelled.

'Yes! Help me! I can't get to the door. The fire's taken hold at that end.'

'Shit,' Jai said. 'I think Kirsty's right. If we open the door at the end of the barn, it'll make it worse.'

I pressed my face up to the slats and shouted, 'Can you keep away from the fire? Are you okay?'

Kirsty came running up behind us.

'Bex is in there!' I screamed.

Kirsty shook her head. 'No. Bex isn't here. She doesn't come to Gritton.'

Was I going mad? Had I been hearing things? But no, she was in there. 'She's in the barn! We have to get her out.' I shouted through the slats again. 'Bex! Are you okay?'

Bex's voice was faint. 'The fire's coming closer.'

The fire was raging at the end of the barn, where the straw was stacked. There was no way we could get Bex through that and out of the doors. I remembered seeing pipes that ran around the top of the barn, supplying water feeders for the pigs. If we could break one of them, maybe it would put the fire out? But if the electricity was still on, it could make the whole building live.

I ran and grabbed Kirsty. 'How can we switch the electricity off? Then if Bex can burst one of the automatic waterers, she can put the fire out. She's definitely in there.'

For a moment, I thought Kirsty was going to argue. Tell me

Bex couldn't possibly be inside. But instead she dropped her shoulders and nodded towards the barn. 'The fuse box is in there. We can't risk water.' How could she be so calm when her sister was about to be burnt to death?

'But can we get Bex to turn the electricity off?' I said.

'No,' Kirsty said. 'The fuse box is at the end where the fire is.'

'So how can we bash the barn wall down?' I wasn't giving up on Bex, like Kirsty appeared to have done. 'At the end which isn't burning too badly. Do you have a tractor?'

'Look, the fire brigade are on the way,' Kirsty said. 'Bex will be fine.'

I'd never seen a relative react like this before. Okay, Bex and Kirsty hadn't grown up in the same house, but they'd spent a summer together. They were sisters. In that moment I hated Kirsty. I'd give anything to have my sister back, and she was prepared to let hers burn.

I heard sirens. 'Oh, thank God.'

Fire engines piled into the yard.

'There's a woman inside,' I shouted.

We watched helplessly while the firefighters worked, one group cutting a hole in the thick barn wall at the far end to get Bex out, another group drawing water from Kirsty's pond and dousing hundreds of gallons of it over the barn.

Kirsty stood recklessly close to the barn while the firefighters worked. But she didn't appear to be concerned – more fascinated. One of the men told her to move away but she ignored him, and he was too busy to insist.

Finally the firefighters managed to remove a panel from the side of the barn. The roof lurched downwards, spitting sparks in our direction. I jumped back. The firefighters were in. The

322

pigs were still squealing and there was so much smoke I couldn't see inside.

Someone was coming back out, dragging a woman behind him. Bex.

The barn made a strange groaning noise. I took another step back.

The remaining firefighters ran from the barn, just before the side wall collapsed.

Bex, Jai and I sat on the dusty ground and watched the firefighters putting out the last of the blaze. Kirsty had been taken away in an ambulance, Frankie with her. Some of the pigs had survived, and Tony Nightingale had come over and was moving them into another barn. I'd offered to help but he said he'd prefer to do it alone, that he could cope better with his daughter being injured if he kept busy. He was setting up metal hurdles to define a path for the pigs to follow. Lots were dead. I didn't want to see.

My phone rang. Fiona. 'We've traced the approximate location of the phone Daniel called you from. Units are heading there now.' I allowed myself to hope that we might find Daniel and that he'd have Violet. That Violet and Daniel would both be okay, even if Daniel wasn't really okay at all.

Bex looked down at her hands. The ends of her fingers were red raw from scraping at the barn wall.

'You need to get those seen to,' I said. 'And get yourself checked for smoke inhalation.'

Bex blinked as if confused. 'Oh. Yes. I will. They said another ambulance is on the way. Dad's going to come with me in that one, so he can see Kirsty too. Did you see what happened to her?'

'A chunk of corrugated metal roof fell on her legs,' Jai said, not very subtly.

I felt a spark of concern for Kirsty, but mainly because she might be the only person who could lead us to Daniel and Violet, and now we couldn't talk to her.

'It's Gritton,' Bex said. 'Bad things happen.'

I pictured her in her cluttered kitchen, surrounded by her saxophone-playing china dogs, saying she'd never come back to Gritton. 'Why did you come back?' I said.

'I didn't want to. But suddenly finding Violet felt like the most important thing in the world. If I could help with that … And I wanted to see my dad and my sister.'

'Did Kirsty know you were coming?'

'No. I phoned but she didn't answer.'

'Why did you go into the barn?'

'I couldn't find Kirsty, and I wanted to see the pigs. I left a message on her landline saying I'd be in the barn.'

'Wasn't the barn locked?'

Bex sighed. 'I guessed the combination. Kirsty always used her own birthday for absolutely everything. But when I got inside, I just …'

'Just what?'

'I didn't expect it to be so … awful. I loved Dad's pigs when I came to Gritton that summer. They were the best thing about the place. They were in cages for a few weeks when they farrowed, and I didn't like that, but Dad explained why it was necessary. For the rest of their lives they were outside. I never realised Kirsty kept them all their lives … like this. I just sat in the barn staring at them. I must have been in a kind of trance. I didn't hear the fire on the moor coming closer. Not until the bales by the door caught fire.'

'How long were you in there?'

'I'm not sure. I sat and stared and stared and then suddenly the straw caught at the end and it went up in a crazy whoomph. I kept trying to get to the barn door but it was no good. The heat was too much.'

'It must have been terrifying,' I said.

She shrugged. 'It was.'

'Are you staying over with your dad?' Jai asked.

'Yes. I arrived this morning. It was good to see him, and he was delighted to see me. He even showed me his pigs playing fetch, just like the old days. But it was all a bit desperate – I think … well, he's not okay about Violet. So I said I'd stay a while. Cancelled my training clients.' She wiped a tear from her cheek. 'It was nice to feel he wanted me around. It wasn't always the case.'

I could see Tony across the yard, gently guiding a pig away from the smoking barn. One of the metal hurdles fell over, and Jai jumped up and went over to help.

'Didn't your dad want you around before?' I said to Bex.

'You know he sent me away to live with my aunt. I'm sure he blamed me for what happened with Tim.'

'Sorry, Bex, you'll have to explain.'

'Tim was the reason our mum had a breakdown and left us. Dad said she never really settled here even before that. That he was a fool to think she'd be happy. He said we're so arrogant in this country – we assume someone from the Ukraine should feel blessed to be here at all. But he was only trying to make me feel better. I know the real reason she left. She couldn't bear to be near me after what happened to Tim.'

'Who was Tim?'

'Tim was my brother. My twin.'

Bex's *twin?* 'Oh no,' I said. 'I'm so sorry, I didn't know.'

'I suppose you wouldn't.'

'Do you mind me asking what happened? How Tim died?'

She took a tissue from her pocket and blew her nose. 'I was only three years old so I don't remember. All I know is what Dad and Kirsty told me. Our mother was tired from looking after us and Tim had been screaming that he could see a white child but nobody else could see it. They thought it was just nightmares. Later, Dad said Kirsty used to tell us stories about the Pale Child and scare us – that's why Tim was upset. Anyway, our mum fell asleep on the sofa. Tim got out of the front door and on to the lane outside …'

I pictured the overgrown front of Tony Nightingale's house. The fence that blocked the route from the door to the lane. The peeling paint and neglect. I nodded at her to continue.

'But it was my fault. Dad tried to say it was because Tim had seen the Pale Child, but I know everyone blamed me. That's why I was sent away to Aunt Janet's.'

So this was the three-year-old who'd fallen victim to the Pale Child: Bex's twin.

'How could it be your fault?' I asked.

She looked at her red raw hands and grimaced. 'I have no idea why I'm telling you all this.'

'It's okay, if you don't want to talk.'

'No, I do. It's a relief. It's been weighing me down forever. I … I liked to paint. I'd been messing about with hand-paint. Blue hand-paint. And later they found blue paint on the lock and the door handle.'

'You opened the door?'

'I only found out later. Kirsty told me. She said it wasn't my fault. I was only three. But I know they blamed me. Everyone blamed me.'

'That's awful. Tim wandered into the road?'

'Yes. He was wearing dark clothes. The driver didn't stand a chance.'

I sensed a shadow over us and looked up. Tony, a smear of dirt on his cheek. He sank down beside Bex and folded her into a hug. 'It wasn't your fault,' he said. 'None of it was ever your fault.'

Bex accepted the hug but then pulled back. 'It destroyed me, Dad. That you didn't support me after the rape. I'd just about coped with you sending me away to live with Aunt Janet, but that ...'

So Tony knew about the rape. He looked down and fiddled with a piece of grit on the floor. 'I'm so sorry, Bex.'

'First the rape,' she said. 'What message does that send? That I was a worthless piece of meat. And then to not be believed, to not be supported. Then you tried to force me to have an abortion even though you knew the baby was the only thing keeping me going, the only thing making me think there was a point to life.'

If Tony had known Bex was pregnant, I wondered why he denied that she'd had a baby when we first came asking about Violet.

Tony took a deep breath. 'I never meant ... I never meant for things to work out the way they did. Please let me make it up to you. Let me take care of you. I always loved you. Everything I did, I thought I was doing it for the best.'

Clearly Tony knew a lot more than he'd let on. And that made me wonder if he knew who Violet's father was. Did he know the identity of the boy? The boy they called the Pale Child.

My phone rang in my pocket. I fished it out and answered. It was Fiona.

'They found bones in the woods,' she said. 'Where the cross and the RIP were marked on that map. And Daniel Twigg has been found too.'

48

Bex – May 2000

Bex lay on the narrow bed in her cramped room, savouring the moment with her baby. But not holding her. That would make it too hard.

A shadow fell over her. Aunt Janet stood in the doorway, her expression sympathetic yet determined, her bulk blocking all exit-points. 'It's time,' she said. 'I need to take her now.'

The baby was in a crib by the bed. Bex had a crazy thought that she could grab her and together they could jump out of the window. She could make a run for it over her aunt's lawn, trampling the borders and crashing through the privet hedge.

But that would be ridiculous.

'Maybe I could manage,' she said softly.

'We've talked about this,' Janet said, 'and you decided to have her adopted.'

Bex said nothing. There was nothing to say. She looked at the crib. The baby's eyes were closed and she seemed to give a little smile, even though Bex knew babies weren't supposed to smile so soon. She reached across and touched the tiny fingers.

'Come on,' Aunt Janet said. 'Don't be silly.'

'But maybe my sister could help?'

'No, Bex.' Janet was very still. 'Not your sister. I'll take her now. It's for the best.'

Bex looked down at the baby one last time. 'Wait a minute.' She fished her brooch out of her pocket. The christening brooch of a pelican digging her beak into her own chest, making herself bleed to feed her young. Bex was doing the same. By giving her baby up, she felt like she was gouging her heart out.

She pinned the brooch to the baby's clothes, lifted her from the crib and gently passed her to her aunt.

49

Meg – Present day
Friday

Clouds gathered overhead as Jai and I drove away from Gritton. The village that had been the site of so much death and suffering. The air was thick with moisture but still it refused to rain. We passed a couple of signs saying, *Protect our heritage! No to the developers!* I thought about the boy buried in the woods.

'Where are we heading?' I said.

'Woodland about ten miles north of here.'

We eventually pulled up in the lane at the location we'd been given, half in a ditch which had been dry for weeks. I found myself not wanting to leave the car, but Jai was already outside, bouncing around like a dog who wanted a walk. 'Are you coming?' he said.

I dragged myself out, clicked the lock, and followed Jai into the darkness of the trees. A path had been marked out with tape. 'These are hideous woods, aren't they?' I said. 'A mess of dark, stinging, spiking unpleasantness.'

'They said you can get in from the other side,' Jai said. 'But this way's easier to walk.'

'Quicker to walk,' I said, extracting my hair from a bramble. 'Not necessarily easier.'

'Are you okay?' Jai said.

'Sorry.' I kicked at a nettle which was tangling its way across the path. I wasn't okay. I pictured Daniel on that narrow ledge, lifting the lamb and passing it to me. Had I really been so wrong about him? 'He phoned me,' I said. 'I should have helped him.'

'You did,' Jai said. 'We found him as quickly as we could. I don't see what more you could have done.'

A small clearing came into view. Daniel's van was at the centre, with a paramedics' van next to it. The force medical examiner met us at the edge of the clearing. I raised my eyebrows at her and she gave a quick shake of the head.

'Overdose,' she said. 'Injected himself. We don't know if it was deliberate or accidental.'

I walked over to Daniel's van and peered in. He was slumped in the passenger seat. The needle was still in his arm. I turned away.

One of the uniforms walked over and said, 'No suggestion anyone else was involved.'

'We can't know that,' I snapped.

I sensed the collective shoulder-shrugging that goes with the death of a drug user. I wanted to say, *But he wasn't what you think. He was functioning. It was for pain relief. He was okay.* But that would do a disservice to those others. Those who *weren't* functioning. Who weren't okay. Those whose deaths were somehow regarded as less tragic than other deaths. And besides, this one was a murderer. No sympathy would be lost here.

'I want us to search these woods,' I said. 'In case he's got Violet hidden nearby.' I may have been devastatingly wrong about Daniel, but I still hadn't given up on Violet.

Richard had asked to see me back at the station. I found him in his room, tending to his cacti, clearly in an ebullient mood. Daniel was dead and everyone was happy. It made me want to retch.

He turned to face me, watering can in hand. 'We have our man then?' he said.

'It's not great news,' I said. 'Daniel Twigg was found dead in his van. In woodland about ten miles north of Gritton. It appears that he died of an overdose. We don't have toxicology back yet, but we know he was on opiate medication for pain relief.'

'We don't know if the overdose was accidental or deliberate?'

'No.'

'But we have very good evidence that he killed Violet Armstrong and Gary Finchley?'

Everyone had given up on Violet. I said, 'We don't know for sure that Violet is dead.'

The toxicology people had said they couldn't tell if there was any anticoagulant in the blood we'd found. Nobody was interested in my theory that she could still be alive. That someone could have put her blood and hair in the pigs' trough to make us think she was dead.

'She's dead,' Richard said. 'We haven't had a single indication that she's alive, have we?'

'No, but I don't think we've got to the bottom of all this. It ties in with what happened in 1999, I'm sure of it. They found bones in the woods, exactly where Anna Finchley said they would be. She was telling the truth. A teenage boy was killed that night and ended up buried in the woods. Gary, Anna, Daniel and

Kirsty have been keeping it a secret ever since. Until Gary told Violet. And now Gary and Daniel are dead and Violet's missing, presumed dead.'

'Well, that gave Daniel a motive to kill Violet and Gary didn't it?'

'I think there's more to it.'

'It's not a Sunday-night drama. It might not all be neatly tied up with a big red bow.'

'I'm sure Kirsty Nightingale knows more than she's told us.'

'I thought she was in a coma.'

'She is. The doctors are going to let us know the minute she regains consciousness.'

'We have our killer,' Richard said. 'The evidence against Daniel Twigg is overwhelming and we have zero indication that Violet Armstrong is alive, or that Kirsty Nightingale is involved in any way. I think we can wrap this up. The bones in the woods are a separate case. We don't need to trouble the Nightingale family any further. They have enough to deal with.'

I looked him in the eye and the realisation hit me like a brick. He wanted this finished and he didn't want us looking at the Nightingales. They were an influential family. They had links with senior people. Richard didn't want us digging around there when we already had our man.

I didn't bother to argue. But I wasn't about to let Violet down.

I pushed open the door to my room, coffee in hand, and was surprised to see Fiona and Craig in the corner by the window. Fiona was leaning against the wall and Craig was looming over her. I heard him tell her, 'Stop saying I'm cheating on my wife. It's not true.'

'Okay.' I stuck my coffee on my desk. 'What's going on and why are you in my room?'

They turned and looked at me with the expressions of dogs caught digging up the flower beds.

'We've all been covering Craig's fat arse with his wife,' Fiona snapped. 'And I'm sick of it.'

Craig spun round to look at her. 'Shut the fuck up. You don't know anything about me.'

I sighed and sat down at my desk.

Fiona narrowed her eyes, and I got a sense of the strength that lay under that amenable exterior. 'I know what I saw,' she said. 'I know you lied.'

Craig advanced on me, approaching belly-first. 'She's got it all wrong.'

I wanted to leave them to their stupid row. To go and see what Bex knew and find out more about Kirsty. I had a very bad feeling about Kirsty. I didn't know how it related to Violet and I couldn't justify any of it to Richard, but even though I'd been wrong about my dad and Daniel, my hunches had a pretty good track record. I was determined to pursue this one.

'Okay,' I said. 'You need to explain now or drop this forever, because we're all sick to death of it.'

'I don't like to see women being cheated on.' Fiona crossed her arms.

Craig lurched forward and slammed his hand on my desk. 'I'm not fucking cheating on my wife.'

My ex had been like this, and to some extent, so had my dad. Those moments of almost-violence. Not touching me but using

335

his physicality, so it was virtually impossible not to shrink in on myself – to grow smaller and take up less space. I wasn't putting up with it from Craig. 'Get your hand off my desk and sit down in that chair,' I said.

Craig angrily did as he was told. I half-hoped this would be the day my guest chair finally collapsed, but it held firm.

Fiona shifted round so she could look at Craig.

I felt like teacher.

'Just tell her,' Craig said. 'And then I'll explain how nosy cows can be wrong.'

'I was in Sheffield and I saw him leaving this woman's house,' Fiona said. 'But when I asked him what he was doing, he lied about it. And he's obviously been lying to his wife, saying he got that injury on his face at work. So now we don't know what to say to her. Do you like being beaten up by prostitutes, Craig? Is that it?'

Craig sighed. 'She's a counsellor, Fiona. I've been seeing her about some stuff I've had going on. Stuff I didn't want to discuss with my wife. I didn't particularly want to discuss my personal problems with you either. Happy now?'

'Not really,' Fiona said. 'Why didn't you want to tell your wife? She's worried about you.'

'That's my business.'

'But, Craig,' I said. 'She does have a habit of involving us.'

He rolled his eyes. 'I know. I've spoken to her about that. It won't happen again.'

50

Bex pulled open the door. 'Oh. Hello.'

'How are you?' I said.

'Oh, you know. Recovering from nearly dying in a fire. My daughter and two friends from childhood are dead, and my sister's in a coma. I've had better weeks, to be perfectly honest.'

So she'd heard Daniel was dead. 'I'm sorry,' I said. 'Could I come in a moment?'

She took a step back. 'Of course. Dad's driven up to the far pig barn.'

She led me into the kitchen and we sat at the table. The heat in there was oppressive, and Bex looked like all the life had been kicked out of her. Her hands were bandaged. 'Did you get checked over at the hospital?' I said.

She nodded. 'I'm fine. Lungs okay. Fingers and hands will mend. But was it really Daniel? Did he kill Violet and Gary?'

My phone rang. I hesitated. It was Fiona. 'I'd better take this,' I said, and picked up.

'We've got some results back on that barn fire,' Fiona said. 'Apparently there are some concerns.'

'What kind of concerns?'

'That it might have been started deliberately. It's not clear cut. There are no traces of accelerant, but they want to talk to Kirsty about why there was so much straw around. The origin was the wildfire, which had spread to the woods nearby. But there was effectively a trail of straw from the woods to the barn. The fire bloke said he thought the insurance assessor would be pretty interested in that. It was an old barn, and it could be quite convenient that it's burnt down. The barn and all the livestock are well insured, apparently.'

'Well, he can't talk to Kirsty right now. She's in a coma.' I mouthed an apology to Bex, and walked out into the hallway, shoving the door shut behind me with a foot. I lowered my voice. 'So we might be talking arson?'

'Possibly. They have concerns. And, Meg, there's another thing. Someone had listened to the message that Bex left on Kirsty's landline, saying she was in the barn.'

'What? Who listened?'

'Kirsty was the only one home.'

'Oh God.' I paused and then whispered, 'If it's arson and Kirsty was the only one around, and she knew Bex was in the barn …' I took myself further down the hallway, further from Bex.

'I looked at the house-to-house again,' Fiona said. 'There was a woman who remembered Kirsty having problems as a child. Behaviour problems. She saw a psychiatrist. But nobody talked about it because she was Tony Nightingale's daughter, and he's like the country gent round here. The landowner. It was a throwaway comment, but it totally made my ears prick.'

'What kind of behaviour problems?' I already had my suspicions.

'It's not very clear. Even now you can see people don't want to talk about it.'

It was a thing I'd noticed in some Derbyshire villages. A deference to the land-owning classes. As if the fact that your great-grandfather made a load of money exploiting peasants somehow made you more worthy. I remembered Gary's wife, Mandy, saying Tony Nightingale had given money to the abattoir. She'd put it down to him wanting to keep everything nice in the village. But what if there was more to it than that? Was Tony paying a price for the villagers' silence about his daughter?

I wasn't surprised Kirsty had had behaviour problems as a child. I'd sensed something off with her from the start. The question was how these 'behavioural problems' manifested now.

'Thanks, Fiona. Can you make sure we've got a good police presence at the hospital with Kirsty, in case she comes round.'

I ended the call and walked back to the kitchen. Bex was sitting at the table staring into space. She jumped when I came in.

'What's going on?'

In my mind's eye, I saw Kirsty's coldness when watching her barn burn, her attitude to her daughter and her sister, Gwen Twigg's fear. I replayed the comments from people in the village about her. She could easily have killed Daniel by doctoring his painkillers, since she supplied them, but there was absolutely no evidence linking her to Gary's death – or Violet's, assuming she was dead.

'Bex,' I said. 'Have you ever had any concerns about your sister's behaviour?'

'My sister? Not really.'

'Did your dad ever have concerns? We've been told he took her to see a psychiatrist when she was a child.'

Bex frowned and shifted away from me. 'No. But if it's Dad, he'd have kept records. Follow me.'

She led me down a panelled corridor and into a musty-smelling study. The walls were lined with books – mainly leather-bound with gold lettering on their spines.

'Dad's meticulous,' Bex said. 'Everything filed away in alphabetically arranged square-cut folders. If Kirsty went to a psychiatrist, he'll have a file. And I know where to find the key to his filing cabinet. I saw when I spent that summer here.'

Bex walked across the room to an antique bureau, pulled out a false base from an inner compartment and fished out a key. She leaned over and unlocked an ugly modern filing cabinet. 'Bingo.'

She opened the top drawer and flipped through some files. 'God, here's one on me.' She fished out a slim beige file and opened it. 'Letters. From Aunt Janet.'

Bex put the file on a leather-topped desk by the window and read from one of the letters. '*Doing well. Better to keep her away from her sister.* What the hell …'

'Your aunt's talking about keeping you away from your sister?' I said.

Bex turned to me and frowned. 'I heard her on the phone once saying that. I thought they wanted to keep Kirsty away from me. I always thought I was the bad one.'

She shoved the file down and rummaged again in the cabinet. Found another file. It was stuffed so full, she struggled to wrench it out with her bandaged hands. 'Ow. This file's huge.'

I suspected this was like with medical records: a fat file was not a good sign.

Bex sank onto the floor, put the file down and allowed the papers to spill out. I sat next to her, shifting my dodgy ankle to get comfy.

340

Words caught my eye on one of the papers: *Callous and unemotional (CU). Non-responsive to punishment. Therapy likely to be ineffective.*

I caught sight of movement at the window but when I looked up, there was no one there.

Bex said, 'But Kirsty was always the golden girl.' She rummaged through the papers. 'My God, all these letters from psychiatrists. What was the matter with her?'

We scrabbled around in the paperwork for a few minutes and then Bex grabbed her phone and tapped a few keys.

She looked up at me, her face drained of blood. 'I've just googled it.'

A thudding noise came from outside. A car door banging shut.

'Shit, it's Dad.' Bex jumped up, hurriedly put the files back together, and stuffed them into the cabinet. 'Come to the kitchen.'

We jumped up, raced to the kitchen and threw ourselves down at the table. A shadow appeared at the door. Tony Nightingale pushed it open and came into the room. He smelled of pig. 'Oh, hello there,' he said. 'Terrible about Daniel. Do you have news on the investigation?'

'It's ongoing,' I said. 'We'll keep you informed.'

'Would you like a drink?'

'Coffee,' Bex said. 'I need coffee. And put some whisky in it.'

'Yes, coffee would be great, thanks,' I said.

'Go into the drawing room,' Tony said. 'I'll bring it through.'

I followed Bex down the hallway into a large room lined with portraits of judgemental old men, and stuffed with antique and no doubt priceless furniture. I sat on a small sofa which had clearly been designed for scrawny Victorians who saw sitting down as a moral weakness. Bex sat on a second sofa by a bay window. A beam of sunlight made a bright, shimmery lozenge on the parquet floor. I felt a glimmer of hope that I hadn't been wrong about Daniel after all. Maybe it had never been him. Maybe he'd been framed.

Tony appeared a few minutes later, handed us the drinks, and headed for the door.

'Hang on!' When Bex raised her voice, I could hear the croak in it from shouting and breathing smoke. 'Dad, hang on. We need to talk.'

'Oh dear, that sounds ominous.' He came back into the room and sat on a wing-back chair.

'What's the matter with Kirsty?' Bex said.

'You know what's the matter with her – she's lying in a coma in the hospital.'

Bex sighed. 'Have you been honest with me about anything, Dad? In my whole life?'

Tony was very still, looking at Bex through narrowed eyes. 'Honest about what?' I felt like an intruder. This was a drama playing out between Bex and her father. But I needed to know. What if Kirsty was behind everything and Daniel had just been a pawn? I sipped my coffee. He'd put whisky in mine too, which was welcome.

'About Kirsty,' Bex said. 'A massive file full of letters from psychiatrists – and I know nothing. So what the hell's the matter with her?'

'Why are you doing this, Bex? Your sister is fighting for her life.'

'Because I want the truth! What's wrong with her that you never told me?'

'She's fine now. She's grown out of it. She had some problems as a child, that's all.'

'What problems?'

'I dealt with it. She's fine.'

'It says she had *callous and unemotional traits*. It doesn't sound fine. It sounds decidedly *not-fine* to me.'

'It sounds worse than it was,' Tony said. 'Our family have always been unemotional. That's why we've been so successful in business. You can't succeed in this world if you spend your whole time worrying about other people. You can't breed pigs for a living if you're over-emotional. The over-emotional children are the worst. Daniel was one of those. And now look what he's done. Killed Violet and Gary.'

'I never knew Daniel was difficult.'

'You weren't here.'

Bex gulped the last of her drink and slammed the cup onto the antique table next to her. 'No! Because you sent me away! You didn't want me.'

'It wasn't like that.'

'So what was it like, Dad?'

'Kirsty was slower to develop empathy than most children. She didn't respond well to punishment. But I know now that punishment's not a good way to change behaviour. She forced me to realise that. To find a better way.'

'For God's sake, Dad, I'm a dog trainer. I know punishment's not a good way to change behaviour.'

'Yes. Well, Kirsty is why I got interested in that kind of behaviour modification in the first place.' He wiped his forehead. 'If you treat these children the right way, they turn out fine. That's what happened with Kirsty.'

'*These* children?'

'Children with ...' He touched his mouth as if he didn't like

343

saying the words. 'Callous and unemotional traits. They find it challenging to think long-term, and they don't respond well to punishment, but they can learn how to behave well in order to get what they want. If you reward good behaviour, it becomes a habit. Like flushing the lavatory. Even *using* the lavatory – children don't toilet-train themselves. You know all this from your dog training. A dog trained with positive reinforcement becomes a good citizen. The good habits become ingrained. The dog doesn't avoid chasing the cat out of any moral imperative or because it's suddenly developed empathy for the cat. It does it because that behaviour has been rewarded so many times it becomes a habit. It's the same with these children. When they're well brought up, they often end up very successful in politics or business. As your sister is, in fact. It's only if they're brought up in a toxic environment that they become …'

'Become what, Dad?'

I knew very well what these children become if they're brought up in a toxic environment.

'Nothing. Your sister was well brought up. She's fine now. All this is ancient history.'

'You clicker-trained my sister?'

'In a way. But isn't that what we try to do with all children? Reward good behaviour? Callous and unemotional children force you to be better at it, like the more challenging dogs do.'

Bex swallowed. 'I thought I was the problem. You kept her and sent me away.'

'I'm sorry, Bex. That wasn't it at all. I sent you away for your own good.'

'For my own good?' Bex scrambled to her feet, puffing with the effort. 'What did you think she might do?'

'She's fine now. She's had no problems for years. This is twenty years ago we're talking about.'

Bex stared at her father. The air felt heavy. 'Are you sure, Dad?' she said. 'Are you absolutely sure?'

He fiddled with a Royal Crown Derby paperweight on the table beside him. 'She was just a little rebellious, Bex. And a thrill-seeker. Don't start thinking all sorts of terrible things about your sister.'

'I googled it, Dad. I know what it means. *Callous and unemotional traits.* I googled it and the first article was called, "When Your Child Is a Psychopath". A psychopath, Dad? You know what else it said? "The condition has long been considered untreatable. Experts can spot it in a child as young as three or four." That's what I found out.' She turned to me. 'That's right isn't it?'

I gave her a non-committal look.

'It's not what you think,' Tony said.

'Fucking hell,' Bex said. 'Aunt Janet told me about the bad people in Gritton, the Pale Child, the boy who died. Was that all Kirsty's doing? Was that why I had to live with Janet? Was Kirsty dangerous?'

'You've got it all wrong.' Tony stood and walked stiffly from the room.

I took a gulp of coffee and looked around. I felt unaccountably tired. A photograph in a gold frame lay face-down on the table by my sofa. I propped it back up. A young woman who looked like Violet. But paler than Violet. She was beautiful in an other-worldly way. Her eyes were brilliant blue, her hair very blonde. My hand shook as I put down my empty coffee mug.

Bex had leaned back in her chair, eyes closed. A grandfather clock ticked.

My phone buzzed. A text from Jai: *Strange result – the boy buried in the woods is Violet's father, as suspected. But he's also related to Bex Smith. Her full brother. Not the twin who died age 3. Looks like she had another brother we didn't know about. Estimated age at death: 13–14.*

I stared at the phone. Another brother? Another brother who Bex didn't know existed? Who dressed in old-fashioned girls' clothes. Who *raped* Bex – his own sister – and fathered Violet. My head spun with it.

Tony was in the doorway. He saw I'd been looking at the photograph, and said, 'Don't you think she's lovely? Like Bex and Violet. She was beautiful then and she's still beautiful now.'

I was feeling woozy. 'Who is she?'

My head fell back before he had time to answer.

51

I opened my eyes. My head was pounding as if it had been beaten. I blinked and tried to focus.

I was in a modern-looking living room, dimly lit by a lamp on a small table. There were no windows. I was lying on a fabric sofa, its weave soft under my skin. The air smelled of vanilla. A faint noise that sounded like drilling drifted down from above.

I dragged myself into a sitting position. There was a kitchen area at the end of the room. Sleek, modern units. What had happened? My mind was in a mush. I'd been with Bex and Tony.

What had Jai's text said? I held my head in my hands and let my thoughts crystallise. Bex had had a second brother. Not her twin who died. Another brother.

I couldn't fit it together in my head. My brain wasn't functioning.

The sound of breathing to my left.

I spun round. There was another sofa. A person slumped on it. 'What …' I peered into the gloom. 'Bex?'

She came into focus. Wild hair, bright eyes.

'Bex! What the hell … Where are we?'

She looked as groggy as I felt. 'I don't know.'

I shook my head. Everything was too confusing. 'What's going on?' I stood, teetering and nearly falling, and then wobbled my way to the far side of the room, where there was a door that looked like an external one. I pulled at the handle, but nothing moved. It wasn't a normal door. It was solid metal. The kind of thing you see in prisons. A thread of panic started forming in my stomach.

I walked back to the sofa and sank down. If only everything didn't hurt so much. I clutched my head. 'He drugged us. Why did he do that?'

'I don't know and I'm so tired,' Bex said.

I turned and looked into her eyes. I could see her more clearly now I'd adjusted to the gloomy light. Was she part of this, whatever *this* was?

A sound from behind me. I turned. There were two doors. Internal doors. One of them opened. Someone was there. A woman in a long nightshirt. A finely chiselled face. Blonde hair with streaks of grey. The woman from the photo in Tony's front room, but older.

She turned to look behind her. Said a few words in a language I didn't understand. It sounded Eastern European.

The door creaked open wider, revealing the room behind. A bedroom. It was dark but I could see the outline of someone sitting on a single bed. A young woman. Slim and pale with light blonde hair, wearing an old-fashioned nightdress, like the one the Pale Child wore. She must have sensed me watching her. She looked up, straight at me, and then shrank away, curling her legs in front of her and gripping them to her chest.

The older woman walked slowly towards us, pulling the door

shut behind her. She was an odd mixture of young and old – her face smooth and unlined, her gait stiff. She came over and sat next to Bex. Bex froze as if scared, but I felt as if I was in the presence of someone wise, like a healer or a Zen master.

The woman reached her hand towards Bex's face. Bex shrank away.

'Rebecca?' the woman said. 'My baby Rebecca?'

Bex was completely still, staring at her. Nobody seemed to be breathing.

The woman whispered words I didn't understand, staring at Bex, her eyes impossibly wide.

Finally Bex softened. Burst into tears. 'Mum?'

The woman reached and pulled Bex to her and they sobbed. I couldn't stop staring. How could this woman be Bex's mother? Bex's mother went back to Ukraine thirty years ago.

'Nina?' I said.

The woman nodded. 'I am Nina. I was Nina.'

Eventually Bex pulled away. 'What's happening?' she said. 'Where are we?'

Nina blinked back tears. 'He wants to keep us safe.'

My brain didn't want to accept this, even though things had started slotting into place when I'd seen the photograph of the woman in Tony's living room. The woman with the pale hair.

Bex stood and took a few strides away, then came back. 'No. No. You're not saying he … You're not saying you've been … here? Oh my *God*!'

'He didn't want me to take you to Ukraine,' Nina said. 'He didn't think you'd have a good life. You or your brother and sister.'

Bex was breathing heavily. 'My sister, yes, Kirsty – you wanted to take her too?'

There was a long silence. 'No. Not Kirsty. She would be better here. Your other brother and sister weren't yet born.'

Maybe it was the drugs Tony had given me. Nothing made any sense. 'The young woman in the room behind?' I whispered. 'Is she …'

'Sofia,' Nina said. 'She's scared of you. Thinks you're the TV people. She's only ever seen other people on the TV.'

Bex spoke so quietly I could barely hear. 'I thought you left me.'

'I never left you,' Nina said. 'I would never have left you. He put me in here. Me and my unborn babies. He thought he was protecting us.'

'I can't …' Bex put her head in her hands.

'There was a boy too,' Nina said. 'Sofia's brother.'

I blinked a couple of times. Tried to clear my head. I didn't want to believe it, even though the solution to the mystery of the Pale Child was starting to click into place in my mind.

'Is that his daughter?' I whispered. 'Has he kept his daughter in this room for her whole life?'

And there had been a boy. I remembered the text from Jai. The bones in the wood. Bex's brother. Bex's rapist. Violet's father. The Pale Child.

'Tony likes us to wear white clothes,' Nina said, 'because Tim was wearing dark clothes when he was run over. White clothes keep you safe. He gives us vitamins. And makes sure we look after our teeth. He has medicine for the pigs that he gives us if we need it.'

'Oh my God, Nina,' I said. 'You've been here over thirty years.' I sank back on the sofa, head pounding.

Bex looked up. 'I should have realised. Ever since Tim died, he's been obsessed with protecting everyone. He's been doing it for years. Protecting piglets from their mothers, protecting the children in the village, protecting me from my sister. It's what he does.'

52

'We've got to find a way out of here,' I said. 'How can we get out?' I was feeling better. Whatever he'd drugged me with was wearing off.

'We can't,' Nina said.

'He has to come some time. I'm going to kill him.' I jumped up and walked over to the kitchen area. Pulled open drawers. 'There are knives here. He's left knives. Between all of us we can overpower him easily.'

'We have knives now because he knows we can't escape,' Nina said. 'He's made it so we can't escape. Because we managed to get Ivan out. Twice. The first time, Kirsty found him and brought him back.'

Despite everything I knew about Kirsty, this made me cold to the core. 'Kirsty knows about this?'

Nina nodded. 'Tony told me she found out when Ivan escaped the first time. He wanted to upset me that my own daughter would know, but not save me. Because he was angry I made Ivan escape through the old lead mining passages under the barn. We would have all escaped but Sofia was too scared of the dark tunnels.' She sighed. 'It was when Ivan and Sofia were nine and Kirsty was fifteen. She is my daughter, but Kirsty is not right. She is the reason I wanted to take you away.'

And that must have been when Daniel's brother, Charlie, saw the Pale Child. Ivan. In a white dress to keep him safe. And then Charlie fell into the reservoir spillway. How convenient.

'After that, Tony closed the tunnels, but Ivan managed to escape a second time. He pushed past his father, and Tony couldn't catch him. But he never came back and I worry what happened because he didn't save us.' Nina wrinkled her brow. 'I pray he escaped but could not find his way back to us. I pray he is alive.'

I couldn't tell Nina and Bex that he was dead. That his bones were buried in the woods. That he'd raped Bex, his own sister, and fathered her child. Fathered Violet.

'How can we get out?' I said. 'There must be a way.'

'There isn't,' Nina said. 'He has codes and the locks work with his fingerprints. And he microchips us.' She lifted her T-shirt and pointed to a scar on her upper arm.

Bex slammed her hand against her own arm. Lifted her T-shirt. A patch of blood. 'Oh my God. He's done me.'

I touched my own upper arms but there was nothing.

'Maybe he's not planning to keep you,' Bex said.

The implications of that churned in my mind. He wasn't planning to keep me. He'd kill me, and make it look like an accident, or suicide. I'd be dead and he'd keep Bex in here with her mother and her sister. Bex who'd told her clients she'd be away for a while.

I turned to Nina. 'What happens if you try to get out? With that thing in your arm?'

She sighed. 'He has a method for … He says it is for humanely … putting us down.'

This felt like a dream. A nightmare. I could barely take it in. *Humanely putting you down?*

'We're below the pig barn here,' Nina said. 'He has a system to feed carbon monoxide into this area.'

'Carbon monoxide?'

'It's a good way to go, he says.'

I looked at her face. 'My God.'

'If any of the microchips go through the doorway, out of this underground place, it closes the vents and activates the carbon monoxide.'

'Fucking hell.'

'Or he can activate it from the barn above. With a code. He told us so we don't try to escape.'

I shook my head. 'Christ, Nina.'

'I should have realised,' Bex said. 'All those years he didn't want me in Gritton. He couldn't risk me finding out. But he was also protecting me. He knew if I stayed, he'd end up putting me in here.' She looked at Nina. 'I'm so sorry. I hated you for leaving me, and all the time you were in here. If only I hadn't been so stupid.'

'But did nobody report you missing, Nina?' I said.

'I had no close relatives at home, and my cousins and friends thought I was happy here. Everyone here thought I'd gone back to Ukraine. And called me a bad mother.'

I shook my head in disbelief. 'You need to tell us everything you know. We have to work out what's going on in his fucked-up head and find a way to make him let us out of here.'

Nina shrugged. 'He thinks it's okay to keep us in here. Like the pigs in the crates. The crates stop them hurting their babies by accident. Same with us, he thinks. He stopped me hurting my babies by taking them to Ukraine. In his brain that was how it worked. Sometimes too much freedom is a bad thing.'

I could hear my own breathing. 'He thinks keeping his family in here is like keeping pigs in crates?'

She nodded. 'We have TV. All the books. Good food. Medicine. Nobody gets shouted at for coming from another place. No children are run over by a car.'

'But …' I didn't know what to say.

'He must know it's wrong,' Bex said. 'But he can't help himself.'

Nina turned to Bex. 'I never thought it was you. Never you. Always Kirsty with the blue on her hands.'

'What blue hands?'

'When Tim died. On the road.'

Bex clenched her face as if trying not to cry. 'I thought you blamed me and that's why you left and Dad sent me to Aunt Janet's.'

Nina shook her head. 'There was blue on Kirsty. Kirsty was bad. I wanted to take you home. Away from here. Away from Kirsty.'

'Kirsty put the blue paint on my hands?' Bex said. 'So I'd get blamed for letting Tim out on to the road?'

A noise from the direction of the external door.

I jumped to my feet, grabbed the smallest kitchen knife and shoved it into my pocket.

The whoosh of a door pushing open.

A man walked in, his face unclear in the dim light from the lamp. Tony Nightingale.

My gut twisted.

'Tony,' I said. 'I know why you're doing this. You're keeping your family safe from harm. We'll take that into account. But it's over now. People are looking for me. They'll come here and find me.'

There was no response. He looked through me as if I hadn't spoken.

'If you let us go now, everything will be so much better for you. Everyone will understand then that you meant no harm.'

'Dad!' Bex stood too. 'She's right. You need to let us go. You can't get away with this. It can't go on any longer.'

He seemed to see us for the first time. 'Bex, you know I can't let you go.' He sounded sad and confused. 'I knew if you came back to Gritton, I'd have to keep you. You'll stay with the others, but first I need to work out what to do with her.'

'Don't be crazy, Dad. You can't keep me. People will look for me!'

'I have your phone. And if people do look for you, Bex, I'll tell them you've gone away for a while.'

'Ugh, this is ridiculous,' Bex said. 'You know you won't get away with it, right?'

A flash of doubt crossed Tony's face. He knew he was in too deep now. He knew he wasn't going to get away with this. But that wasn't a good thing. The statistics on family annihilations were pressing themselves into my mind. It was almost always men who killed themselves and their children. Men who couldn't see a way forward. If Tony realised there was no way back from this, would he take us all with him?

He pointed at me. 'I don't think I can keep her. But obviously I can't let her go.'

'Dad, she's a detective. Someone will come for her. You can't hurt her. You're not that person. Let us go and we won't tell anyone about the others. I promise. If you let us go now, you can still keep them. Otherwise it's all going to be over, and what will happen to your family then? They won't cope.'

He shook his head. 'You know I can't do that, Bex. And I'm afraid I don't believe you.'

A crash from behind me. I spun round. It had come from the room I hadn't seen inside. The other bedroom, I assumed. The door banged open and a teenager shot out. With a shaved head, but dressed like the others in a long, white garment.

53

The teenager saw me and ran to me. Grabbed my arm. Screamed, 'Help! Help me! You've got to get me out of here!'

'Oh my God,' I said.

Tony watched with cold eyes. 'Don't be silly, child. You're safe here.'

'Violet,' I said gently, as she clutched my arm and sobbed. I felt a glimmer of joy that Violet was alive. The bloody Scottish sheep wasn't black after all. But I realised I was crying too, because how could we get her out? Tony was going to kill me and keep her and the rest of her family in this luxury prison under the pig barn.

'How could I let you go, Violet?' Tony said. 'Once you told me you were famous on the internet. Parading around in a bikini. As soon as you told me that, I knew I'd have to protect you. It was a rash decision, but how could I not?'

Violet turned to him and screamed, 'I don't want your fucking protection, you fucking psychopathic bastard!'

'You have to stay here with the others, Violet,' Tony said. 'But the detective can't be with you.'

Violet sobbed and grasped my arm. 'He shaved my hair off.

He took blood from me. I came round and he had my blood in a massive syringe. And he stole my clothes. And he was talking on the phone to Kirsty about it. What was he doing to me? Why did he do that?'

He was talking to Kirsty. Could she have masterminded everything? I pictured Daniel living in his caravan, building his rock sculptures, drinking tea with oat milk, desperately trying to do the right thing. Trying to make up for past sins. Had he been Kirsty's sacrificial lamb?

Tony fished a set of handcuffs from the pocket of his coat and pointed at me. 'I need to put these on you.'

I hesitated. Violet started backing away from me, crying. The others stared wide-eyed. Tony was banking on the fact that if I killed him now, we couldn't get out. I held out my arms.

'Hands behind your back,' he said.

I reluctantly let him cuff my hands behind me. He pulled me towards the door.

'No!' Violet screamed. 'Don't leave us!'

'Let him take her,' Bex said under her breath. 'It's our best chance.'

Tony pulled me towards the door. Pressed his thumb onto a pad. The door swished open. We both went through and it closed behind us, leaving us at the base of a set of stairs. We climbed them, me desperately trying to make a plan. I wasn't in a strong position. The knife was in my pocket but I couldn't get it out.

At the top of the stairs was another door. Tony reached up to press a code into a keypad. I tried to see the numbers he pressed, but he shielded them from me. The second door opened, and we were out. In a large gloomy barn that smelled strongly of pig.

I swung my leg back and kicked at Tony's knees with all my might. He yelled and crumpled forward. I kicked out at him again, but with my hands behind my back, it was hard to put any force behind it. He yanked at my arms and dragged me towards a wall. A creature squealed. The barn contained pigs. Pigs in cages. I lost focus for a moment and Tony shoved me to the floor. Attached to the wall was a chain, on the end of which was a single cuff. There was brick dust on the floor below. That must have been the drilling earlier. He'd been preparing to chain me up.

Tony was fiddling behind my back, trying to get the cuff onto my wrist. He was struggling to get it on with the handcuffs already there. I lifted my foot and kicked at his head, but he managed to duck.

He grabbed my torso and slammed my head into the wall. Everything went dark.

I opened my eyes. I must have blacked out for a few moments. Pain filled my consciousness. I was aware of nothing except how much my head hurt.

I forced myself to focus. The pigs were making frantic grunting noises and gnawing at the bars of their cages.

I could feel metal encircling my wrist. I yanked at it. He'd cuffed me to the wall, but he'd had to remove the handcuffs. I now had one hand free. My head was still spinning and so painful I felt it would explode, but this was my chance.

Tony was checking my wrist. He didn't notice my other hand moving. I inched it forward and grasped the knife. Happy that I was firmly attached to the wall, he gave the cuff one last pull and then shoved something into his coat pocket.

I whipped the knife forward, rammed it into his stomach, gave it a twist, and pulled it out.

At first, he didn't react. Then slowly he looked down, registering the red bloom which was spreading outwards on his shirt like ink on blotting paper, part-hidden by his coat. He shuffled away from me, an expression of surprise on his face. He crashed into the corner of one of the pigs' cages, but somehow managed to stay on his feet.

I watched transfixed as he dragged off his coat and dropped it on the floor. He pressed his hand flat against his stomach. Blood was everywhere. 'What have you done?' he gasped. 'They'll starve to death if I die.' He lurched over to the far barn wall. Through the gloom, I could see that he was leaning over, tapping on a keypad. My heart pounded. He was typing in a code. Oh God. The carbon monoxide.

I clutched my knife, stood up, and tried to follow him, but the metal cuff was around my wrist. I yanked at it, but couldn't get it off. I was chained to the wall.

Tony stopped typing on the keypad and there was a deep click, followed by a hissing and a whirring noise. Still clutching his stomach, he slipped through the barn door and slid it closed behind him.

I screamed. 'Bex! Violet! Nina!'

Frantic voices from below me, muffled and hard to make out.

A faint ripping noise, and then Bex's voice. 'Can you hear me now? The vents are solid metal, and he's sound-insulated them. I've ripped the cladding off, but there's a piece of plastic between us still.'

'I can hear you. I stabbed him. He's badly injured. But he's put the code in, Bex. I think it's the carbon monoxide. I can hear it hissing.'

A pause. Then Bex: 'Can you get out and get help?'

'He chained me up. I can't get away.'

More muffled voices.

Beside me was a large gas cylinder. A tube extended between it and a sealed hole in the floor. The cylinder was labelled 'CO'. Carbon monoxide. The hissing was coming from it. Carbon monoxide was flowing from the cylinder and presumably into the sealed basement area.

I shouted, 'Is the gas coming out? I can hear it.'

Muffled voices. 'Yes. We're trying to block the inlets but there are lots.'

'I stabbed him,' I said. 'It's my fault. He's done it so that if he dies you don't starve to death.'

My eyes had adjusted to the gloom. I peered down at my wrist. The cuff looked unbreakable. It was very clear he'd planned to put me here. But why? Was it so he could work out how to get rid of me in a way which looked like an accident? So nobody would come looking and find his little family.

I tried again to pull my hand through the cuff. I had slim hands. But it wouldn't go. Not even close. I yanked at the chain, but it was firmly attached. I looked around for an implement to smash it with, but there was nothing within reach. Just a couple of coats hanging on hooks, and a pile of bagged pig pellets.

I pulled to the end of my chain and lay down, twisting to push my feet towards the blood-soaked coat Tony had discarded. I was sure he'd put the key to my cuff in the pocket. But I couldn't reach it. Even stretched out fully, I was nowhere near. 'I can't reach. I can't reach his coat. The key's in his coat but it's too far away.'

The pigs had calmed down and were grunting softly and shifting side-to-side, which was as much movement as they could manage in their tiny cages. The cages had metal dividers which would separate the mothers from their babies once they were born. Perhaps I could use one of the dividers to reach Tony's coat? But without even trying, I could see they weren't big enough to bridge the gap between me and the coat.

Maybe Jai or Fiona would come looking for me. Surely I'd been gone a while? But they weren't expecting me back at the station. If Dad had still been at my house, he'd have wondered where I was. But he wasn't at my house and he certainly wouldn't be wondering why I wasn't answering his calls.

Nobody would be missing me.

It hit me then. This was it. I would die in this barn with these desperate people and equally desperate pigs.

At least Hamlet was with Hannah. He'd be okay. Maybe she'd keep him.

The carbon monoxide tube was within my reach. If I could pull out the tube and plug the hole, I could stop the carbon monoxide getting to the people trapped below. I could use the coats to block the hole. If I did that, I'd be poisoned instead. 'I can save you,' I shouted. 'I can pull the tube out.'

Voices from below. 'But then it'll go into the top barn and you'll die.'

'If he survives, he'll kill me anyway. At least this way I'll have carbon monoxide in my bloodstream. He can try and make it look like an accident, but he won't get away with it. And then they'll come and find you.'

'No! You can't do that.'

'There are four of you,' I said. 'And only one of me. And six pigs.'

I wondered if I could make myself do it. Pull the tube so the carbon monoxide killed me and the pigs instead of the people

363

below. If Tony died, I thought we'd eventually be found, but it would be too late for me. If Tony didn't die after all, he'd come back and kill me and dispose of my body and keep the others. If I'd breathed in carbon monoxide, he'd have to be really clever. Make it look like my Victorian boiler did me in, perhaps? I doubted he'd get away with it.

I thought Bex was considering what I'd said. If I was going to die, I wanted to take Tony Nightingale down with me. I clutched my knife and remembered another case I'd worked on where a murder victim had managed to communicate that it wasn't an accident. I'd do the same. I'd carve it on my skin. Under my arm where Tony wouldn't look. I'd carve a message that told them it was him and made them look in this barn. My body would be the clue that made them find the others. It was almost poetic.

A voice from below: Bex. 'Don't you dare save us and kill yourself. We don't want this life! We'd rather die.'

Was that what they all thought? Or just Bex? Nina and Sofia had already survived thirty years of captivity.

Bex's voice came louder from below. 'Can you reach to let any of the pigs out?'

I looked at the pigs in their cages. I was chained to a wall in a dark barn but I still had more freedom than the pigs. I stared into the eyes of the closest. She gazed back. There was a patch on her face. She had an intelligent look. A creature in a tiny cage with such an intelligent eye. There were too many horrors bound up in that thought. 'Yes,' I said. 'I can reach the nearest one. But she can't escape. The barn door's closed.'

And then I remembered. The pigs had been taught to fetch. 'The pigs …' I said. 'Could the pigs help us?'

A murmuring from below and then Bex spoke again. 'What's within your reach?'

I looked around me. 'There are some bags of stuff. Pig food, I think. And a couple of coats hanging behind me. And a few empty hessian sacks.'

'Have you ever trained an animal?'

I looked at the pig, the huge pig, and felt a flush of adrenaline in my stomach. 'I clicker-trained my cat to do a high five.' I pictured neat little Hamlet raising his paw. A very different proposition to a pig the size of a small car.

'Can you hear me clearly? I'm right by the grille.' Bex's voice was quieter. Speaking rather than shouting, but I could hear her.

'Yes,' I said.

'Right. *Do not* mess with that carbon monoxide. We need you to be able to think. You're going to get us out of here. You and that pig.'

54

'These pigs can fetch,' Bex said. 'I know exactly what Dad taught them.'

'Right.' My voice came out as little more than a whisper.

'I'll coach you through it. We're going to get the pig to fetch Dad's coat. She's going to get us out of here. She's bloody well going to get us out of here.'

My breathing was coming fast. 'I'm not sure I can … She's massive.'

'Yes, you can do it.' Bex sounded confident, as if she'd switched to work-mode. This was what she did, and she was good at it.

My heart thudded steadily. If I diverted the carbon monoxide and Tony died, he'd be found and they'd look in the barn. If they found him quickly and the lower barn was reasonably airtight, the others would be saved. I'd be dead but they'd be saved. But if he survived and came back, he'd either kill them or they'd stay locked up, and Bex claimed they didn't want that life. Or if it took too long for people to come, everyone would die. I didn't have the energy to make the decision. I let Bex take over.

'You'll have to give me a running commentary,' Bex said, 'but I know you can do this.'

'What do I have to do?'

'You're going to release the pig, and you're going to reward her for touching one of Dad's coats. Use one of the ones behind you. Then you're going to move that coat towards the coat with the key in it, and reward her for touching that coat. Then you'll only reward her if she bites it. And then if she pulls at it. She can drag it to you.'

'Oh God.'

'Do you remember how you trained your cat to high five?'

'Yes.'

'Thank God you did that. You'll be fine. This is the same. But it will happen fast once you free her. She'll be excited and we need to tap into that. She can't get to the food, can she?'

'No, it's behind a barrier.'

'Okay, rip open one of the bags of feed, and put a load of pellets in your pocket. Leave the bag open so you can get more pellets. We've got no time to waste.'

'Okay.' It was like a dream I have where I'm about to do an exam but I'm completely unprepared and usually naked. This time I was completely unprepared and chained to a barn wall, surrounded by vast, scary pigs.

'She'll be free to wander,' Bex cautioned, 'so she needs to work out quickly that you're the source of rewards. Now get one of Dad's coats.'

I did that, reaching up awkwardly with my unchained arm. 'I've got it.'

'You're going to let her out, and then throw some food at her. Okay? Can you open the cage at the front and let her out? Stand back. She might be a bit over-excited. Can you imagine how you'd feel if you'd been trapped in there?'

I fiddled with the catch and pulled open the door of the cage nearest me.

The pig shot out and barged into me, knocking me off my feet. She was enormous and seemed completely unaware of me. The other pigs grunted and pushed at the fronts of their cages.

I scrambled up, bruised and now scared of this panicked animal. I told myself she was scared too. We needed to help each other get out of here.

The pig looked around the gloom of the barn. Her attention was everywhere but on me. She was heavily pregnant. Frighteningly big. She stood, listening. An ear flicked in my direction. I chucked a handful of food towards her. It landed on the concrete floor and the pig looked down at it warily. She didn't go for it immediately, but looked back up again. Although I was focused on the pig and on what Bex was saying, part of my brain kept telling me I might be about to die, and wondering if Mum would be okay. She'd have to cancel her trip to El Salvador.

'If she's too stressed, she won't eat,' Bex said. 'Which means we're pretty much screwed.'

Something in the pig's body softened and she reached down and snuffled on the ground, picking up the food.

'She's eating it!' I told Bex.

'Chuck her some more. She needs more time to settle.'

'Yes, okay. Except we don't have more time.'

'Well, do you have any better ideas?'

The pig ate and then looked up. Her body language had softened some more. I chucked a few pellets at her. She'd registered my presence. I made an effort to slow my breathing and project calmness towards her. I didn't know if it would help but it was making me feel better.

The pig shuffled in my direction. 'She's coming towards me,' I said. I wasn't scared of pigs, but this one was enormous and looked flighty, and I was chained to a wall.

'You need to get her to notice the dummy coat. Hold the coat out towards her.'

I held the coat out. 'She's not going to bite me, is she?'

No reply.

I shoved the coat at the pig and she initially jumped back, but then hesitated and stepped forward to sniff it. I clicked and threw food. I knew I needed to tell Bex what I was doing, but it was taking all my concentration watching the pig and rewarding her for doing what I wanted.

I rewarded the pig when she focused on the coat, or touched the coat. Once she even mouthed it.

'Put the coat on the floor,' Bex said. 'We need it to move towards Dad's coat, and we need her to bite it, so we can eventually get her to drag Dad's coat to you. She can do it, because she knows how to fetch a dog-toy.'

'Don't panic me! It's too complicated. But she's touching it.' I tried not to think about Tony out there. Patching up his wound. Coming back to finish the job he'd started. How could he have kept his family locked up for thirty years? Ivan had tried to escape, but had been so horrifically damaged by his life that he ended up raping Bex, his own sister. And Kirsty had known. I was sure now that Kirsty and Tony had killed to keep this secret. And my instincts had been right about Daniel after all. He'd been framed.

The pig snuffled at the coat on the floor. I rewarded her.

I knew the principles. We needed the pig to start biting the coat or she'd never pull it anywhere. But this was hard. I remembered with Hamlet. Not rewarding the paw movement he'd been rewarded for before. Waiting a little longer. Hoping he'd raise that little black-and-white paw higher so I could click and give him one of the Dreamies cat treats he loved so much. Thinking about Hamlet made me want to cry. Would Hannah want him? Or Mum? Because there was no way this insane plan was going to work. No way I was getting out of here alive.

'Don't be afraid to withhold the click,' Bex said. 'It might not be the best training, but biting's what a pig naturally does when she's frustrated.'

The pig bit the coat. Yes! I clicked and threw food, while in the back of my mind, I was wondering if I should have lived differently. Was Mum right when she said I was a workaholic? Should I have worked less and lived more? Seized opportunities for happiness? I thought of all Jai's subtle overtures that I'd ignored. Had I been wrong?

The pig bit the coat and inadvertently dragged it slightly towards me. My pulse quickened.

'She dragged it,' I said, 'but I need to get her to drag your dad's coat, not this dummy one.'

'Can you throw the dummy coat near to Dad's coat? Just keep away from her teeth.'

I picked up the coat and threw it close to Tony's discarded one. The pig was now totally focused on it. She knew it was the answer to getting food. She touched it, bit it, then pulled at it. She dragged it towards me. I could feel the excitement rising. For the first time, it occurred to me that this might actually work.

I threw the food nearer to Tony's coat. We were getting there, but it was taking too long. The carbon monoxide was flowing into the room below. I tried to slow my breathing. To stay calm.

The pig reached for her food and in doing so noticed Tony's coat. She froze. Confusion. Which coat should she focus on? She stood still. Thinking. She was going to panic.

'I think it's the blood,' I said. 'Your dad's coat's soaked in it. She's just standing there.'

'What's happening?' I could hear the anxiety in Bex's voice.

Then I heard someone moving outside the barn.

55

'Bex, are you okay?' I called. 'Are you still okay?'

Bex was losing some of her calm composure. 'We'll be fine. You have to keep going, Meg. All you can do is keep going.'

The pig twitched one ear towards Tony's blood-soaked coat. We were back on. My breath was coming fast and my heart pounding. I rewarded every tiny step the pig made. When she swivelled one eye towards the coat. When she twitched her nose at it. When she took a tentative step towards it.

In the background was the gentle hiss of the carbon monoxide being released into the sealed room below me.

The pig made a sharp movement and I clicked too soon. She hadn't been going for the coat.

The pig froze. Gave me a look as if to say, *You're the worst trainer ever, but I think I've got it.* Then she very deliberately leaned forward and bit Tony's coat. I felt like screaming, but I calmly clicked and threw a big handful of food at her.

'She bit your dad's coat,' I said.

There was no reply. The pig munched on the pellets.

I heard another noise outside the barn.

'Shit,' I said. 'I think he's coming back.'

I tried to control my breathing, keeping calm for the pig. She needed me to watch her every muscle twitch. My timing had to be perfect.

The pig snuffled into the coat, not biting at it but getting her face deep into its folds. I took a chance. Didn't click. The pig gave me a slightly pissed-off look and pawed at the coat. Oh God, another behaviour I didn't want. I didn't click. Couldn't speak. I tried not to listen to the sounds from outside the barn. To the hissing of the gas.

The pig bit the coat. Thank God. She bit and pulled. She dragged the coat slightly towards me.

Thankfully, the pig never tried dragging the coat in the wrong direction. She knew that good things were coming from me. She pulled it closer. And closer. I was ready to get it as soon as it came within reach.

'I think I can get it.' I was only talking to myself now. There were no more noises from below.

I shifted forward, quickly but smoothly. 'Oh my God,' I whispered. 'I've got it. I don't fucking believe it.' I threw a huge handful of pig food on the floor, scattering it for the pig to eat.

I dragged the coat to me and pulled the key from the pocket.

I fiddled with the key and eventually managed to shove it into my handcuff. It flipped open.

Hardly able to believe I was free, I crept to the other side of the barn and looked at the keypad. I didn't know how to shut the carbon monoxide off. And I couldn't get into the basement without knowing the code.

I ran to the edge of the barn, slid the door open an inch, and peered out. I was sure I'd heard noises from outside the barn a few minutes earlier. Tony was out there somewhere and I didn't know what state he was in. What's more, as a farmer, he most likely owned a shotgun.

The barn was isolated from the house, on the edge of the woods. It was approached by a dirt track that you could drive along, and Tony's car was parked at an angle with a door open. He was nearby.

I inched the barn door closed again, and crept back in to look for some kind of weapon.

The pig was still snuffling around hoovering up the last of the pellets. The other pigs were grunting softly, and the hissing was steady in the background.

The blood-soaked knife was on the floor where I'd dropped it when I'd stabbed Tony. I picked it up.

A noise outside.

I dashed back to the wall and slumped down where he'd chained me earlier. The knife was next to me, hidden from sight.

The barn door slid open.

Tony walked in. He was moving stiffly, and a bandage encased his middle. He was wearing a coat identical to the blood-soaked one on the floor. He must have had a few of them – standard-issue farmer-coats.

He was carrying a shotgun.

His eyes flicked to the pig, who was trying to get the remaining pellets, snuffling and stamping on the coat on the floor.

Could Tony see that the coat was closer than when he'd left, close enough for me to reach? He gave no indication that he'd noticed.

He walked over to me, holding the gun loosely. It hadn't occurred to him that I might not be chained any more.

I peered at the shotgun. It looked like the safety catch was on.

A noise from the cellar below. Tony turned towards it.

I hurled myself at him, knocking him to the floor. The gun fell and I grabbed it.

Tony struggled to his feet. Tried to lunge at me. I kicked him in the face and pointed the gun at him. I shifted away so he couldn't reach me, keeping the gun aimed at him.

'You're going to walk to the wall,' I said, 'and you're going to put that cuff on and lock it. The key's still in it. Go on. Move. I'm watching.'

He eyed me. I wasn't close enough that he could leap at me, or knock the gun from my hand.

He took a step towards me and held his hand out. 'No, come on, give me my gun.'

I thought of his wife downstairs, kept there for thirty years. His daughter who'd never seen daylight. 'I fucking mean it.' I flicked the safety catch off. 'I won't hesitate to kill you.'

He stepped back and sank down against the wall. 'You can't leave me here. The carbon monoxide ...'

I kicked the knife away so he couldn't reach it. 'Put the cuff on,' I said.

When he looked up at me again, I could see the fight had gone out of him. He slumped and reached for the cuff. Put it around his wrist. I waited while he locked it and threw me the key.

'Show me it's locked,' I said, and he tugged at the cuff. 'Tell me the code to stop the carbon monoxide.'

Tony looked up at me and opened his mouth, but then his eyes glazed over and he slumped sideways, eyes closed.

'Tony!' I yelled. 'Wake up! Tell me the code!'

There was no response. He lay wedged against the wall.

'I'll shoot your legs off,' I shouted.

No response. Maybe he really had passed out. We were so close, but the women were going to die if I couldn't get that door open. I fired the gun at the pipe carrying the carbon monoxide. The loose pig careered across the barn and the other pigs squealed. I whispered an apology to them. The gun had blasted a hole in the tube. I ran and opened the barn door wide. But there was already too much carbon monoxide in the basement.

I crept towards Tony. He hadn't jumped when I'd fired the gun. If he was unconscious, I needed to get his keys from his pocket and open up the house to get access to a phone.

'Bex!' I shouted. 'Are you okay?'

No response. I pictured them dead or brain-damaged.

I put the gun down, and the key to the handcuffs. If Tony was faking, I couldn't risk him grabbing those. I crept closer to him. Still no sign of life.

I reached out and slipped my hand into the pocket nearest me. No keys. I groped around to the other pocket. No keys. My pulse was pounding in my ear. I slowly unzipped Tony's coat and slipped my hand inside to feel for the inner pocket.

He grabbed my arm. And punched me in the face. I gasped. The agony in my nose blinded me. Colours spiralled through my head – reds and purples and exploding golds – and my ears roared. He hit me again.

I pulled back and lunged at his stomach, where the knife had gone in. Pulled off the bandage.

He kicked me, and connected with my bad ankle. Always my bad ankle. I cried out and plunged my hand into his side. Into his wound. He screamed and fell back.The loose pig let out a squeal of alarm and shot out of the barn door.

I staggered away from Tony and grabbed the gun.

My voice was low and full of pain and fury. 'I swear to God, you fucker, I will shoot your arm off and use your thumbprint. Just tell me the fucking code.'

He was clutching his side. 'Okay, okay. Get us out of here.'

I ran to the door and waited. He shouted a six-figure code and I tapped it in to the keypad. The door popped open.

'What's the code for the bottom door?' I shouted.

'The first five primes in reverse order.' And he passed out.

'Oh for God's sake.' I dragged myself down the steps, blood smearing my vision. Hesitated while I convinced myself he wouldn't have included the number 1, and then typed 11, 7, 5, 3, 2.

The door clicked and I pushed it open. 'Bex! Violet!'

There was no sign of them.

I rushed forward and pulled open the door to one of the bedrooms. Nothing.

Oh God, were they already dead in the other room? I opened the door.

They were there. Still alive.

'Oh my God,' Bex spoke far too slowly. 'You did it.'

They were groggy and pale, their lips an uncanny cherry red. Violet staggered ahead of us. I took Nina's hand and Bex took Sofia's. We dragged them up the stairs and into the barn.

Ignoring Tony's shouts, I wrenched the barn door wide open, to the first daylight Nina had seen for thirty years.

Sofia stopped at the edge of the barn and refused to move, her pale skin and hair looking unearthly in the pink light. We couldn't delay; there was too much carbon monoxide inside the barn. Bex and I released the remaining pigs, and then the four of us dragged Sofia whimpering into a world she'd never seen.

56

Meg – A Week Later

'I never meant to hurt anyone.' Tony Nightingale spoke quietly, looking at his hands which were curled in his lap. He'd survived the stabbing, with a little help from the NHS. He looked tiny in our interview room, much smaller than he'd seemed in his own house or when he was trying to kill me. He had his own solicitor, but the man kept giving him shocked sideways looks as if he couldn't quite comprehend what Tony had done. There had never been a case like this in the UK before.

The recording apparatus was on. Jai was next to me. My eyes and nose were still bruised, my wrist painful and my throat not quite right, but I was okay. Ready for this. We had plenty on Tony. What I was after was evidence of Kirsty's involvement. We didn't have enough on her, even though I was sure she'd killed Gary, wearing Daniel's overalls, and then doctored Daniel's painkillers to murder him too. If she ever recovered I wanted her in a secure psychiatric unit for the rest of her life.

Tony looked up and caught my eye before looking down again. 'How is Nina?' he asked. 'And Sofia?'

'As well as can be expected,' I said. 'They're being looked after.'

'Sofia might not cope,' he said. 'With being outside.'

'You can let us deal with that. You've done enough. Now you'd better tell us what happened with Violet Armstrong.'

'Will it help me if I cooperate?' He looked at his solicitor, who gave a quick nod.

'It will definitely be taken into account,' I said. He'd be going nowhere for a long time either way.

Given that he was being interviewed by the person he'd drugged, punched, knocked out, chained to a wall, and imprisoned with his family who he'd kept locked up for thirty years, Tony seemed to realise he wasn't in a strong position to deny anything. He let out a breath of air. 'What do you want to know?'

'Do you admit to abducting Violet Armstrong and holding her against her will?'

'You make it sound terrible. They had everything in there. A good life. A safe life.'

'You abducted Violet?'

'She told me she made videos,' he said quietly, almost beseeching-ingly. 'People were threatening her. How could I let her go again, knowing she was going to get hurt? It was the same with Bex. Why did she have to come back to Gritton?' He wrung his hands together, squirming in his chair. 'I didn't want to have to do it. I couldn't help myself.'

'You drugged Violet?'

He said nothing, his breathing coming heavily.

'You drugged her, Tony?' I made my voice loud and he shrunk back, playing the poor old man. As if I was going to buy that after what he'd done to me.

He nodded slightly. Glanced at the recording apparatus and whispered, 'Yes.'

'And then what?'

Tony swallowed.

'And then what? I'm not buying this feeble old man act. Tell us what you did next. When did you call Kirsty?'

He shook his head. 'It was me. I did it all. Not Kirsty. But I only did it for Violet's own good. She was putting herself in danger.'

'It's all right, Tony. We know Kirsty came up with the plan. We know it was her idea to put the blood and hair in the pig troughs. Violet heard you talking to her, remember? Kirsty wanted to make it look like Violet had been fed to pigs. It was very clever of her.'

I saw a flush of parental pride. Unbelievable. He spoke softly. 'It wasn't Kirsty's fault. I did it, not her.'

'What did she tell you to do?'

'It was all my idea.' He was still protecting Kirsty. Denying what she was.

'Tell us then. What did you do?'

'He deserved to be punished for what he did to Lucas. He was living on borrowed time. I made it look like he killed Violet.'

I kept my voice steady. 'Daniel Twigg?' My misery and anger was so strong I had to clutch the table to steady myself.

Tony nodded. 'Yes. He killed Lucas. So because of that he deserved to die.'

I wanted to scream at Tony. *You stupid, gullible, crazy fucking man. Daniel was a good person. He didn't deserve to die.* Tony didn't even believe this crap – it had come from Kirsty.

Instead I said calmly, 'What did you do?'

Tony raised an eyebrow at his solicitor, who nodded. There was really no defence for any of this.

Speaking in little more than a whisper, Tony said, 'I put gloves on, and overalls and a hat, and foot covers.'

'Speak up please,' I said.

Tony coughed. 'We have foot covers for going into the house in muddy boots. And … er, I shaved off Violet's hair, and I got some of the big syringes the vet gives us, for taking blood samples from the pigs. The ones with anticoagulant in them. And I …' He hesitated. 'I took as much blood from Violet as I could, while she was still drugged with the pig-sedative.' He looked down at the table and coughed again. 'She started waking up. I took off all her clothes and her necklace and put everything in a plastic bag.'

This was utterly chilling, but I tried not to react. I wanted him to speak freely. 'Okay. Then what?'

'Can we take a break?' he whispered. He looked dejected, almost as horrified by what he'd done as we were. I was sure Kirsty had come up with this plan, but he was the one who'd carried it out.

'Not yet,' I said.

He sighed. 'I am sorry. I never meant for it to get so out of hand.'

'What did you do next?'

'I took a sack of pig pellets, and Violet's keys and I drove her car to the abattoir.'

So someone else had driven that car. He must have put the seat back and then moved it forward again, but too far.

'Did you deliberately drive past Mrs Ackroyd's house?'

He nodded quickly. 'Poor woman never sleeps. But you can't see who's driving the car from her house. The street lamp reflects off the windscreen and she's short-sighted anyway. And there's a camera on that road too.'

I nodded. 'And you gave yourself an alibi?'

He looked surprised for a moment, then said, 'Yes. I pulled over just after I passed the CCTV. My robot has a camera so I could see what he was doing via 4G. Luckily there's a signal in that area. He has twelve servo-motors so his arms move almost like a human. He can make coffee. Dialling Bex wasn't hard. And he has a microphone and a speaker so I could talk to Bex's answerphone.' Some of Tony's natural confidence came back as he said that, and I was more certain than ever that the sad-old-man act was faked. I guessed this bit had been his idea, not Kirsty's. 'And I got my robot to watch TV,' he added.

Without even being consciously aware of it, we'd been fooled by the unmodernised house, the old phone, the man who'd aged before his time. And we'd assumed, with it being an old-fashioned dial phone, that he must have been there to make the call.

'So you let yourself into the abattoir and fed your bag of pellets to the pigs?' I said.

He nodded. 'As many as they'd eat. So it would look like they'd had a big meal.'

'And then?'

He looked down. 'I put the blood and a few hairs in the trough.'

I nodded. 'And then …'

He took a gulping breath and said, 'Okay. I found the cubicles where the workers kept their belongings, and put Violet's car keys, laptop and bag in hers. Daniel lives in a caravan so he showers and shaves at the abattoir, and keeps a stack of spare overalls there.

And his razor was there too. He hadn't even locked his cubicle. I took one of his overalls and put some of her blood on it, put that and the razor in the bag with Violet's stuff, and put it in the Cat 2 waste. And I put some of Violet's blood on Daniel's boots and left them in the locker.'

Daniel had been sacrificed as if his life was worth nothing. A good life had been ended. And he'd died before he'd had the chance to make peace with himself.

'Did you know the usual company who took the waste had been changed?'

'No. The bag – actually it was a bin liner, as you know – was supposed to have been found more quickly. We expected it to be found. You can't put plastic in the rendering machine.'

He'd said 'we'. 'Go on,' I said.

'It goes in with other farm waste in a huge lorry. You'd have no chance of finding the stomachs from these particular pigs.'

And that would have been the case had Gary not changed the company who took it away.

'You and Kirsty thought it all through.'

'Just me. Not Kirsty.'

'You said "we", Tony. We know she was involved. So you did all this and then what, walked home afterwards?'

'Yes. I smashed the CCTV and took the hard drive home with me. That's in the slurry pit at my farm.'

'And what about Gary?' I said.

'Yes, I killed him too. He was always a silly boy. He caught sight of me leaving the abattoir that night, as he arrived. Tried to blackmail me.'

'How did you kill him?'

'I … I'm quite tired. Can we take a break?'

'Not yet. We know Kirsty killed him, Tony. She wore Daniel's overalls.'

Tony shook his head but there was no conviction in it.

'She killed Daniel too,' I said. 'She supplied him with drugs, didn't she?'

'If she did, it was only for his pain. The doctors wouldn't give him enough.'

'We know she's a psychopath, Tony.'

He slammed his hand on the table, a shock move that made both me and the solicitor jump. 'Don't say that word! She's not one of those!'

I slowed my breathing again. 'But you sent Bex to her aunt to keep her away from Kirsty?'

'I never believed Kirsty hurt Tim. That all came from Nina.'

'So Nina thought Kirsty let Tim onto the lane deliberately, but you didn't?'

'Of course not. There was paint on the key from Bex's hands. But nobody blamed her – she was far too young. She should have been watched, but Nina was struggling. Not getting enough sleep. She was imagining things. Kirsty isn't bad, just different. My father and my grandmother were like her.'

'But you sent Bex to your sister Janet, and you locked your wife up.'

'I didn't mean it to be permanent. I did it to stop her leaving with Bex. But then I realised she was pregnant. She would have taken all my babies to the Ukraine. I couldn't let that happen. I'd already lost my darling Tim. I couldn't bear to lose any more children. I'm not a bad person. Once I knew Nina was staying there, I made it nice. It's much better equipped than my own house. And I never ...' He looked down and fiddled with a scratch on the table. 'I never forced myself on her. She didn't want ... There were no more children.'

I couldn't respond to that. 'And we know Kirsty found out what you'd done, the first time Ivan escaped.'

Tony hesitated. 'I *trusted* Nina. But she orchestrated it, I'm sure. I felt very betrayed by that. Luckily, Kirsty found him. Kirsty could see the benefit in our ... situation.'

'But Daniel's brother, Charlie, saw Ivan in the woods,' I said. 'So Kirsty put Charlie down the spillway in the reservoir.'

Tony looked at his hands again, fingers squirming in his lap. 'I'm sure she didn't do that.'

'And then a few years later Ivan escaped again. The night of the barbecue. And things got very nasty.'

'I feel bad about that. After that I introduced much better security. I couldn't risk anything like that happening again.'

'Ivan raped Bex? And then Lucas killed him?'

'I didn't know Bex had the child. I *told* her not to, again and again. Beseeched her not to. But she didn't listen. Kirsty and I did everything to stop her having that baby.'

'So she had the child of an incestuous rape.'

'But Violet's fine, isn't she? Very beautiful, in fact. When in-breeding works well, it can work very well. Ask anyone who deals with animal stock.'

'Right.' I sat back, repulsed by him. 'You're admitting to imprisoning your wife and children for thirty years, kidnapping and imprisoning Violet Armstrong, and conspiring to murder Gary Finchley and Daniel Twigg?'

'I'm not fighting. I know I'm going to prison for a long time. I suppose I deserve it.'

57

I sat on the hospital chair and focused on my breath. The unique smell still made my heart beat faster and my muscles tense. Sent me spiralling back to the day they'd diagnosed Carrie. I closed my eyes and let myself remember. The undercurrent of my parents' hushed conversations that felt like it could throw me across the room. The numbness in my head that spun into disbelief and then horror, getting stronger and stronger until I knew in my bones that nothing would ever be the same again. I let the feeling sweep through me and then fade.

'Well, if it isn't Dr Dolittle.'

I flipped open my eyes. Kirsty was attached to drips and monitors – stable, but I'd been instructed by a stern-faced nurse not to upset her. The white sheet was flat where her legs should have been. Sepsis had taken hold and they'd had no option but to amputate. We probably didn't need the cops who were guarding her room.

'I've been catching up on the news,' she said. 'You're quite the hero. But my father did an impressive job on your face.'

I tried to gauge from her eyes whether the mask had finally

slipped because she was too drugged or in pain or generally beaten down to maintain it. There was a coldness that made my chest tighten. 'Word of advice,' she said. 'Don't stand under a collapsing pig barn.'

She'd spoken first. Maybe she'd continue. This wasn't a formal interview. I couldn't make her talk, and she could get me evicted at any time.

'Frankie will be better off without me,' she added. 'Bex is looking after her. I do care about her, contrary to what you think, but she's not one of us. Not one of the esteemed "callous and unemotional" branch of our great family. We're dying out. It's a shame because we're what made the Nightingales great.'

I nodded, hoping she'd carry on talking. We had the room to ourselves and it was quiet. I could just hear the faint clattering of a trolley in the corridor and muffled shouting from a nearby ward.

Kirsty pulled herself up on her pillows and fixed me with that icy gaze. 'Oh, you love to think we're this terrible blight on humanity, don't you?' she said. 'You Normals. When in reality you need people like us. Who do you think runs the factory farms, heads up the profitable corporations, takes the risks to start businesses while you Normals sit around pretending to be so nice and compassionate and letting us do your dirty work for you?'

I felt like saying, *But some of us don't want people like you to do the dirty work while the rest of us pretend it's not happening. We don't want to be able to eat factory-farmed meat while letting you be the only one to look in the pigs' eyes, or buy cheap products while people like you manage the slave labour.* But there was no point. And maybe she was right. Most people still bought the cheap meat and the bargain electronic goods. We were all complicit in some way.

'You think the rest of Gritton didn't suspect?' Kirsty said.

'You really think that? At least I'm honest about what I am, not like the rest of you.'

In my mind I said, *You killed innocent people. You took Daniel from me.* But I wanted her to keep talking. 'Maybe you're right,' I said.

'You know I'm right. It's another reason I despise Normals. You turn a blind eye to things you pretend to condemn, because you're all so scared of being ostracised from your little social groups. Luckily, it allows us to manipulate you.'

Clattering from the corridor. I wanted information from her before we were interrupted. 'I assume you removed some bones from the troughs that time you fed lamb to the pigs,' I said, hoping her urge to show off would be stronger than her instinct for self-preservation.

'Yes. I wasn't expecting you to come along. I only expected to show Anna. That was quite fortuitous.' Her lips curled into a slow, predatory smile. 'You've hit the jackpot here, DI Dalton. I'm only telling you these things because I have no intention of living like this. Being a *cripple* really isn't my style.'

I winced inwardly, but I wanted her to carry on. 'Do you have evidence that anyone in particular in Gritton knew what your father was doing?'

'Not the kind of evidence you want. But they had a good idea. And they chose to let it happen. They chose to carry on accepting his money, letting him create the perfect village for them. Lovely parks and playgrounds – a *library*, for goodness' sake – in a tiny village like that. Even the abattoir was the best in the country. All down to his money. They chose it. What a clever myth my father created. *If you see her, turn away! Don't let her see your face!* People in the village already talked about the Pale Child. I'd had some fun telling Bex and Tim stories about her when they were young. Poor Tim was a little scared, I'm afraid. But my father changed the story to suit his needs. Clever. A few lives were sacrificed for the good of the many. Isn't that what happens in society?'

'Did you sacrifice Gary Finchley's life for the good of the many? And how about Daniel Twigg's?'

'Are you allowed to do this, Detective?'

'You don't have to tell me anything. You can ask me to leave at any time.' If she was as bored as I suspected, she'd not want me to go.

She paused as if weighing me up. 'What I can tell you is that Gary Finchley was not a nice man. I didn't mean to kill him initially, but the stupid man tried to blackmail my father after he saw him at the abattoir. It's not a good idea to blackmail people like us. No, he was asking for it. And he trusted Daniel, so when he got a text from Daniel saying to meet him in the woods, he wasn't concerned. And it's surprisingly easy to kill someone with a heavy rock. I thought the pig's head mask was a nice touch though, didn't you?'

I didn't respond to that.

'As for Daniel Twigg – he got what he deserved for killing Lucas,' Kirsty said. 'I know he didn't mean to and it was a long time ago, but he'd been living on borrowed time ever since. So yes, I was fine about sacrificing him too.'

I started to speak and then realised there was no point. I'd felt more for Daniel in the few days I'd known him than she'd felt for anyone in her whole life.

Kirsty put on a fake sad face, lips turned down. 'Sorry about Daniel,' she said. 'But you really shouldn't have feelings for suspects.'

I froze. Kirsty laughed. 'We're perceptive too,' she said. 'Poor little DI Dalton. Did you like Daniel a lot? He wasn't worth it. He was a rather pathetic creature.'

I looked into her cold eyes and shivered.

'But you Normals aren't as nice as you like to make out,' Kirsty said. 'Even sweet little Anna. She puts on a good show, but when we were young, she encouraged me to take Gary to the betting shop. She wanted him to go off the rails so she could get her hands on the business. That's not terribly nice, is it?'

My mind drifted to Anna with her cupcakes and flapjacks, and I wondered if that was true. It didn't matter now.

'And they made it so easy for me,' Kirsty said. 'Daniel was always leaving his phone lying around in a crappily secured caravan. It was easy to break in and take it while he was at work.'

I'd thought it was weird the way that phone was turned on and off. And I could tell from the state of the door that someone had broken into Daniel's caravan.

'I turned the phone on to text Gary from the abattoir and then off again when it went home with me, and on again in the woods that night,' Kirsty said. 'I wasn't sure how accurately you could track the thing, but no point being silly about it.'

Kirsty was right. I had hit the jackpot. She was happy to talk. But I believed her about not wanting to live like this. Most people wouldn't follow through on that, but she would. There'd be no day in court on this one.

'So you wore Daniel's overalls and made sure you left fibres and one of Daniel's hairs on Gary's body?' I said.

'It's so easy to research now isn't it?' she said. 'On the internet. I bet you detectives hate that. I knew you'd check for fibres. And I gambled that if I put the overalls in the bin near Daniel's caravan, and the phone back in his caravan, you'd find them. I couldn't make Daniel look *too* stupid, but I thought I'd get away with that.'

I pictured Daniel's face. His rock-balancing art. The man who'd spent his whole life making amends. Working in an abattoir, trying to make the last hours of the animals' lives as bearable as possible. A very special man. I blinked. I didn't want this monster to see that I was upset.

'But you could have ended up going to prison.' I said. 'Why would you risk that to cover up for your father?'

'I'm not averse to risk. It keeps life interesting. And I thought I'd get away with it. If it had ever looked like I was going to end up in prison, we'd have sent proof that Violet was still alive, and that would have been the end of your case. I must admit I didn't anticipate Gary seeing my father at the abattoir. It was silly of me to kill him.' She laughed. 'But never mind.'

'What happened the day Tim died?' I asked.

The mask snapped back into place. I'd messed up. Probed too deep. 'It was a terrible accident. My father loved that boy so much. So much more than he ever loved Bex or me.' Kirsty smiled.

She'd deserved to lose her legs.

58

Jai flipped on the wipers as he pulled onto the Via Gellia. Finally it was raining. A motorbike roared past us, narrowly missing a quarry truck thundering the other way.

'Do you think they actually want to die?' I said. 'Rain after a drought – they must know it's prime biker-death conditions.'

'Especially on this road,' Jai said. 'I suppose it's natural selection.'

'You can drop me at Mum's, if that's okay,' I said.

'No problem.' Jai took the right turn to head up to Eldercliffe. 'Does your mum know about your spectacular pig-based escape?'

'She does. She's very proud.' I spoke as if that was a joke, but it was the truth. I even felt proud of myself for once. Myself and that incredible pig.

'It's so like you to be rescued by a sodding pig.'

'Yeah, no knights in shining armour for me. But I don't plan to make a regular thing of it. There were a few dicey moments.'

'You're not planning to recruit a pig as part of your team then?'

'She was faster on the uptake than some I could mention, but let's not go there.'

Jai flicked me a quick sideways look. 'I'm going to stick to free-range and organic. I can't give it up completely – bacon and that.'

'It just tastes too good?'

'Yeah, but …'

'No, that's amazing, Jai. I'm really pleased. If everyone did that, there'd be no pigs in cages. Good on you.'

'Fiona's doing the same.'

I felt it wash over me. Affection for them. My team. 'I'm welling up, Jai.'

'It's only right. Pigs being practically our colleagues now, rather than just what we get called.'

'Well, it's made me very happy. You're good guys – you and Fiona.'

'Enough already. You're starting to embarrass me.'

'Did you ever find out what's up with Craig?' I said.

'No. Just that he's seeing a counsellor and doesn't want his wife to know.'

'There's clearly deep-rooted stuff going on in his psyche,' I said. 'I suppose I should try to feel sorry for him, but he acts like such a dick.'

'I know.' Jai fell silent but the air was full of him preparing his words. 'I wasn't going to tell you this, but I've been worrying about it. I wondered if he's been violent towards his wife and that's what he's getting counselling about?'

'Oh shit, really? Do you think that's why Tamsyn keeps approaching us? Does she need help? Shit.'

'I'm not sure. I thought it might be.'

'Is that what you said to him when he hit you?'

'Yeah. He hit me for accusing him of being violent. He doesn't have a finely developed sense of irony.'

'God, I hope Tamsyn's okay. She must know how hard it can be to get action taken against violent cops. We have to help her.'

'What can we do? We've got no evidence. I might be totally wrong.'

'Just keep a close eye, I suppose. And if she contacts us again about anything, I'll try and get it out of her.'

We carried on along the tree-lined lane towards Eldercliffe. The rain was making the stony, muddy ground on each side encroach upon the tarmac, narrowing the road to the point where meeting one of the vast quarry trucks would be genuinely hair-raising. Luckily the road was empty apart from us.

'Also, I'd been meaning to tell you …' Jai said.

'What?'

'Er, me and Suki split up.'

'Oh no! I'm so sorry.'

'It's for the best. You see, Meg, I was going to say to you. I wonder if we—'

'You're right,' I said. 'Cops are better not having relationships. It's too complicated.' But what I meant was that I was just too tired to think about this. Even if it could be really good. Because I was exhausted after Gran, and this case. And I wasn't over Daniel, but I couldn't say that because I couldn't admit to my feelings for him. And anything that involved effort, that involved one or both of us changing jobs, no matter how good it could be, was too much. 'Detectives are better off single,' I said.

Jai sighed. 'I'm sure you're right.'

And we sat in silence, listening to the sound of the tyres on the rain-soaked road.

Jai steered around a rock, then said, 'I found out who Richard went on holiday with.'

I felt awkward saying it. 'Is love in the air?'

'Apparently not. Maybe he agrees with you on the subject.' Just a hint of snark. 'He went with a male friend. He had a bit of a rant to me. Said the guy was a widower and they're just friends and seriously, if Richard was gay, he'd be perfectly happy to tell us, his daughter's transgender for goodness' sake and he's fine with that, do we seriously think he'd have a problem with being gay, so could we just drop it because this bloke is a friend and Richard has no desire to meet anyone for a relationship anyway, and they had a fantastic time on their safari, thank you very much, now shut up about it.'

'Accurate replication of a Richard-rant there, Jai. And I like it. Great outcome.'

Jai pulled up outside Mum's house. Drizzle was drifting sideways through the trees. 'It's difficult to imagine we had all that hot weather,' I said. 'It was like a different country. Do you want a cuppa?'

'You don't want some time to talk about … your dad?'

'That bastard? No, I'm done with him.'

We splashed up the drive and knocked on the door. It opened to a frazzled-looking Mum, but her face lit up when she saw Jai. 'How nice! Are you having a cup of tea.' With Mum there was never a question mark at the end of that sentence.

'That would be lovely, Mrs Dalton,' Jai said. 'Shall I give you a hand making it?'

'Oh for God's sake,' I spluttered. 'She already thinks the sun shines out of your arse.'

'Meg, really.' Mum led us through to the kitchen, and then noticed my face. 'Oh, good heavens. You have been in the wars, you poor thing.'

We sat at the kitchen table and Mum bustled around. I realised she wasn't frazzled – she was excited. Buzzing with energy.

'Are you going to sit down for a few minutes?' I asked, pretending to be irritated. She was more herself than she'd been since Gran died. Possibly more herself than she'd ever been, and I was happy for her.

Mum ignored me. 'How's that girlfriend of yours?' she said to Jai.

'Oh. Um. Yes, actually we decided to call it quits. It's fine.'

'Oh goodness,' Mum said, putting tea mugs in front of us and sitting at the table, still for the first time in God knows when. 'I'm sorry.'

Jai glugged some tea. 'She doesn't like my kids. At first we avoided the issue, but it's kind of a deal-breaker. And she was going to want kids of her own, and I don't want more. Two is plenty.'

'Yes, I can see that,' I said. 'Sorry, that sounded wrong.'

'So you're both single,' Mum said.

'It's the best way for cops.' Jai took a biscuit. 'Isn't that right, Meg?'

I looked into my tea and didn't comment.

Jai coughed. 'When are you leaving for El Salvador, Mrs Dalton?'

'Jesus, Jai,' I said. 'Stop calling her *Mrs Dalton*. You sound like you're trying to sell her double glazing.'

'Day after tomorrow. I'm so disorganised.' That was not true. Everywhere I looked, there was a list on the back of an envelope, or a pile of neatly categorised stuff. 'But we don't need to talk about me. I want to talk about Meg.' She reached and touched my hand. Jai smirked. 'I mean, goodness me, you saved those poor women. I'm so proud of you.'

I felt like crying. I'd been pretending I was okay, but it had all been so hard. The Violet case, the abuse directed at me, and then the stuff with Dad. I swallowed, unable to talk.

'I think you're exhausted,' Mum said. 'After this, go home and go to bed. But I hope you've given yourself a pat on the back. Has she, Jai?'

'I hope so too. She had a visit from the chief constable.'

'Gosh, that's nice. Good. She works so very hard.'

'I am here, you know.' I gripped my tea mug so tight I felt like it might smash into pieces.

Mum put her serious face on. 'Are you okay though?'

'I am, Mum. Justice for Violet have self-destructed in a puff of *being totally bloody wrong about everything*, the Animal Vigilantes have calmed the hell down, Bex and Violet are making sure Nina and Sofia are looked after. And Dad's sodded off back to Scotland in a cloud of shame. What's not to like? We've even managed to arrest most of the animal killers and the bastard who threatened Hamlet.'

'Well, that's excellent. I'm glad. I just need to say one more thing to you.'

'Oh God.' I half laughed, so as not to cry. 'Am I going to be told off?'

'About your father.'

I looked into my mug. Jai's presence beside me felt good. Reassuring. I wondered if I'd made the wrong decision.

'He did try to con me out of money too,' Mum said, 'but I was more cynical than you. You managed to cancel that cheque?'

I took a breath and looked up. 'Yes. It's all cancelled. Although I'm not sure my neighbours have forgiven me for his wounded-buffalo bellowing when he realised I'd locked him out and chucked his clothes out of the front window. Their Great Dane can be a bit excitable.' It still made me feel queasy what I'd done to Dad, even though he was a bastard of the highest order.

'You need to know it's not you,' Mum said. 'He was being pursued by money-lenders. He was absolutely desperate. But I hope this helps you realise you're worth ten of him. There's no point you trying to impress him because he's only ever focused on himself. The best thing you can do is be proud of yourself, forget about him, and get on with your life.'

Jai had been very quiet, sipping his tea. 'My family are an absolute nightmare as well,' he said. 'I think it's character-building.'

'Just not the character I wanted,' I said.

59

The pigs were in an outdoor pen with their piglets, the hazy evening sun highlighting the blond hairs on their backs and the flakes of mud where they'd rolled. The one with the patch over her eye was there, rooting around with a quiet determination. Our saviour.

Bex and Violet sat opposite me on a picnic bench, one of Tony's creations. They were close to one another as if they'd known each other for years.

'How could he not see it?' Bex said. 'Even if the occasional piglet gets crushed, which if you give them enough space they don't, this is so much better.'

'Will you be taking over the farm then?' I asked.

She grimaced. 'No. We're both staying away from pigs for a while. But Dad's paid for this lot to go to a sanctuary to live out their lives.'

'Oh, thank goodness,' I said. 'I was going to offer to help with that. Old Patchy here saved us. I wasn't going to let her spend another minute in a cage.'

'No,' Bex said. 'It's a drop in the ocean, but at least we can save these.'

Violet looked up. 'No more barbecue videos for me,' she said. 'I don't know why I ever got into that in the first place. I'm going to use my notoriety to campaign against factory farming. And I've got the right look for that now.' She touched her head. Her hair was beginning to grow back and she looked stunning – the benefits of good bone structure.

'How are you feeling?' I asked.

'I'm okay.' The fading light touched her cheekbones and for a moment she looked much older, as if I was seeing the woman she would become. 'It's funny how much you appreciate simple things like the sun on your face. And I've got a birth mother, a grandmother and an aunt I never knew I had. Also a grandfather and another aunt, but I'm not sure I'll be keeping in touch with them. And I've sorted things out with my parents – my adoptive parents.'

'Good,' I said. 'I'm really pleased.'

'Yes, but …' She was different. The naive confidence was gone. It used to burn out of her eyes in her barbecue videos – the faith that everything would always be okay for her. 'I'm trying to get my head around being Ivan's daughter. I was seriously freaked out about it, but … well, I suppose I just have to get used to it. He had more excuse than most for his behaviour.'

'It doesn't mean anything,' Bex said. 'You're clearly fine. We're the product of nurture more than nature and Ivan had no chance to be normal. What a tragic life he led.'

'I know,' Violet said. 'It doesn't mean he's passed on … anything to me.' She looked over at the pigs and smiled. Two of the tiny piglets were chasing each other round like puppies.

'Frankie's coming to stay with me,' Bex said. 'I'll make a crappy mum-substitute but I suspect even I'll be better than what she's used to.'

'That's great news' I said. 'And how about Nina and Sofia?'

Bex shook her head slowly. 'I can't imagine ... More than thirty years trapped under a barn. All that time I thought she'd abandoned me, she was there. If only I'd realised.'

'You couldn't have known,' I said.

'He was obsessed with keeping water out of that barn.' Bex looked up at the sky, which was beginning to deepen into pink. 'I remember when I visited when I was sixteen, he directed it to flood the house rather than end up in the barn. I can see us all sitting in the kitchen, me soaking wet and shocked and wondering why on earth I'd even come to Gritton, and Daniel having a go at Dad because he'd let the old books get wet. The books that were rescued from the manor house. I thought Dad was concerned about the pigs.'

She took a deep, shuddery breath. 'Talking to Nina, it's obvious she never gave up. She played the long game, and pretended she'd resigned herself to her life, so Tony would trust her, but all the while she was waiting for her chance. Even though, once he micro-chipped them, it was pretty much impossible. If Tony hadn't perpetuated the rumour about the Pale Child, someone would have found Ivan the first time he escaped and worked out what was going on. But people ran away from him. It makes me sick. Sick to my stomach that he's my own father.'

I wasn't sure what to say. Not sure how these women were supposed to cope with finding out the truth about their family. 'I should have spotted it,' I said. 'We saw from the drone footage that there was a septic tank for that pig barn, but we just assumed it had been converted to a home.'

'Well, you wouldn't exactly expect there to be people imprisoned there,' Violet said. 'It's not your fault.'

'I think Aunt Janet must have worked out there was a problem with Kirsty,' Bex said. 'She never wanted me to come to Gritton. Said it wasn't safe, but I never knew why. I thought it was to do with the pigs.'

I nodded. And then she had warned Violet's parents to keep her away from Gritton, which they did for as long as they could.

'I keep thinking about Sofia,' Violet said. 'Locked up for her whole life. I can't imagine. He gave them TV, but Sofia didn't realise the TV people were real. She thought it was all made up, even though Nina did her best to educate her.'

'Nina's an incredible woman,' I said.

'They were kind to me,' Violet said. 'I'll help them adapt any way I can.'

'And Dad's money can pay for whatever they need,' Bex added.

'The bastard can at least do that.' Violet gave a shallow smile.

Bex turned to look at Violet and said, 'He did it for love, you know. The kind of love he was taught by his father on the farm.'

'Yeah,' Violet said. 'Misguided, fucked-up, Gritton-style love.'

Author's note

Most of this book is the product of my fevered imagination. However, the keeping of pigs in tiny cages is not.

In the UK, over half of sows are kept in 'farrowing crates' from up to seven days before they give birth until the piglets are weaned at around three or four weeks of age. The crates are sized such that the mother pig cannot turn around, reach to nuzzle or lick her piglets, or even lie comfortably. The floor is usually hard and slatted, even though a mother pig has a strong motivation to build a nest before giving birth. The crate also prevents the mother pig from being able to move away from her piglets or push them away, for example if they bite her teats.

If you eat pork but would prefer not to support this, look for products labelled 'organic' or 'free range'. If you choose 'outdoor reared' or 'outdoor bred', the sows are not kept in crates, although the pigs they give birth to are still kept indoors for at least some of their lives. Compassion in World Farming has good information – https://www.ciwf.org.uk/your-food/meat-poultry/pork-and-bacon/

UK pig farming has a long way to go, but it is better than in much of the rest of the world. In many countries, it is common for a pregnant sow to be kept in a sow stall (also called a 'gestation crate') for the whole of her sixteen-week pregnancy. A sow stall is a metal cage – usually with a bare concrete/slatted floor – which is so narrow that the sow cannot turn around, and she can only stand up and lie down with difficulty. Larger pigs cannot even lie on their sides as they sometimes like to, and must lie on their fronts. Sow stalls were banned in the UK in 1999, with a partial ban enforced in the EU from 2013. Unfortunately, following the UK ban, supermarkets increased imports of low-welfare meat from other countries, putting UK producers in an impossible position unless consumers specifically chose higher-welfare meat. It is unclear what will happen in the future, but it is likely to be even more important to check carefully what you are buying.

Acknowledgements

Writing the acknowledgements gets harder with each book. So many people have helped me in so many ways and it's all hugely appreciated, but I can't mention everyone.

Massive thanks to everyone at Marjacq, especially my fantastic agent, Diana Beaumont. The longer I work with her, the more I realise how incredibly lucky I am!

Thank you to my brilliant editor, Emily Kitchin, who has had huge input on this book, making it so much better, and who never says anything is too weird or taboo (well, not so far!) Also, to my excellent copy-editor, Anne O'Brien, and the whole HQ team, including Lisa Milton, Janet Aspey (the right Janet), Lucy Richardson, Lily Capewell, Joe Thomas, Melanie Hayes, and all the others who work tirelessly to support our books.

Again, Jo and Ducky Mallard were indispensable on the CSI side of things and are always (perhaps worryingly) happy to speculate on how to commit a perfect murder. Seriously, you do not want to get on the wrong side of these guys. And thank you to the other wonderful police people who've helped me, including but not limited to Paul Callum, John Tanner, Phil Blood, and Claudia Musson, who helped with detail but also understood that I have to leave out the boring bits! Any inaccuracies are totally mine.

The Doomsbury writing group have kept me sane(ish) and helped me laugh about the ups and downs of publishing, so huge thanks to Sophie Draper, Fran Dorricott, Jo Jakeman, and Louise Trevatt. Louise may not have written her book (yet) but her work saving dogs from the meat trade in South Korea is truly inspirational. It's sometimes depressing not being able to save them all, but if more people were like her, the world would be a much better place.

All my friends have been brilliantly supportive, including Ali and the lovely Paws (RIP), who inspired Hamlet, and all the rest of the Alderwasley crowd (thank you, Jane, for offering to get me an inside view of an abattoir, and sorry I couldn't quite face it!) Also Chris Scott, Sally Randall, Ruth Grady, Emma Goodchild, Sarah Breeden, Susan Fraser, Estelle Read, Corrine Baker, Keren Hill, Helen Chapman, Gemma Allen, and Alex Davis and the people I met on his courses, including Glenda, Peter, Ray and Carl.

Thank you to Sir Richard FitzHerbert of Tissington Hall for being the first person (and I hope not the last) to send me a message saying, 'You must see my cesspit'. It was indeed a fantastic place for disposing of things. Also, the patent attorney community have continued to be hugely enthusiastic, especially with suggestions for future victims (trade mark attorneys and solicitors seem popular). Thanks also to the wonderful clicker-trainer community, whose creative approaches to problem-solving inspired one of the more unusual parts of this book! And huge thanks to the wonderful Compassion in World Farming for fact checking my author's note.

The crime writing world is famously supportive over a drink or two and in online groups. Thank you to all the writers who are such fun to be around and who also took the time to read and comment on my first two books – there are too many to mention but you know who you are. Likewise, the incredible book bloggers who do so much to support authors, and those who are involved with book groups in the real world and online, and those who take the time to post reviews – it really does make a huge difference. These include (among others) Jacob Collins, Kate of 'For Winter Nights', Vicki of 'Cosy Books', Noemi Proietti, Julia Wilson, The Book Doctor, Abby Slater-Fairbrother, Rosie McCall, Ruth de Haas, Tina Pritchard, Pam Gough and Beccy Bagnall.

Also, my local bookshops, especially Waterstones Derby, Meadowhall, Sheffield and Chesterfield, and Scarthin Books, my local libraries plus the wonderful one in Newport, Pembrokeshire, and also Radio Derby for thinking of me when you need vital contributions like being pedantic about apostrophes.

Thank you to Rob for supporting this unexpected and at times overwhelming career change (and no, Craig is not based on you – well, not entirely), my mum and dad, Julian and Marina, and Katia and Maxim for ongoing periodic sidewaysing of my books.

Finally, thank you to my readers, who've been so enthusiastic and encouraging. It's been heartening (and yes, a little bit stressful) to be asked so many times when this one is coming out! Thank you for choosing to read this book – I really hope you enjoyed it.

Turn the page to read an exclusive extract from the first book in the DI Meg Dalton series, *The Devil's Dice*...

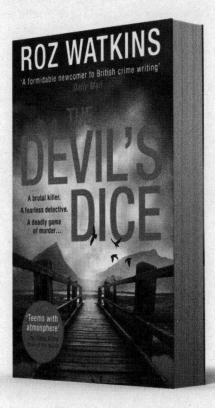

Available to buy now.

PROLOGUE

The man clambered into the cave on shaking legs, sucked in a lungful of stale air and stared wide-eyed into the blackness. When the dark mellowed, he shuffled inside and sank onto the seat that a long-dead troglodyte had hewn into the cave wall. The familiar coldness seeped through his trousers and into his flesh. The discomfort pleased him.

He fished out his torch and stood it upright, so the light beamed up and bounced onto the glistening floor. Bats hung above him, their tiny feet grasping at the rock, furry bodies tucked into cavities.

The solitude was soothing. No judgemental glances from colleagues. No clients clamouring for his attention like swarms of angry insects. No wife shooting arrows of disappointment his way.

He placed the book by his side. Eased the cake from his pocket, pulled open the crinkly plastic wrapper and took the soft weight in his hand. He hesitated; then brought it to his lips, bit firmly and chewed fast. Another two bites and it was gone.

The air went thick. His throat tightened. He leant back against the cave wall. There wasn't enough oxygen. He gasped. Clamped his eyes shut. An image of his long-dead mother slid into his head. Slumped in her wheelchair, head lolling to one side. And an earlier one – way back when his memories flitted like fish in shining water – smiling down at him and walking on her legs like a normal parent.

He rose. Stumbled to the back of the cave, grasped at the ferns on the wall, fell against them. His stomach clenched and his upper body folded forwards. He was retching, choking.

More snapshots in his head. Kate's face on their honeymoon. Beaming in the light of a foreign island, laughing and raising a glass to sun-chapped lips. He gasped. Air wouldn't come. Drowning. That time in Cornwall, still a child. Beach huts against the bright blue sky and then the waves throwing him down. Dragging him along the sea bed, his terror bitter and astonishing.

He crashed to the cave floor. An image of a childhood cat, orange-furred and ferocious, but loved so much. The cat dead on the lane. Now a girl hanging deep in the Labyrinth, the noose straight and still. Please, not his girl.

A terrible burning, like maggots burrowing into his cheeks. He clawed at his face, nails hacking into skin, gouging into eyes.

Blackness coming in from above and below. The image of his mother again, in bed, both emaciated and swollen. Suffocating. Pleading.

Chapter 1

I accelerated up the lane, tyres skidding in the mud, and prayed to the gods of murder investigations. *Please bestow upon me the competence to act like a proper detective and not screw up in my new job.*

The gods were silent, but my boss's voice boomed from the hands-free phone. 'Meg, did you get the details? Body in a cave... almond smell... philosophy book...'

I squinted at the phone, as if that would help. Richard's monologue style of conversation meant he hadn't noticed the bad signal. Had he really said 'philosophy'? Our usual deaths were chaotic and drunken, with absolutely no philosophy involved.

Another snatch of Richard's voice. 'Scratches on his face...' Then the line went dead.

I swerved to avoid a rock and dragged my attention back to the road, which climbed between fields sprinkled with disgruntled-looking sheep and edged with crumbling dry-stone walls. A mist of evidence-destroying drizzle hung in the air. As the farmland on the left merged into woods, I saw a couple of police vehicles in a bleak parking area, and the sat nav announced that I'd reached my destination.

I pulled in and took a moment to compose myself. Of course it was terrible that a man was dead, but if he'd had to die, at least he'd done it in an intriguing way, and when I happened to be nearby. I was an Inspector now. I could handle it. *Mission 'Reinvent*

Self in Derbyshire' was on track. I took a fortifying breath, climbed from the car, and set off along a corridor marked with blue and white tape.

The path sloped up towards the base of an abandoned quarry. I trudged through the fallen leaves, the mud emphasising my limp and sucking at my feet with an intensity that felt personal. I needed to rethink my fitness regime, which mainly consisted of reading articles in *New Scientist* about the benefits of exercise. It wasn't cutting it in my chubby mid-thirties.

Through the trees I saw the face of a cliff, tinted pink by the evening light. An area around its base was enclosed by ribbons of tape stretched between rocks and shade-stunted oaks, and a police tent squatted just outside. I walked over and encased my genetic matter in a protective body suit, face mask, overshoes and two pairs of gloves.

The duty sergeant was a bearded man who looked slightly too large for his uniform.

'Sergeant Pearson,' he said. 'Ben. No evidence trampled. All under control.'

I didn't know him, but I recognised the name. According to the (admittedly unreliable) Station grapevine, he was extensively tattooed. Nothing was visible but apparently his torso was completely covered and was the subject of much fascination, which just demonstrated the poor standard of gossip in the Derbyshire force.

'DI Meg Dalton,' I said, and looked around the taped area. There was no-one who was obviously dead.

Ben pointed to the cliff. 'In the cave house.'

A narrow set of steps, smooth and concave through years of use, crawled sideways up the face of the cliff. At the top, about fifteen feet up, a dark, person-sized archway led into the rock.

'There's a house up there, burrowed into the rock? With a corpse in it?'

'Yep,' Ben said.

'That's a bit creepy.'

4

Ben squeezed his eyebrows together in a quick frown. 'Oh. Have you heard… ?' He glanced up at the black entrance to the cave.

'Heard what?'

'Sorry. I thought you said something else. Never mind. It's not important.'

I sighed. 'Okay, so what about our iffy body?'

'Pathologist said he died within the last few hours. And SOCO have been up.' He nodded towards a white-swathed man peering at what looked like a pile of vomit at the base of the cliff.

'Who's been sick?'

'The dog. Seems to have eaten something nasty.'

'The dog?'

'That's how they found the body. Bloke lost his dog. Searched everywhere for it. Eventually heard noises up there.' Ben thumbed at the gap in the rock. 'Climbed up, saw the body, found the dog licking something.'

'I hope it wasn't tucking into the corpse?'

'It was a Labrador, so I don't suppose it would have turned it down. But I think it was the plastic wrapper from a cake or something. Looks like it might have been poisoned.'

'Is the dog okay? Where's the owner? Has someone taken a statement from him?'

'It's all here for you. They've gone to the vet, but the dog seems fine. Only ate a few crumbs, he thought.'

'Interesting location for a body,' I said. 'I've always been kind of fascinated by cave houses.'

Ben inched towards the cliff and touched the rock. 'This area's riddled with caves. Not many of them were ever lived in, of course.' He hesitated as if wondering whether to say more, given that a corpse was waiting for my attention.

'I'd better press on,' I said, although I wasn't looking forward to getting my bad foot up the stone steps. Besides, there was something unsettling about the black mouth of the cave. 'What were you going to say earlier? When I said it was creepy?'

Ben laughed, but it didn't go to his eyes. 'Oh, don't worry. I grew up round here. There was a rumour. Nothing important.'

'What rumour?'

'Just silliness. It's supposed to be haunted.'

I laughed too, just in case he thought I cared. 'Well, I don't suppose our man was killed by a ghost.' I imagined pale creatures emerging from the deep and prodding the corpse with long fingers. I forced them from my mind. 'I was told the dead man smells of almonds. Cyanide almonds?'

'Yep, slightly. You only really get the almondy smell on a corpse when you open up the stomach.' Ben's stance changed to lecture-giving – legs wide apart and chest thrust forward. I hoped he wasn't going to come over all patronising on me. I wasn't even blonde any more – I'd dyed my hair a more intelligent shade of brown, matched to my mum's for authenticity. But I was stuck with being small and having a sympathy-inducing limp.

'Yes. Thanks. I know,' I said, a little sharply. 'So, do we have a name?'

Ben glanced at his notes. 'Peter Hugo Hamilton.'

'And he was dead when he was found?'

'That's right. Although I've seen deader.'

'Can you be just a little bit dead?'

Ben folded his arms. 'If there are no maggots, you're not that dead.'

'Okay, I'll have a look.' I edged towards the steps and started to climb. A few steps up, I felt a twinge in my ankle. I paused and glanced down. Ben held his arms out awkwardly as if he wanted to lever my bottom upwards, a prospect I didn't relish. I kept going, climbing steadily until I could just peer into the cave. A faint shaft of light hit the back wall but the rest of it was in darkness. I waited for my eyes to adjust, then climbed on up and heaved myself in.

A musty smell caught in my throat. The cave was cool and silent, its roof low and claustrophobic. It was the size of a small room, although its walls blended into the darkness so there could have been tunnels leading deeper into the rock. A tiny window and the slim door cast a muted light which didn't reach its edges. I pulled out my torch and swooped it around. I had an irrational feeling that something was going to leap out of the darkness, or that the corpse was going to lunge at me. I scraped my hair from my clammy face and told myself to calm the hell down and do my job.

The dead man lay at the back of the cave, his body stretched out straight and stiff. One hand clutched his stomach and the other grasped his throat. I shone my torch at his face. Scratches ran down his cheeks and trickles of blood had seeped from them. The blood gleamed bright, cherry red in the torch light.

A trail of vomit ran from the side of the man's mouth onto the cave floor.

I crouched and looked at his fingers. They were smeared red. Poor man seemed to have scratched at his own face. Under the nails were flecks of green, as if he'd clawed his way through foliage.

Resting near one of the man's bent arms was a book – *The Discourses of Epictetus*.

A plastic wrapper lay on the stone floor. I could just read the label. *Susie's Cakes. Dark chocolate and almond.* I lowered myself onto my hands and knees and smelt the wrapper, wishing I hadn't given up Pilates. I couldn't smell anything, but I didn't know if I was one of the lucky few who could smell cyanide.

I stood again and shone my torch at the wall of the cave behind the man's body. Water seeped from a tiny crack in the cave roof, and in the places where light from the door and window hit the wall, ferns had grown. Some were crushed where it looked as if the man had fallen against them, and others had been pulled away from the cave wall.

I felt a wave of horror. This was a real person, not just a corpse in an interesting investigation. He was only about my age. I thought about his years lost, how he'd never grow old, how his loved ones would wake up tomorrow with their lives all collapsed like a sink-hole in a suburban garden.

I breathed out slowly through my mouth, like I'd been taught, then stepped closer and pointed my torch at the area where the ferns had been flattened. Was that a mark on the stone? I gently pulled at more ferns with my gloved hands, trying to reveal what was underneath. It was a carving, clearly decades old, with lichen growing over the indentations in the rock like on a Victorian gravestone. It must have been completely covered until the dying man grasped at the ferns.

Something pale popped into my peripheral vision. I spun round and saw a SOCO climbing into the cave house. His voice cut the silence. 'We found a wallet with his name and photo driving licence. And a note. Handwritten. It said, *P middle name.*' He showed me a crumpled Post-it, encased in a plastic evidence bag.

'Has the back wall been photographed, where he pulled at the ferns?'

The man nodded.

'Okay, let's see what's under there.' I pointed at the marks I'd seen in the rock.

Together we tugged at the ferns, carefully peeling them off the cave wall.

The SOCO took a step back. 'Ugh. What's that?'

We pulled away more foliage and the full carving came into view. My chest tightened and it felt hard to draw the cold cave air into my lungs. It was an image of The Grim Reaper – hooded, with a grinning skull and skeletal body, its scythe held high above its head. The image was simply drawn with just a few lines cut into the rock, but it seemed all the more sinister for that. It stood over the dead man as if it had attacked him.

'Hold on a sec,' the SOCO said. 'There's some writing under the image. Is it a date?' He gently tore away more ferns.

I crouched and directed my torch at the lettering in the rock. A prickling crept up my spine to the base of my neck. 'Not a date,' I said.

The SOCO leant closer to the rock, and then froze. 'How can

that be? That carving must be a good hundred years old – the writing the same – and covered up for years before we cut the foliage back.' His voice was loud in the still air, but I heard the tremor in it. 'I don't understand... The dead man's initials?'

I didn't understand either. I stepped away from the cave wall and wiped my face with my green-stained gloves.

Carved into the stone below the Grim Reaper image were the words, 'Coming for PHH'.

ONE PLACE. MANY STORIES

Bold, innovative and
empowering publishing.

FOLLOW US ON:

@HQStories